The Creed Room

A NOVEL OF IDEAS

Daniel Spiro

AEGIS PRESS

Aegis Press

P.O. Box 3023
Del Mar, CA 92014

www.theaegispress.com

Design and layout
BBD / Jonathan Gullery
9 Washington Avenue
Pleasantville, NY 10570

Library of Congress Cataloging-in-Publication Data

Spiro, Daniel, 1960-

The Creed Room : a novel of ideas / Daniel Spiro.-- 1st Aegis Press ed.

p. cm.

ISBN-13: 978-0-9747645-2-8 (alk. paper)
ISBN-10: 0-9747645-2-3 (alk. paper)

1. Idea (Philosophy)--Fiction. 2. Forums (Discussion and debate)--Fiction 3. Debates and debating--Fiction. 4. High school teachers--Fiction. I.= Title.

PS3619.P577C74 2006

813'.6--dc22

2005034229

Manufactured in the United States of America

First Aegis Press paperback edition published 2006

Alas! If All Men Were Wise
And Of Good Will As Well –
The Earth Would Be a Paradise,
Now It Is More a Hell.

*Inscription on the front wall of the
Spinoza House, Rijnsburg, Holland*

CHAPTER 1

THE INVITATION

Some people are born fools. Some achieve foolishness. And some, like my friends and me, have foolishness thrust upon us.

At least that's the way things look right now.

Here we were, a tiny group of people, brought together by a man known to us as "the Benefactor." We were mostly undistinguished and hardly of one mind. But when we came together, we actually believed we could unify this society based on common sense, logic and compassion alone.

Many might say we failed beyond our wildest nightmares. I say, the jury is still out.

ॐ

When I think back to the '99-'00 school year, the most momentous year in my life, I remember so many events. Yet one stands out above the rest—the warning my group received about our "Benefactor" and essentially disregarded.

Lately, I've been wondering a lot about that warning. If we all knew then what we knew now, what would we have done? Would we have simply killed our group in its tracks? Personally, that group has been the greatest thing that's ever happened to me. But I'm haunted by the effect that it has had on our country and our world.

In a nation of nearly 300 million people, a switch of 60,000 votes in Ohio would have swung the Presidential election of 2004. I was in Akron on Election Day working to ensure that every African-American vote would be counted. The Democrats around me were giddy with enthusiasm. "This turnout is amazing," they'd say. "We're definitely gonna win this thing." But I knew better. I knew the other side well. I knew they had begun organizing back in 2000. And I knew *how* they organized, and how successful they'd be in getting out their own vote.

The GOP owes its victory to but a few causes. One, obviously, was 9/11. Another was the work of the Creed Room.

"Guess what, Mr. Kramer? I'm so, so, so relieved. I finally got my period. I was, like, a week late. *A week.* That never happens to me."

Jenny Davis was 15, and I had always thought she was a young 15. She was also the second girl who had told me about a late period since the start of the school year. "That must be a relief," I said.

"You're telling me, Mr. Kramer. I'm Catholic. My folks are, like, totally pro-life. I don't see how I could have gotten an abortion. Could you see me walking around every day with a belly out to here and everyone looking at me like I was white trash? All so I could give the baby up for adoption?"

"You might want to think about that for a while before—"

"Yeah, I know. I also know I'm gonna be late for class if I don't run. Bye, Mr. Kramer."

She left me standing in the hallway wondering if other teachers are told when students get their periods, or whether it was just me.

In fifth period, my psychology class was having an animated discussion about what it means to be normal when Ms. Cratchett, from the classroom next door, interrupted. Cratchett, or "Crotchrot," as the students called her behind her back, had 40 years of tenure in the school system. "I'm not going to ask you again!" she said, standing at my doorway. "My class is trying to view a film on the Revolution. Keep it down, or I'll go straight to the principal."

"Sorry, we'll be good," I said. I was embarrassed, but also annoyed by the fact that Cratchett spent so much time showing movies instead of actually teaching.

After school, Ryan Bolog, a senior known primarily for his abs, approached me with his girlfriend Sara Barber. She was wearing a tight shirt with spaghetti straps and the words "Porn Star" across her chest. "Hey Kirby," Ryan said, addressing me by a nickname the students often called me simply because one of them thought I looked like a "Kirby." "I wanted to talk to you about normal."

"So you liked the psych discussion today?"

"No, not that normal. N-O-R-M-L—the National Organization for the Reform of Marijuana Laws."

"Oh *that* NORML. Sorry if I didn't recognize the name. I'm more into heroin."

"We're serious, Kirby. We want you to sponsor a NORML group at Takoma Park High." Ryan said.

"You what? You must think I'm stoned right now."

"No really," Sara said. "We were thinking you'd agree that pot should be legal."

"You do, don't you?" Ryan asked.

"I think kids your age shouldn't be allowed to smoke the stuff. *That's* what I think."

"I'm turning 18 in four months, Mr. Kramer," Sara said.

"What about then?"

I had to think for a bit. "I like the way they deal with it in Holland. It's not legal, but it's decriminalized. Then again, they don't have the kind of poverty problem we have. That's all this country needs is more pot."

"You're beating around the bush, Mr. Kramer," Sara said. "Do you think America should legalize pot, or don't you?"

"No, I don't. We've got too much poverty. And even if I agreed with you, I wouldn't dare sponsor your club."

"Come on, Mr. Kramer," said Ryan. "You're the coolest teacher in the school. If you won't help us—"

"No dice," I replied. "But let me recommend a book for you: John Stuart Mill's *On Liberty*. He argues that if you're not hurting another person, but only yourself, the government shouldn't stop you from doing what you're doing. Check the book out. It's a classic."

"Whatever," Sara said. "Let's go, Ryan."

Wisdom begins with dreams. As a child, mine was to be a school teacher.

On Saturday, September 25th, 1999, I was a month into my fourth year of living that dream. I taught social studies at a suburban public school in Chase County, Maryland, having dropped out of law school four years earlier, at the age of 25. My school was so close to the nation's capital that Tiger Woods could have teed up at the front entrance and hit the D.C. line with a golf ball.

I was living alone in a drab one-bedroom garden apartment in Rockville, Maryland, about twenty miles northwest of my school. Aside from my mother, no woman had come to the apartment in months, but I figured that was just as well, given all the clothes, dishes, and other clutter that hadn't been put away.

Opening up the morning paper, my ritual was always the same. Read the front section, then study the Sports page. Some days that would be the extent of my newspaper reading, but on that particular Saturday I turned to the Style section. That's where I saw the advertisement.

LOVERS OF HUMANITY. SEEKERS OF WISDOM.
ATHEISTS. THEISTS. LIBERALS. CONSERVATIVES.
Come learn and grow together.
Formulate a new creed for humankind.
The excitement begins Tuesday, September 28th, at 7:30 p.m.
The meeting place is 6201 Buckingham Drive, Garrett Park, Maryland.
YOU ARE MOST WELCOME.

That was all it said. No phone number. No organization taking responsibility for the ad. Just an invitation. But the words attracted me. I cut out the ad and placed it on my bedroom bureau.

From time to time that weekend I wondered about the ad and, on Monday morning, stuffed it in my pocket while dressing. I showed it later in the day to my closest friend on the faculty, Joe Wong. "Odd," Joe said, looking at the clipping. "They don't even give you a clue what it's about."

"Sure they do," I said. "It's some kind of study group."

"Studying *what*, Sam? Creedology? I think this sounds bizarre."

"Yeah, maybe so," I said, "but it got my attention. Besides, what do I have to lose?"

Though it took me less than 15 minutes to get to Garrett Park that Tuesday, I felt like I'd entered a different world. Most of the homes in my area had been built within the past few decades and had virtually no personality. Not so in Garrett Park. The houses there were large two- or three-storied Victorians with cylindrical towers. They were at least 100 years old. Driving down the roads of that town, I saw mostly large oak trees that shaded the homes and created a feeling of privacy unusual in suburban D.C.

When I arrived at 6201 Buckingham Drive, I noticed that a large room on the second floor was well lit. So was the top of the third-floor tower on the right side of an otherwise two-storied Victorian. Otherwise, I saw no signs of life at all. I waited a full minute after ringing the doorbell until I was finally met by a tall, powerfully-built, 40-ish man. His arms were adorned by gaudy tattoos. In fact, he looked like a refugee from a motorcycle gang. "How ya doin'?" he said, unsmiling. "You're the first. Let me get some lights on and then I can take you where you need to go."

He flipped a few switches, and I looked around. The house seemed to be a relic of a past century. Its spacious living room was filled with antiques—furniture, paintings, objets d'art and statuary. The walls in the main hallway were papered with an old-fashioned print. An impressive molding of detailed animal figures lined the ceilings.

I was ushered up a stairwell and into a chamber. It was the well-lit room that I had observed from the front of the house. "Take a seat," said the man with the tattoos, motioning towards a large oval table in the center of the room. "Relax. You'll have company soon enough." With that, he left me alone to my thoughts.

The room could easily have been exhibited in a museum. A mahogany table that stood next to the front window held photographs of a man and a woman from a different era. In front of the side window sat a maroon couch suitable for at least three well-fed guests. On the ceiling opposite the front window was a video camera. Though it appeared to be turned off, it still made me uncomfortable. On the walls hung a number of paintings that looked to me to be valuable antiques. This was my kind of art—in the style of old Holland, and Rembrandt in particular. Could it be, I wondered, that they were original creations of Rembrandt's school?

As I was examining a landscape painting, the doorbell rang. At last, company. Seconds later, the door to the room opened and five people walked in. I recognized one, Art Sherman, as a member of my county's School Board. I was sure he didn't know me from Adam. Three of the guests were extremely attractive women in their 20s. I smiled at them as long as I could without being rude. Then, after they took their seats, I went back to browsing the art.

My favorite painting in the room was a portrait of an elderly lady. When I looked at her, she stared back with a riveting expression suggesting that she had been deeply wronged but hadn't lost her dignity. I was transfixed by her face until, finally, someone lost patience waiting around for no apparent gain. In Washington, D.C., one of the world's most restless cities, people don't indefinitely sit still in an unfamiliar house looking at art, regardless of its quality, without a darned good reason.

"Are we supposed to just sit here all night?" asked Allison Schwartz, a striking Semitic woman in her mid to late 20s. Her facial features were classically Ashkenazic, as was her long, wavy, jet-black hair, yet her skin was as fair as any Swede's. As beautiful as she was, she was equally fit. I had noticed her toned leg muscles the moment she walked into the room.

As the senior member of the group—I had them all by

about four minutes—I felt a duty to respond. "I'm sure things will start soon."

"What things?" Allison asked. "Do you know what this is all about?"

No sooner had I shrugged in response to her question than the doorbell rang. And it rang several more times over the next 15 minutes. The first three of the new arrivals were shuttled to our room; the others were either turned away or taken to another part of the house.

At 7:45, with nine of us around the table, the man who had answered the front door came back and passed out questionnaires. He told us that if we wanted to participate in the program advertised in the paper, we had to complete every item. Then he left the room again.

The questionnaires began by asking for all sorts of biographical data. We also had to identify our favorite historical figure (I said "Spinoza," the 17th century Dutch-Jewish philosopher), academic discipline (in my case, philosophy) and hobby (spectator sports). We even had to mention an unfavorable fact about ourselves (my nasty temper). Finally, we were asked whether we had any other commitments on Tuesday evenings. I couldn't think of any.

Shortly after we completed and turned in the questionnaires, two people were asked to leave and were quickly replaced. As soon as the replacements sat down, the man who brought us to the room cleared his throat. "My name's Dave McDonald," he began, in a stern monotone. "I don't own this place. I just take care of it." He then pulled a document out of an envelope. "Your host asked me to read this:

Welcome and thanks for coming. It honors me that you took time out from your busy lives to respond to my invitation in the Washington Post. I hope to repay that honor, if you give me the chance.

I'm fast reaching the winter of my life. It has been very rich in many ways. But I don't feel satisfied or complete. For that, I need help from each of you. In return, I'd like to offer you an opportunity to earn $42,000 in eight months.

All you have to do is participate in a weekly discussion group. The group will meet Tuesday evenings between now and May. Each session must be at least two hours long. There will be 28 meetings in all, and you won't be asked to come during the weeks of Thanksgiving, Christmas or New Year's, or the second week of April.

Those of you who agree to participate will set the agendas for the meetings. But I am hereby supplying the overarching goal of this project—for you to join together in creating a creed, a philosophy of life that can inspire the human race as we begin a new millennium. The nature of that creed is up to you. I don't want any hand in the decision.

Simple enough, wouldn't you say?

I have chosen not to reveal my identity at this time. But rest assured that none of you know me, or at least I can safely say that I don't know any of you. At the group's final meeting on May 23rd, I'll join you in person. That evening, I'll expect an oral presentation and a transcript of that presentation. Its length is for you to decide.

As soon as the composition of the group has been determined, this session will be recorded on video tape. So will all future sessions. I may watch the tapes with a few friends, but believe me, they'll *never* be made public.

I've decided to pay for your participation because I need your attendance. You'll each receive $1,500 for every session you attend. I'll give you checks for $500 by the end of October and $10,000 at the end of the first ten sessions. On May 23rd, I'll pay the rest of what I owe you. But these promises come with a condition. If at any time you miss a total of three sessions, you'll stop getting paid altogether. The same applies if you miss two sessions in a row. Of course, if you can't attend because of a real, documented emergency, I'm sure we can work something out.

That's my proposal. Tonight, I need you to make up your minds. If you have *any* doubt that you can meet the attendance requirements, please tell Mr. McDonald immediately. This project can only succeed if those requirements are honored.

But let me not end on a sober note. This is a cause for celebration, not worry. Some of you are about to embark on a journey that you'll never forget. And with your help, I'm about to learn a new way to look at my world. I look forward to it.

Yours truly, C.F.

When he finished, McDonald asked if there were any questions. Nobody uttered a word. I, for one, was too stunned to say anything. "Fine," McDonald said. "I'll let you think about it a few more minutes. But remember—if you say you're in, you'd *better* be in for the duration."

After McDonald left the room, the group remained silent. I'm sure we were all asking ourselves the same questions. Why were we, a group of random people, being offered such a huge chunk of change? Would we ever see a penny of it? Was this some sort of psychological experiment? Or a practical joke?

Finally, Allison Schwartz broke the silence.

"Are these guys for real?"

"Oh, they're real alright," answered Scott Shaw, a gangly African-American with an impressive, throwback Afro hairstyle and wire-rimmed glasses. "They're real con artists, if you ask me."

"I wouldn't be so sure," Art Sherman said. "I bet they're on the level." Sherman was a tall, distinguished-looking man of medium build, with gray hair and a noticeable paunch. He spoke with a trace of a Southern accent. I guessed he was in his mid-50s.

"Why do you say that?" Allison asked.

"Just a gut feeling. McDonald doesn't have the face of a con-man."

"What about his boss?" Shaw said. "How can you trust an offer that crazy?"

"See if he pays the first couple of checks," I answered.

"I'd still bet they're crazy," Shaw said.

"So what if they are?" I asked. "This isn't about them, it's about us."

We continued for the next several minutes debating the sanity of McDonald's proposal. Some members of the group seemed skeptical. Others, like me, were enthusiastic. Then, at Art Sherman's suggestion, we all introduced ourselves. After everyone had a chance to say a few words, McDonald returned. He was barely inside the door when Paul Choulos, a grey-haired man with a noticeable foreign accent, fired off a question. "Why so much generosity?"

"Does it matter?" McDonald said.

"I'm curious. In Greece, where I'm from, people don't pass out money without a good reason."

"What can I say, pal? Your host isn't Greek."

"I want to know *why* he's doing it," said Choulos.

"That's not your business," said McDonald.

"Sure it is. It's all of our business. You want us to spend dozens of evenings in this room. We've got a right to know what's going on."

"Look," said McDonald. "You know what's going on. A man with a whole lot of money wants to use some of it to sponsor a group. He'd like you all to think up a new creed. He doesn't want to influence what you come up with. It's that simple. If that doesn't work for you, there's the door." McDonald stared at Choulos. I waited for Choulos to respond, but he didn't.

"Well, can you tell us something about the guy?" Allison asked. "*Anything?*"

McDonald took a deep breath. "He's my cousin."

"What else can you say?" asked Allison.

"He's a good man. And you'll be happy to know the two of us don't have much in common."

After fielding a few more questions, McDonald said that it was getting to be time for us to make some decisions. "I'm going downstairs," he added. When I come back, let me know if you want to stay or go. I've got other people down there who are willing to join up if you're not."

Fred Keister, a short and muscular middle-aged man with a bushy mustache and shaved head, was at best ambivalent. He wore a T-shirt with the words "Proud to Be a Redneck" on the front and, as I saw later, "Gus's Gas 'n Guns" on the back. "I'd like to ask y'all a couple of questions," Keister said, after McDonald left the room. "Any of you not go to college?" No one replied. "How about not *graduated*?" Still, no response. "I figured. Folks, I barely finished high school. I ain't going to add nothin' to this group."

"Oh please. That's bull." Shaw said.

"Excuse me?" Keister replied. "You don't know me at all."

"I can't believe I'm saying this to a white guy," Shaw said, "but this group needs diversity, and *you're* it!"

Keister rolled his eyes. "I'm telling you. I'd be a potted plant wastin' that dude's money."

"But you could use that money, couldn't you?" Shaw asked.

"Yeah, so?"

"Then stay with us. You need the money and we need someone who hasn't gotten their common sense and their balls beaten out of them in college."

"I agree," Allison said. "If our benefactor only wanted college grads, you'd have been out of here already."

That seemed to quiet Keister down, but then Sherman started chatting quietly with the woman next to him, whom he had previously introduced as his wife. She was a petite woman, approximately the same age as her husband, with short, dyed-blonde hair and delicate features. "I really appreciate your showing me that ad," I overheard her say. "I know you came here for my sake."

We talked a bit longer about what we thought of our host's proposal until, finally, all nine of us agreed that we'd stick with the project. Allison announced our decision to McDonald when he came back once again to ask for an update.

"You're all *sure* you want to do it?" McDonald asked.

"Positive," said Allison.

"Very well, then," McDonald replied. "You'll excuse me for a moment." He was gone for less than a minute when a light appeared from the ceiling. It was the video camera—my acting career had just begun.

When McDonald returned, Art took it upon himself to be the group's first performer. "Mr. McDonald, if I may introduce myself, I'm Arthur Sherman. After looking the people in this room in the eyes, I'm certain that they'll make an outstanding commitment to accomplishing the goals that our benefactor has established. We're all quite appreciative of the opportunity we're receiving. On May 23rd, I can guarantee we'll return the honor –"

"Give me a break, will you?" McDonald's voice was low, but commanded attention. "I don't care if you want to try to impress these people with your speeches. Don't bother with me."

"Please," continued Sherman. "I only wanted to express my gratitude—"

"Look, man," McDonald said, once again interrupting. "Spare me the B.S. I'll let you in on a secret, Sherman. You wanna know how I got this gig? Your host didn't want to fool with what you people are gonna talk about, and he knows I'm gonna stay the hell away from you. I got no desire to fool with mental masturbation.

"What I *do* like is making money. And I can promise you all that the money here is real. Even the people downstairs will get 50 bucks just for showing up."

"Speaking of money," Sherman continued, before turning to look straight into the camera, "allow me to address my next comments to our host. This is indeed a rare privilege you have bestowed upon us. While I dare say –"

"Knock if off!" For the first time, McDonald's voice sounded hostile. "Do not address *him* again in this room. If *he* wanted to be addressed here, he would have joined the group himself. This is *your* group. Do you understand me?"

"Fine. Whatever you say," Sherman replied, with a look of disgust on his face.

McDonald asked if we'd like to look at our completed questionnaires in order to get to know each other. When we nodded, he passed them out and then left us alone for the rest of the evening.

The group took a few minutes to browse the questionnaires and say a bit more about ourselves. Art Sherman called himself a "traditional" Christian and an American patriot. He had earned most of his income as the chief lobbyist for ATTA—the American Telemarketing and Telefunding Association. Dolores Sherman, Art's wife, had been a member of an ecumenical women's spirituality group for years. "Think of me as a Christian," she said, "only my Christianity and Art's are very different."

Scott Shaw was my age. He identified himself as a screenwriter, but one who hadn't sold a manuscript. Shaw earned his living working at a book store. I couldn't help but smile when I read that one of his hobbies was "muckraking." When introducing himself, he slaughtered just about every sacred cow of the religious right.

Keister was a 45 year old construction worker who grew up in the Allegheny Mountains of central Pennsylvania. He told people to feel free and tell him whenever he was "talkin' like an idiot, which will probably be most of the time." The two of us shared a passion for sports, but not the same ones. I've always been addicted to watching ball games. In his favorite sports, you only win when an animal dies.

At 65, Choulos was the group's oldest member. He referred to himself as a businessman and an observer of the human condition. "I see people for what they are, not how they want me to see them. Maybe that's because I speak seven languages, and each one opens up another world for me. I'll say this: McDonald, he's a typical American—*uncivilized!*"

"If that's what you think about us, why haven't you gone back to Europe?" Art said.

Choulos glared at Sherman before replying. "Maybe I'm something of an anthropologist, yes? Maybe I like to study simple, primitive people. Big shots, beggars, it doesn't matter. Most Americans are children. We'll see if this group is different."

The three young women were all close friends and third year law students from Georgetown. Allison Schwartz introduced herself by saying that "theology, philosophy and political theory are in my blood," but she also described herself as a party animal. "Of the three of us, I'm the one who likes to get out the most, wouldn't you say, ladies?" Her friends smiled. "Usually that means going to a restaurant or a club in the city, not some Scooby Doo house in the 'burbs. But it's always fun to try something different."

Allison came from a group of elite institutions—Stuyvesant High School in New York City, Columbia University and, finally, Georgetown Law Center. This was one woman whom my mother, another New York Jew, would have liked me to get to know better.

Eileen Mitchell was fit, like her two friends, yet she had soft features and a slightly rounded face—quite a contrast to her friends' sleek angular looks. Eileen's hair was blonde, and her blueish-green eyes were anything but intimidating. In fact, her entire appearance invited relaxation. She was a native Minnesotan who identified herself as a lover of music, animals and philosophy—both Eastern and Western. Of the nine people in the room, Eileen was easily the most reserved. I wondered how her voice would be heard.

Linda Smith was the third member of the "Georgetown

Triumvirate" and probably the most attractive. A tall and slender African-American with light brown skin and legs as long as mine (and I'm over six feet tall), she looked like a supermodel. Her facial features were classically proportioned, except for a prominent chin. Whenever Linda spoke, the room was riveted. She had an air about her that commanded attention; it wasn't just her appearance.

Linda grew up in Boston and expressed an interest in politics, maybe even in running for office. "It wasn't my idea to come here tonight. Blame that on Eileen. Girl," Linda said, facing her friend, "thank you, thank you, thank you! I have to say, I can *really* use the money. And I can't wait for the discussions." Linda identified as an unfavorable fact about herself that she wasn't nearly as smart as her two friends.

After we finished introducing ourselves, a number of us had "now what?" looks on our faces. Art was the one to break the silence. "We need a moderator, someone who can impose a little structure. I've been in groups that lack structure. They don't work."

"D'you want to take that on?" Keister asked.

"I'd love to, but I better not. I don't have the time to do it right."

"I nominate Linda," Allison said. "I've known her for two years. She'd be a natural."

"I agree 100 percent," Eileen added.

"Well, how about it?" Art said, addressing Linda. "You seem to be comfortable here. Let me ask you point blank: Do you have it in you to serve as our moderator?"

Linda considered the matter for only a few seconds. "All right. I can do it if no one else wants to. Anybody?" No one responded.

"Fine, I'll be the law around here," Linda said, laughing.

"But I want to point out one thing. I'm no Jefferson. I can bang the gavel, but I can't bang out the Declaration. I'm not a philosopher, and I'm not a poet."

"Fred, she doesn't do construction either," Allison said.

"All right, all right," said Linda. "I just wanted everyone to know my limitations."

"Don't let her rope-a-dope you boys," Allison said. "She can hold her own."

At that point, Linda led us in a brainstorming session that we continued for the rest of the evening and the next Tuesday. We decided to organize all our sessions around presentations that one or two people would give. The speakers would have to e-mail something to the group about their talks a few days in advance of each session. During the year, we'd discuss religion, politics, economics, American culture, psychology and philosophy.

Before the session ended, Linda proposed that we meet each week from 7:30 to 9:45 p.m. Nobody objected. So we had a plan.

In fact, we had more of a plan than the Benefactor knew. After we left the Victorian, Choulos stopped the rest of us on the front lawn. He volunteered to perform a special service: digging up info on our host. "When I'm done," Choulos said, "I'll be able to tell you what kind of undergarments he wears." Once again, nobody objected.

I received a note in my box to see Principal Ericsson during lunch. When I walked into his office, he was steaming.

"Why on earth would you recommend a book to students calling for the legalization of drugs?" he asked. Ericsson was tall, slender and had very little grey hair for a man in his early 50s.

Throughout my tenure at Takoma Park, he had remained popular with the teachers, students and parents. But on that afternoon, I resented the hell out of him.

"Come again?"

"You heard me."

"I don't know what you're talking about. I've never recommended any book about drugs."

"Last week a couple of kids asked you to sponsor a marijuana rights club—"

"Oh crap, Jim. I know what you're talking about," I interrupted. "I just told the students to read *On Liberty* by John Stuart Mill, that's all. Have you read it?"

"No, I'm not familiar with it."

"It's one of the classic works of British philosophy. It explains the basis for civil libertarianism. It's not a book about drugs."

"I had to answer to the mother of one of those kids," Ericsson said. "There was nothing I could say. She was right. You gave them information to help them make better arguments in support of the legalization of marijuana. You used *terrible* judgment."

"Terrible judgment?"

"Listen. Drugs are off limits here. Do you get that?"

"I never said they weren't."

"You don't understand what I'm saying. We can't take any chances with this topic. As far as this school is concerned, there are no good reasons to legalize pot. None!"

I spent the rest of the day seething about what a dense bureaucrat Ericsson could be sometimes. It was a relief when my last class was over. As I approached the final corridor on the way to my car, one of the school's toughest football players was heckling an honor student, Jerome Haupt. Jerome was on both teams that I coached—forensics and tennis. The football player, George London, was the son of Charlotte London, who served with Art Sherman on the county's school board.

London was holding court with a couple of his cronies when Jerome walked by. "What-up, faggot?" London said. "You're looking mighty sexy today. Maybe I should help you out and rip you a new one with my snake." While London was laughing at his own wit, one of his friends chimed in. "I don't know, G. I think you'd have to fight off half the football team first."

By the time I reached London and company, I was loaded for bear. They must have been able to tell because they turned to walk away.

"Where are you boys going?" I asked. "I need to talk to you."

"What do you want?" London said. He spoke to me, but his eyes followed Jerome, who continued walking.

"I heard what you said. You can't talk that way around here. You understand me?"

"Yeah," he said. "I hear ya."

"If I catch you harassing Jerome again, or anyone else for that matter, you're going to be in *huge* trouble with the principal. Is that clear?" Those were my words, though as soon as I said "principal," my stomach turned.

The boys nodded, but London still didn't meet my eyes. I followed his gaze and saw Jerome look back over his shoulder briefly. London managed to establish eye contact, and his expression made his point quite clearly. They'd be resuming their conversation soon enough.

As I continued down the hall to leave the building, my thoughts shifted from London to Art Sherman and the question of whether he could possibly be a friend of London's family.

George was a young punk; Art, a pillar of the community. I imagined them sitting together at a dinner party, with George adopting a persona that he thought the Shermans would like. I suspected he could pull it off. In my experience, bullies are the biggest phonies around.

❧

I had no plans for the weekend. My intent was simply to begin generating ideas for the Creed Room. Certainly, there was nothing in my apartment to distract me. The furnishings were barely worthy of a college dormitory.

Just as I sat down to write out my first idea, I got a call. It was from the most important person in my life—a walking and talking superego.

"Hello?"

"Hi, sweetheart."

"Oh hi, Mother."

"Did you have a good week, honey?"

"Yes and no."

"What's wrong?" she asked.

"I had some tough moments at school. But believe me, I'm still having fun. I knew I'd have to take the bad with the good when I went into teaching."

"Don't bring up that decision, Sammy." All the warmth in her voice disappeared. "You know what I think about it."

How could I not? She brought up the topic in just about all of our conversations. It drove me to distraction. "Mother, I wasn't trying to—"

"You could be making $200,000 a year or more now. You could own your own house. You could spend vacations in Rome, Italy, not Rome, Georgia."

"I've never been to Rome, Georgia. But then I think you

knew that."

"I know that when you're older you're going to regret every year you spend teaching and not earning a real living."

"Tell me, Mother. Do you value anything other than money?"

"I'm not like that, Sammy. I don't have to tell you how many causes I care about and how involved I am with gun control."

"I know how many causes you *talk* about. You only seem to care about one."

"Don't confuse the issue. I'm your mother. I've every right to worry about your future. How are you going to take care of yourself when you're my age? You won't have the money to travel. You won't be able to retire until you're old, just like I can't. Of course, with all the stress you put on yourself, you'll probably never get to be old."

"Mother. You're getting worked up over nothing."

"Nothing? I'll tell you what's nothing. The respect you teachers get. It's not just the money. I know your working conditions. No office. No secretary. If you're going to teach, at least be a professor."

"Mother. Do I have to—"

"High school teaching's no job for someone with a real brain. It's a waste of your talent."

"Mother, you're crazy. You know you're crazy."

"No, *you're* crazy! You tossed away so much potential. You could have done anything you wanted. Law. Medicine."

"Do you hear yourself?" I asked, finally beginning to lose my composure. "You talk like I rob banks for a living. I'm a school teacher. I can make a difference—"

"Just the other day I was listening to Rose Bernstein talk about her son. He teaches political science at Yale. I don't know how much he makes but at least he's allowed the time to write articles, lecture at conferences, teach whatever he wants. Oh, you should hear Rose. She goes on and on about Joshua's awards and honors. It was the same way with her daughter, the surgeon. What's she making now, $800,000 a year? And here you are—"

"MOTHER! Will you shut the hell up! You're out of your mind, do you know that? I don't give a crap about your friends' children. Do you hear me? I help kids become thinkers. And I like it. OK? It's none of your goddamned business what I do anyway!"

"Don't speak to me like that, Sammy."

I tried to calm myself, but it wasn't easy. "Now how should I speak to you when you treat me like a five year old?"

"Don't you speak like that to me. You show me some respect. I'm not going to listen to you curse at me and ridicule me."

"*You're* the one who's being abusive. I was trying to relax and you call and berate me for the millionth time about how poor I am and how lousy my career is and how wonderful all your friends' kids are and all that other bullshit. What do you want me to do?"

"I'm telling you not to speak like that to me, Sammy! I let you go to college 3,000 miles from home. I put you through Stanford. I watched you get into Harvard Law School. A dream, Sammy. A dream! Now I have to sit back and see you throw it all away on a job for people who have half your brains?"

All I could do was shake my head in awe at her ability to disrupt my sanity. "Mother. I can't take it. Will you stop?"

I could hear her take a deep breath. "Alright, alright. I don't like this any more than you do. You *know* I'm not going to be able to sleep tonight. But I'll tell you this, Sammy, I won't put up with your language. I can't live like this. Do you understand what I'm saying?"

"Yes, Mother. I'm sorry to yell at you, but you've got to stop berating my job. Deal with it. Your only child's a school teacher. Not a professor, a teacher. Good night, Mother."

"Listen, Sammy—"

"Good night, Mother!" I had to stay firm with her or she'd keep me on the phone for another hour. Thankfully, she relented.

"Good night, Sammy."

CHAPTER 2

THE PLUNGE

*L*uigi's was my favorite restaurant in Rockville. It was an oasis in a stomach-turning suburban mall. For me, the Maplewood Mall and the Victorian were polar opposites. The Victorian fostered reflection and a respect for the past. Maplewood celebrated materialism and all the latest fads. At the top of the mall, you could find its signature store—The Player's Palace. That's where herds of teenagers and young adults gather in a video games Mecca. It's noisy, hectic and dark. It's also *incredibly* popular.

Just as the Victorian's art evoked images of Amsterdam, so did Maplewood. It had one worthwhile store in addition to Luigi's—a huge bookstore called Newberg's. To see Newberg's and the Player's Palace in the same mall reminded me of Holland's largest city, where within a relatively small area you can take in the Van Gogh, Rembrandt and Anne Frank Houses, on the one hand, and the Hemp Museum and Red Light District, on the other. Obviously, the Dutch are civil libertarians; Americans are more Puritanical. But since the Player's Palace doesn't promote sex or drugs, we affirm its right to exist. Then again, that doesn't mean we all have to respect it or like it. Snobbery may not be fashionable, but it'll do in a pinch.

I had been seated at Luigi's for nearly a half hour when

Allison walked in. She looked unbelievably sexy. That was due to her self confidence, mostly—that and one of her signature skirts that didn't go nearly as far down as her knees. Of course, I already knew that Allison was a workout warrior. What I hadn't seen before was how beautiful and warm her smile could be.

Three days before, I had e-mailed to the group an essay introducing my presentation at the next Creed Room session. In the e-mail, I invited the others to meet me for dinner at Luigi's, which wasn't far from the Victorian. Allison was the only one who showed up.

My essay discussed the religious views that I grew up with in an atheist-Jewish family. I explained that while my beliefs had changed since childhood, I've always thought you can't really understand anyone's world view until you know where it has come from. "Maybe I can only speak for myself," I wrote, "but what I was taught as a child about religion formed the foundation of what I've thought ever since."

I went on to say in the essay that my parents worshiped science and ascribed all of life's mysteries to natural laws. They taught me that believing in God was like believing in Santa Claus. Just as kids picture Santa Claus as the perfect grandfather who gives us whatever presents we need, so adult Believers imagine God as a father who perfectly serves our needs on a cosmic scale. He tells us what He wants out of us. Then, if we act like good little boys and girls, He promises to deliver us happiness—if not in this life, then in the next. "Such a deal!" my mother would say, mocking anyone who expected a divine payoff.

My parents, I wrote, told me to submit every idea to the crucible of reason. When I did, all the talk of God as a Cosmic Santa Claus withered away. The concept of an all-wise, merciful and powerful creator seemed ridiculous after Auschwitz, unless, by mercy, we mean the mercy of the ovens; they were, after all, a respite from the torture of the death camps. God, I decided, was but a figment of our imaginations. We created Him in our own image to provide a road map for how to behave. As for the idea that He sent plagues against the Egyptians or promised land to the Jews, I concluded that the founders of Torah Judaism had no respect for the truth. They wanted to manipulate us to do good things. If the truth got in the way, then the truth be damned!

Despite all their criticism of Torah Judaism, I explained in the essay, my parents raised me to observe the Jewish holidays, become a bar mitzvah and associate myself with the Jewish people. Their Judaism-Lite didn't satisfy me, but perhaps it kept my flame burning, because I remained fascinated throughout my childhood with the basic issues of religion—like whether God exists or whether we have an immortal soul. Even as an atheist, I remained open-minded, always ready to believe that the old religious sages knew something that I didn't. In college, I "graduated" from atheism to agnosticism and explored several religions, but none seemed to fit the bill. I explained that it wasn't until after college that I came to embrace the idea of God. But even then, I couldn't get comfortable within any religious community.

Sitting across from Allison at Luigi's, I wondered what she thought of my essay. I didn't have to wonder very long.

"I want to talk to you about what you wrote," Allison said.

"No problem."

"I've got to know whether, if I criticize it, you're going to get defensive. Because if you are, I'd rather just say how great it was."

"You don't have to patronize me if that's what you're asking."

"Good," Allison said, smiling. She went on to explain that she thought the picture of Judaism that I painted in my essay didn't do the religion justice. But she wouldn't tell me why. Instead, she made a proposal: that she act in the role of "destabilizer" after my presentation.

"What does Linda have to say about that?" I asked.

"Oh, Linda. I'm glad you brought her up."

"Why's that?" I asked.

"Guess what she got in the mail last week? A beautiful hand-crafted pair of African earrings. From *you know who.*"

"Our benefactor?"

"The very same. And he sent a note. It said something like: "Dear Linda. Thank you for accepting the job of coordinator. I won't pay you any extra. I can tell that, for you, virtue needs no reward. But I wanted at least to acknowledge your efforts with a little gift. Do me a favor and wear them to the next session. Sincerely, Your Loyal Viewer."

"So I guess I'll see the earrings tonight," I replied.

"I reckon so," said Allison. "Getting back to your question, it was Linda's idea that I play the destabilizer. She figured the group sees the two of us as pretty similar—both liberal Jews in our 20s. If we can go at each other, everyone else will start speaking their minds too."

"I'm OK with that. I've always liked to argue. That's probably why I went to law school."

"I didn't know you went to law school," she said.

"For almost two years. I didn't like it enough to stick around."

"Where were you?"

"Harvard."

"And you dropped out to be a school teacher?"

"I'm nuts, aren't I?"

"You wouldn't be the first person who hated law school. Anyway, here's my plan. Let me attack what you wrote. Then you counterpunch. Hit me back hard if you'd like. I don't care."

"You'd probably like it," I said, smiling.

"Probably so. I can tell you this. If we all show up each week just to agree with each other, I swear I'm bringing my sleeping bag."

"I wouldn't worry about that. Not with this crew."

"I'll do my best to attack your *ideas* and not resort to the ad hominem," she continued. "If I slip once or twice, ignore it. Whatever vinegar I'll bring won't be personal, just business."

"Thank you, Godfather," I replied.

"Assuming you can still stand me after this evening," she said, "I want you to come to my apartment this Friday night. I've got a treat for you. A piece of Judaica. How about it?"

Of course I accepted. Are you kidding?

It took me a while that evening to get used to how quickly Allison spoke. At times I almost struggled to follow her. After we paid our checks, she told me that she'd need a lift to that "creepy mansion" since she rode the subway to get to the mall.

"You think it's creepy?" I said. "I kind of like it."

"Oh, it's creepy. Mostly 'cause of that Dave McDonald. You wouldn't understand. You've never been approached by a large hulking man who asks you to give him a hummer."

"McDonald did that?"

"No. But he reminds me of someone else who did. Same mannerisms exactly."

"Do you think we'll ever see Choulos again?" I asked. He never showed up at the group's second and third sessions, so according to the house rules, he could be disqualified from getting paid.

"Good question," Allison said. "I'd just as soon he stayed

away. That's guy's totally full of himself."

"I was kind of looking forward to hearing what he'd come up with on the Benefactor."

"Oh yeah," said Allison. "Choulos was supposed to dig up dirt, wasn't he? I tell you what. Maybe in a couple of weeks I'll have the time to do some digging."

Allison and I also talked about Baruch Spinoza, the philosopher. She brought him up because she remembered that I had mentioned Spinoza in my questionnaire. Allison said she had always associated Spinoza with stoicism and thought it was odd that I identified myself as having a bad temper but also said that I loved Spinoza.

"Do you really have a temper, or are you just not as stoic as Spinoza?" she asked.

"No. I've got a temper. I never said I was some sort of model Spinozist. I just like him."

"So you're not wearing one of those 'What Would Spinoza Do?' bracelets?"

"Sorry. I left it at home next to my 'What Would Descartes Think?' necklace."

Allison smiled. "I'll tell you what he'd think—that you philosophize too much when it comes to religion. But I don't want to get into that now. I'll talk about that in Garrett Park."

We got to Buckingham Drive exactly when the session was supposed to start. Allison asked me to drop her off and then drive a block down the road before parking. She didn't want the rest of the group to see us together.

McDonald met me at the front door. He said gruffly that I was late. I nodded and took the stairs two at a time.

"Sam, we were just talking about how much we liked your

essay," Linda said, as soon as I walked into the Creed Room. She was, indeed, sporting exquisitely carved earings. One was in the shape of an antelope; the other, a gazelle.

"Thanks," I said. I had no idea how the group would react to it.

"I think you know that when you're finished, Allison's going to present a response," Linda said. "I say go ahead and start. You've got the floor."

"I wanted to speak to you tonight about *labels*," I began, standing by the front window. "My written presentation was full of references to them. Take, for example, labels for God. I referred to God as the Cosmic Santa Claus or the Perfect Father. People who buy into the concept of God I called Believers. Those who don't, I called Atheists.

"A label was used for the belief system of my distant ancestors—Torah Judaism. I used a whimsical label for the way my parents raised me—Judaism-Lite.

"Obviously, I like to play with religious labels. But many people would rather scrap them altogether. They'd tell you it's impossible to create religious labels without over-simplifying the profound or attempting to describe the indescribable.

"Fair enough. Religious labels are crude. And yet I'm here to speak on their behalf. It's not because I especially like them. I simply can't imagine thinking about life without them. They're like democracy and capitalism—hardly ideal, but the alternatives are horrid.

"Religious labels are designed to clarify, to distinguish. They help give us a sense of identity, and allow like-minded people to find each other and form a fellowship. They can also help reasonable people explore their differences. If I say I'm a Muslim and you're a Jew, it means we care enough about what those words mean to identify ourselves with them. If we're lucky enough to enter into a discussion about them, we open our minds to the views of someone else. That's how we test our own views. That's how we allow ourselves to grow.

"For most of us, once we blow off religious labels we start blowing off religion altogether. Labels give our beliefs their shape, their meaning. They also galvanize our passions.

"Lest I sound too positive, there's one religious label that I *can't* stand—agnostic." I looked around and was happy to see that nobody seemed put out. "I once used that word to describe myself, so I understand why people use it. I just happen to hate it.

"We need conversation *starters*. That's the whole point of religious labels—to spur dialogue—either with ourselves or others. I'd love to live in a society where, at parties, whenever things got boring, someone would bring up religion and all of a sudden the conversation would get lively. When I imagine who'd participate in those conversations, the last group I think about are the agnostics. You'll almost never hear an adult use that word as a conversation starter. It usually means 'I don't know and I don't care. There are no answers to those questions anyway, so why worry about them?' That's the attitude that alienates me. If a person doesn't care about what fascinates me most in life—worse yet, if he feels intellectually grounded in not caring—how can the two of us ever build a bridge?

"Agnostics might deny that their attitude is grounded in apathy. But facts are facts. Just about every adult who calls himself an agnostic gets bored silly every time the topic turns to God.

"If I wanted to be charitable about agnosticism, I'd think about agnostic teenagers. A lot of them aren't apathetic at all. When I used the term for myself, I cared a lot about whether God exists. I only wanted to make the point that we can't know the answer for sure.

"That sounds harmless enough, doesn't it? Lord knows it's the truth. Obviously we can't answer the deepest religious questions with any degree of certainty. Big realization there. If I had my druthers, we'd kill agnosticism with kindness. Next year on July 4th, everybody would go to their county courthouse at High Noon and proclaim in unison, 'WE CAN'T KNOW WHETHER GOD EXISTS WITH ANY REASONABLE DEGREE OF CERTAINTY. SOME QUESTIONS JUST CAN'T BE ANSWERED LOGICALLY.' There you have it. A truism. If we all say it once, perhaps none of us will have to say it again.

"Forget the need for certainty! Certainty and religion don't go together. Whenever you see them combined, you see the face of close-mindedness, bigotry, fanaticism. But forget agnosticism too. It begs the questions that really matter. Do you or don't you live life as a believer in God? Do you love your God? Does your love for God inspire you in any way?

"If the answer to those questions is 'no,' then damn it, say so! I'd respect your right to have that attitude. It's a whole lot more courageous than to call yourself an agnostic and then quickly change the subject back to the world of business or politics or the stinkin' weather.

"If you're tempted to refer to yourself as an agnostic, try this instead: call yourself 'open minded about God.' That conveys a wonderful message—even though you can't answer the question of God, you're interested in learning more about it. The problem with the word 'agnostic' is that it *connotes* that since we can't know the ultimate truths about religion, there's no reason to think about or have feelings for God. That's the attitude I want to fight."

I went on to talk a bit about atheism. I explained that it takes guts to call yourself an atheist. It means you're taking a stand, and an unpopular one too. By rejecting God with an exclamation point, atheists at least show that they care about the topic.

"So I'm not alienated by atheism," I continued. "But I'm no great fan of that label either. It doesn't go far enough in staking out a position. It doesn't say much about what you believe or how you live. It only identifies something you reject: a particular type of God worship.

"Fine, atheists. Reject the old god. What do you put in his place? When you're not thinking about God, what *are* you thinking about? Tell us something about yourselves affirmatively, not just negatively. That's a conversation *starter*.

"When I hear people describe themselves as Secular Humanists or Ethical Culturists, I'm intrigued. I want to know more about their beliefs and how those beliefs affect their lifestyles. I want to know how much they give a damn about their faith, how passionate they are. Those are labels I applaud even though they reject something that I love deeply.

"There. I admitted it. I believe in a God. Maybe mine is a lot like your God; maybe not. If you believe in a God who's been anthropomorphized, you'll probably think of me soon enough as an atheist. I wouldn't care if you do. I don't let anyone else define God for me.

"I'd love to discuss where we stand on the ultimate questions, but tonight, I wanted to address something even more fundamental. Those stances divide us. I want to help us come together. We have only seven months to do that, so we'd better build a foundation quickly. Since we all responded to an ad inviting us to start a new creed, we should at least be able to agree on a common enemy: apathy. The name of this game is to be committed to the idea that religion *matters*. That politics matters. That every topic we discuss in this room matters.

"I see this as some sort of intellectual wrestling club where independent thinkers are forced to butt heads. If we're going to make this work, we better be ready to be turned on by everything we hear in this room, as long as it's expressed logically and with conviction. As for our dogma, we'd better check all that baggage at the door. Now!

"Before closing, I want to share with you my favorite label: Student of Philosophy. When I hear people describe themselves that way, I know we're kindred spirits. You can't be a Student of Philosophy if you don't share the values I'm praising. You can be a professional philosopher, but they're not all students of philosophy any more than all lawyers are students of law. It could be just a job, not a love affair. True students love their subjects. Students of Philosophy love the open-minded search for wisdom even if nobody's paying to know what they've found."

At that point I turned to Allison and said, "Your argument, counselor."

Allison got up and approached where I was standing. Our eyes met for a second. She had the look of a fierce competitor in a one-on-one battle, and I was clearly her intended prey.

"You would *too* care if we saw you as an atheist," she said to me in front of the group.

"Maybe a little," I acknowledged. "Just a teeny bit."

Allison nodded her head. It was her first victory of the evening.

She was just about to begin her speech when the doorbell rang. I wondered if she would start anyway, but she didn't. "You don't think it could be Choulos, do you?" she asked the group.

"It's probably a friend of McDonald's," Linda said. "Go ahead and get started."

"Fine," said Allison. "I was asked tonight to respond to Sam's *written* presentation, and that's mostly what I'm going to do. But I've got to say I liked what we just heard. I agree with his point about agnostics and apathy. I definitely second what he said about the need to check our dogma at the door. That'll be easy for me. I don't have much dogma to check. I've always hated it as much as Sam hates apathy.

"I'll even agree with Sam about the value of labels. The problem is that when you use them you ought to know what you're talking about, which brings me to Sam's essay. A lot of it focused on the label of Torah Judaism. But what I know as Torah Judaism and what he wrote about are very different things. His Torah Judaism is a strawman, something he thought up himself so that he could rip it apart. Mine's a great religion."

At that point we heard shouting from the ground floor. Allison stopped talking, and we all listened. Choulos had indeed returned, and it sounded like McDonald wouldn't let him come upstairs. I struggled to make out their words but had little success. Finally, Shaw said that he wanted to see the insanity, and after he left the room, the rest of us followed. When I got to the ground floor, I saw Choulos waving his finger in McDonald's face despite being barely half our custodian's size. McDonald responded to the scolding with resolve: "You broke the rules. You missed two consecutive meetings. You're no longer welcome here. Now leave!"

"Listen to me," Choulos replied. "I had personal business to attend to. I give you my word on that. I'm here to give this group my full attention. My problems are behind me. I'm ready to turn my attention to the creed, I swear to you. I will make you proud. I will make you *all* proud. So I will take my rightful seat now, yes?"

"Don't push me, little man," said McDonald. "I discussed your so-called 'emergency' with my cousin, and he said it didn't qualify. You're out of the group. End of story."

Choulos wouldn't take no for an answer. He darted up the stairs and into the Creed Room, with McDonald chasing after him. "Everyone out of here," McDonald said. "I mean everyone. Choulos and I have some business to take care of." What kind of business was clear enough.

"Are you threatening me?" Choulos asked.

"Take it any way you want to," McDonald replied.

"In my country, if you make a threat, you had better be man enough to accept the consequences. Are you?"

"Out of this house. *Now!*" said McDonald.

"Very well," said Choulos. "Have it your way. For the moment." And with that, Choulos left the room. Seconds later, he slammed the front door with authority.

We didn't get back to the subject of religion for quite a while. With the video camera running, we discussed what McDonald did. Most of us thought he should have been more flexible. Then again, it wasn't our money at stake, nor McDonald's. As Keister pointed out, McDonald didn't make the rules, and he probably didn't have the authority to change them.

After we had dissected the McDonald-Choulos exchange to death, Allison resumed her talk. "That jackass is a tough act to follow," she said. "And I don't mean you, Sam."

I smiled. Hopefully, we all knew whom she meant.

"I was saying that Sam didn't do Torah Judaism justice when he talked about it in his essay. Keep in mind, I don't describe my religion as Torah Judaism. I'm just a garden variety Jew. In some ways, I'm traditional; in others, I'm modern. Certainly in appearance I'm modern."

Allison laughed and so did I. Then I glanced at her thighs. The idea of an elderly Talmudic sage setting foot in the same room with her without constantly averting his eyes would be an absurdity.

"Now I'm no rabbi, but my father is. He taught me a lot about Judaism over the years, enough so that I don't like to hear people talk about it the way Sam did. Sam, if you're going to insult our religion, at least get it right.

"A Jew always has the Torah to cling to. I can't say exactly what it meant to my ancestors. But most modern religious Jews don't draw from it the belief that God created eye-popping miracles that mocked the laws of nature. Who buys into that anymore? Just the Orthodox, and not all of them either.

"Sam speaks as if Judaism breeds stupid Pollyannas who think of religious myths as literal truths. That's not Judaism. The Jews I know take the myths as myths. But they're still important. We use them to build a common body of knowledge from which we can weave beautiful webs. With one, we teach about morality. With another, we create awesome holidays. With a third, we learn enlightened approaches to birth, death or marriage. Our myths have nothing to do with brainwashing ourselves to believe in nonsense as long as it's in the Torah.

"It's a book of stories, that's all. It just happens to be *our* book of stories.

"I'll tell you one thing about the Torah. There's nothing in that book half as ridiculous as the stuff Sam wrote about God. Remember when he talked about God being like Santa Claus? Really, Sam's God is more like Geppeto, and we're supposed to behave like good little puppets.

"I'm sorry, Sam, but gag me. Jewish people don't think that way. At least the Jews I know don't think like that. You must be hangin' with some pretty strange ones."

I had to interrupt. "I've known a wide range, actually."

"So have I," Allison fired back. "And most of them don't have their heads up their butts.

"Sam's big mistake is that he confuses religion with philosophy," Allison continued. "We heard him call himself a Student of Philosophy, and I wouldn't doubt that label for a second. But he thinks that makes him qualified to criticize a great religion. It doesn't.

"Philosophy and religion are different animals. One's about reason; the other's about wholeness. The best philosophers know the difference. Religion appeals to *every* part of our soul. Philosophy only appeals to our intellect. That's why the great religions center around spiritual leaders, not builders of complex, intellectual systems.

"Western philosophy takes profound religious symbols and strips them down to propositions. The propositions are then analyzed for truth or falsity, rationality or absurdity. It's a sport that dates back to the ancient Greeks. Tonight we've heard from one of its disciples. Not a Jew but a Greek. And I'm not talking about Choulos."

"No, we heard from him too," Art interrupted. "Hopefully for the last time."

Allison nodded and continued with her talk. "Please get this: religion isn't above all a search for truth. It's not a search for anything. It's an awakening to what's right in front of our eyes. You don't dissect it or analyze it. You embrace it, talk to it, listen to it. You recognize in it our common source of unity, and the meaning we've found in our lives. Sam doesn't want us to anthropomorphize that source of meaning. Believe me, neither does Judaism.

"Jews shouldn't be thinking of God as human. God transcends us. We can't begin to appreciate how transcendent He is.

And yet we've got to face facts. We're limited by our humanity in whatever we do, and if we hope to relate to God, we'd better allow ourselves to *experience* Him in a way that makes sense to us. That's why we talk and listen to Him through human language. That's why we think about him as all-wise, merciful and powerful. That's why we assume He feels the best of human emotions, like compassion. It makes Him *real* to us. It lets Him touch our hearts.

"What's Sam's alternative anyway? Approaching God as if we were computers, always acting in accordance with the rigorous demands of logic. Heaven help us if we'd ask God for a favor. How philosophically incorrect. How gauche!

"Religious Jews want our God to be near us. Otherwise, He's not worthy of the name God. We're human, so perhaps we treat Him a bit like one too, but we don't forget common sense. We appreciate that God isn't one of us and that the Torah doesn't do away with the truths of science. Think of how many Jews are great scientists. We can have our God *and* science.

"But most importantly, we have our way of life. Above all else, that's what Judaism is—a set of guidelines for living the good life. The Jew that Sam sculpted in his essay provides an example of one lifestyle—the lonely thinker who even at an early age was fascinated by the ultimate philosophical questions. I don't begrudge Sam his hobbies. I only want to point out that our religious lives don't have to be that lonely. Judaism emphasizes community. It offers a path for people to *celebrate* life together, not just to learn. We pray. We sing. Mostly we rejoice in what God has given us. Every sunset, every bite of food, every smile. Each of those things is worth far more than any true or false proposition—even the proposition that 'God exists.'

"Words can do justice to most propositions. But the transcendent can't be captured in words. We can only approach it through our feelings, like when we recognize in a sunset the same source of beauty that we see in a smile."

At that point, she walked back to her seat.

I didn't know how to react at first. I wanted to reflect on what she said. But then I realized that Allison wanted me to engage her. And whatever Allison wanted, Allison got.

"You've never been an atheist, have you?" I asked her.

"Can't say I have. My dad taught me how to come to God in my own way. I had no reason to be an atheist."

"That's what I figured. You sound like someone who assumes that everyone else gets the whole point of religion just because you did."

"I wouldn't say that."

"Wouldn't you?" I said. "Most of the bright people I meet have totally given up on religion. They're sick and tired of all the pie in the sky about the Biblical God and miracles. You can romanticize it and call it myth, but a lot of people take those myths as fact. And they're peddling that stuff everywhere you look."

"There are ignorant people in the world. So what?" Allison asked.

"So they're dominating the discourse, that's what! When you hear a rabbi wax poetic about God without ever explaining who he's talking about, do you think he's providing a service? Maybe he knows that God doesn't think or feel like a person, but his flock doesn't. Half of them still think of God as Santa Claus. Most of the others are looking at their watches and wondering how they get dragged to synagogue week after week to listen to a bunch of junk."

"Where do you come up with this stuff? Do you work for the Gallup Poll?"

"Let's put it this way," I replied. "I can't stand the fact that so many people still think the way I used to. They want to believe in a God but can't bring themselves to buy all the traditional junk, so they become alienated from the whole process. They're the ones I'd like to reach."

"And you think they can be reached through philosophy?" Allison asked.

"Many of them."

"I doubt it. I think you're a little unusual, Sam. Most people come to religion through the desire to celebrate, not to philosophize."

"I'm not trying to convert people," I replied. "I only want the thinkers of the world to know that there's a place for them in religion."

"I guess if you set your goals low enough," she said, "you're more likely to meet them."

After another minute or two of fencing between Allison and me, Linda asked that we take a break. Art was the first to speak when we resumed. "I've got a question," he said. "Let me see a show of hands. How many of you are Christians? *Believing* Christians?"

Art and Dolores both raised their hands. Keister started to raise his, but then waved it from side to side as if to say "maybe yes, maybe no."

"That's what I suspected," Art said. "Folks, I'm very concerned that Christ's message isn't going to be taken seriously around here." At that point, Dolores told her husband, in essence, to take a Valium, and she was immediately seconded by Scott Shaw.

"Here's the bottom line," Shaw said. "Nobody should care if they start off in the minority. Say what you have to say and assume people will listen with an open mind. Whether your point comes from Christ, the Buddha or my Uncle Lionel shouldn't matter."

"Is your Uncle Lionel a minister?" I asked.

"He's a drunk," Shaw said. "But he comes up with a few gems now and then."

As the discussion continued, some of the Creed Room's less opinionated voices opened up a bit. After Eileen said that she was still looking for the right label to describe herself, Keister asked if she believed in God. "That would depend on how you defined the word," she replied. "I don't get much sustenance from the Biblical God. Mine is more like some sort of *force*, some positive spirit inside of each of us."

As I listened to Eileen, I noticed her uniqueness for the first time. This was ironic, since I viewed some of her words as clichéd, especially that last statement about God. She spoke with such purity and openness of heart that I somehow felt free to interrupt her in mid-sentence.

"May I make a suggestion?" I asked, while she was talking.
"Sure."

"You spoke of God as a force inside us, but I'd suggest you flip that around. Don't just view God as in us. Why not view us as in God?"

"I'll think about that. Thanks." She actually seemed to welcome the interruption.

Keister spoke next. He went on at length about his experiences with Christianity. There was a time, he said, when he went to church every Sunday, but that ended when his wife died from cancer. "Even before the cancer, I wondered about believing in *miracles* with a capital M—like Jesus rising from the grave or Moses parting the sea. I'd already been thinkin' that this world don't look like it was made by a God we'd want to believe in. After my wife got cancer, I'd be thinkin' that stuff even more. That cancer just tore me apart.

"Right now, I don't know what to believe. Sam, I won't call myself an agnostic, but ... well, I know people who would."

"That's OK," I said, smiling. "As long as *you* don't."

"Let me say this," Keister continued. "People can say all they want about how there's no God and how Jesus ain't God's Son, but there's somethin' about bein' Christian that seems to do good things for folks. The guys at the site who don't believe in Christ, I wouldn't trust 'em as far as I can throw 'em. You see 'em hittin' on women or drivin' drunk. They're plain nasty. The Christians are different. Most of 'em got somethin' inside that stops 'em from acting like animals. I reckon it comes from the message of Christ. It's a great message. That's why I still more or less think of myself as a Christian. I'm happy to think about what's underneath this world—only if you take away Jesus, I ain't sure I want to be around to find out."

The last person to speak during that session was Linda Smith. She told us that the concept of God didn't do much for her. Instead, her religion focused on human beings.

"I believe in hard work and treating people with respect. My politics are a fair amount farther to the right than most African-Americans'. You can say I'm obsessed with the idea of individual responsibility. If people took responsibility for their actions and their fates, believe me, this would be a completely different world."

At the end of the session, Linda said she wanted the next session to be devoted to Christianity. Art passed on the opportunity to do a presentation, saying that this would be a particularly bad week for him work-wise. Then he turned to his wife. "What about you, Dolores? You'll have some time after you finish eating your daily bon-bons, won't you?" She didn't look thrilled with the bon-bons comment (I suspect she'd heard it once or twice before), but she agreed to give a talk. Personally, I wanted to learn more about Christianity and was pleased that Dolores, and not her husband, would be the presenter.

As we walked out of the Creed Room, Allison approached me, glanced around to confirm that nobody was watching, and put a piece of paper in my hand. I opened it when I arrived at my car. It said, "1920 17th St., N.W., Apt. 305, 6:30 p.m., Friday, October 22. Don't be late."

CHAPTER 3

THE WARNING

"*H*ello my friends," said a voice from behind a large oak tree in the front yard of the Victorian. "I've got a present for you." We couldn't see him, but Choulos's accent was unmistakable.

"You know what they say about Greeks bearing gifts," Art mumbled.

"I've got a letter for each of you," Choulos said, finally presenting himself. "After McDonald threw me out of the house, I drove home and typed it up on my computer. I think you'll find it very, very interesting." Here's what it said:

YOU STAND WARNED

Your benefactor's name is Charles F. Feaver.

You might want to think of him not as a benefactor but as a malefactor.

He speculates in art, and quite successfully. He once sold a Vermeer painting for $15 million.

He is known to have sold paintings that resemble 17th century Dutch art but are, in fact, modern reproductions.

He is believed to be a member of a secret society called the Empire Club. Only the rich and powerful may join.

Please give him this message, through his servant, McDonald:

Woe unto the stubborn.

He who does not bend, shall break!"

"You got any evidence for this?" Shaw asked, voicing exactly what I was thinking.

"You believe I made it up?" Choulos said.

"I didn't say that," Shaw replied. "I just want to know your sources."

"I got his name from the county real estate people. I went on the Internet. I made phone calls. I put on an act, alright? I pretended I was looking into buying artwork from this man."

Just then, McDonald walked out of the house. He spotted Choulos right away.

"I told you to get off this property! How deaf and *dumb* are you?"

"No problem. I'm leaving," Choulos said. "My business here is finished."

McDonald didn't appear to notice the letters in our hands. Until the moment Choulos drove away, McDonald looked at no one else.

That night, I went to bed awed by Allison's speech and confused by Choulos's warning. I was also thinking about something Linda said in our very first session, when she announced that she wasn't up to taking on the role of the group's Jefferson. I had Jefferson on my mind for two reasons. First, because I was planning on teaching my next Honors U.S. History class about him. And second, because I had visions of doing for the

Creed Room what Linda thought she couldn't, though instead
of drafting a Declaration of Independence, I would pen a
Declaration of Unity.

Jefferson may not have been the most ethical or courageous
of our Founding Fathers, I told my students the next day during seventh period, but he remains the quintessential American
genius. Put aside that he wrote our defining political document. That's just the beginning of his accomplishments.
Whether you're a lover of art, music, philosophy, science,
anthropology, religion, nature, language, architecture or literature, you're mining ore that Jefferson explored at a deep level.
I've always loved that line from President Kennedy when he
brought in a number of Nobel laureates for a formal dinner
and announced that this was the greatest assemblage of intelligence at the White House since Jefferson dined alone.

While toasting Jefferson's lifestyle to my students, I was
compelled to point out how much it was supported by the
institution of slavery. Still, more than the other southern aristocrats, Jefferson created a day-in day-out routine that was
remarkable for how it enabled him to cultivate so many schol-
arly and aesthetic interests and still have time to attend to the
affairs of the state. Jefferson strived to create a nation whose
citizens could live in freedom, think for themselves, worship
whomever they wanted, and develop their talents as much as
possible. For the vision of a statesman, I asked my class, what
could be greater than that?

After offering some general ideas in praise of Jefferson, my
plan had been to focus on one specific aspect of his thought—
his views on education. Unfortunately, I never got there.

"How many of you have been to Monticello?" I asked. A few
students raised their hands.

"It's my single favorite place in the United States, and it's less than a three hour drive away," I said. "The place is amazing. The history, the architecture, the views, all of it.

"When I was a kid, I especially loved Monticello's inventions, like the two doors that open when you only pull one handle. Today, I marvel mostly at the books. He once owned 6,000. Jefferson was like the lead character in 'Good Will Hunting'—pick any subject, he'd learn it quickly and never forget what he'd learned. At Monticello, you can see *how* he learned it. He surrounded himself with beauty, and he treated every hour as a divine gift.

"Sometimes when I go there, I turn to face D.C. And I try to keep this in mind: Jefferson wasn't content just to lift himself up. He felt a duty to help the rest of us too. He and his friends forged a vast wealthy republic unlike any this world had seen. Jefferson was truly a great man."

"That's it. I can't listen to this any more." The words were spoken loudly, defiantly. They came from Lorraine Jackson, a 17-year-old who hadn't missed either the school's honor roll or the McDonald's All American basketball team in two years and who was usually an absolute joy to teach. "This has got to be the most biased, ridiculous lecture I've ever heard."

"So, Lorraine," I said, taking a deep breath. "What's the problem?"

"Oh come on, you know the problem. You talk about this guy like he's some *god*. How do you think he was able to live like one?"

"If you're talking about slavery, I've already acknowledged that without slavery, there wouldn't have been a Monticello."

"Sure, you mentioned it for a couple of seconds. I guess that's all the time it was worth."

"It's not like Jefferson was the only white southerner who owned slaves. If you were wealthy and southern in those days, you had them. That's the way the world was. Washington, Madison, Monroe, they all had slaves."

"You don't get it, do you? Jefferson enjoyed his life because he was willing to break my ancestors' backs. You've pretty much ignored all that, and you've *totally* ignored that the man was sleeping with his slaves."

"But Lorraine—"

"Let me finish!" she said, her hostility growing by the minute. "This is the same jerk who wrote 'all men are created equal.' What an unbelievable hypocrite!"

"Again, you're not judging the man according to the values of his times."

"Who says I have to? I've heard a lot about Jefferson from my dad. I don't need to like this guy no matter when he lived. It's bad enough that he said we were dumber than white people. Why did he have to write about how the orangutan male is more attracted to black women than other orangutans? Look it up, Mr. Kramer. I did. Jefferson wrote that. Do you think that maybe, just maybe, he thought that my people are *apes?*"

"All right," I said. "Let's put this in perspective, shall we? First, I never said Jefferson was a god. If you had let me finish, I'd have spoken about Sally Hemings, the slave who Jefferson slept with. I'd have spoken more about slavery, too. We all know Jefferson was human. That's one of the reasons he's so interesting. Nobody deifies him, not like they deify Washington. That's a good thing.

"Secondly, the same kind of number your dad did to Jefferson could be done to almost any historical figure. They all had skeletons in their closet. This guy insulted blacks, that guy insulted Jews, the other guy insulted Catholics. That's just the way life was back then."

"If you say so, Mr. Kramer."

At that point I went to my desk and pulled out one of my history books from college. "Lorraine, I assume you think of Lincoln as a good guy. Am I right?" She didn't answer. "Let me read to you a passage from one of his speeches. He gave it in 1858 in South Carolina.

"I am not, nor ever have been, in favor of bringing about in any way the social and political equality of the white and black races. ... I am not, nor ever have been, in favor of making voters or jurors of Negroes, nor of qualifying them to hold office, nor to intermarry with white people. ... And inasmuch as they cannot so live, while they do remain together there must be the position of superior and inferior, and I as much as any other man am in favor of having the superior position assigned to the white race.'"

For the first time in minutes, the room was silent. Several students looked to Lorraine to respond, but she didn't right away. When she finally found the words to reply, her voice had lost much of its earlier passion. Instead of showing defiance, she showed exasperation.

"Are you crazy?" she asked. "Lincoln is a hero to my people. Right near the top. I can't believe you're trying to trash him."

"I think you missed my point."

"Oh, I got your point alright."

"*I doubt it!*" I blurted out, finally showing annoyance. "I'm not trashing Lincoln. I love Lincoln. But I love Jefferson too. They're both heroes to me. I just won't judge them based on today's standards. That's all I'm saying. I don't think we have to belabor the point."

Perhaps not. But after my colloquy with Lorraine, I couldn't teach my lesson about Jefferson's theory of education. The mood was ruined. That lesson would have fallen flat.

I went on to talk about Jefferson's impact on U.S. history,

but my lecture was pedestrian at best. Lorraine had thrown me off my game. As I walked to my car after school, I cussed myself out for the way I had handled things during seventh period. But to ensure that some good came from that experience, I also made a vow: I'd take my praise of Jefferson seriously and gain inspiration by his example. In other words, I'd follow through on my vision of the night before and be ready to become the Creed Room's Jefferson, if only Linda would give me the chance.

When I got home, I needed to vent, so I called my college friend, Steve Jamison. We were both raised on the East Coast, but after we graduated from Stanford, Jamison stayed in the Bay Area. He has always looked like a Californian—tanned, blonde and chiseled. Less than a minute into the conversation, Jamison tried to persuade me, and not for the first time, to move back.

"It's not happening, man," I said, reverting to my college voice. "D.C. feels like home."

"Have it your way. If you don't mind, I'd rather spend my time outside in great weather hanging out with beautiful women, and not necessarily sober. But that's just me, brother. If you'd rather spend the day in Rockville reading the New Republic, more power to you."

"So Steve," I said, shifting gears. "I made a jerk of myself in school today."

"What happened?"

"I was teaching a class on Jefferson, singing the guy's praises, when this precocious black girl chimes in with all this stuff about Jefferson being a hypocrite."

"That's a stunner. You couldn't have seen that coming."

"I mentioned the slavery issue. I just didn't give it nearly enough attention."

"You screwed up a little," Jamison said. "So what?"

"After we argued about Jefferson, I felt the need to show he was no worse than anyone else. So I pulled out this segregationist quotation by Lincoln. After I read it, the girl asked why I was trying to tear down a hero to the black community."

"Why were you?"

"I wasn't thinking, that's all. I got caught up in the need to win the argument."

"I can understand that," Jamison said. "I get that way too. I think everybody does."

"So who are you seeing these days?" I asked, shifting gears. The variety in Jamison's love life has always amused me.

"Oh, a couple of women. Amy and Naomi. Amy's really smart—she's a physics grad student at Bezerkely. Naomi, let's just say she's really *talented*, and leave it at that. How about yourself?"

"I haven't been dating anybody," I replied. "But I am seeing a woman Friday night."

"No kidding," Jamison said. "What do you have planned?"

"I'm going over to her place. I think we're going to discuss Judaism."

"Sounds thrilling," he replied. "Sorry I can't make *that.*"

"Don't get the wrong idea," I said. "She's not a geek."

"Hey, whatever works for you is cool by me," Jamison replied. "I just get the feeling that you don't have to worry about me stealing her away, if you get my drift."

"So how do you think the Redskins are gonna to do this year?" I asked.

"They'll suck. Oh that reminds me, I got season tickets to the Niners and Warriors."

"Whoa. The Niners *and* the Warriors?"

"You got it," he said.

"I couldn't do it, even if I could afford it. I just don't have the time."

"No argument here. I can see you gotta put in extra hours planning those great lessons."

"Jamison, has anyone ever told you you're a prick?"

"Moi? No, I'm just a guy with a lot of leisure on my hands. Not bad for a 30 year old who makes twice as much as the President, huh?"

"Tell me, what would you do if the software business went soft?"

"I'd land on my feet. You know I would. So, are you making more than ten grand yet?"

"It's not that bad. It's at least half a garbage man's salary."

"Poor baby," Jamison sighed. "But you made your own bed. Besides, don't you get to coach girls' volleyball?"

"I hate to tell you, but a woman's got that job. Can you believe it?"

"What a waste," he said. "Anyway, the 'Skins are finishing dead last in their division. You can bank on it. And I've gotta go."

"Good luck with Amy," I said, laughing. Of course, Naomi was the one I was imagining.

That Thursday, I learned that I was going to have a visitor. Mother called, telling me that she had decided at the spur of the moment to come to Rockville for the weekend. "You need to pick me up tomorrow night at the subway. I'll be there around 8:30."

"I can't get you then, Mother. I'm busy that night."

"What are you doing?"

"I have a date."

"Really?" my mother's voice perked up more than I'd heard in a while. "Is she Jewish?"

"Yeah. I think you'd like her. She's beautiful, she's brilliant and she's a lot of fun."

"What's wrong with her?"

"Nothing, as far as I know. But I'm still getting to know her."

"I'll keep my fingers crossed. So what does she do?"

"She's a law student at Georgetown."

"A law student," Mother groaned. "I've heard that one before. Does she plan on finishing, or just teasing her parents a bit and then dropping out?"

I rolled my eyes at my mother's predictability. "Very nice. This keeps your streak alive. That's 121 conversations in a row in which you've reminded me of dropping out."

"I wish we could turn back the clock," she said. "This time, I'd put my foot down."

There were usually at least two or three times in a conversation with my mother when all I could do was shake my head and laugh. That was one of them.

"The cross you have to bear, Mother. How do you face your friends when they start bragging about their kids?"

"It's not about me, Sammy, it's about you. Do you know what lawyers make these days?"

"Enough with that," I said. "Let's get back to tomorrow evening."

"Fine. I want to talk more about this bionic woman. What's her name?"

"Allison. There isn't that much to talk about. We haven't known each other very long."

"Where did you meet her?"

I had chosen not to discuss the Creed Room with my mother until I received the first $500 check, which I expected within the next week. The idea of getting ridiculed about the whole experience didn't excite me. "We, uh, have some mutual friends. Mother, I've got to run. I haven't eaten and I'm tired. Can't we figure out our plans for the weekend?"

"Alright. How about this—invite Allison to your apartment. I'd like to meet her anyway. I'll call you from the subway when I'm ready for you to pick me up. I'll just talk to her for a couple of minutes, then I'll be out of your hair."

"An insane asylum," I muttered. "That's got to be my best option."

"What? Sammy? I can't hear you."

"I'M NOT PICKING YOU UP AT THE METRO! Do you hear me *now*?"

"Sammy, by the time I get to Maryland, I'll be exhausted. I'll have to work most of the day, take the train to Manhattan, take another train to D.C. and another one up to Maryland. And you're not even going to pick me up at the subway? Your own mother?"

"I'm sorry. Allison and I aren't getting together at my apartment."

"Why not? It's perfectly presentable if you pick up the place a bit."

"No! Do you hear me? No! You'll have to take a cab and let yourself in. You haven't lost the key, have you?"

"I've got a key. But I'm not taking any cab, Sammy. They're goniffs, those cab drivers. I'm not paying those prices."

"Then take a bus. Walk. Rickshaw it. I don't care how you get here. I'm busy."

My mother asked me a couple more times for a ride home on Friday. Finally, she relented after I suggested that she should come down some other weekend instead.

"That's alright, Sammy. I'll fend for myself."

"One more thing, Mother. I don't know when I'm getting back home. Maybe 9 or 10, maybe a lot later. Just put yourself to bed and plan on seeing me in the morning."

"Don't come home too late, Sammy. I don't care how wonderful she is. You need your sleep. And you have crazies on the roads late at night."

"I'll come home when I want to. It could be early. We might have a lousy time."

"I hope not. You're not getting any younger. One of these dates had better work out. By the way, I have our Saturday planned already. There's a program on the Holocaust at the Rockville Jewish Center. Maybe Allison will want to come."

"I doubt it."

"Suit yourself, sweetheart. I'll see you soon. Good night." Those were the last words I heard from her until Saturday morning.

Dupont Circle is one of my favorite neighborhoods in D.C. Most of the others remind me of how dominated the city is by the government. Lawyers, policy wonks, lobbyists, journalists, politicians—they're the people Washington seems to be made for. But not Dupont Circle. Sure, you see some suits and ties there, but you also see same-sex couples holding hands and smiling as if they never got the memo that said they were committing a faux pas. Even more than Georgetown, Dupont feels like a college town.

When I arrived at the door of her Dupont Circle apartment, Allison greeted me in a short sleeveless red dress and an even broader smile than I had seen at Luigi's. I couldn't help but be impressed by her home, which we toured as soon as I walked in. It had two large bedrooms and an enormous living room. Allison had a roommate, a Georgetown Law student who was usually out of town on weekends visiting her boyfriend. Still, I wondered, how could even two students afford such an apartment?

After the tour, Allison made us both a vodka martini and joined me in the living room, where we talked for a while before dinner. "Have you tried to verify what Choulos said in his letter?" I asked.

"Not yet. But Linda's got his address and phone number. She, Eileen and I plan to meet him at his jewelry store and find out if he can back up his claims."

"That sounds good," I replied.

"Are you worried about all this?"

"Curious," I said, "not worried. Even Choulos says the Benefactor's rich. All I really care about is that he pays us and gives us a place to meet."

"But aren't you concerned about what's going on with that guy? What if—"

"I've said it all along. This is about *us*, not him. Besides, Choulos hasn't given us proof of anything. He's just pissed off and he's spreading rumors. Big deal."

Allison was obviously more disturbed by Choulos's warning than I was, but she was too preoccupied with dinner to continue the conversation. She threw me the remote control to her TV and said that she had all the ESPN channels. "I'm sure you can find something to watch while I finish the meal." With that, she left for the kitchen, and I daydreamed about my hostess.

Periodically, Allison would step into the dining area and fill the table. I could tell how much pride she took in her cooking, and for good reason. She served a delicious Middle Eastern meal.

"You're not by any chance one of *them*, are you?" Allison asked, glancing down at the lamb she had prepared.

"You mean a vegetarian?" I asked.

"Uh huh."

"It's a little late to ask now, isn't it?"

"Not at all," she said. "I made enough veggies and grains."

"Well, I'm not a vegetarian. I've never been motivated to take the leap."

"I'm glad. I know enough of those people. It drives me crazy to cook for them. You know who's a vegetarian? My buddy Eileen. Ethical reasons."

"Good for her," I said.

"Oh please. It's fun to eat animals, and if we didn't, people wouldn't raise them. So we're saving their lives, right?"

"You sound like the old soldier who destroyed the village in order to save it. Personally, I think it probably is wrong to eat meat. It's not like we *need* to any more, given what we know about nutrition."

"But you'd like me to pass you some lamb anyway, right?

"Yup."

"Good boy."

"While we're on the subject of carnage," I asked, "are you a fight fan like I am?" Allison had put on her questionnaire that she loved sports, and I was curious about how far that extended.

Allison laughed. "Not exactly. But I can appreciate good smash-mouthed football."

"You'd rather watch a 10-7 game than a 31-28 game?"

"I don't know about that, but my favorite play in football is a sack."

"What about the sacks where the quarterbacks spring right back up afterwards?"

"Those don't count," Allison said, smiling.

I pictured entering Stanford Stadium with Allison at a college reunion. The weather's always nice there on fall Saturdays, and she'd be showing a lot of skin. My friends would be fighting to sit next to her so that they could ogle her from behind opaque sunglasses. But once the ball was in play it would be all football, and she'd be right in there with the rest of us.

Allison got up from the table and made herself another martini. She asked if I wanted one, but I declined. "I'm very picky about the guys I hang out with. They've got to have something between their ears, but they can't bore me or make me feel guilty about being myself. It's a good sign that you eat meat, only you don't seem to be much for liquor. That's a concern."

"What can I say? I don't really like to drink."

"What do you do for a release?"

I laughed. "I get a coffee buzz sometimes."

"Oh no, not *coffee*," she said, rolling her eyes.

"Seriously, what are you asking me? I exercise. I watch football games and yell like a Banshee. Oh, and I know, sometimes I read the Op-Ed section of the Post and imagine my fist in George Will's face."

"Now *that's* cathartic," Allison said. "What about Krauthammer? What do you want to do to him?"

"I don't read him. Why bother? He just spews out the right wing party line. It's totally predictable."

"Are you afraid Art's going to be like that?" Allison asked.

"I don't know yet. The thought's come to mind, though. I won't deny it."

Allison got up and returned to the living room. She put on a CD, one that I instantly recognized. It was the soundtrack to *Fiddler on the Roof*. "Sam, pour yourself something—a soda if that's what you want—then come back in here. I want to return a favor."

"What favor?"

"You shared with us how your religious views have evolved, and all you got from me was ridicule. Tonight, I want to share with you where I come from."

"From *Fiddler on the Roof*?" I asked.

"Yeah. In part. I told you before that my dad's a rabbi. My mom's a retired anesthesiologist. She's always been a great mother. But my dad's the one who's influenced me the most. For about 20 years, he's been the head rabbi at New York Hebrew Congregation in midtown Manhattan."

"That's a Conservative shul, isn't it?"

"The biggest in New York. For as long as I can remember, he told me stories and talked about books. He made sure I read the classics. That's why I've read your Spinoza's *Ethics*."

"I'm impressed," I said.

"This CD you're listening to was Daddy's favorite teaching tool. Actually it wasn't the CD, it was the video tape, but this has all the highlights—the songs."

"They're great," I said. "I love this musical."

"Daddy's lectured me about it since I was in diapers. He'd say the idea of a fiddler on a roof was a symbol of all the angst and alienation that Jews experience."

"I gather that describes your dad?"

"To a T. He'd tell me that if a Jew wants to get off the roof, throw away his yarmulke and shave his beard, he could pass for a corporate executive at an Episcopal school fundraiser. But Daddy would rather stay on the roof, so he's had to figure out how to cope as an outsider. He says the best way is to develop a relationship with God."

"You don't mean Spinoza's God either, do you?"

"Not a bit. Think about how intimate Tevya was with God. Tevya didn't address some philosophical Absolute whose life was sucked out of him. Daddy said Tevya was an authentic Jew because he treated God as his *partner*."

"I can see that. Tevya was always questioning God and consulting with Him."

"Right. Any time something important came up, Tevya spoke to God about it. That's my daddy's Judaism. It puts us at the center of God's life, just as it puts God at the center of ours."

"How does your dad feel about Tevya treating his daughter Chava like she was dead because she married a non-Jew?"

"Daddy never held that against Tevya. It's not like anyone else in the shtetl let their daughters marry out of the faith."

"Would you ever consider intermarrying?"

"I doubt it. My father would pretend he's OK with it, but he wants a Jewish son-in-law. I won't deny him that. Anyway, I'm mostly attracted to Jewish guys, so it's no big deal."

I couldn't help but smile at that comment.

"Guess who's my favorite character in the musical?" I asked.

"Not Tevya?"

"Try again."

"I don't know, Yenta?"

"She's a hoot. But it's Motl, the tailor."

"You're kidding," said Allison. "That little nebbish?"

"Yeah. I loved when Motl stammered his way to ask Tevya for his daughter's hand. Tevya didn't want to listen, but finally Motl was able to say, 'I'm a human being. You can't treat me like a God-damned slug.'"

"Not exactly in those words, though."

"Close enough," I said, laughing. "It's a message I've felt like delivering many times in my life. I don't think it'll ever get old."

"It's time to change the entertainment," Allison said. She turned off the CD and popped a tape into the VCR. It was an interview with one of the 20th century's greatest Jewish thinkers, Abraham Joshua Heschel. NBC filmed it only weeks before Heschel died in 1972.

We watched it in total silence. When it ended, Allison asked what I thought.

"Fascinating. I've been an admirer of Heschel for years."

"He played the same role in my father's life that my father played in mine," Allison said.

"How so?

"Daddy studied under him at the Jewish Theological Seminary, and he helped Heschel write *The Prophets*. Daddy says that the prophets' writings are the cornerstone of Judaism and that Heschel was a modern day prophet."

"I can't believe you, Allison. You call yourself a garden variety Jew, but you spent your childhood listening to Heschel's disciple preach about the essence of the religion. What kind of garden are you talking about?"

Allison simply ignored me and asked me how I would describe Heschel.

"A prototypical Jewish holy man. Pious, intimate with God, humble, marched with Martin Luther King, obsessed with social justice."

"How old do you think he was in that video?"

"Well, let's see. He looked like Father Time. I'd guess from the number of wrinkles on his face that he was in his late 80s. Then again, his mind was razor sharp."

"Why shouldn't it be? He was only 65."

"You're kidding. That Methuselah was 65?"

"That's what happens when you take his approach to Judaism to heart."

"And that's your dad's form of Judaism?"

Allison nodded and looked down at the ground. "Daddy

calls it *Prophetic Judaism*. It's all about suffering. Even Daddy's God suffers. Most people assume God spends most of his time thinking about great, eternal ideas that are way over our heads. Not Daddy's God. He spends more of his time concerned about the plight of widows and orphans on earth."

"So your dad and Heschel are masochists, is that what you're saying?"

"Let's say they're empaths to the nth degree," she replied. "Do you recall that line in the video about how Heschel doesn't want to be deaf to the cries of any oppressed people? That's a lot of cries to be listening to. More than I care to hear on any given day." Allison rewinded the tape and replayed the portion in which Heschel said, "The greatness of man is that he faces problems. I would judge a person by how many deep problems he's concerned with."

"There," she resumed. "That one statement explains why the man you're looking at is 65 going on 90. Prophetic Judaism means to devote your life to confronting deep, painful problems. That aged-beyond-your-years' face, that's what you get if you practice what my daddy preaches."

"Maybe that's why we have so many religious hypocrites," I said. "It's hard *not* to be one if this is the alternative."

Allison jumped to her feet and went into the kitchen. When she returned, she had a big chocolate cake in her hands—she called it a "torte"—and that trademark smile on her face.

"Do you like Hegel?" she asked.

"That's what you're smiling about? Hegel?"

"I was smiling about the cake, you idiot."

"Sorry," I said. "I prefer cakes to Hegel, if that's what you wanted to know."

"His writing almost always goes over my head, but I like his idea of the dialectic. As a kid, my *thesis* was Prophetic Judaism, but after a while it left me gasping for air. So I found an *antithesis*. And I guess you can say I'm open now to finding a new *synthesis*."

"I take it the antithesis wasn't something your dad would approve of."

"Not at all. Once I entered puberty, I stopped wanting to be just like him and paid more attention to my friends. In college, I had a blast. Late night parties, weekend ski trips, you name it."

"Drugs?" I asked.

"You bet. I decided that there was more to life than obsessing about the poor. There wasn't a whole lot I could do to help them anyway. Look at my daddy. He preaches to a bunch of rich people. Do you think he makes much of a difference?"

"He probably does, Allison. You sound so cynical."

"I'm just realistic, that's all. I doubt a few guilt offerings from Midtown Manhattan are really going to change people's lives."

"So where are you now?"

"I'm not as apathetic about spiritual things as I was as a teenager. I pray a lot. I care more about politics. I vote Democrat, like my daddy. I oppose capital punishment. I'm anti-gun."

"But—" I interrupted.

"The 'but' is that I don't buy all this stuff about how you judge people by the number of deep problems they're concerned with. I judge myself mostly by my capacity for joy. And that means I don't wake up each day worrying about the poor, the sick, or anyone else.

"One more thing. I hate thinking about God as depressed. My God's at peace."

Before I left that evening, I thanked Allison for sharing so much about herself and providing such a great meal—particularly the torte. I also said that I'd love to see her again soon.

"How about Sunday?" she replied.

"Sure," I said. We arranged that I'd call after I dropped off my mother at Union Station.

When I got home, the matriarch was asleep. I lay awake for a while that night thinking about this whirlwind of a person I was just getting to know. Once she gets to know me, I asked myself, what will she think? Would she want me to be more than just a friend? Could I give her what she needs from a man?

The one question I had no trouble answering was whether I'd enjoy a relationship with Allison. She offered me vitality. Whenever I was with her—whether she was telling stories or engaging me in debate—I felt incredibly alive.

Mother and I spent the next day together and had a great time, as I had the sense *not* to talk to her about Allison. Oh, she asked, but driving home the night before I made a commitment to avoid the topic like the plague.

In the past, whenever I introduced my mother to a new girl, she'd discourage me from getting involved. Mother would tell me the girl lacked a spark, a future, a dependable character, or maybe that she just wasn't right for me. Ultimately, that was always the bottom line. Mother saw the whole process as a day at the mall. My job was to find the highest quality merchandise. The idea that *I* might not be good enough for a girl would have never entered Mother's mind.

Here I was, a law school dropout, prone to angst, incapable of cooking, unable to change a tire, lousy at sports and poorly paid. Yet, in my mother's eyes, I was the supreme catch. She justified this delusion by thinking that I was endowed not only with talent but with the best of characters. And why not praise my character? I've never been convicted of a crime of moral turpitude. So there's no objective way to argue when Mother calls me a prince of a man.

What I don't understand is this: I've always known my mother's judgment about me is biased, yet somehow I take her praise seriously. What is it about Jewish mothers, anyway? Do they cast a spell on us that allows us to take their ridiculous superlatives to heart? Despite all the frustration that she's caused me, despite her complaints about the decisions I've made, the fact remains that her support of my talent and character has done wonders for my ego.

At the Rockville Jewish Center that Saturday afternoon, we ran into an old friend of hers from FLAG, Freedom Lovers Against Guns. For years, Mother had done odd jobs as a FLAG volunteer—mailing letters, answering correspondence or manning the phone bank. When she saw a fellow traveler, the two spoke for nearly an hour, mostly about their sales pitches. Mother's included guilt trips; "if you don't give to FLAG, and you hear about a kid being shot in school, will you be able to live with yourself?" Somehow, I wasn't surprised.

After Mother and I left the RJC, we went to the house of her older brother. Lenny has always been one of my favorite people. He lived in North Rockville, and I'd often go to his house to watch ball games and listen to him spout off about the latest bit of evil wrought by the Republican Party—the "Let 'Em Eat Cakers," as he calls them. Lenny would honor me with some of the crudest jokes and comments I've ever heard. I've wondered whether he gets annoyed whenever he goes to a public bathroom and finds no graffiti. I can't imagine where else he, as a septuagenarian, would ever get fresh material.

The craziest thing about getting together with Lenny and my mother is that she's always treated him like he could do no wrong. "Lenny was the first Rosenberg to earn a PhD," Mother told me. "Dr. Rosenberg. It has such a wonderful sound." Mother refers to her older brother as "brilliant" and even giggles at his raunchy jokes. "He's entitled," she once said. "He's so responsible, to a fault, really. I'm sure he needs to crack filthy jokes to help him let go of stress. Besides, who am I to judge?" This from the woman who judges everyone else.

That evening I told Lenny that I recently received a grant to teach philosophy during the next semester. Hopefully, I told him, it was just the first step in my quest to become a Grant Guru. "The more grants I get, the more likely the school will think of me as indispensable and leave my classroom the heck alone. That's my goal."

He understood the sentiment entirely. "You're on the right track, kid. Find a niche. That's the only way to survive in a bureaucracy." Lenny knew about bureaucracies. He had spent 20 years as an economist for the Department of Energy before retiring in the mid 1990s.

"Unless you're going to spend your career as a tuchis licker," he said, "you've got to make 'em think you're absolutely necessary. Otherwise they'll beat you down like they did me. Of course, there's one other way to get ahead in a bureaucracy, but you lack the requisite tits."

Lenny was a study in contradictions. He was normally upbeat, except when the subject of bureaucracies was raised, in which case he turned into a misanthrope. He was also spiritual, but you'd never believe it from his salty language. Lenny was a role model to me in that he, too, grew up as an atheist but found God later in life. After I mentioned that Mother lectured me earlier in the day about the irrationality of religion, Lenny couldn't resist the temptation to preach.

"It's not about truth, Ruth," he said, laughing at the silliness of the rhyme. "None of us can know the truth. But we can all find *meaning*. That's the whole point of life, when you think about it. So why believe in nothing? What's the percentage in that?"

I looked to my mother for a reply, but she said nothing. Perhaps she wanted to show me how to listen to someone preach without responding. I almost never extended her that courtesy.

Sunday morning was both slow and pleasant. Mother and I hung out in my apartment, watching TV and reading the newspapers. She preferred the New York Times; I, the Washington Post. We had each spent years living in both cities, yet she was a New Yorker, charmed by its pace and culture, and I was partial to Washington. I've always felt that the center of the earth is somewhere between 1600 Pennsylvania Avenue and Capitol Hill — and I don't mean the IRS Building, which is the only place in D.C. that many New Yorkers care about.

After I dropped my mother off at the train station in the early afternoon, Allison and I met up at the National Gallery of Art. We agreed it wasn't nearly as incredible a museum as New York's Metropolitan. Then again, the good people who run the Met don't let everyone in for free like they do at the National Gallery.

I had arranged to meet Allison in the Dutch Masters section, and that's where I found her, staring at a Jan Steen. "So," she said, before even saying 'hi,' "do you think he sells fake art?"

"My guess," I replied, "is that the guy's got class. Choulos is the one who doesn't."

Allison and I walked around the National Gallery for a while and then strolled up to Chinatown for dinner. While we were eating, she asked me if I had ever been to a Poetry Slam, and I replied that I hadn't. "I guess that settles what we're doing tonight," she said.

From the minute we walked into the Lotus Restaurant to witness the Slam, Allison was treated like a celebrity. One person after another walked over to us and asked whether she was going to compete. They seemed disappointed when she said she was there only to watch.

I liked a lot of the poetry we heard that night, if in fact the proper word for it was "poetry." Most of what we heard were angry diatribes against bigotry, selfishness or injustice. The Slam's winner, a beatnik, approached Allison after the competition and said that if she had competed, the best he could have done was second place.

Allison told me she had been performing Slams for two years since the summer before law school until she finally burned out. During her hey day, she'd always assume a character when she recited a poem. "Sometimes I was an earth mother. Other times, I was a suck-up attorney at a big firm trying to make partner. My most popular role was the tough feminist bitch. That one was a blast!"

"I'm having a little trouble picturing you as a feminist bitch."

"Oh, it was easy. My bitch had so much energy that the judges would give me a high mark even when my writing stank. Last year, I won the city championship."

I suggested that Allison take some of the energy that used to go into poetry and channel it toward the Creed Room instead.

"I think that'll be more your thing than mine," she said.

"But we'll see."

After driving Allison to her apartment, I intended to stop by only long enough to drink a cup of tea and watch her recite a couple of poems. She performed them in the voice of her feminist bitch. It was an awesome spectacle. The poems were brilliantly crafted and delivered with passion. Allison assured me that the bitch role wasn't the real her, or at least not much of her. To prove she was anything but a man hater, she walked over to me, rubbed my back, gently stroked my hair and, finally, gave me a long kiss—the first of many that evening.

CHAPTER 4

THE ONE TRUE FAITH

$\mathcal{M}$cDonald began the next session of the Creed Room by handing each of us $500 checks. That put everyone in a good mood—at least for a while. Believe me, it went away soon enough.

"Hey guys, we're changing our plans a bit," Linda said, introducing the evening's activity. "Dolores has agreed to yield some of her time to her Rock of Gibraltar, and ever-loving husband, Arthur. Those are her words, not mine. So without further ado, I give you the Rock himself."

"Thanks, Linda," Art began. "Hello everybody.

"I've got to be candid. After talking to Dolores about her presentation, I became concerned about the impression she'd give you of Christianity. I'm not here to put her down. Freedom of thought is what makes America great, and I've always encouraged Dolores to think for herself. But the Dolores I married and the woman you see here today don't see eye to eye when it comes to Christ. Her views are no longer in the mainstream of our religion.

"My wife and I spoke about my concerns, and we decided that I'd begin by presenting the traditional Christian perspective. Then she'll give her side of the story.

"Let me start by telling you what Christianity is *not*. It's not a religion based on finding the right human role model. Now please don't misunderstand me. For my money, Jesus' teachings represent the finest guide to human conduct *ever*. I know what a difference his moral code has made in our family. For six years, we took a series of Latin American exchange students into our home. There's no way I would have agreed to that if not for Jesus.

"So to those of you who say that Jesus is a role model second to none, I'm with you. But Jesus is far more than a role model. With all due respect, anyone who thinks of Him mostly in that light is missing the main point of His life on this planet.

"Another thing Christianity is *not* is an opiate for the masses. A *traditional* Christian is at odds with most people in society. Because of that, our lives aren't easy. Still, this much I can't deny: Christians *know* we've found the one true faith. And that knowledge brings incredible joy.

"So Christianity is not primarily a mentoring program, and it's not an opiate either. Now let's talk about what it *is*. It's a religion that celebrates God Almighty. Christians give thanks to God for the gift of creation, and we learn about Him from His only Son, Jesus Christ. God put Jesus on this earth for one purpose, and that was to save souls. Because of Jesus, salvation is available to everyone who has an open and humble heart.

"Folks, I know this isn't popular these days, but I've got to say it. The Scriptures teach that all people who lack faith in Christ will be condemned. Even before Christ came to Earth, God condemned people who lacked faith in His promise that someday a Messiah would be sent here as a Redeemer. Jesus came to make the ultimate sacrifice. He died so man can live in an eternally blessed state linked with His Father. We all have free will and, if we hope to be saved, we'd better use our freedom wisely. We'd better accept Lord Jesus as the Christ.

"I realize you probably *despise* those words."

"Now you're speaking the truth, brother," Allison said. "I guess you just had to get warmed up."

Art simply ignored her. "But I'll say it again. *Only* through Christ can a human soul be saved. Every other soul is condemned to an eternal state of separation from God. And that state is more painful than life on earth, where God's grace is given to us all."

"Funny," Allison said. "I never read that in the Bible."

"You might want to read more thoughtfully," Art replied. "Look, people, I hear what's being said about Christians these days. We're called arrogant, sanctimonious, Neanderthal ... or worse. We're told our religion divides at a time when we should be uniting. We're laughed at by the very souls we'd like to see saved.

"So why do we hold on to this crazy idea that only through Jesus can someone be saved? Because of honesty. We Christians must always be honest with ourselves. And we believe the Bible is the truth—not just our truth, but *the* truth for everybody, whether they want to believe it or not. Our duty is to preach the word that has been planted in our souls. To teach anything else simply because it might be more convenient to our lives is not an option."

I waited for Allison to respond—or Shaw—but heard nothing.

"Last week," Art continued, "you all said you'd be open minded. That won't mean anything unless you come to Jesus with an open heart. I know that what I've said isn't going to change what you believe. I can see that in your faces. But here's my challenge. Don't take my word for anything. Read the New Testament for yourselves. And read it with a *receptive heart*. Just try it once. If you let in a single ray of light from that Book, you'll be blinded by truths more powerful than the sun. And this power will last, both in this life and the hereafter.

"So that's my request—read the Bible in the privacy of your own home. Nobody's going to brainwash you. It'll just be you and the word of God. I can promise you this: if you open your heart to Christ Jesus, you'll never be the same person again."

I wouldn't give Art the satisfaction of admitting this out loud, but I had never read the New Testament without a strong bias against Jesus's divinity. I wondered how many Jews have.

Before sitting down, Art turned to his wife and said, "I now yield back the remainder of my time to the gentlewoman from Potomac, Maryland, Dolores Sherman." He looked satisfied, yet despite his talk of openness, Art kept a distance from the rest of us. "The Rock of Gibraltar" seemed impregnable to anything that we could have done or said. Perhaps he felt the need to steel himself a bit if he hoped to share "the truth" with a world that had become increasingly antagonistic to his message.

Dolores smiled at her husband and walked to the front of the room. Her bearing was so different from Art's. Whereas he stood erect and exuded a commanding, almost regal, presence, Dolores's shoulders were rounded and her head tilted forward as if to signify her desire to get closer to us.

"Arthur and I," she began, "were both raised Presbyterians in conservative, Southern homes. We still worship together at a conservative, Presbyterian church. The church's basic doctrines are what you just heard. That's what I believed for many years.

"Now I find myself disagreeing not only with Arthur and our church, but my parents too. They even question whether I'm a Christian. Arthur knows not to say that to me, but I sometimes wonder if that's what he believes." Art kept a poker face. "The truth is that I love Jesus as much as ever. I just don't buy into some of the things that the Church says about Him.

"Here's what happened to me. In '91, a friend invited me to join a discussion group. Through that group I've come to know dozens of wonderful women. Some are Christian, but we also have Jews, Muslims and Buddhists. We even have Wiccans who call themselves witches—two of the sweetest women you'll meet. Everyone in the group is devoted to developing her spirituality and respecting the ideas of all religious traditions.

"After a few weeks in this group, I began looking at Christianity differently. It will always be a very special religion to me, but I stopped looking at it as a *better* faith than the others. It just happened to be the one I was raised in as a child, so it speaks to me the most.

"It only makes sense that I'd keep my religion. Growing up Christian, I became attuned to the religion's beauty. The fun of the holidays. The thrill of the music, whether gospel or Bach. The stained-glass windows. The steeples. All of it. Why should I give that up? Christianity is a perfectly good faith. It just needs to mature a bit.

"After I'd been in the women's group for a while, those of us who are Christians joined another organization. It's part of a national movement of Christians who'd like to see the religion change to the point where *all* Americans can feel good about it. We're speaking out against a number of traditional church doctrines, especially the one Arthur talked so much about tonight.

"Speaking for myself, the thought that a Christian could meet people like the Dalai Lama and Ghandi and decide that their souls will be eternally separated from God unless they convert to Christianity ... that seems ridiculous."

"It seems *insane*," Shaw interrupted. "Am I wrong?"

"I'll answer you this way. If Jesus came to my door in the

flesh and told me that the Church was right all along, I'd probably rethink my love for Jesus."

"Amen," Shaw said.

"Do you know what else I don't like about Christianity?" Dolores continued. "The proselytizing, which of course follows from this idea that Christianity is the one true faith. The problem is that we're supposed to be humble. What does it say about our humility that we think we know what's the best religion for somebody from Borneo or Chad? Actually it's worse than that—we think we know the best religion for *everybody* from Borneo or Chad. *That's* insane.

"Anyway, let me change courses here. Friends, Romans, countrymen," said Dolores, smiling, "I didn't come here to blame Christianity, but to praise her! Besides, I don't want Arthur to kick me out of my own bed tonight."

I wanted to ask why that would be such a bad thing, but I held my peace.

"More than anything else," Dolores said, "I look at Christianity as a set of values. I hope everyone here knows what values I'm talking about. Loving your neighbor as yourself. Treating others with kindness even if they've been mean to you. Having faith in the goodness of the creator of life. Loving that creator. Being humble and modest. Being respectful to all people. Giving liberally to charity. I could go on and on, but you get the point."

"Don't *all* religions preach most of those values?" Eileen asked, raising her hand.

"No question, but they don't all have the Christ of the Gospels," Dolores replied. "Like Arthur said, as a role model, he's magnificent. That's why our movement is trying to change the focal points of the religion into the values Jesus taught and the way he taught them.

"You may not believe this, but another thing I really love about Christianity is the concept of the Trinity. Some people think it's an example of bad math. I think of it as *God-plus*. The Trinity says there's one God, *plus* it tells how God can come alive to us. For me, the best way to make that happen is to relate God to Jesus.

"In Jesus's *person*, we have a wonderful role model: loving, peaceful, caring, forgiving. In Jesus's *divinity*, we learn what it means to be made in God's image. I like to think about God becoming flesh—peaceful, loving, human flesh. It reminds me that we can all walk in the ways of God and peace. I also like to think about God's only Son being sacrificed in order to save the rest of us. It's a great way to remind us that God really does love people, and that helps us come to love God more in return.

"Remember, you don't have to take everything that's said about God and Jesus literally. I don't. Like Allison said, myths can be incredibly powerful."

"What about the Holy Spirit?" Keister asked. "How come you hardly ever hear about that, even in church?"

"It's a missed opportunity, plain and simple. Here's how I see the Holy Spirit. For every force in the physical world there's one in the spiritual world. Now what's the strongest force in the physical world? Gravity, correct? So think about gravity as a spiritual force. It's like a magnet pulling our souls closer and closer together. That's the Holy Spirit at work. It's everywhere, just like gravity. It's in every earthly being and in the spaces that connect us to each other. Even as our stubbornness pulls us apart, the Holy Spirit works to make a connection.

"I think the problem is that the 'Holy Spirit' sounds like such a formal term. We need one that's softer. How about '*holiness*'? We all have it in us if we're willing to recognize it."

"You know, I've asked people about the Holy Spirit before,"

Keister said. "That's the first answer I got that actually made some sense."

"I'm glad," Dolores said, warmly. "One of the things I love most about Christianity is how it speaks of the Holy Spirit in the same sentence as God and His Son. We're supposed to find holiness wherever we happen to be—just like Allison said about her faith.

"Let me conclude by saying again that I can't defend Christianity's claims to be the *one* path to heaven. But I can say that, for me, Jesus is the single most beautiful role model of all. And if we think about Christian doctrines in the light of the Gospels and not the dogma of the Church, we can find wisdom that truly brings people together instead of tearing us apart.

"That's all I have to say. Thanks for listening." With that, Dolores walked back to her seat and visibly exhaled. I could tell she wasn't the Sherman who was used to making long speeches. I felt fortunate to have heard her expound for as long as she did.

During the Shermans' presentations, Shaw had been getting increasingly restless. Once Dolores sat down, his voice took center stage.

"I like the portrait you're painting, Dolores," Shaw began. "But I've got to say, it's not Christianity. Where I'm from, if you don't believe in Jesus as the only possible path to God, you're not a Christian."

"Believe me, she's been told that before," said Art, who must have been surprised to find Shaw as an ally on any issue regarding religion.

"You can't ignore Christianity's history," Shaw said, addressing Dolores.

"Religions can change just like people can," Dolores replied.

Shaw raised his voice. "I'm *telling* you, you're fighting an uphill struggle. Compare your religion to Judaism. The Jews can accept diversity of thought because they're about ethnicity, not dogma. As long as you're born a Hebrew, you'll always be a Jew. I've talked to too many Christians who tell me that once they give up the dogma, they feel like they don't belong."

"Trust me," Dolores said. "There are *so* many kinds of Christians in the world. You're focusing only on part of the community."

"Maybe, but it's the vocal part. The rest of you don't have tongues."

"That's what my group is trying to change."

"You might be trying," Shaw replied, "but nobody's listening."

"So what's your point? That we should just give up?"

"Not on spirituality, just Christianity. Some things are best buried."

"So all your talk about openness is just bull?" Art said.

"You had to be honest with us, I'm only being honest with you. How can I help but associate Christianity with plantation owners telling us to perk up, pick our cotton and smile? 'Cause we's all gonna go to Heaven just like massa's preacher says."

"Young man, you've got to get over that stuff. It's blinding you," said Art.

"Then help me see the light, Arthur. I've got some questions for you."

"Go ahead," Art sighed.

"For starters, I've never understood this idea that your Lord Jesus was making such a sacrifice. Here's a guy who seemed certain that the world was just about to come to an end. And his 'sacrifice' was to allow himself to die a bit early, knowing that after his death he'd experience total bliss for all eternity. What kind of sacrifice is that?"

"That's a novel argument. Did you get that from the back page of Atheists' Weekly?"

"Seriously," Shaw said. "I can see that if he were willing to endure Hell for eternity so that the rest of us could be saved, *that's* a sacrifice. But he gets to go to heaven after a few hours of pain. Sounds like a good deal to me."

"Let me get this right," Art replied. "Jesus endured one of the most painful deaths imaginable. And you're suggesting He did this for His own sake? If you keep your heart closed, don't blame me for the consequences."

"That's me. Closed-hearted," Shaw said. "But I wonder how open-hearted you'd be if the shoe were on the other foot. Let's say Jesus wasn't the lily-white Nordic your ancestors created out of whole cloth. Let's say he was a bit more swarthy—a real Jew with a big nose, like the one he probably had. No, wait a second. Let's say Jesus' image wasn't stolen by white artists but by African ones. And this missionary from Zaire comes up to you and Dolores and says, 'There's this black guy. Here's His picture.' When you look at the picture you notice that he's got thick lips and a flat nose and ebony skin."

"You know," Art interrupted, "everything's not all about black versus white."

"Now please," Shaw said. "The missionary's not finished talking. Where was I? Oh yeah. So the missionary says, 'It so happens that this black man's the one and only Son of the Creator of everything in the universe. And this Creator's been killing folks for doing the littlest thing wrong and sending 'em where they can fall and burn, fall and burn, for eternity.'"

Art looked like he had an abdominal disorder, but he let Shaw finish his story.

"This black guy, He's here to help you," Shaw continued. "He suffered for a day or two so that all folks, black and white, red and green, can be happy forever—like they're spending all of eternity piggin' out on ribs. Only there's one catch: If you want to be happy, if you want to avoid fallin' and burnin', you've gotta believe that this black dude's your Lord and Savior. You've gotta believe He's the Creator's only boy. Just look at that face. Those big negro lips. All you've gotta do is have faith that He's your meal ticket, and you're set for life ... *and* death.'

"That's the kind of option you've given me, Art. It seems kind of silly. Why should anyone believe that the Dude With the Big Lips—or for that matter the Pale Man With the Twirpy Beard—is part of God's nuclear family? Because some missionary is threatening you with Hell if you don't? So call me closed-hearted. Or closed-minded. I'm actually trying to open my mind to possibilities that seem a bit less silly."

"Are you done?" Art asked, a few seconds after Shaw stopped talking.

"I don't know," Shaw replied, smiling. "It depends on what you want to say."

Art spoke in a low voice at first. "You're just cheating yourself, son. You have a wonderful chance to save your eternal soul. All you have to do is read Jesus's magical words." Then a snarl appeared on Art's face. His voice picked up in volume as well. "But you won't read the Scriptures, will you? You'd rather mock Jesus and fight some stupid race war. You're angry because you've never done anything with your education except sit on your fanny in a bookstore and ring up the cash register. So now you have to rev up all the other ticked-off black people and set them at the throats of the white man. That's your idea of religion, isn't it? A holy war."

"I've got nothing against white skin. I just can't stand to see some folks try to dominate others, especially if they don't have the guts to admit what they're doing. I want equality."

"You might want to worry less about equality and more about your soul. I know *I* do."

"Thanks for the advice," Shaw said. "You know, it's not really about race, it's about power. It's bad enough that folks like you can buy as many BMW's as you please while people of color still live in poverty. When I hear you rich Christians say that black people will suffer forever unless we worship your lily-white God, I get a little miffed. When I hear you people tell us that it's good to be meek, I get more miffed. And when I hear you fat cats say all that stuff and then claim that yours is a religion of humility, I stop getting miffed and start going crazy. It's amazing you all lie so much and you still have smaller noses than Sam here."

I couldn't help but laugh at that little dig, and Keister's guffaw was even louder than mine—a little too loud for my taste—but Art wasn't amused. "You miserable little punk. Now you've lumped all traditional Christians together as liars. Oh, I forgot. We're not just liars, we're hypocritical power-crazed liars."

"You got it, Art. I guess you *are* open to the truth."

"Amazing," Art said, shaking his head. "This country became great because of all the inspiration we've received from the Scriptures and Christ. But you've got no sense of gratitude."

"I'm supposed to have gratitude when—"

"Now you let *me* finish!" Art exclaimed. "You talk about poverty, but you're as blind as a bat. The poor blacks you whine about are still a heck of a lot better off than they'd be in the jungles of Africa or wherever the heck they'd be if they hadn't been brought to this country and taught Christianity. Look at the standard of living in black Africa. Then compare it to the way your people live here. You live like kings and queens compared to your African cousins. Deep down you know it too. That's why you people won't jump on a plane and go back.

"This is a Christian country and always will be, despite ingrates like you. The Lord will make sure of that. And whether you know it or not, you've been the beneficiary. Once you die, you'll be in God's hands. Then you can kiss your sorry little soul goodbye."

"Nasty, aren't we?" said Shaw, whose mood was only then turning as sour as Art's had been for minutes. "I thought your Jesus was supposed to plant love in your heart. Your Christianity must run about as deep as a bath tub."

Art's face contorted worse than I'd ever seen it. But before he had a chance to fire back at Shaw, the light from the camera started flashing. Seconds later, I heard McDonald's footsteps rushing toward the Creed Room.

"What's wrong with you?" McDonald yelled at Shaw, upon entering the room.

"Me? What about him?" Shaw said, pointing at Art.

"Just worry about yourself, not him," McDonald replied. "And what about you, Madam Coordinator?" McDonald said, facing Linda. "*He's* counting on you to keep the peace around here. You can't let things get out of hand like this."

"Your right," Linda said, humiliated. "I'll take care of it."

McDonald left the room, and yet it took Linda several seconds before she could compose herself and address the group. "We're on film and you two are acting like this? Aren't you the least bit embarrassed? I know I am.

"Let's take ten. I think we all need a break."

Several people bolted out the door. After Linda, Art was the next to leave. He was followed by Eileen and Keister. A couple of seconds later, Shaw departed, laughing under his breath and shaking his head. That left Allison, Dolores and me.

I closed my eyes and took a deep breath. The interchange between Art and Shaw was the last thing I wanted to hear after

Dolores's presentation, which had left me more sympathetic toward Christianity than I'd been in some time. My eyes opened when I heard Allison's voice. "Well, Dolores, all I can say is you're a lot more patient than I'd be."

"Pardon?"

"I don't mean to pry," Allison said. "I'm just curious. You're a progressive woman and he's a die-hard fundamentalist. Yet you guys stay married. I'd find it a real challenge."

"Excuse me?" said Dolores. "I only ... I mean..." She stopped to collect her thoughts, and then looked back at Allison. "The last I checked, my marriage was none of your business."

"Whoa, I wasn't putting you down. There's no reason to take offense."

"You insult my marriage, and you don't expect me to take offense? I'd appreciate it if you left my marriage alone."

"No problem," Allison replied, laughing. "He's all yours!"

"What's that supposed to mean?"

"Nothing at all. Forget I said anything."

But Dolores wasn't finished. "When Art and I agreed to join this group, I didn't think he'd have to deal with people mocking his faith and calling him a liar." Dolores's voice caught, but she continued. "That guy basically told Art that everything he stands for is garbage."

"Scott needs to smooth out the edges, I'll give you that," Allison said. "But your husband might want to join the 20th century before it ends."

That was all Dolores could take. She got out of her chair, tears streaming down her face, and left the room. I couldn't believe what I was witnessing. And it was all on tape.

Linda was right. This was embarrassing.

During the last part of the break, we all quietly sat in our seats, except Linda, who had gone downstairs. Dolores's eyes were red, but she had regained her composure.

Upon returning, Linda set out to resume control over the inmates. "It's safe to say that some of us are having no trouble sharing our feelings. At the rate we're going, we'll soon be insulting each other's looks. Oh wait, we've already heard reports about Sam's face, so we need another idea. I know. We can dump on each other's mothers. Scott, do you want to start?"

"No thanks," said Shaw, fighting off a smirk. "I've vented enough for one night."

"I should think you have," Linda replied, visibly annoyed.

At Linda's suggestion, everyone said a few words with the goal of bringing a little civility to the proceedings. Keister, for example, praised Dolores' talk. "Good stuff," he said. "Bein' raised a Christian, it made me proud."

I was more long winded. "We need a unifying principle. Otherwise, we'll just be talking past each other, which is basically what just happened. Art made his speech and Scott made his, but there was no effort to reach a synthesis.

"I say, if we want a unifying principle, let's go with the voice of *reason*. Allison said last week that philosophy was about reason, and religion about wholeness. I say if we want a creed that's whole—I mean, *internally consistent*—we'll have to embrace philosophy. We'll have to analyze the essence of every topic and figure out what arguments are the most sensible and the hardest to refute.

"If Art wants to talk about Scripture, that's fine. But just because an argument is grounded in Scripture doesn't make it sensible. If Scott wants to react emotionally to an argument because of the experiences of slavery or Jim Crow, that's fine too. Emotions can teach a lot. But they may not carry the day around here, because we've all had different experiences. So what touches Scott might not touch Art, or even Linda."

Neither Art nor Shaw replied to my comments. Shaw simply reached out his hand to Art and said, "No hard feelings." Art shook the hand but didn't crack a smile.

Then, Dolores said, "I hope we've all learned that we need to tread a little more lightly."

"But not *overly* lightly," said Linda, smiling. "We still have to be ourselves."

CHAPTER 5

SWEET VIRGINIA

*T*he Creed Gang met seven more times in 1999 after the Christianity session. In reaction to that meeting, Linda took an active role in planning the sessions so as to turn down the heat and encourage us all to bond.

Eileen was chosen as the person most able to soothe the savage beasts. She was asked to lead two full sessions, and both were excellent. Eileen was well spoken, but her communications in the group were primarily non-verbal. Even when she was giving a lecture, she would pause between thoughts to make sure we were all connecting. It wasn't something I was used to, and yet I felt comfortable with it. As Allison once told me, Eileen has a way about her that not only puts people at ease, but also makes them feel like they're in the presence of what Dolores would call "holiness."

In her first session, Eileen led a discussion about Eastern religions. We talked about Buddhism, Taoism and Hinduism. Eileen explained that immediately after college she had studied these philosophies, and particularly Buddhism, for the better part of a year in Nepal.

The group was very well behaved. Perhaps that's because the topics were exotic enough that they didn't rub salt into Shaw's wounds or threaten Art's imperial vision. Art, in fact, was a pussycat who showed a genuine appreciation for learning. Even Shaw had to be impressed.

As a person who hates to see God anthropomorphized, I was especially interested in one part of Eileen's talk. "Before my trip," she said, "I couldn't wait to see the people in towns and villages and learn how their religions shaped their lives. When I got there, I felt let down. Other than the monks, nobody seemed to practice the religions that brought me to the Far East in the first place. The villagers' gods were human—maybe their bodies weren't, but their minds were. I can't tell you how many fantasy myths and stories I heard about a god's passions or heroism.

"It made me wonder why the ancient Eastern teachings have had such little impact on people's day to day lives. I've had the same question about Western philosophy. People in America know so little about it. Why is that? It frustrates me because that stuff moves me, and I don't like to think about it as 'secret wisdom.' Secret wisdom doesn't do much for the world."

At times that evening, Eileen reminded me of a college professor. In our next session, though, she turned the house into a New Age retreat. Instead of teaching with words alone, she presented New Age techniques designed to develop spirituality. The activities were incredibly relaxing. I couldn't decide whether to stay awake and listen, or close my eyes and dream.

Eileen began with a demonstration of what she called aromatherapy. Periodically that evening, she changed the scent. Eileen also brought in two "Tibetan Singing Bowls" that produced beautiful, haunting sounds. She gave us a tutorial on how to make the bowls sing, and we each took a shot at it. I was by far the slowest to catch on, which is hardly surprising, since I'm so inept at working with my hands. Then, Eileen showed us rune cards, tarot cards, and some sort of Native American inspired cards, which she said were wonderful tools for exploring our intuition. I had never before thought about the need to do that, but did my best to suspend skepticism and practice what I preached about open mindedness.

Eileen ended the session by teaching us how to meditate. For me, this was the evening's highlight. I had attended a transcendental meditation session a couple of years earlier. The TM teacher presented scientific evidence that meditation can do wonders for both your mind and body. Then, he presented the four-figure asking price for his services, and I was history.

Eileen, by contrast, taught her class for free. We'd all leave the room except one person. When it was my turn, Eileen directed me to sit still as she chanted Sanskrit, burned incense and cut flowers. Then, she walked up to me and whispered a mantra into my ear. "I have to whisper because nobody else may ever learn your mantra, including *him*," she said. After we each got our mantras, Eileen brought the group back together and taught us how to use them so as to empty our mind of thoughts, relax and, hopefully someday, achieve a higher state of consciousness.

I began to see why the TM people charge so much. As Eileen might say, I "intuitively" could tell that meditation could be deeply enriching for people willing to stick with it, and nothing motivates us to do that quite like having to pay up the nose for the privilege of participating.

As we left the Creed Room that evening, I'm sure everyone felt honored. We were students in a wonderfully-taught class designed to purify the soul and delight the senses. To cap it off, we were each $1,500 richer than when we arrived that evening.

It's a nice job if you can get it.

During the next two sessions, Linda supervised a series of exercises designed to draw out our personal philosophies. For example, she posed a series of moral dilemmas in order to reveal our ethical compasses to the group in a non-threatening manner. Later, she selected historical figures, gave us a few minutes to think about them and then asked us to discuss what they meant to us. She also directed a free-association game in which we were each given a word—like love, God, justice or freedom—and told to rapidly unleash a stream of consciousness on what that word meant to us. Linda gave us a chance to ask follow-up questions, but we couldn't stop laughing at the absurdity of so many of the responses.

What I loved about those sessions was that, for the first time, we were addressing Creed Room topics playfully. Chimes, meditation, incense and Eileen Mitchell may have helped me relax, but it wasn't until we all made fools of ourselves together that I began to feel truly at home in that room.

In December, the group discussed the topic of "The Human Animal: Actual and Potential." Shaw led the first discussion, concentrating on the heart versus the mind; altruism versus egoism; the role of faith, knowledge and intuition; and the sources of human fulfillment and agony. Fred and Art led the next two discussions. They analyzed various virtues and vices, and discussed the extent to which moral truths are absolute or relative.

While I felt engaged by the "Human Animal" discussions, my favorite moment came immediately after they ended: McDonald walked in and passed out $10,000 checks. It was the last thing that happened in the Creed Room that fall.

Back at Takoma Park High, the second half of the fall semester had passed quickly. I spent every spare moment preparing for my new philosophy class, so the pace of my day was insane—teach a class, take four minutes to breathe, teach another class, do some lesson plans, teach another class, and so on until the final bell.

I was fortunate that my last class of the day was U.S. History. While I've always liked teaching honor students, I had a special fondness for that group of kids. By the close of the semester, everyone appeared to be excited about history. I credit this, above all else, to the unit on the Civil War and the efforts of one Lorraine Jackson.

Lorraine's role in my Civil War unit was spawned by her bitching and moaning about Jefferson in October. I was determined to teach my pet lesson on Jefferson's theory of education and feared that she would disrupt me once again. So I offered a deal to coopt her: she'd let me do my thing on Jefferson, and I'd let her help plan the Civil War unit. The idea worked like a charm.

"When you all think of education, what word comes to mind?" I asked the class, to begin my lesson on Jefferson. "Just call out your answer. Don't bother to raise your hand."

"School," a couple of students replied. A few others nodded their heads.

"Personally, I would have said 'citizenship,'" I said. "But I'm glad to hear your answer, because schools are exactly what I've come here to talk about. Before I start, please indulge me for a moment. A number of you have been referring to me as Governor Jefferson. I request instead that you call me Thomas. Truly, I am not worthy to be addressed any other way by members of this illustrious legislature."

"What legislature?" asked Alice Stepowski, a short redhead

who was never shy about speaking up in class.

"My good man," I replied, "is this not the Virginia State Legislature? Do you not want to hear about my proposed Bill for the More General Diffusion of Knowledge?" One by one, the students caught on.

"Governor, I mean Thomas," asked David Rice. "Could you tell us today's date?"

"Why, sir, it's June 28th."

"And the year?"

"Well, you know the year, I'm sure. I must say, jocularity is most atypical for this chamber, but I rather like it." And I truly did appreciate the question, since it gave me a chance to show off. "The year. Let's see. It's been three years since we declared independence, 348 years since Joan of Arc was burned at the stake, 713 years since the Battle of Hastings, and—give me a few seconds—2,177 years since Socrates drank the hemlock. Is that right? Yes. That's right. It's now 2,177 years after 399 B.C. Well, what year did you think it was, my friend?"

David looked at me for a moment before responding. "I guess it's, uh, 1779."

"Congratulations, sir. That's quite a guess. It is indeed June 28, 1779. A fine day to consider how to enable Virginians to become the best educated people in all the *eleven* states.

"As I trust you know, education and schooling are very different things. Education is a necessity; schooling, a mere luxury. Schools are very expensive to keep up, and when our young people are in school, they're not helping their family earn a living. If I were to propose that all poor children attend school, most people would say that's as absurd as a two dollar bill.

"But that is precisely what I am about to propose. Let us be ambitious, my good sirs. Let us try to push ourselves. What if I told you we could raise taxes to send every free child in

Virginia to school? How many years of schooling do you think we could give them?"

Again, Alice spoke. "OK. I'm game. How about 13 years?"

"Thirteen? I was told you would not support *any* years of schooling for the poor. Now you say 13? Ah, you must be playing with me, my good fellow. You almost had me, sir. My bill is more modest and thus more practical. So hear me on this, I beseech you. I propose that all boys and girls in the Commonwealth—other than slave children, of course—would receive three years of free education at primary schools. In each primary school, one poor boy would be chosen to attend a secondary school free of charge together with more affluent children. After two years of secondary school, each poor boy would be given a test, and the top performer at each school could stay for four more years. Finally, at the end of the six years of secondary school, the better performing half of the poor boys left in the system would be allowed to attend my alma mater, William and Mary College, at the Commonwealth's expense.

"Any questions?"

Rebecca Cohen, my Congressman's daughter, had one. "I heard you mention girls getting an education in the primary school, but what about secondary school and college?"

"I think you'd find that if you, sir, tried to push in this illustrious body public funding for girls to receive a higher education, you'd never, *ever*, be re-elected. Really, secondary schooling for girls? If I may be so bold as to make a suggestion, sir, perhaps you need to spend more time investigating the domestic virtues of the fairer sex."

I asked for other questions or comments, but heard none. "Nary a word from any of you? Alas, I'm afraid I know what you're thinking. Men of means should not be forced to bear the burden of supporting poor children. I admit, gentlemen, that my proposal would involve paying a fair sum of tax dollars. But think of what is at stake.

"Three years of public education is all I'm asking for. Children would be taught the basics in reading, writing and arithmetic. This would give them the tools to become *educated voters* for the rest of their lives. They could read newspapers, for example. I've always seen the newspaper as the cornerstone of a democracy."

Once again, Rebecca Cohen raised her hand. "Do you know how many years I had to go to school before I could read a newspaper? Seven, maybe eight. Do you really think three years is going to make a difference?"

"You're missing the point, sir. Three years of school won't make a person educated. But it should be enough to give children basic skills and, what's more, it will teach them to adore the process of learning. The children would teach themselves to read progressively more advanced writings on their own."

Rebecca shook her head and laughed. "You're a dreamer."

"I've been called worse. A lot worse."

"I'm sure you have, Kirby," said David Rice, much to the delight of his classmates.

I smiled and resumed my lesson. "We've been talking about my proposal for universal primary schooling. But I've got to say a few words about my provisions for secondary and university education. The students who would benefit from those provisions are among our natural aristocrats. Simply because they happened to be born poor does not mean that our society can survive without their stewardship. If anyone here thinks otherwise, I would suggest that he leave this chamber and breathe the fresh air of the Commonwealth. Meet the people we condemn to ignorance. You will find golden nuggets there, as surely as you will find them in the opulent bedrooms of the nicest plantations."

At that point, I went out of character, and the kids became more comfortable participating in a discussion. I told them that the Virginia legislature waited until 1796 to approve a single part of Jefferson's proposal, the one involving primary schools. And no sooner was it approved than it was emasculated. The legislature decided to let county courts decide whether and when to introduce the program, and the courts refused to tax the rich in order to educate poor children.

In short, Jefferson the Progressive swam upstream when he threatened the wallets of his peers. But, as I explained to my class, what moved me the most about Jefferson's bill had less to do with distributive justice than with the hallowed nature of education.

First, I love the idea that three years of schooling would be enough to create a learner for life. Of course it's utopian. But think about what it says about Jefferson. He clearly believed in the addictive nature of learning. Years before Mark Twain, he taught us that when it comes to education, schooling should be the tip of the iceberg.

Second, I love to imagine what it would have been like to have been a poor boy who survived Jefferson's gauntlet and matriculated at William and Mary. The analogy to Charlie in the chocolate factory wouldn't do justice to his euphoria. Heaven might be a closer analogy. I told my class to contrast that attitude with the way kids approach college today. There's no sense of being privileged or gulping down as much learning as possible. Kids mostly revel in the opportunity to get away from their parents and hang out more with their friends.

The attitude that education is all about rights and not privileges applies not only to college but to schooling generally.

As a result, we feel less honored at being given the chance to learn. And when school's over—either the school day or our career as students—most of us feel that we've spent enough time learning and want to use our free time to "relax" or "have fun." The idea of devoting a lifetime to intellectual pursuits seems almost silly to most young adults.

Worst of all, I said to my class, people no longer feel compelled to serve as active citizens. We may be able to read, but we're not educated, at least not as voters, and that's why we elect politicians based on 30-second sound bites. Even those of us who cherish our right to vote aren't likely to be committed to public service in the way Jefferson was. That's why hardly any of our most talented, charismatic people dare to even think about pursuing careers as statesmen.

"The choice is yours," I said. "You're the bulwark of this democracy. Are you going to view citizenship only as a birthright, or as a joyous honor too? And how many of you are going to try to emulate Jefferson's natural aristocrats and pursue politics not as spectators, but as players?"

I ended the class with a pronouncement. "There's no holier vocation than politics, but only if it's pursued with a fair amount of integrity, intelligence and courage. Jefferson had all the brains he needed. He just could have used a bit more of the other two." Right then, I looked at Lorraine, hoping she understood that I recognized Jefferson's limitations as well as his strengths.

After the bell, Lorraine walked up to me, smiled and said, "It's not about his lack of integrity or courage, Mr. Kramer. It's about his selfishness and greed." Then she turned her back on me and walked away before I had a chance to respond.

After the Jefferson lesson, I left school like a bat out of hell. It was the day before Thanksgiving, and I'd arranged to spend the entire weekend with Allison.

We met at the B&N bookstore in downtown Bethesda, a few miles south of my apartment and not too far from the D.C. line. That area had a number of the best restaurants in metropolitan Washington. It was enough of a drawing card that an urban snob like Allison was often willing to see me there. I had a devil of a time motivating her to visit me in Rockville, where I lived, or Takoma Park, where I taught.

Allison was pulling a suitcase on wheels, having agreed to use my apartment as her home base for the weekend. She planted a big kiss on my lips and told me how thrilled she was to get out of the city for a few days and leave the law behind. "I didn't bring one God-forsaken law book," she said.

"You're being redundant," I replied, recalling how much I hated those case books.

"Oh my God," Allison said, before she shoved me Elaine Benes-like into the wall. "Guess what. We've *finally* arranged a meeting with Choulos. And he's got *documents*."

"What are you talking about?"

"I'm telling you, he's gathering his evidence. County real estate records, Internet clippings. He's also got his notes from the conversation with the guy who bought the Vermeer."

"You're kidding."

"No. Choulos told us that after he types up his notes we should go ahead and call that guy. Apparently, he was really friendly."

"Can you imagine plucking down $15 million on one painting?" I asked.

"And that was back in the '80s. The Benefactor should have probably hung on to it. It could be worth twice as much now."

"I'll bet," I said. "Vermeer didn't paint very much, and each one is amazing. By the way, did you know he was born in the same year as Spinoza?"

Allison rolled her eyes at that fun little fact and headed for the literature section. I made a bee line for philosophy. A half hour later, while still browsing, I saw another member of the Creed Gang stacking books.

"Kramer! What the heck are you doing here?" he practically shouted.

"Hey, Scott. I didn't know you worked here."

"Don't rub it in. The pay sucks and there's no privacy. But at least I get to be around books, and my schedule's pretty flexible. Speaking of which, I'm off in a few. Are you doing anything for dinner?"

Just as Shaw asked that question, Allison came up the escalator and saw us. "My God," she said, smiling. "If it isn't the Creed Room's answer to John Brown. How's it hangin', Scott?"

"To the left, babe. As always. Wait a minute," he said, with a puzzled look on his face. "I haven't seen anyone from our group here before. Now I see both of you. Is this a coincidence?"

Allison and I looked at each other. Then she smiled and said to Shaw, "Actually, we've been seeing a lot of each other lately."

"I see," Shaw muttered. "So I guess that means you *are* busy for dinner, huh Kramer?"

"Don't let me get in the way of male bonding," said Allison. "I'd love to go to dinner with both of you handsome gentlemen. That's assuming I can choose the restaurant."

"How about it?" I said to Shaw. "Are you game?"

"Sure. Give me 15 minutes. Then we can go wherever the lady wants."

Allison chose the Cancun Grille, a popular Mexican restaurant. We stood at the bar while we were waiting for a table. By the time we were able to take our seats, Shaw and Allison had nearly finished their second drinks.

"So," Shaw said, "how do you lovers like the Creed Room?"

"I've had fun," Allison said. "I really liked your presentation last week, especially that stuff about myth of altruism."

"Oh, come on, don't butter me up," Shaw replied, after he ordered yet another drink. "That presentation was a sleeper. I'm kinda afraid to liven things up right now. You recall what happened when everyone's favorite religion came up."

"Now whose fault was that?" I said.

"Not mine," Shaw said. "I was only adding a little balance, that's all."

"You call that *balance*?" I replied. "I call it a machine gun."

"Please, they deserved it," Shaw said. "I'll leave the missus out of this, although she's an enabler as long as she stays married to that jackass and spends his money. Let's talk about A-Hole Art. Everything about him is offensive. His job, his attitude, and especially his so-called 'faith.' He should damned well be ready whenever someone has the guts to call him on it."

"What about his job?" Allison asked.

"Are you serious?" Shaw replied. "That guy's the number one lobbyist for the stinking telemarketing industry."

"Doesn't he also lobby for charitable fundraisers?" I asked.

Shaw laughed. "Oh my. The telefunders? Do you really give to those people?"

When I replied that I had, Shaw laughed even louder. "Do you know what fraction of each buck they raise actually goes to the charity? Twenty cents if you're lucky."

"Why would the charities put up with that?" I asked.

"'They're getting money for doing nothing. It's win/win for

everybody except the marks like you. If you'd given directly to the charity, you could have quintupled your investment."

"I wonder how much Art makes a year," Allison said. "What d'you think—400? 500?"

"More," said Shaw. "And no social utility either. Pretty impressive."

"So, Scott," I said, "what do *you* think about the Creed Room so far?"

Suddenly, Shaw seemed to sober up almost immediately. "I'm withholding judgment until we get to the meaty topics."

"The meaty topics?" I repeated.

"I'm waiting until we talk politics in the spring. Right now, I can't tell whether we're going to give The Man some real smack or just another sales job."

"What are you talking about?" I asked.

"Let me spell it out for you, Mr. Tele-Mark. I'm looking for the group to remind Daddy Warbucks that a whole lot of people in this world *and in this country* don't have the kind of scratch he does. And as long as they're in poverty, nothing else matters."

"Poverty equals injustice," Allison said. "That's a Jewish concept. Are you sure you're not a tribesman?"

"Me?" Scott asked, laughing. "Y'all wouldn't want me. I don't have the right pedigree."

Allison and I looked at each other. We decided to leave that comment alone.

When Allison changed the subject to sports, Shaw was definitely in his element. He went on and on about University of Maryland basketball to the point where Allison finally grew tired of the topic and asked him about his career. Then, Shaw became melancholy. "Do you *really* think I want to work in a bookstore forever? I'm just biding my time until one of my screenplays sells."

"I hear you," Allison said. "If I thought I could make a living writing screenplays, I'd do it in a heartbeat."

"Hey, don't sell yourself short," Shaw replied. "You always know the words to use to put a man in his place. There's no more important skill for a woman writer than that, is there Sam?"

"Not these days," I replied.

Shaw faced Allison again. "Maybe you can become a screenwriter when you get tired of kissing ass at the law firm."

"Oh, I don't know," Allison said. "Some things never get old."

I had a great time that entire Thanksgiving weekend, and it was all thanks to Allison's vivacity. She appointed herself the Thanksgiving fun director. Wednesday night's dinner out would be followed by indoor sports back at the apartment. Thursday would also be spent mostly at the apartment—reading and listening to tunes, checking out some football, and cooking and eating turkey—before winding up the evening at the movies. We'd spend Friday and Saturday on day trips; the first would be her choice, the second, mine. Finally, we'd spend most of Sunday at the Redskins game. It had been sold out for ages, but Allison pulled some strings and got us both tickets.

On Friday, Allison schlepped us to western Virginia where we spent the day hiking in the Blue Ridge. Late in the afternoon, she checked us into a motel where we could change clothes and ready ourselves for the evening's activity—a visit to a Reform synagogue in Charlottesville.

Allison knew I had a lot of problems with Jewish liturgy. I didn't believe, for example, that a God created or sustains this world in accordance with a human-like will, which seemed to be the basic premise behind all the traditional prayers. But when Allison announced that evening that we would be going to services, I caught a break. The service was led by a guest rabbi from Jerusalem with a marvelous voice. Rather than conducting a traditional ceremony, he spent most of the evening leading us in the humming of melodies without words. I was completely entranced—by the melodies, the feeling of being a part of a spiritual community, and the sense of being in the presence of a man drunk with divinity. I didn't dare ask Allison how this service compared to one led by her father. It wouldn't have been fair to Rabbi Schwartz.

On Saturday, we visited the homes of some of the Old Dominion's most venerable statesmen—Madison, Monroe and, of course, Jefferson. Before that weekend, I'd been to Monroe's Ashlawn three times, Madison's Montpelier four or five, and Monticello perhaps as many as ten. But I never enjoyed them as much as when I went with Allison.

Over and over again, she'd ask the docents questions. Sometimes she'd ask about minutiae, such as why Jefferson slept on such a small bed if he were such a tall man. Other times she was more provocative, like when she asked why Montpelier's caretakers didn't show Madison the respect of restoring the entire house to look like it did when he lived there.

I told Allison how much I'd love to have someone like her in one of my history classes.

"Oooh, I'd like that too," she said. "If I were in your class, I'd probably be one of those naughty girls who's got a crush on their teacher. When I'd see you looking at me, maybe I'd lick my lips a little. Or maybe I'd stroke your arms sometimes when I'd leave your classroom—"

"That kind of thing happens all the time," I replied, giving her a taste of her own medicine. "You know, we're supposed to flirt too. It gets the kids more involved in the school."

"OK, OK," she said, laughing. "I'll stop."

"Seriously, did you do much dating in high school?" I asked.

"I had a steady boyfriend during most of my senior year. Junior year, I had a couple of boyfriends. Nothing too exciting. You?"

"I didn't date at all. In fact, I pretty much hated high school."

"Wait a minute. You hated high school, but now you teach there? What's up with that?"

"Teaching was something I wanted to do for as long as I can remember."

"But why high school? Why not college?" Allison asked.

"The better question is why not middle school? I like trying to get through to kids before they've decided whether to be thinkers or mindless bores. By the time they're in college, they've already decided."

That weekend, I had so much fun that the only thing left for me to neurose about was whether Allison was feeling the same way. Late Sunday evening, I asked her directly what she got out of having me as a boyfriend.

"I don't know. I don't analyze that stuff. Let's see. You're cute, you're engaging, you probably even remind me of my dad."

"Is that a good thing?"

"Sometimes. Other times the angst gets on my nerves."

"Sorry."

"Don't apologize, sweetheart. That's the way you're wired. That's the way he's wired. It's true with me too, only I'm trying to pull out the wires—I'll take my chances without them."

"You've got more balls than I do, Allison."

"No, just bigger ones," she said, smiling.

❧

"Hello, Mr. Kramer?" the voice began, in his best imitation of a 16-year-old girl, half tart and half ingenue. It was the Monday after Thanksgiving. "My mommy and daddy are gone this weekend and I was wondering if you could come over and teach me about Webster, Clay and Calhoun. I'll just be wearing a thong. Nothing else—just ... a thong."

"Well, well," I replied. "If it isn't the most eligible bachelor in Silicon Valley. Have you had your annual STD test yet, Steve?"

"It's scheduled for next Monday," said Jamison, not missing a beat. "A few of the girls were going to pick me up in a van and we were all going to get tested together. Wish me luck."

"So what's up?"

"I'm going to come visit you."

"Awesome! But I thought you told me your days of monument stomping were over."

Jamison started laughing. "You thought I'd be coming to *that* self-important backwater? Come on, guy, get real. I'm talking about seeing you during Christmas week in a *real* city. You are going up to visit your mom, right?"

"You know it. She'd have a coronary if I didn't."

"Then that's where I'm headed. Take in a game or two at the Garden, hit a couple of shows on Broadway, check out the Met and the MOMA. Doesn't that sound like more fun than listening to some pompous Washington Bureau Chief talk about the Middle East?"

"OK. I'm following you. What day are you coming?"

"I was thinking the 26th, and I'd stay through New Year's Day. You don't have any special plans for that week, do you?"

"Well, my friend, I've been dating a girl whose folks live in Manhattan. We're finally going to meet each other's families."

"So it's serious?" he asked.

"I like her *a lot.* I'm telling you, she's great."

"Is there a problem with me coming out then? Three can be a crowd."

"Believe me, I'll still have plenty of free time. And I know my mom would be happy to put you up."

"You think I'll need to *stay* at your mom's house for the week? Nooooo. I just meant that I'd visit you there. I'll be checking into a nice mid-town hotel, dude. My days of free loading off your mom are over."

"You sure?" I asked. "For some strange reason, she likes your company. Maybe it's because you're the only one in the world who flatters her."

"My pleasure," Jamison said. "So how's teaching going?"

"Pretty well. I wonder whether I'll want to do it in ten years, but for now it's fine."

"That's cool. I have to say, I can't imagine what else you'd be doing. The profit motive is beneath you, so you can't go into business. You can't be a lawyer 'cause you won't advocate only one side of an issue. You can't be a doctor—that would take too much time away from your philosophy reading."

"So I'm stuck, then," I said, playing along. "Teaching history. Turning whining nerds into master debaters."

"Hey, I know you're a great teacher," Jamison said. "I don't doubt you can entertain your kids, and I bet some of them even understand what you're saying. If the rest of us have to supplement your salary with welfare checks, so be it."

The next day at school, I brought in my two best history

students, Vijay Gupta and Lorraine Jackson, to help design the Civil War unit. In addition to assisting me with lesson planning, they were told that they'd command the two armies. Vijay won a coin flip and chose the North. He and Lorraine selected troops from among their classmates. Lorraine later told me that she avoided picking any African-American students for her army because she didn't feel comfortable forcing them to argue on the side of the Confederacy.

As it turned out, I enjoyed everything about the Civil War unit and especially its climax—when representatives of the two sides met at Appomattox, Virginia to discuss how the war would be resolved. I let the class vary from historical fact in choosing who would do the talking at Appomattox and on what terms the South's surrender would be accepted.

The students impressed me a lot by staying in character. One after another, the "grey" ones mangled southern accents, but at least they tried to sound authentic. One of the "blue" students, playing the role of a former slave, walked down the aisles of the classroom, wagging an accusing finger at the southerners for treating blacks like cattle. "I want proof that you're gonna change your ways. *Proof!* All men are created equal, my butt!" he yelled. Fortunately, Cratchett didn't teach a seventh period class, or surely she'd have come in to complain.

The high point of the exercise for me was Lorraine. She played the role of a lower-middle class shopkeeper's wife, and somehow she managed to state the essence of the South's argument without losing her integrity in the process. You might say that only weeks before I began teaching philosophy for the first time, Lorraine drummed into my consciousness exactly what it meant to be a philosopher. It was a lesson I kept in mind not only when I taught philosophy but also when I tried to practice the values of a philosopher in the Creed Room.

"Slavery, slavery, slavery," Lorraine began. "That's all we're hearing about today. You'd think that was all this war was about. It's not. I'd rather not even talk about slavery. I didn't come here to defend it, and I didn't come here to attack it. Like a whole lot of white families in the Confederacy, mine never had slaves, but we supported the Confederate Army anyway. That's because there was a lot more at stake in this war.

"No matter what you think about slavery, the Confederacy had no choice but to defend our land, and we defended it well. You outnumbered us, but we darned near beat you. Don't think for a second we've lost our pride. And don't think that you can get away with treating us without mercy. If you don't show us mercy, you can forget about this union becoming a big happy family. You'll be tearing it apart, guts and all.

"Trust me, if you abuse your power, you won't be worrying only about angry Southerners. You'll know that just as you once bullied your brothers and sisters to the South, some day, maybe some other country's going to do the same to you. It'd be their right, wouldn't it? You'd be saying that whoever has power can use it anyway they want to.

"The choice is yours. Forgive us, and send the message that all Americans should come together as equals. Or invite the English, the French and the Spanish to take back their land— as soon as they get the muscle to do it. If you humiliate your own families in places like Virginia, Alabama, and my own beautiful North Carolina, you'll deserve whatever's coming to you.

"We can't read your minds and tell you why you fought this war. Maybe you fought over slavery. Maybe you had some other reason. But please take us at our word. We fought over the right of the people who live in a particular place to decide for *themselves* how they should live. It's the same reason we revolted against England. We didn't want the English king, who didn't even live here, to tell us what to do. It's our land, so it should be our choice what to do with it."

Lorraine continued for a couple of minutes, explaining that even if the Northerners hated slavery, they'd have to admit that if people started invading other people's lands every time they found something they didn't like, there wouldn't be anyone left on the planet. She ended by saying, "The South understands that slavery has to go, whether we like it or not. Let that be your only trophy from this war. Accept us as equal members of your family, and you won't be sorry."

The class remained quiet as she took her seat. I had already presented the South's perspective on the war in my lectures, but it must have jarred everyone's ears to hear Lorraine of all people advocate the South's cause. Watching her do it without having to come across as being pro-slavery couldn't help but impress her classmates, particularly the African-Americans. As for me, I was dazzled by her ability to get right to the heart of an issue, see all the possible sides, and then communicate precisely what she's seen. If that isn't the hallmark of a philosopher, what is?

CHAPTER 6

FUN CITY

*A*llison and I drove up to New York on Christmas Day. It was a great time to travel; even the Jersey Turnpike was relatively empty. When we stopped off at one of the Turnpike's rest areas, it looked like we'd come across a synagogue group out on a retreat. The only tie-up all day was when an elderly woman slowed up the line at Hardees for several minutes, demanding her money back for a half-eaten chicken sandwich that she said was too cold.

"I can't place her," Allison said, "but she reminds me of someone."

"Yeah, me too—most of my family," I replied.

I dropped Allison off at her parents' Midtown condo in the afternoon. She invited me to stop by for a few minutes, but I decided against it. I wanted to be able to spend a while with her parents when we met for the first time, and I had promised my mother that I'd get to Brooklyn before the sun set. Allison and I arranged that she'd meet the two of us for a long lunch the next day, and I'd plan on seeing her folks later in the week.

My mother owned a modest duplex in the lower-middle class neighborhood of Midwood. This was the house where we had lived together with her parents in the mid to late 80s. Back then, we had always felt cramped, but ever since my grandparents died the duplex had seemed spacious to me. Lord knows, it also felt familiar. Mother has never changed anything about it—not even the appliances, unless they were beyond repair.

When we originally moved into the house from the D.C. suburbs, my grandparents sold their furniture so that we could bring in our own. Consequently, the Midwood home had much of the same feel as the house in D.C. where I grew up. Most people would call its furnishings drab and out of date. To my mother, though, they were tremendously comforting. They connected her life in New York with the life we had before in Washington.

Sitting in her living room that Christmas Day, I was happy to relax and listen to her banter. Oh sure, she graced me with little else than her latest kvetches about friends, politics and co-workers, but I enjoyed what she had to say. As comfortable as her ugly home furnishings were to her, my mother's chatter was to me, unless, of course, I was the object of that chatter.

After dinner, we watched a Bowl game on TV. She had no reason to care about either college, but that didn't stop her from reacting as if one of her kids played for Kansas State.

Allison was already seated by the time Mother and I arrived at the restaurant on the corner of 59th and 5th. It was a Jewish deli, one that serves large quantities of sodium-laden, fatty meats. "Just what I need for my Ashkenazic intestines," Mother said. She's often complained that her irritable bowel syndrome was the product of centuries of Jewish cuisine.

I was struck by the excellent conversational chemistry between the two women. They'd talk passionately about one topic, then seamlessly move on to another. Mostly, though, they spoke about Allison's dad, whom my mother once heard lecture on the topic of Israel. Mother gushed her praise of Rabbi Schwartz, and Allison glowed with every compliment.

After the meal, I left the table for a couple of minutes. When I got back, the conversation's intensity had kicked up a notch. I knew what they were talking about as soon as I saw the look on my mother's face, which was at once bitter and wistful. It was a topic I had avoided discussing with Allison.

"What a beautiful ceremony it was," my mother said. "They held it at a Reform temple on Queens Boulevard. Benny's brother Morris was the happiest groom you could imagine, and my friend Miriam was absolutely stunning. It's no wonder Benny and I felt so romantic when we first met at the reception. That kind of mood is contagious.

"Less than a year later, we were married. It was a big wedding, lots of meshpukah. Nobody had to travel very far. I grew up in Brooklyn. Benny was from the Bronx.

"We got married in June 1958. Our first home was in the City, on 20th St. near the East River. Then in '65, Benny got a chance to open up a small accounting firm with an old CCNY classmate. So we moved to Rockville, only a mile or two from where Sammy lives now.

"The D.C. area was nice then. It had wonderful museums, an active theater community, even a passable newspaper. It wasn't congested either. Today, oy gevalt, it takes forever to drive around there. They've never heard of building highways other than that one stupid beltway.

"I got a job at a public library. Benny was doing people's taxes. We made a decent living. When we had Sammy, everything was perfect. He was such a nice boy, really a gem."

"Oh, come on Mother," I said, embarrassed.

"You were a *wonderful* child. You never made any trouble.

"For the first ten years after Sammy was born," Mother continued, "we were about as happy as three Jews can be, if you know what I mean. Then Benny's business partner died. He had a massive heart attack, right in the office—Benny saw the whole thing. Afterwards, life wasn't the same. Benny may have been a whiz at accounting, but he wasn't much of a schmoozer, so when his partner died, the clients who needed the schmoozing took off."

"That destroyed my father," I added. "He was like a different person."

"Year after year, our income went down," Mother said. "It came to the point where even with a lousy librarian's salary, I earned more than Benny did."

"And you often reminded him of that too. Didn't you Mother?"

"I don't recall doing that."

"Believe me, you did."

Mother glared at me and then resumed. "I was hoping that Sammy's Bar Mitzvah would cheer Benny up. It did for a bit, but not for long. He started drinking. A lot. I couldn't believe my eyes. Who's ever heard of a Jewish alcoholic? Gamblers yes, even mobsters. Not alcoholics. Just our luck, Benny was the exception. He ..." my mother's voice tailed away for a moment. Then tears rolled down her face. "He never beat me. Never. He couldn't possibly hurt another person. He couldn't even hurt a fly. Only himself."

"You're forgetting the plates, Mother. The vases."

"Fine," she said, fighting off tears. "He had a temper. Alright? Sometimes he'd break things. *Things*. He never touched either of us."

"That's true," I acknowledged.

"I asked him to get counseling, but Benny wouldn't go. He

said he just needed a few more clients. I told him to go to Temple and try to hustle up business, but he wouldn't do that either. Like I said, Benny wasn't much on small talk. And he was way too proud to beg for business. 'I'm not a schnurrer,' he'd tell me.

"In November of '85, Sammy was 15. Benny took off from work for a week. He said he needed a little break and that his clients wouldn't miss him. That Wednesday, as I was cooking dinner, I heard a horrible noise. I didn't know what it was. I ran into the study, but before I got there I could see Sammy standing near the door. He was frozen. When I looked in the study, I saw Benny. His head was blown apart. And blood was ss... spilled all over the walls."

She was crying too hard to continue, so I finished her story. "He put the gun in his mouth. Pointed it straight up. And blasted the living ..."

That was the last word from either of us for well over a minute. Mother was sobbing, and I couldn't stop seeing the image of my father's face severed from much of his head. I reached over to hug her. It was an embrace between two people who realized that nobody else in the world could possibly share their pain. Allison offered a few words of compassion. But really, what could she say?

"You know," I said, regaining my composure, "there's one thing about my father's death that almost makes me laugh. He had a suicide clause in his insurance policy, so when he died young, he didn't leave us with any money. When you consider what happened to his accounting business, I guess it's fitting that he couldn't even manage to make his death look like an accident."

For another minute or so, we sat in silence once again. Mostly, I was feeling shame that Allison needed to hear that story from my mother and not me. All that I said to Allison back in D.C. was that my father was an accountant who died when I was a teenager.

After we finished talking about my father, we tried to continue the conversation, but it was no use. The three of us might as well have spoken in different languages.

On the ride back to Brooklyn, Mother was as subdued as I'd seen her in years. It wasn't until bedtime that she showed signs of life. "Allison seems like a beautiful person, a real delight," she said, smiling. "I'm happy you two found each other." I wondered at that moment how Allison could possibly have felt the same way about me.

I had a good time with Jamison when we met up at the Metropolitan Museum of Art and then had dinner with a couple of his friends in Greenwich Village. Afterwards, we headed off to an upscale club and listened to a local blues band. The band sounded great, but I'm not exactly hard to please when it comes to live blues.

I was disappointed that Allison couldn't come to the club that night. She had family commitments. In fact, after the deli meeting, Allison and I didn't see each other until the 30th. That's when I met her at her parents' home.

The Schwartz's lived right off Central Park on the ninth floor of a large building called the Independent. I was greeted at their door by a middle-aged woman. She wasn't what I expected Dr. Schwartz to look like. Her features appeared to be Eastern European—but Slavic, not Jewish. Also, she bordered on the obese.

"Dr. Schwartz?" I asked.

"Oh no, no. I'm Marta. I'm helping Wendy with the meal

today. Come in, come in."

Marta led me through a wide, plushly carpeted hallway and then opened the door into a spacious, formal living room. "Please, have a seat," she said. "You're Mr. Kramer?"

"Yes, that's right," I said. "Call me Sam."

"The Schwartz's have been expecting you. Allison said she'll be out in a moment."

I hadn't seen such opulence since my last trip to the Victorian. Abstract sculptures graced two corners of the room. Striking Judaic paintings lined the walls.

I learned later that much of the Schwartz's artwork was painted by the rabbi's younger brother. It only stood to reason that a family as fortunate as the Schwartz's would produce their own court painter. In my family, you'd probably have to go back centuries before you could find even a half-decent artist.

Allison and I spent several hours with her parents that day. Dr. Schwartz was a highly attractive woman who looked to be in her 40s but was actually in her late 50s. The rabbi was as grey and prematurely wrinkled as Allison had described him. But I didn't see the anxiety she had led me to expect. What I saw instead was the affection he felt for his wife and daughter.

Dr. and Rabbi Schwartz regaled me with stories about Allison. One had to do with her beloved pet, Jacob, a 16-pound poodle whom she named after her favorite Biblical character.

Allison trained her dog all by herself, Dr. Schwartz explained. "She was ten when she asked for a dog. She said 'Get me one, and I'll do all the training.' The only thing we did is pay for a trainer to come to our home. Allison took care of the rest."

"Remember when Allison would put her dinner on the ground and eat out of one bowl while Jacob ate out of the other?" the rabbi asked.

"Of course," Dr. Schwartz said. "They were inseparable."

"She also taught the dog to howl when she didn't like one of my sermons," the rabbi said. "After we came home from shul, she'd say something to Jacob, and he'd howl for ten minutes. She wouldn't stop him. She said she owed it to the congregation."

"Did your sermons improve?" I asked the rabbi.

"Of course. I couldn't stand to hear that noise."

After they finished the tale about Allison the Dog Trainer, the Schwartz's turned to a story about Allison the rabbi. When she was 12, the family had a big dinner party, and they invited a prominent rabbi from a neighboring synagogue. "Before the party," Rabbi Schwartz said, "I made the mistake of telling Allison what I really thought of the man—how the only thing he liked was the cut of his own jib. You know the type."

"They're as common among rabbis as perverts among priests," Allison said.

Rabbi Schwartz looked askance at his daughter and then continued. "Allison made a monkey of the man. He went on and on with some theory about the Book of Esther, and she just pounced on it. She'd ask him one question after another, and he'd brush her off. But her questions were interesting. For example, he said that Esther was a parable about good and evil, and its moral was that we must recognize and eradicate evil whenever we see it. Then Allison asked, 'Don't we all possess both good and bad qualities, meaning shades of grey? And aren't the religious fanatics who are obsessed with eradicating evil the true evil doers?' He wouldn't answer.

"Eventually, a couple of the other guests responded to Allison. And the next thing you knew, we were having a lively conversation centered around her ideas. Everyone participated but the rabbi. He probably figured none of us wanted to be enlightened."

"It was an awkward situation," Dr. Schwartz said, "but I have to admit I was proud of Allison. We've always taught her to stand up for herself."

"And don't forget the best part of the story," Allison added. "A few years later, the windbag was convicted of tax fraud."

Before I left the Schwartz's condo, I was able to speak to the rabbi at some length about philosophy and theology. As learned as he obviously was, he was just as respectful. I found myself wishing he could move to D.C. so I could hear him preach, but I realized he belonged in New York. If the Big Apple isn't the Mecca of Judaism today, it's at least the Medina.

On New Year's Eve, Jamison picked Allison up at her parents' condo and brought her to my mother's house for dinner. Our plan was to hang out until nine or so, jettison my mother, and then head back to the City. One of Allison's high school friends was hosting a lavish party in her mid-town apartment. "She's from old money," Allison told me.

Jamison and Allison had never met prior to that evening, but by the time they arrived in Midwood, they seemed to be fast friends. I wasn't surprised. Steve has always known how to charm women. He can disarm them at will with his humor, but he also knows when to show them that he shares their values. For example, even though Jamison normally doesn't care to talk about politics, he joined right in with Allison when she bashed right-to-life politicians. I was tempted to ask if his pro-choice views were based on self-interest, but I held back.

During dinner, I boasted about Allison's stature as the reigning D.C. Poetry Slam champ. When Mother said that she'd once attended a slam, Allison's eyes widened in surprise.

"It was God awful, there's no other way of putting it," Mother said.

"What happened?" Allison asked.

"I went there to keep my friend Mildred Lipschitz company. Her son Henry was competing. He talked about an evening he spent at Martha's Vineyard making love under the stars. And he didn't spare any details. Mildred was completely humiliated."

Allison sighed. "He shouldn't have asked his mother to come."

"Henry was just the appetizer. A young black man got up and ... what a bastard he was. He talked the whole time about the Israelis. They kill babies. They bulldoze houses. It was three minutes of absolute anti-Semitic ranting and raving."

"I hate to see poetry slams abused like that," Allison said. But my mother was more interested in talking about anti-Semitism than poetry slams.

"When you think about all we've done for those people during the civil rights movement. Back then, if you found a white person working for civil rights you could be sure he was a Jew. Now, the worst anti-Semites in the country are black."

"How do you know that, Mother?" I asked, skeptical about her expertise.

"I read the papers, Sammy. I see what their leaders are saying. It's the same michigas that came out of Germany. The Jew is cold, calculating, money-crazed, selfish, dishonest ... we all know the stereotype. We've been the world's number one scapegoat for 2000 years."

"So get back to the poetry slam, Ruth," Jamison said. "What happened?"

"I sat and waited for this idiot to shut his mouth. Excuse me—I waited for the 'poet' to complete his act of 'self-expression.' Isn't that the politically correct way to put it?"

"Close enough," Jamison said, smiling.

"Then the audience gave him a raucous ovation, and the loudest applause came from the competitors—not Henry, but some of the others. Personally, I wanted to pull that man by the ear into the bathroom and wash his mouth out with soap."

"I'll bet you did," said Jamison, laughing at that image.

"Thank God one of the judges slammed *him* or he might have won. The other judges gave him top scores."

"I guess that's the last poetry slam you'll ever attend," Allison said.

"I didn't stay for the second round. I thanked the judge who stood up to the schmuck and left poor Mildred sitting alone. I had to get out before I went meshugah."

"You stuck around long enough," Jamison said.

"No kidding," I said. "Could you imagine what that black guy would have done if Lipschitz had been spewing out venom about *his* people?"

"Could you imagine the audience applauding after Henry finished?" asked Mother. "Let's face it. Anti-Semitism's always in vogue. Now, it's Israel bashing. A hundred years ago it was the Jewish bankers. Some things never change."

I looked over at Jamison and could tell his attention was wandering. He had walked over to the window and looked out. When a guy who lives overlooking the Pacific Ocean feels the need to catch the view outside of a Midwood duplex, you better believe he's restless.

Mother must have noticed that because she began peppering him with questions about his software company and all the expensive things he'd been able to buy lately. Then, it was my turn to get bored, but I kept it to myself. Mother has often seemed to live a bit vicariously through Jamison's nouveau riche status, and I enjoyed seeing her happy. Besides, Jamison's talk of a beautiful coastal house, big Mercedes Benz, and state of the art electronics didn't push any of my buttons. I was quite content having none of the above.

The evening was going about as smoothly as I could have hoped until the instant when I noticed my mother set her fork down next to her plate with a purpose. She crossed her legs and turned toward Allison. Mother was obviously ready to get down to business.

"So, Allison," she said, "what do you plan to do with your law degree?"

"Work at a firm," she replied. "I want to do general litigation. Trial work, appellate work, all of it. I want to learn to be the best litigator I can be."

"Why litigation?" Mother asked.

"It's where the action is. I like to mix it up a bit—a few pointed words here, a little drama there, whatever it takes to get the job done."

"Sure, that makes sense," Mother said. "You're the poetry slammer."

"You know, litigation's not all about drama and making speeches. A lot of it is figuring out what questions to ask to bring out a story. I like that part too. I've enjoyed all my litigation training."

Mother glowed at Allison's response. "It's wonderful that you're so excited about your career, and such a nice choice—great pay, lots of prestige. Tell me, within the field, what do you see yourself doing, say, over the next 20 years?"

"I figure I'll work at a firm for a few years, learn the tricks of the trade, make some decent money, then maybe go to a U.S. Attorney's Office or the Justice Department. It would have to be a high-level job—no way I'd want to be a worker bee in that hive. Then who knows, maybe try for a judgeship or go back to a firm. I'm trying to stay flexible. There are a number of things in the law I wouldn't mind doing."

"And you can make some serious change too," said Jamison. "Pull in a quarter mil a year by the time you're 30; maybe 6-700K by the time you're 40. You can live OK on that."

"It'd be pretty strange to bill people $500 an hour and actually hear them tell you you're worth it," Allison continued. "I can't imagine being worth that kind of money." That's what she said, but I didn't believe her. I assumed she envisioned the day when she'd be as much of a pillar in her own profession as her parents were in theirs.

"I can see you as a trial attorney," Jamison said. "No question about it, you could kick some serious tush in the courtroom. You've got flair. I don't see that in too many lawyers."

"I agree," I said, focusing on the issue for the first time. "You're a natural, Allison."

"Thanks. I'm pretty pumped to get started."

"Tell me this," Jamison said with a puzzled look on his face. "Why are you thinking about working for the government down the road? What's the attraction?"

"Variety. Like I said, I wouldn't go to the government for just *any* job. I'm not crazy."

Mother had been content to let Allison and Jamison carry the conversation, but the mention of government employment raised her antennae. "I'm a government employee, you know, and I understand exactly what Allison's talking about. Working in a public library, I can't tell you how badly the place is run. The people in power don't know the first thing about libraries.

"And my brother Lenny—he's worked an eternity as a government economist. You should hear him talk about bureaucracies. Trust me—if you're not running one, avoid 'em like the plague. They'll sap your energy to the point where none of us would recognize you."

"Give her six years in the Department of Veterans Affairs," Jamison said, "and I bet *you* could beat her in a poetry slam, Ruth."

"I wouldn't be surprised," Mother replied. "They'd break her will."

Jamison laughed, picked up his wine glass and downed all the contents in one gulp. Mother laughed along with him. Then she turned to face Allison. "I don't see you slaving away for Uncle Sam. Not now, not ever. You have too much sense for that."

"You could be wrong," said Jamison. "Maybe she wants to make a difference in people's lives." I knew Jamison was being tongue-in-cheek, but I don't think my mother did.

"She can do that in the private sector. There's a lot of good work to be done at firms. She'll just have to find the right cases. She's smart enough. She shouldn't have any trouble."

Ever since the conversation had turned into a public service bashing session, I had been getting progressively annoyed. Finally, I couldn't keep quiet any longer.

"Mother, you're so naive. Don't you get it? You argue the cases your clients hand you. Sometimes you're on the right side, sometimes the wrong side. That's the way it works."

"There's your cynicism again, Sammy. I'm not buying it. You should hear Debby Scolnick talk about her daughter's work at Jones & Falk. She raves about that job. Exciting work, *good* causes—."

"Spare me," I interrupted, while getting up from the table to stretch my legs.

I was hoping someone would change the subject, but Jamison didn't see the need to take a break. Turning to Allison, he asked, "Have you ever thought of teaching?"

"Nah. I've no interest in teaching law."

"You're not, uh, going to quit your profession and teach high school, are you dear?" asked my mother.

"Oh come off it, Mother."

"Can you imagine a woman like that in your school, Sammy?"

"She'd do great."

"Please. She'd be wasting her time, just like you do."

"Watch it, Mother," I said, beginning to feel my blood pressure rise. "Not tonight. OK?"   But my mother never was very good at impulse control. "Allison wants to make something of herself. Can you blame her?"

"I think it's very noble what Sam does for a living," Allison said. "This society needs inspiring high school teachers."

"So let it pay for them, then," Mother said. "It's crazy to do that work for peanuts."

"Ah, the voice of wisdom," Jamison chimed in. "It can really *smart*, can't it, Sammy? Your momma just nailed you right between the eyes. I've always told you to make a fortune first, then you can choose whatever you want to do and you won't have to worry about how much it pays or even *if* it pays. Doesn't that make sense, Ruth?"

"Obviously. Sammy, you should listen to your friend Steve. It's not too late."

"Mother, enough," I said. "Enough!"

"You know, every time I try to talk sense into your head you refuse to listen," she continued. "Just calm down and listen to reason. We're all saying the same thing."

"Darned right," Jamison said, his own impulse control compromised by the wine he and Allison had been drinking from the moment they walked in. "Sam could make the same kind of money I do. He's plenty smart enough. By the time I'm 40, I won't have to worry about money for the rest of my life. Then, if I wanted to, I could go teach college, or high school, or for that matter, *romper room*."

"Don't mention romper room," Mother said. "You'll put ideas in Sammy's head."

That was it. I started hollering.

"Listen, Mother. I'm sick of your God damned shit about what I do for a living. I'm helping people out who need a good education. It's as simple as that."

"Don't speak that way to me!" she shouted back. "Who do you think you are, talking like a drunken sailor? You show me some respect. You show your guests some respect!"

"Guests? One of my guests is as full of crap as you are. Jamison, you and your piles of money can get *really* annoying, did you know that? You'd think with all your bragging that you've accomplished something. You've just sold some stupid software to a bunch of rich assholes."

"What?" asked Jamison, clearly non-plussed. "Dude, leave me out of your problems. I make what people need. And not just rich people, *all* people."

"First of all, that's not true. A lot of people can't afford your technology. Second, it's not like technology is saving anybody's soul, certainly not their humanity. It's only making people slaves to all the junk they own. I'm not so sure that's progress."

"I'm not saving people's *humanity*? Man, what kind of God complex do you have, anyway? Say all you want about how great it is to teach at a public school, or work at the welfare office or do whatever other lousy public sector job meets your moral demands. I ain't buying it."

"Sammy, you're wrong about technology," Mother said, still fuming. "But I don't want to talk about that. I want to talk about your lack of respect."

"Like you show me any."

Mother must have reached her limit too, because she paused a while before responding. "It wasn't my idea that you throw away everything you worked for and drop out of Harvard. That was *your* act of insanity. Well, I guess you came by it honestly. Like father, like son."

At that point, the vision of my father's brains plastered on the wall of the study took over.

"God damn you!" I yelled. "You're *fucking* crazy, you know that?"

"Sammy," she replied, quietly. "I've got to find you help. Professional help."

I had to leave that apartment. I wanted to ask Allison to get out of her seat, put on her coat and leave with me, but I had no confidence that she'd do it. So I got up, grabbed my own coat and headed straight for the door. "You all have fun," I said. "I've got to take a walk."

I was gone for nearly a half hour. When I got back, the only person left was my mother, who sat in silence. After our eyes met, she shook her head over and over again. We didn't say a word to each other all evening.

Allison had originally planned to drive home with me the next day—Saturday, January 1st. I waited until 4:00 on Sunday afternoon for her to call, but she never did. So I said goodbye to my shell-shocked mother and drove home alone, as alone as I had felt in years.

CHAPTER 7

LADY PHILOSOPHY

Mother and I made up pretty quickly after New Year's Eve, but I didn't speak to Allison for several days. Lord knows, she didn't reach out to me. Feeling the need to hear her voice, I finally called her. She had no interest in staying on the phone, let alone in getting together. We spoke for all of two minutes.

Fortunately, I had something else to occupy my mind. Allison may have been my latest infatuation, but philosophy was my lifelong passion. Finally, I was given the chance to share it every day with my students. What an opportunity this would be, I told myself—much more fulfilling than designing a software package or making a witness's story fall apart on the stand.

My philosophy class was scheduled for first period. It was set up that way to accommodate the administrators and curriculum planners who would frequently sit in, which was the custom whenever grant funds were involved. On the first day of class I caught a break. There were no adults in attendance, just students—and, for the most part, smart ones. In fact, several of my best students signed up for the course, including Lorraine Jackson.

As the students took their seats, they saw eleven words at the center of the blackboard:

***P**robing*
***H**onest*
***I**ndependent*
***L**onely*
***O**pen-minded*
***S**peculative*
***O**bservant*
***P**rovocative*
***H**igh-minded*
***E**rudite*
***R**ational*

At the upper left of the blackboard, in smaller writing, they saw the following:

Please be absolutely silent until I begin to speak. Avert your eyes from your fellow students. Focus entirely on the front of the classroom.

I waited two full minutes after the bell rang before beginning class. I heard giggles but ignored them, and simply sat at my desk contemplating the words on the board.

Finally, I walked over to the board and erased the small writing at the upper left corner, leaving the remaining words for the class to examine as they pleased. "I'm here to talk to you about my first and greatest love," I began. "Her name is Lady Philosophy." At that point laughter erupted, but once again, I ignored it.

"The Lady is old and experienced. Believe me, she's been around. People have known her for thousands of years. They say her birthplace is Athens, Greece. But they're wrong. You'll find the Lady on every planet in every galaxy where there's intelligent life, or to be more precise, *self-conscious* life. She has no one birthplace.

"I speak a lot to the Lady. But she's not quite so talkative. She always leaves it for me to figure her out for myself. So I consult books. Whenever I meet smart, reflective people, I consult them too. Mostly, though, I'm left to my own ideas. I've been trying to understand the Lady for the better part of my life."

"Have you succeeded?" asked Lorraine.

"Somewhat. But God, is she a tease! She'll have you thinking you've figured something out. Then you run into new information, and you realize just how little about her you understand. She can be *really* frustrating."

"Sounds like my ex-girlfriend," said Joey Waylan, one of the leading wisecrackers in my fifth period psychology class. "What does this chick look like, anyway? Is she worth it?"

"I don't have a picture of her in my mind, except for her eyes. They pierce through your soul—always challenging you, making demands.

"That's what she does, you know. She stares. And the way she stares is amazing. She goes deep, like a laser beam, always looking for the essence of everything. Whatever it is she's thinking about, whether it's math, music, even football—she's interested in going right to the heart of it. Trivia's not her thing.

"But she doesn't just go deep. She looks outward too, as far as she can see. She trains her eyes to picture the whole forest and not just hone in on a few trees."

"Is that what you're going to teach us?" Lorraine asked. "How to get those eyes?"

"That's what *you're* going to teach yourselves. A philosopher's greatest teacher is himself. Or herself. Don't ever forget that."

I asked for volunteers to define the word "philosophy." Several students threw out suggestions—pretty good ones really. Then I gave them my favorite definition. It comes from the German philosopher, Karl Jaspers:

"The Greek word for philosopher (*philosophos*) connotes a distinction from *sophos*. It signifies the lover of wisdom (knowledge) as distinguished from him who considers himself wise in the possession of knowledge. This meaning of the word still endures: the essence of philosophy is not the possession of truth but the search for truth, regardless of how many philosophers may belie it with their dogmatism, that is, with a body of didactic principles purporting to be definitive and complete. Philosophy means to be on the way. Its questions are more essential than its answers, and every answer becomes a new question."

"By the time you complete this course," I said, "you'll be expected to understand what Jaspers was saying. You're going to learn the difference between the love of the search for wisdom and the love of the possession of knowledge."

"Are we getting tested on it?" asked a student whose name I hadn't yet learned.

The question hit me like an uppercut to the jaw. Still, I dared not belittle the importance of tests, not in this environment. "If I were you, I'd assume that whatever you learn in this class that has meaning to you, you'll want to remember it for tests. Sure.

"If I can get back to Jaspers's definition, you'll notice he mentioned love. I know it sounds corny, but that's what philosophy's about. Philosophers spend a lot of time figuring out what's wrong with the world—all the B.S. we have to put up with. But when they think about that B.S., they still need love in their hearts. It's quite a trick to pull off.

"When I was a teenager, I was obsessed with the B.S. in life. I wanted to understand it so that when I was older, I wouldn't foist it on the next generation. Any of you guys like that?" Most of the students raised their hands.

"You might think any teenager who's obsessed with the B.S. would fall for the Lady. It's not true. Kids often react to the B.S. by getting hateful or resentful. Then the Lady turns her back on them. She's scared of people speaking in her name if they're not full of love.

"Do you know why?" No one answered. "It's because doing philosophy is all about exercising wise judgment. Without love, you can forget wisdom. At least that's what she tells me."

"Mr. Kramer," said Janice Stansmith, an excellent student whom I knew by reputation. "Don't people think you're a geek if you're really philosophical?"

"Laughing at philosophers is a time-honored tradition. It goes back to ancient Greece. Aristophanes wrote a play called *The Clouds* that made the great Socrates look like an absent-minded dreamer whose head was always in the clouds. That's still how a lot of adults think of philosophy—just a silly diversion from the real world.

"This class will ask you to decide for yourself whether philosophy is just an elaborate diversion. Do we *need* Lady Philosophy's inspiration? Do we even *want* it?"

"That depends on whether she inspires us to *act*, or just to think," Lorraine said.

"What do you mean by that?" I asked.

"I'm a doer, Mr. Kramer. I believe in thinking in order to figure out what to *do*. Otherwise, philosophy seems like a waste of time."

"You're reminding me of Marx's statement, 'Philosophers have always tried to interpret the world. The point, however, is to change it.' I guess you agree with Marx, right?"

"Definitely."

"Actually, I do too," I said, smiling. "I'd like to think that *true* philosophers try to change the world. But when I make that statement here, in America, I'm reminded that our country isn't known for its philosophers, and some would say that's because we're people of *action* instead. Movers and shakers. We gave the world the airplane, the car, the movie, the H-bomb. We're too busy to sit around thinking about questions that no one can answer.

"Obviously, that's not my attitude. I don't see it as an either/or deal—either you're a thinker or a doer. I say you can be both. In fact, this country needs doers who *think*. And we need them desperately!"

"I know what you mean," Janice said. "The people who run this country don't think through what they're talking about. Like you'll hear this politician call himself 'pro-life,' and then he talks about how he loves to hunt like a real man and is in favor of capital punishment. So what does he mean by pro-life?"

"He doesn't have to tell us, does he?" I replied. "We don't require politicians to say what they're *really* thinking. When I was your age, I'd listen a lot to the politicians and talking heads on TV, and I'd almost always get annoyed. I was happier reading a great novel or listening to a great singer. But even then, even when I was listening to Bob Dylan longing for peace or justice, something was always missing. I had this itch for more. It was the Lady talking to me.

"She'd always say the same thing: *Go for it!* Don't beat around the bush. Don't sidestep—a little symbolism here, a little hint there. Have some guts. Say what you're thinking and *why* you're thinking it. Get right to the heart of the matter. Make all the arguments, even if they contradict each other, and make them as clearly as you can. Analyze, analyze, analyze! Then when you're finished, draw your conclusions and express them with pride, whether they're popular or not. That's philosophy. There's no substitute for it."

After finishing my rhapsody, I stopped talking for a few moments to let everyone collect their thoughts. Then we began discussing the words on the blackboard. The students had a lot of questions. I answered all of them except one—when Joey Waylan asked me to define the word "erudite." I wouldn't give any more definitions.

"If you want to be erudite," I told Joey, "you're going to have to look the word up in the dictionary. That's what students of philosophy do—they spend a lot of time looking up words, and once they see what Webster's says, they come up with their own definitions. Like when Spinoza defined 'hatred' as 'pain, accompanied by the idea of an external cause,' or 'love' as 'pleasure, accompanied by the idea of an external cause.' Once I heard those definitions, I've never thought of the words the same way since."

"Come on, Mr. Kramer," Joey said, with his typical impish grin. "Give it up on erudite. I got that itch for knowledge, and you gotta scratch it."

"How about this?" I said. "I won't define the word, but I'll tell you a true story about how to become erudite. When I was in college, I talked for a few minutes to this guy who came to my dorm campaigning for the school senate. He asked me twice to define a word I'd used. I couldn't believe my ears. Nobody did that at Stanford. Everyone was so concerned about looking stupid. But not this guy—he wanted to know what every word meant, and he didn't care what people thought of his intellect. Wouldn't you know it? A year later, he won a

Rhodes Scholarship.

"Now *that* guy's got the making of a philosopher."

After we discussed all the words on the blackboard, I told the students to work silently for the rest of the period on their journals, which I said would be a major component of the course. As she was leaving the room, Lorraine looked over at me. I asked if she found the class interesting. "Most of it," she said. "I think challenging is a better word."

"Good," I replied. "If I'm not challenging you in this course, I should spell out 'FRAUD' instead of 'PHILOSOPHER.' Let me know if I need to start thinking up five words."

"You've got a deal," she said, smiling. "I'll see you in seventh period."

?⟩

The first month of philosophy class was the most enjoyable. I wasn't fazed in the least when adults sat in, whether I knew them or not, and the students seemed able to ignore them too.

January 2000 was, in fact, one of the most exciting months of my career as a teacher. However, as I reminded myself in February when it served my interests to do so, there's more to life than our jobs. January was also an agonizing time for me romantically—and yes, I knew full well who to blame for my plight.

The first time I saw Allison after New Year's Eve was in the Creed Room on January 11th. She was sitting next to the evening's presenter, Dolores, who had volunteered to talk about American culture.

It took a while for me to focus on Dolores's presentation. My mind was elsewhere, on Ms. Schwartz. Not only had she stopped calling me, but when I saw her in the Creed Room she practically treated me like a stranger. A big part of me wanted to write her off for good. Yet that wasn't possible. I was clinging to too many memories.

My reverie ended with a jolt when Dolores began paying tribute to old musicals—shows like Oklahoma, the Sound of Music and West Side Story. Many of the images she evoked were beautiful. But the others, well, let's just say they dealt with her husband, Art.

We all learned that night that Art loved to walk around singing old musical numbers—in the shower, to the kids, even in the bedroom. I can still picture the image of that man taking a break from touting telemarketers by falling onto his knees and serenading Dolores with the song "Maria" from West Side Story. Then again, I also can still picture what my stomach looked like when I had shingles.

Dolores commended the old-fashioned musicals for the ways that they celebrated love. Just look at the *Sound of Music*, she said. It offers us not only the love of music, but also of nature, family, country, and, of course, romance. According to Dolores, when you watch an old musical and listen to two lovers put their emotions into song, you're able to appreciate much of what she was trying to say in October about Christianity.

"Remember the words to 'Maria' in *West Side Story*," she said. "Sing the name one way and it fills your senses with pleasure. Sing the name another way and you're engaged in prayer. It's such Christian imagery. The one you love—the flesh and blood beloved—opens your eyes to God.

"Think back to the Christian idea of holiness. If that word's going to have meaning to us, we'd better know of something real that we can relate it to. It can't be totally abstract. Since we're human beings, it only makes sense that holiness would involve the human ideal, which for me is Jesus. For Tony, Maria personified at least a glimmer of that ideal."

What happened next was eerie. I had been envisioning Natalie Wood's ravishing smile, when that vision was suddenly replaced by the mug of Art Sherman. Wasn't that what Dolores was implicitly suggesting: that everyone's romantic beloved (in her case, Art) is their personal gateway to the human ideal? Before I could grimace at the thought, Shaw beat me to the punch.

"Oh man!" he growled, audibly enough to be heard, though I doubt that was his intent.

"We know what made Tony fall in love with Maria," Dolores continued. "It was her face. He saw it from the opposite end of the dance floor, and instantly, he was in love. There was something about that face that melted him and captured for him the human ideal.

"When we fall in love, there's always at least *one* holy thing that we see in the other person. Maybe it's their face, maybe their sense of humor, or it could be the sound of their singing voice. In my case, I think it's something about Arthur's traditional, wholesome attitude toward life—his loyalty, his chivalry, even his appreciation for romance.

"Obviously, the chemistry has to be right. But when it is, and we see something holy and exemplary about another person, it draws us in with unbelievable power. Tony thought he could always count on living amidst incredible beauty. It's as if he owned the Mona Lisa and could display it in his living room. I call Arthur my rock because he's my source of stability. When everything else is going wrong, I know I can rest on his old-fashioned values.

"So far, I've been talking as if romantic love is all about possessing a holy object. But that's only half of the equation; our beloved possesses us too. He reaches out and says, 'I want us to be there for each other. Forever.' Maria said that to Tony with her smile. Think about it—not just a human being but a representative of holiness was offering herself to him alone and honoring him by begging for his devotion in return.

"Talk about an irresistible force. Talk about a *movable* object.

"Some of you might think I'm crazy, but I'm going to say this anyway. Even if our minds don't believe in God, our hearts are programmed to melt at the thought of His love for us. We especially feel that love when a person who reminds us of holiness chooses us as his beloved.

"So let me sum up. Romance to me is all about the ideal and the holy. It meets our emotional needs and gives us an incredible feeling of honor. But please don't confuse what I'm saying. None of this means that we think *everything* about our beloved person is perfect. Even my Arthur," she joked, "has his issues."

After relating Arthur to Jesus and Natalie Wood, Dolores discussed the way movies and TV currently present romance—through sex, not song. The celebration of love, she said, is no longer depicted through the man singing alone in the street, or the couple holding hands, each of them sporting a "how can I be so lucky" look." A romantic affair is now not so much celebrated as *consummated*. We see it through the come hither look; the long, wet kiss; the throbbing of naked bodies under the sheets and sometimes above them. According to Dolores, watching Hollywood's depiction of romance these days is nothing more than an exercise in voyeurism.

Dolores went on to lambast Hollywood's gratuitous violence. Then she spoke about the general failure of the culture to foster active, creative pursuits. "We're getting dumber and lazier," she claimed.

The rest of the Gang was pretty much on board with

Dolores's message. She didn't lose us until she started listing all the "decadent" ways our society makes us passive and uncreative. The mutiny began when she took on the "ridiculous" national obsession with spectator sports. It turned out that most of the Gang were serious fans of one team or another. In fact, everyone chimed in against Dolores's anti-sports diatribe; everyone, that is, except Eileen Mitchell, who had yet to enter into *any* of the Creed Room frays.

That was one of the few times that Shaw and Art Sherman were on the same side of a debate. "Honey, you can't mess with our love for football," Art said.

"Especially not during the playoffs!" Shaw added.

After we filed out of the house at the end of the session, the Triumvirate quietly led us to the oak tree in the front yard— the Choulos Oak, as we came to call it. I had heard from Allison something about what they were going to say, but now for the first time the news was being passed on to the whole Gang. Linda was the spokesperson.

The Victorian was definitely owned by a man named Charles F. Feaver. Linda, flashlight in hand, had the records to prove it. She also presented Internet clippings demonstrating that a "Charles F. Feaver" sold a Vermeer painting in 1988 for $15 million. "Dutch art, people," she said. "It's got to be the same guy." Linda spoke to the painting's buyer, James Roy, who mentioned that he had heard rumors that Feaver had sold "fakes." But the Vermeer was unquestionably authentic, he added.

Roy passed on still other rumors about Feaver's membership in the Empire Club, yet he could find little information about that society. Their interest piqued, the Triumvirate enlisted Eileen's father, a recently retired FBI Special Agent. Mr. Mitchell learned that the Empire Club is so secretive that even its members know only a small number of their colleagues. They gather in local cells and are aware solely of the identities of those in their own cell, plus one or two members of a tiny central body thought to be based in the New York area.

Only men with money to burn are invited to join the Empire Club, Eileen's father said. The group is supposed to have roughly 300 members across the country. It claims to be devoted to the "health, strength and unity of the greatest country that this world has ever known."

"So how do we know that Feaver is in this group?" Art asked, when Linda finished speaking. "Because this Roy heard *rumors*?"

The Triumvirate looked at each other and shrugged their shoulders. "I guess that's one way of putting it," Linda said. "Roy got his information from speaking to people in the art business. It's not exactly something you can confirm from the newspaper, or even from the Internet."

"Rumors and tumors," Art replied. "I don't know which are worse."

"Yeah," I sighed. "There's a lot of smoke here, but not much fire."

"Come on, Sam," Allison said. "You don't find this disturbing?"

"Sure, it's disturbing. But what do we do about it? You've got nothing solid."

"Maybe not *yet*," Allison said. "But we will."

One by one the Gang disbursed, beginning with Art, who waved his hand at the Triumvirate as if to dismiss their revelation. Then Allison approached me and took me to where we could be alone.

"I can't really talk tonight," she said. "They're waiting for me, and I have to get home."

"No problem," I said. I didn't mean it, but it sounded like the right thing to say.

"I do want to see you," she said. "I've just been so busy."

"How about sometime this weekend?"

"I'm not sure that works, but we'll do it soon, very soon. I'll give you a call."

She called the next Monday, arranging to meet with me later in the week. But then she had to reschedule, as her mother was coming to town. That meant that other than in the Creed Room, I didn't see her from New Year's Eve until January 29th—four excruciating weeks.

During that time, my obsession with Allison grew and grew. I realized I didn't want our relationship to end. In so many ways, I thought the world of her. She was beautiful, monstrously talented, fun-loving, self-confident, and, therefore, incredibly sexy. I could go on, but why bother? She had more than enough positives. Her problem was the other side of the equation.

In that regard, I often found myself thinking of her as a narcissist and a snob. Once, I let my paranoia run wild and imagined Allison as a prosecutor and myself as the accused. "Fine," I said to her, "You got me. I've got issues with my mother. She often drives me crazy. And I vent, OK? Does that make me unworthy of you, one of the Central Park Schwartz's?"

The two of us barely interacted during the two late-January Creed Room sessions. They were devoted to human diversity and led by the tag team of Smith and Keister, who discussed social conformity; the value of diversity; affirmative action; and various 'isms,' including racism, sexism, sexual preference-ism (aka homophobia) and social class-ism.

The sessions were entertaining, as much to see who stood up for which position as to hear the arguments themselves. I especially enjoyed watching Linda's spirited debate with Shaw over affirmative action. She was opposed; he, of course, was in favor. Occasionally, I'd look over at Art's face. His grimace whenever Shaw opened his mouth was unmistakable and, for my money, quite grotesque. Art said little to Shaw, preferring instead to watch Linda carry the banner for "meritocracy" instead of "reverse discrimination." At one point, though, Art couldn't stop himself. He blurted out that Shaw didn't want affirmative action so much as charity, and suggested that he needed to swallow his pride, grab a hat and take to the streets, so he could get his handouts with integrity "like the other bums."

That gave me a new vision to associate with Art. I could wipe out the image of him as a blissful balladeer walking down the city streets singing a tribute to his beloved. My new Art was a smirking suit, walking with equal bliss down the same streets, disdainfully ignoring the homeless and other beggars while contemplating his own financial well being, superior status and time-honored morality.

Art's entry into the debate must have inspired my leftism. I suggested that affirmative action, if properly limited, had nothing to do with charity. It involved justice and equal opportunity. Charity, I said, channeling Shaw, is only relevant because earlier in our history, white people begged the Demon of Greed for the right to deprive other races of their human rights. The whites got the handout they were looking for, thanks to brute force, but they didn't call it charity. White people, I concluded, only call it charity when they give, not when they *seize*.

Allison smiled when I made that point. Then she seconded my comments, and we actually carried on a bit of a conversation in front of the group. Other than that, I don't remember us saying a word to each other during the human diversity sessions, and I was fine with that. I didn't want to talk to Allison in a group. I needed to see her alone.

CHAPTER 8

THE CASUALTIES
OF LOVE AND WAR

_W_ hen I opened the door, a face appeared that had been absent from my life since December. There she was, the Allison I remembered from the fall: relaxed, playful and beaming. We hadn't planned an agenda in advance, but I could tell she had one in mind. She had asked me to reserve both the day and the evening, and leave the rest to her. When she made that request, I had an inkling the old Allison might return, and that thought put me in a great mood.

Allison seemed anxious to hit the road from the moment she arrived. She wouldn't tell me where we were going, only that it would be outside. The gods provided a gorgeous day. The high was expected to top 60 degrees—quite unusual for D.C. in January.

Before long, we were in Allison's car heading northwest. She was behind the wheel and very much in charge of the CD player. Led Zeppelin was her first choice of driving music, which she turned to the appropriate volume: not ear popping, but not exactly conducive to conversation either, so I didn't try to make any. Once we reached Frederick, Allison flipped the CD to softer music—the Dave Matthews Band—and we began to chat a bit. She seemed to be as excited and upbeat as I'd ever seen her.

When Allison turned off the highway, I could tell we were headed to the Antietam National Battlefield Park. "Have you ever been to Antietam?" I asked her.

"Nope."

"Cool. How'd you come up with the idea?"

"I wanted to see you in your element, and I thought a battlefield would be fun."

"Why this one?" I asked.

"I checked with my dad. He knows some historians. I asked him to find out the best local battlefield to visit."

"*Best*?" I repeated.

"The one with the best combo of scenery and historical value."

"He's probably right," I said. But I was less struck by the merits of Allison's choice than by the absurd notion that in our society, everything is becoming yuppified—even the choice of battlefields. Apparently, what Ben and Jerry's is to ice cream and Heineken to beer, Antietam is to mid-Atlantic battlegrounds. Leave it to a true connoisseur like Allison to find what is *objectively* best in every consumable good, service or killing field.

After picking up a map of the battlefield, we took the driving tour and stopped at the more famous landmarks. Allison was particularly moved by a sunken road that is commonly known as "Bloody Lane." She had read before coming to Antietam that Bloody Lane was the site of literally thousands of casualties on both sides and became the focal point of the Civil War's single deadliest day. I shared with her the persistent rumors that this narrow piece of grass has been haunted by ghosts ever since. But Allison didn't want to be bothered by ghost stories. She sought only an image: a vision of Bloody Lane as it must have appeared shortly after the battle.

We sat silently for minutes. When she finally broke her silence, she said that she'd been picturing the Lane with dead bodies, one on top of another, and appendages and organs strewn throughout the nearby field. She told me she was determined never to lose that picture in her mind, lest she become overly cavalier about the horrors of war. "Americans," she said, "had better remember this kind of place. We've forgotten that war is hell. Because we make war on everyone else. No one makes war on us."

Allison told me that Antietam was only the second battlefield she had ever visited, having gone to Gettysburg once on a school field trip.

"Your father never took you?" I said, stating the obvious.

"Are you kidding? He hates war, everything about it. He's basically a pacifist."

"A Jewish pacifist?"

"What's that supposed to mean?" Allison replied. "Do you think of us as bloodthirsty?"

"No. It's just that Jews should understand the lessons of history. Think of the old cliché: if the pacifists had taken over our government in the 30s, we'd all either be Nazis or dead."

"Oh please, that was a unique time," Allison said. "If you want to understand the Jewish attitude toward war, look at Israel. The Palestinians have given us every incentive to blow them all to Hell. But Jews won't take innocent lives. We don't practice genocide."

"Israel doesn't have a choice," I replied. "If it nuked Gaza, *all* the Muslim countries would declare war, and sooner or later there'd be no more Israel. The only Jewish homeland left would be Brooklyn."

Allison looked at me and, quite out of the blue, said "I bet you think about your dad as much as I think about mine."

"Hardly a day goes by when I don't."

"Do you dream about him?" she asked.

"All the time."

"That's one thing about your life I can't begin to relate to," said Allison.

"I can make it simple for you. I live to make my father proud. Even though I don't think he's aware of what I'm doing, I try to act in a way he would approve of. I don't know why that matters so much to me, but it does."

We left Antietam by mid-afternoon. Allison wouldn't divulge the next destination, and I was content not to ask. She headed back to the D.C. area and got off the highway at the Rockville exit, yet instead of heading to my apartment, she drove to a miniature golf course. I knew the course well. It's county-owned and officially open only during the summer, but that didn't deter Allison. She had brought along two putters, a couple of balls and even a scorecard.

I've always thought of myself as pretty good at miniature golf, especially after going through a stretch during high school when I practically lived at a Putt Putt course. That afternoon, I got off to a decent lead, but couldn't completely shake Allison. Up by a stroke with one hole left, I choked and got a four. She, on the other hand, sank a five footer for a par two.

For the next 20 minutes, she sassed me like I've never been sassed before. My mistake was in claiming before the game that I was a decent player, which only added to her glee when she won. It was cute at first, even arousing, but I was relieved when she finally gave it a rest.

After golfing, we headed to the city. She dropped off her car near her apartment, and we walked around Dupont Circle for a while before sitting down to dinner. Allison was happy to let me choose the restaurant, but she wouldn't let me in on her plans for our post-dinner activities. "Trust me, you'll love it," was all she said.

We were on the Red Line, just past Metro Center, when she announced that ours was the next metro stop. "The MCI Arena?" I asked.

"I bet you were afraid I was taking you to Georgetown Law Center," she replied, laughing. "You don't have to worry about that." At that point, Allison reached into her purse and pulled out two tickets for the night's show at the Arena: a U2 rock concert.

I nearly shrieked like a 12-year-old girl when I saw the tickets (which would have been practically a first on the Metro, where a staid demeanor appears to be a requirement of admission). I'd been a U2 fan for years but had never seen them in concert. They were awesome. They played for over 2½ hours, and Bono, their lead singer, threw his guts into every song. Allison hardly sat still from the opening song to the last encore. I wanted to touch her but thought better of it. We had to talk first and figure out what in blazes happened over the past month. Besides, who needs to think about women when there's top quality rock n' roll?

I was in an incredible mood when we got off the Metro and walked toward Allison's apartment on perhaps the warmest night of the winter. When we came to her building, she could tell I planned to go inside. "Sam," she said, "I think it's best if you don't come up."

"Are you sure?" I asked, taken aback.

"Yes, honey. Not tonight." She said it with a kind voice, though the words wounded me just the same. "It's been such a great day. I ... I don't think it would be a good idea."

She had always invited me in before when I walked her to her apartment. In fact, I was used to spending the night with her. "Last chance," I said, while putting my hand on her cheek.

"Sorry. Listen. I really did have a wonderful time. I mean that."

Before I could respond, she leaned over and kissed me on the lips. It was a short kiss, but a warm one, and for those few seconds that warmth meant everything in the world to me. "I'd like to see you soon," I told her. "How about tomorrow, for the Super Bowl?"

"I can't. I already have plans."

"How about Tuesday, then? Before we go to the Creed Room?"

"I have a presentation that night... I tell you what, let's meet after the session is over."

"OK," I said. "My place on Tuesday night."

"Sounds good."

❧

The next Creed Room session was the first of a two part series on "Liberty and its Limits." Allison made both presentations. She addressed issues such as gun ownership, abortion, drug use, prostitution, capital punishment, school vouchers and religion in the schools.

Allison took a pretty straight civil libertarian slant—except when she spoke about guns, a topic that was obviously close to my heart. She took on Keister and Art Sherman in arguing for as many government restrictions on guns as possible.

Keister didn't seem frustrated by Allison's gun-control comments so much as amused. "You can put down guns all you want," he said. "Ain't gonna matter. This is America. We love our guns here. You know we do. These liberal politicians talk about three-day waitin' periods and bannin' assault weapons. What they really want is no more guns except in the hands of cops, only they can't argue that 'cause they'd never get re-elected.

"Must be pretty depressin' bein' a gun control lobbyist, wouldn't you think, Art?"

"You've got that right," he replied, grinning. "There can't be too many of them. Probably just a couple of guys who were fired by the NRA and got angry."

I didn't care to hear them gloat about the country being awash in guns, not after my father's suicide. So I broke my silence. "Tell me, Art. You ever seen anybody shot dead?"

"On the news, sure."

"I mean in real life—not through the media."

"I can't say I have."

"How about you, Fred?"

"'Not dead. Injured, but not dead. What's your point?"

"Maybe you need to see a person shot dead with your own eyes. Then we'll see if you've got the guts to gloat that it's so easy to buy a gun and kill yourself or someone else."

Fred's face turned bright red. "No one's gloatin' about nothin'. I'm talking facts! Outside of the liberals in a few cities, *everybody* believes in the right to bear arms. Even some of those liberals got guns; they just won't admit it. They got 'em at home so that if a criminal comes in their house they can blow him away in a flash. They'd enjoy doin' it too, believe me."

"Absolutely," Art said.

"You mean to tell me you don't have a gun, Sammy?" Keister resumed. "You don't itch to blow away some scumbag when he comes through your window feelin' like Superman and lookin' to take you for all you've got? You'd rather let him rob you blind?"

I stared at Keister for at least a couple of seconds—a real

baleful stare—before I addressed him. "How about you watch someone close to you die from gunshots, and I don't mean shots fired by cops or criminals. Then you can come in here singing the praises of guns. Just don't forget to bring in the picture for show and tell. You'll need that for your credibility."

"Well what do we have here?" Art said. "I thought you were Mr. Voice of Reason. If I didn't know better, I'd swear you were dealing with this issue emotionally."

"'Course he is," Keister added. "It only makes sense to let people protect themselves from criminals."

"That's the bottom line," Art said. "There's only one rational way of dealing with guns. Prosecute criminals. Let good people protect themselves. End of story."

I was too upset to respond. Besides, unlike my mother, I harbored no illusions about gun control. The gun lovers have lobbyists, money and two centuries of romantic American lore to draw from. What does our side have? Marches and corpses. It's not hard to keep score. In this culture, all we can do about the gun laws is try to make sure they don't get any worse.

Allison and I didn't arrive at my apartment until after ten. I had hoped to get out of the Creed Room earlier, but Shaw wouldn't let her go. She had apparently entranced him with her presentation—hardly surprising, given that Shaw had seemed to be hot for her ever since we all had drinks together in Bethesda.

The first thing I did when we got inside was put on a CD, the Greatest Hits of Crowded House, an obscure New Zealand band from the 80s. "Oh, I love this stuff," Allison said, after hearing the first few measures. "I didn't know you owned any Crowded House."

"That's because you haven't spent any time here lately," I replied, equally surprised that she recognized the music. "I just bought this CD a few weeks ago."

"Eileen sings some Crowded House songs," Allison said. She had previously told me that Eileen—yes, quiet Eileen Mitchell—had a beautiful voice and was an excellent guitar player.

Allison and I made small talk for a couple of minutes. I was the first to raise the topic of our future. "All I can say is that I like being with you, and I want *us* to continue. When we're together, I feel good about myself." Finishing that sentence, I started thinking about Brooklyn, and then laughed. "Well, most of the time. No relationship is perfect, right?"

I expected a quick, witty response to that rhetorical question but didn't get one. Instead, Allison took on a deadly serious demeanor, took a deep breath, and said, bluntly, "I don't think it's going to work, Sam. Not in a romantic sense."

"You ... you what?"

"I can't say why. I just know how I feel, and I've got to trust my intuition when it comes to this sort of thing."

I searched for a way to respond with dignity. Finally, I asked, "Don't you have fun with me?"

"Of course I do. I don't fake emotions. But it's not enough that we have fun. I'm looking for a relationship that has a chance to last. This one can't. Our values are too different."

"What's that supposed to mean?"

"Sam, we're just different, that's all."

"You're copping out. What are you *really* saying?"

"You want me to add insult to injury?"

"I want you tell me the truth. If it's insulting, so be it."

"Fine," she said. "Have it your way. Your little act with your mother was appalling."

"Go on."

"And all this stuff about philosophy, you're no philosopher; you're a fountain of opinions. How can you keep your mind open if you're so passionate about everything you believe?"

"You're pretty opinionated yourself," I replied.

"Well, I don't call myself a philosopher, do I?"

"Me neither."

"Excuse me—a *student* of philosophy. Remember in the Creed Room, when you took off on agnostics and anyone who's apathetic? You sounded like one of those glib talking heads on the radio. Those acts get old, do you know what I mean?"

"Now you're warming up," I said. "What else?"

"You're a masochist, aren't you?"

"I guess I'm a Prophetic Jew, like your dad."

"Let's leave my dad out of this, alright? Look. I'm not trying to judge you—"

"Of course not," I interrupted.

"I mean it. I'm judging our compatibility, not *you*. I'm looking for someone who's more tolerant and less opinionated— more philosophical in the true sense of the word. And I absolutely can't deal with the way you treat your mother."

"Tell me this," I said. "Had you decided about our relationship before Saturday?"

Allison let out a sigh that seemed to take five seconds. "Yeah. I had."

"So why Saturday, then? What in blazes were you thinking?"

"I wanted to see if my other instincts were right—about the friendship. I'd like us to try to keep that going. Because I agree with you—we *do* have fun together."

With every sentence she spoke, I was getting more confused. Perhaps, I thought, she was right about our relationship. Then again, maybe she was monstrous for letting Saturday happen. Did I even want to be her friend?

Just before Allison left my apartment, she told me she was having a party a week from Saturday at eight. "I'd love for you to make it. I'm inviting the whole Creed Gang. Do you think you can come?"

"I don't know," I said, quietly. "We'll have to see." I wanted to demonize her for dumping me, but here she was, blithely inviting me to her party. It was enough to make a man scream.

CHAPTER 9

AUTONOMY

*A*rriving at my classroom the next morning, I thanked God for Takoma Park High School. The entire Allison mess was eating up my inner organs. I needed to be in the one place that could take my mind off my love life.

Philosophy class began that day with four adult spectators walking in. As always, I tried to ignore them. Our first task was to review the unit we'd just finished on the ancient Greeks. One of my students asked what Socrates and Plato would care most about if they came back to life today as high school students. The consensus response was "sex."

"Yeah, but what kind?" said Joey Waylan. "Mr. Kramer, remember when you told us that Socrates and Aristotle were gay, but Plato was straight? Do we really *know* that?"

"I heard it from my college philosophy professor, that's all I can tell you." I never knew whether to believe that rumor either, but it sounded nuanced and, therefore, credible.

Once the subject of Plato and Socrates as teenagers was raised, it was hard to get the class to focus on anything else. I have to admit, though, that I found their perspectives eye opening. For example, I learned that a teenage Plato would be a dream date. He'd probably be a musician—a singer, song-writer, guitar player, that kind of guy. Maybe he'd write short stories on the side. A teenage Socrates, on the other hand, would be too ugly to date but would be a big hit at parties. The kids recalled from the *Symposium* that Socrates could drink like a fish and never get sauced.

It was the silliest discussion we'd had to date, and yet the exercise I'd planned for the second part of that class was even sillier. While one of my students was talking, I pulled out a bushy fake mustache from my desk and slapped it on my face. Then, in the thickest German accent I could summon, I introduced the class to a new philosopher.

"I've been listening to this inane discussion and I can't believe my ears!" I said. "You've had a chance to talk about two of the greatest philosophers who've ever lived. And you're talking about their sex lives? And their alcohol consumption? Are you people ignoramuses?"

Lorraine Jackson had seen enough of my role plays over the course of the year. She practically yawned when she asked, "Alright, Mr. Kramer, who are you today?"

"Who *am* I? You wouldn't know, would you? Because you don't read the classics of world literature, many of which I've written. And why should you read them? They'd only spark your interest in living the way life was meant to be lived. Intensely and courageously—as if you walked a tightrope between life and death and your choices each day determined your fate.

"No, you best not read my books. They'd get you out of sorts with your precious peer group. You couldn't converse with your puerile friends. They'd say you're not *cool*, and you'd be miserable. So please, don't read my books. Enjoy your herd. Graze on, children. Graze on."

I didn't hear a word for a few seconds. Then several of the students laughed. One even said, "Tight. Kirby gets high."

"Yes. There it is again," I said, mocking my accuser. "The same tired refrain. Everyone who doesn't act like a herd animal must be crazy, or on drugs. I've been laughed at for years. People tell me I'm a loon. And yet when you go to a book store, you'll see more of my books than any other philosopher's—except for that Jesus guy. Even now he gets read. Amazing!"

As I paused to allow the students to figure out who I was imitating, the noise level in the room steadily grew.

"Same question, Mr. Kramer," said Lorraine. "I haven't a clue who you're supposed to be."

"My name is Friedrich Nietzsche. I was born in 1844. They say I died in 1900, but look at me—alive and well, and ready to take on a new millennium. Now I have a question. I've been told that some people, even today, worship God. Could that be true?"

"I almost never hear the name of God in this school," said Janice Stansmith, "but—"

"Good! So news of His death must have spread. Death by irrelevance. I understand that during the last 100 years, tens of millions of people have been slaughtered by human hands. You want to know why no God was there to stop it? It's because He died back in the 19th century."

"You didn't let me finish," Janice said, annoyed. "I was about to say that some of us haven't abandoned the Lord and won't either. And you, Mr. Nietzsche, are the one who's dead."

"Oh, aren't we original? 'God is dead!'—Nietzsche; 'Nietzsche is dead!'—God. I read that the other day on a bathroom wall. What a clever point you make. If I were born in 1844, I must be dead. And God must be alive, since He's the All-Powerful.

"In the name of Goethe, young lady. Open your eyes! I'm alive in the mind of everyone who's had 'enough' with playing 'follow the leader.' I'm alive in the mind of everyone who puts aside Christ and God and Plato's Transcendent Forms, and grabs on to the world that's before our eyes. Don't let any pseudo-sage fool you. The one thing we all understand is *this world*—not some metaphysical realm but the world of our senses. I'm its greatest fan.

"As for the old God, you religious people can worship Him all you want. Project your highest ideals and hopes onto Him. Keep the same tired mythology. Be my guest. Your kind has little to teach me any more. I'm on to you and your little power grab."

"Mr. Kramer, I gotta say," said Waylan, "with that mustache you look gayer than Socrates."

"My good man," I replied, continuing to speak in a German accent, "I'm not going to dignify your comments with a substantive response. 'Gayer than Socrates,' huh. Tell me, why is it you Americans are so obsessed with other people's sexuality? Sexuality and guns, that seems to be all you care about. If some kind of pistol isn't involved, you people are unconcerned.

"Rather than explore my private liaisons with your sordid minds, I'd rather discuss my mission back in the 1880s and how it's evolved since. In those days, I preached a new faith. It had no gods, just heroes. I called them Ubermenschen. You may call them Supermen. My task was to paint a portrait of these Supermen and explain why they alone shall rule over this planet.

"You who've studied the traditional religions would hardly recognize my Superman. He's a very different hero than, say, Jesus Christ, pitifully stretched out in pain, bleeding to death. Jesus is a role model for the dying. The Superman is creative, vivacious, fearless and, above all, powerful. He has cast out from his heart any trace of pity for the weak. The Superman is a man full of great contradictions that he isn't afraid to embrace, for whatever doesn't kill him shall make him stronger. He seeks out obstacles as challenges to be overcome. He has enough self-confidence to master everything in his way and mold the world according to *his* will, and his will alone. Sure, he's willing to share power—but only with his equals.

"These Supermen aren't like politicians and priests. When they finally arrive, they won't need propaganda and trickery to rule the world. And they won't seek followers with pie-in-the-sky predictions either, like when Jesus proclaimed 2000 years ago that the kingdom of heaven was near. Funny, God's boy missed on that one, didn't he?

"Heaven is one thing the Supermen won't be concerned with. They care only about reality, which they'll have no trouble affirming with a resounding YES!"

I paused for a few moments to let the students reflect a bit. Then I pulled off my mustache and resumed speaking in my regular voice.

"When you think about Nietzsche, think about him issuing a challenge: to decide for yourselves what you believe and how to act. Be creative. Follow the flow of your thoughts. Don't fear where you're heading. If you think that your parents or teachers won't like what you're coming up with, don't let them stop you.

"Then take a break. Think long and hard about the world you've left, the world of your parents and teachers. Consider all the things you *like* about that other world. And realize that maybe there's a way to combine the best of both worlds—the traditional and the creative, the way of the herd and your own way as an individual.

"The old Nietzsche is truly dead. He was merely an *antithesis*, a reaction against tradition. We have a lot to learn from him. But we have a lot to learn from tradition too.

"Find a new *synthesis* using the teachings of the old Nietzsche, but also those of Plato and Socrates, and Jesus and Moses too. Be creative, but be respectful. Assume that the things which existed for thousands of years couldn't be completely without value. Take God, for example. If you have a problem with the way people speak about Him, think about coming up with a God of your own. Redefine the word, if you have to. See if there's a way it can make sense for *you!*"

Five days later, I received a note. It told me to come to Ericsson's office immediately after the final bell.

When I opened Ericsson's door, I had the pleasure of seeing all four adults who had observed my Nietzsche role play. This time, unfortunately, I couldn't hide behind a moustache.

"Come in, Sam," Ericsson said. "I'm sure you know Bill Jones on my right." Jones was the county's Director of Social Studies. "I think you also know Mary Leeds, Bill's Deputy," Ericsson continued. "To Mary's right is Scott Gerwitz, who just moved to the county from Ohio to take over as Inspector General. Whenever the county gets a grant, Scott is charged with making sure we use the funds as we said we would in the grant application."

I turned to Gerwitz. "I trust you've found no fraud yet."

"None so far," he said, "though I can't say my trips to your room have been uneventful."

"We try," I replied.

"Let me get on with it," Ericsson said, looking at his watch. "Sam, your philosophy class isn't working out the way I'd hoped. Something has to be done about your teaching methods."

"Have the students been complaining?" I asked.

"I've received complaints from various circles, including the people in this room."

"I asked about the *kids*. How many complaints have you gotten from them?"

"We can't tell you that," said Gerwitz, a gruff, heavy-set man. "County policy precludes us from providing information that could cause a teacher to seek retribution against students when they complain about a teacher's methods. All you need to know is that the county has received at least one student complaint."

"Richard," I said, ignoring Gerwitz, "can you please tell me what this is about?"

"We witnessed your Nietzsche presentation," Ericsson replied. "We heard your review of Plato and Socrates. Frankly, with each philosopher you discuss, you get yourself and this school in more and more trouble."

"The students are learning. They're enjoying themselves—"

"*The students*," Ericsson interrupted, "are listening to theatrics that heap all sorts of abuse on their parents' religions. If that's not bad enough, you're introducing references to sex that have no place in the classroom. Frankly, your lack of judgment is astounding."

I froze for a moment before responding. "Let me get this right. You've attended my class, you've seen the kids wide awake and opening their eyes to philosophy, and all you have to say is it's filthy and sacrilegious?"

"Sam, I'm not here to critique all the upsides and downsides of your approach," Ericsson said. "What I'm saying is you've crossed the line. Big time. Take your comments about Socrates and homosexuality. Or the pleasure that you seemed to get from talking about Christ like someone only a fool could worship. You're taking way too many liberties."

"I'm Jewish, and I found your Christ baiting offensive," Gerwitz said.

"I was trying to teach Nietzsche authentically. He didn't beat around the bush."

"Scott's only voicing how a lot of parents would have felt had they sat in on your class," Ericsson said.

"You people just don't get it. I sing a philosopher's praises one day, and the next day I'm tearing him down. My students know the drill. I'm there to expose them to all kinds of perspectives and teach each one with passion. My job is to make the kids *care* about this stuff. I leave it for them to figure out what to believe."

"You're the one who doesn't get it," said Gerwitz. "I've worked in public school systems for 25 years—since before you knew the difference between Plato and Play-Dough. This isn't adult theater. We're here *in loco parentis*. They trust us with their children, and you're abusing that trust. You need to create an environment that *each and every parent* would agree is acceptable for their kids. Nothing else will be tolerated."

"That's unrealistic," I said. "Some of these parents don't know anything about education. They certainly don't know anything about philosophy. Teachers have to be trusted to use their own judgment about how best to inspire the children. We're the professionals, aren't we?"

Gerwitz started laughing. "It is *Mr.* Kramer, right? Not *Dr.* Kramer," he said. "I've got a newsflash for you—you teach *high* school. Do you think you can grasp that, or do you need me to write it out for you? We don't believe in absolute academic freedom here. You teach the way *we* say to teach. If you don't like it, go back to Harvard! Maybe they'll hire you to teach metaphysics to grad students."

The laughter went a bit too far for Ericsson, I could tell. He realized it was time to cut the session short. "Sam, let me make the message simple. Tone down the rhetoric. And remember what Scott's been saying: don't teach anything that parents would find offensive. I trust you know what I mean by that. Also, starting a week from Thursday I want to see a copy of your lesson plan for each week by no later than the Thursday morning of the previous week. That's probably not a bad idea for any experimental course. It's definitely appropriate here. Are you following me?"

I thought for a minute. Do I try to bargain with them? Reason with them? Then I relented. "Yeah, I hear you. Is there anything else?"

Ericsson looked around. "No, that's it. Thanks for your time this afternoon."

The walk from Ericsson's office to my classroom was one of the most intense in my career. After contemplating the feel of my hands around Gerwitz's throat, I seized upon the picture of a certain woman in Brooklyn. She was wagging her finger and saying "I told you so"—not with glee but with genuine despair. The image of my mother depressed me and sapped me of a bit of my anger.

That was fortunate, as it turned out. Just like the last time I left the principal's office after a lecture, I heard the voice of one of the few students I truly couldn't stand, George London. "I'll see you fags tomorrow," London said to a couple of scrawny sophomores. "And I'll expect a little more money than I got today."

"What did you say?" I hollered, finally reaching the corridor. "Are you extorting money, you son of a ..." The last word never got out of my mouth. Thinking about my mother made me too subdued to finish that sentence. London then denied the charge, and his victims backed him up.

I thought about pressing the matter further, but London got me on the right day. The bureaucrats had thrown me off my game. So, against my better judgment, I let him go with hardly another comment. My glare would have to suffice.

The day after the Gang of Four session at school, I saw Allison for the first time since she ended our relationship. She was giving the presentation in the Creed Room, and I was in no mood to listen to her, or anyone else for that matter.

The session went painfully slowly. I tried to hide my pain, but I'm sure the group could tell something was up. Even when they discussed public school vouchers, I didn't participate. People would look in my direction, anticipating some perspective on the issue, but for once I kept my thoughts to myself.

Shaw put me on the spot, and not just once. He had expected me to side with him in opposing public funding for private schools. Perhaps he even counted on me to do the heavy lifting so that he and Art could take the night off from pugilism. "Sorry, Scott," I said, beginning one of the very few sentences that I spoke during the evening. "I'm not weighing in on this tonight. I'd rather just take in what everybody's saying."

"Don't cop out on us," Shaw pleaded. "We know you've thought about this stuff."

"Christ, man, I don't cop out on many topics. You know that. This is one where my feelings are mixed, if that helps you. Sometimes there really are two sides to an issue."

"Care to give 'em?" Shaw asked.

"Not really," I said, before heading back to my oblivion. I then struck a pose, copying as well as I could Rodin's Thinker. But that was just a smoke screen. My head was occupied by daydreams and emotions, not thoughts. I asked of myself only to last the evening without having to jump up, scram, and then scream, Munch-like, as soon as I got back in the car.

In school the next morning, I went through the motions, but my heart wasn't in it. The bureaucrats had alienated me from the teaching experience. As a result, I approached everything I taught with extreme vigilance. Social studies became for me a mine field; all of my instructional ideas seemed like potential explosives.

I hadn't spoken to Jamison since New Year's Eve but couldn't bring myself to call him. I wasn't ready for whatever flippant spin he'd put on the situation at school and *really* didn't want to talk to him about Allison. Nor did I want to discuss those topics with my mother. Whenever she asked about Allison, I rebuffed her, causing her to complain that I was closing her out of my life. Better that, I thought to myself, than engage her and lose my sanity.

By the time Saturday rolled around, the weekend offered nothing pleasant to anticipate. It was freezing outside, there was little to watch on TV, and I was hardly in the mood to relax in front of a good book. At dinner time, having spent the day alone, I wondered for the first time whether to make an appearance at Allison's party.

From a hedonistic standpoint, it seemed stupid to go. Small talk was never easy for me, and given my state of depression, I was liable to chew out some law student for saying nothing but innocuous drivel. I would have stayed home had I not heard the whisper of Nietzsche's voice. It told me not to hide from problems and return to the womb of non-existence.

After listening to the dead philosopher, I felt compelled to go to Allison's apartment and mix. If venom were to come out of my mouth, so be it. Lord knows it had seeped out of

Nietzsche's from time to time, and he was my role model of the moment.

I got to the party well after nine. Allison met me at the door, smiling with pride like a conqueror receiving tributes. She said that except for Fred and Art, the whole Creed Gang was on the premises. So were at least three dozen others, including a few who were well into their 50s, if not older. Don't tell me Allison invited some professors, I wondered. Man, she really *is* going far in this world, isn't she?

Allison led me over to the nearest opportunity for male bonding—two 20-somethings in preppie attire. I was with them for less than five minutes and during that span learned that they were both 3-Ls, on the Law Review, and enrolled in the same Commercial Transactions class. One of them claimed to be the lust object of their professor, a buxom blonde in her late 30s. "Get this. She sees that the lectern is blocking my line of sight," he boasted, "so she smiles and says 'now, that won't do,' and moves the lectern so I can have a clear view of both grapefruits." Not to be outdone, the other 3-L enlightened me with a valuable lesson from their class. "Did you know that if I wrote a check to Samuel 'Penis' Kramer, and you signed that name on the check and tried to deposit it, your bank would have to let you keep the money?"

On a normal day I'd have more patience for that kind of banter, but on that evening I was hardly in the mood. "It was Nietzsche who brought me here," I said to myself, "so let's seek out a more Nietzschean experience. Let's find Shaw."

He was in the kitchen, stuffing his face and talking to Linda. As soon as he saw me, he became animated. "Now there's the guy that went AWOL on us last Tuesday. What happened? Did you misplace your vocal chords or something?"

Linda and I looked at each other. It was obvious she knew

all about Allison and me. "Sam's having issues," she said, warmly. "Aren't you, Sam?"

"You can say that," I replied.

"Really?" said Shaw. Then his light bulb went on. "You mean with Allison?"

"Now *that's* a question." I said, hardly surprised by his characteristic directness. "And they call us Jews nosy."

"I'm not nosy, just concerned."

"Fine," I said. "If you must know, Allison and I are on the rocks. Maybe it would be more accurate to say we've fallen off the rocks and into the sea."

Shaw's face took on a deep glow. I already knew about his feelings for Allison, but my God—wouldn't a little feigned pity have been in order?

Shaw asked to excuse himself; no doubt, he made a bee-line for Allison. As soon as he left, Dolores walked over, sporting a broad smile and carrying a tall drink. Obviously, she had forgiven Allison for her comments in the fall about Dolores' marriage.

"Linda," she said, "you've got to tell your friend to stop plying me with alcohol."

"Are you kidding?" I said, laughing. "Allison lives to get people drunk. I don't see why she gets off on it so much."

"Rabbi's daughter," Linda said. "It's that simple."

"Thou speaketh the truth," Dolores said, slowly. "I'll drink to that."

Then Allison came over with Shaw in tow. "So, are you gonna answer my question yet?" she said to Dolores, "or am I going to have to whip out the Tanqueray?"

"You give me that and I'll toss my cookies," Dolores replied.

"Then tell me vat I vant to know," Allison said.

"OK, OK," said Dolores. "Here goes. Every couple of

months, he goes to one of these meetings late in the evening. Everything's all hush, hush. When I ask where he'll be, he says he can't tell me."

"Sounds like the Empire Club to me," Allison said.

"I don't know that. Honest," Dolores said. "I've never heard those words in my house."

"Who does he meet with?" I asked.

"You got me. I swear, I'm never invited. For all I know, they're people we hang out with. Or maybe I wouldn't recognize them. They call him on his cell phone and give him all the information he needs on the meetings. I think they hold them at different locations."

"Can you tell *when* they meet?" asked Allison.

"Pretty much. He usually goes to sleep early, but on those nights, he's out until three."

"Have him tailed!" Allison said. "C'mon, I'll chip in. We can get to the bottom of this."

"You think I'm going to pay someone to tail my own husband?" Dolores said, laughing. "You really don't understand me, do you?"

"No, no. I do," Allison said, frustrated. "I'm just desperate to find out what's going on."

"Let's say he is in the Empire Club," Dolores said. "So what? That doesn't mean he knows Feaver, or even that he knows why Feaver sponsored us. Remember about the cells? Maybe they're in different ones."

"It was his idea to come to these meetings, right?" I asked Dolores.

"He showed me the ad, yeah. What does that prove?"

"Have you asked him point blank whether he's in the Empire Club? Or whether he knows the Benefactor?"

"Of course. He said he'd never heard of Charles Feaver. And

he wouldn't lie to me. He also told me he couldn't tell me the name of his group. He was sworn to secrecy about that."

"That's an answer," Allison said.

Just then Shaw pulled me aside so Dolores couldn't hear him and said, "I never trusted this 'benefactor,' and I never trusted Sherman either. But I don't see anything they can do to us. We say our piece, get paid and go home. It's not a bad deal, really."

"Oh my God," Allison exclaimed, looking at her watch. "I've got to start the show."

Before I could ask what she was talking about, Allison began to yell. "Everyone into the living room! Let's go! Now!"

The kitchen cleared within seconds. Everyone moved into the living room and dining area. By the wall, sitting on a chair with a guitar on her lap, was Eileen Mitchell. She wore blue jeans and a white pullover—as usual, nothing flashy.

"Hi, everybody," Eileen said. "I've been asked to play a few songs for you. I think you'll recognize most of them. Feel free to join in."

Even though I had been told Eileen was a singer, I still couldn't believe my eyes. Shaw might think I had been vocally challenged that past Tuesday, but Eileen was vocally challenged almost every Tuesday. Yet here she was, about to make her voice the center of attention.

"This first number," Eileen said, "is dedicated to a hillbilly in our midst. June, where are you?" A zaftig woman across the room with a "Mountaineer Fever" sweatshirt raised her hand. "Here you go," Eileen continued. "This is for you and any other West Virginian out there." Eileen went on to sing and strum "Country Roads," by John Denver, a tribute to our nearby state. She got quite a sing-along going during the chorus, and at one point asked June to stand up and solo the chorus for us, which she did with abandon.

Eileen played five more songs that night. The first three were pop classics—"Landslide," by Stevie Nicks, "Carolina In My Mind," by James Taylor, and "Mr. Tambourine Man," by Bob Dylan, whom she introduced as a fellow Minnesotan. Her voice was rich with emotion and so gentle on the ears. The more she sang, the more transfixed I became by her performance.

After warbling Dylan, Eileen took a sip of water, looked down, and spoke: "This next tune is not as well known as the last few, but it's by one of my favorite bands. I hope you enjoy it." With that, Eileen began to sing.

"I'm really close tonight.
And I feel like I'm moving inside him.
Lying in the dark..."

Instantly, I recognized the song. I looked at Eileen, smiling, and she looked through the crowd of people and met my eyes. She answered my smile with one of her own, but then returned to the mood of the song, which was wistful, as are so many other tunes that Neil Finn wrote and sang for Crowded House. After she finished "Fall at Your Feet," she played another Crowded House song, which she dedicated to "all the dreamers in the audience." It was the band's only hit single in the U.S., "Don't Dream It's Over." I was incredibly moved by Eileen's soprano and impressed with her guitar playing. But as pleasing as it was to listen to her, I enjoyed even more the raucous applause she received when she strummed her last chord.

While many of us continued to clap, Eileen was quickly enveloped. Allison and her roommate rushed to congratulate her, as did one of the men I assumed was a professor. "Excellent work," he said. "Truly a superb effort." Yup, I decided. Definitely a professor.

I stood alone at the side of the room while Eileen received more and more tributes. Gradually, I could see her tiring. Her replies became more cursory. Her eyes began to wander. Perhaps ten minutes elapsed before she was finally left alone. She looked exhausted—happy, but exhausted. I decided she needed one more well wisher.

"Too bad you didn't have a keyboard player for that last song," I said, smiling.

"Do you play?"

"No. I just like the keyboard parts in that song. Even without them, you sounded great."

"Thanks. It means a lot to me that you liked it." Then she paused and said, in a low voice, "I know you've been going through a tough time lately."

"So Allison's filled you in, huh?"

"Pretty much."

"Did she tell you our relationship is over?"

"Do you want it to be?"

I thought for a moment before answering. My mind turned to Eileen's final song, and whether "dreaming it's over" felt like a nightmare. "I don't know," I said in frustration.

Eileen and I looked at each other for a few seconds, but I couldn't think of anything to say. Finally, she reached out to touch my shoulder, just a friendly pat. "You'll figure it all out," she said. "For what it's worth, Allison has spoken *so* well of you. She really has."

Those were the last words I heard from her that evening. As she walked away, I responded "thanks," but it couldn't possibly have been audible.

Just then I noticed Dolores. She was starting to look less cheerful and more dizzy. I knew she couldn't drive home. "Can I give you a ride?" I asked.

"That would be great," she said, and planted a kiss on my cheek. It smelled of alcohol, but it was appreciated just the same.

Without saying goodbye to anyone, I helped Dolores out of the apartment and took her home. When we got there, I asked if she could do me one favor.

"Name it," she said.

"I've tried not to get too caught up in this intrigue about the Benefactor, or Feaver, or whatever you want to call him. But that's because he's not in our group. Arthur is. And if he's some kind of plant who's spying on us, that I need to know. Do you think you can find out?"

"I'll try," she said. "Promise."

Driving home that night, I had company; Nietzsche rode shotgun. "So, was it worth it? he asked. "Are you glad you didn't lie around feeling sorry for yourself?" I had to say 'yes.' I had had an interesting time. But most importantly, I realized I may have made a new friend. Allison's party helped me see Eileen in a different light. Before that night, she was always the third member of the Triumvirate, the quiet one. I had thought of her as a good soul, just somewhat lacking in muscle tone. No, I'm not talking physically—in that way, she kept herself as fit as Linda or Allison. But in the Creed Room, she ducked one fight after another. At first, I thought she was simply turned off by the combat—too Zen-like, if you will. Yet even when the discussions were harmonious, her comments were relatively brief and uncontroversial, as if her preference was to watch and learn, rather than participate and teach.

That Saturday night, the passive Eileen had disappeared. She was in her element, equally at peace with both music and words, sound and silence. I realized then that Eileen was a person for whom comfort in her environment was all important.

No wonder she hated law school, as Allison once told me. I found it even more difficult to imagine her there than myself.

After arriving back home, I went into the kitchen to fix some tea before watching SportsCenter. That's when I noticed a call on the answering machine.

"Sam, this is Allison. I'm soooo frustrated you left without saying goodbye. Thanks for coming, though. For a while I worried you wouldn't, and I *really* wanted you to hear Eileen play her songs. When I told her last week that you liked Crowded House, she told me she was going to play a couple of their songs for you.

"I wish we could have spent more time together, but you know how it is when you throw a party. You never really have a chance to talk to anyone, at least not for long. Hopefully, we can get together sometime soon outside of the Creed Room and just hang out—maybe with Scott, or Eileen or Linda. Or Dolores, if she'll get drunk.

"So thanks again, and I'll see you on Tuesday."

The message's tone was so ditsy, so Valley Girlish. It made me wonder why I ever thought the two of us were right for each other. But no sooner did that emotion pass than a new set of images entered from the previous Thanksgiving weekend. I recalled Allison throwing all her clothes on the floor except her underwear and jumping into my arms with a smirk on her face and a request on her lips. "You pretend you're Martin Heidegger, and I'll pretend I'm Hannah Arendt. Let's make philosophical love. German to Jew."

Boy, did I miss that Allison.

CHAPTER 10

THE HAND
OF PROVIDENCE

*I*f Linda could have removed the breakables from the Creed Room, she'd have done it before the February 15th session. This was the night Shaw had been waiting for all year. He and Art would be speaking about the American economic system.

The Creed Gang received nothing in writing in advance of the session. The one exception was that Art, who would talk first, was directed to send Shaw an outline of his speech.

"If you're the type of person," Art began, "who blames Hitler's parents for his actions; if you'd like to see the Constitution amended so that Clinton can be President for life, and I mean Hillary, not Bill; if you get a warm feeling whenever you hear the word 'welfare'; if you think property is theft or that theft should be punished by a slap on the wrist; if you think golf is more obscene than cock-fighting or that boxing should be banned and prostitution legalized ... then this talk is especially for you!"

Art looked around. "C'mon that doesn't even merit a chuckle?" Actually, Keister chuckled a bit, but he was the only one. The rest of us were surely wondering about Art's bona fides in our group. Was he an Empire Club spy or wasn't he? In any event, I knew I had to stop asking that question. Part of *our* club's code was to consider everyone's words on their own merits, regardless of who authored them. It was time to practice what we'd all been preaching.

"I'm a Christian, conservative, American patriot," Art resumed. "I can say that with pride, even though I know that to most of the so-called 'creative' community or the self-proclaimed 'intellectuals,' that makes me *the enemy*.

"Those who demonize us call themselves 'progressive.' They say they stand for progress. They style themselves champions of the downtrodden, mother earth, and justice—things that supposedly don't mean anything to me and my buddies because they don't matter to the bottom line, and that's all we heartless hypocrites care about.

"Those stereotypes bother me, but what bothers me even more is what these so-called progressives are doing to my country. They tolerate all sorts of decadence—like drugs, street crimes, abortions, Hollywood smut, welfare mothers and schools without God.

"It's funny, I guess. The progressives don't lose any sleep over those things. What they *can't* tolerate is American affluence. That's what they consider to be decadent.

"It's a simple fact that most Americans live pretty well. But that's seen as a sin as long as there's *one* soul who's poor. It's not just our affluence that sticks in the progressive's craw, it's also our commitment to competition. When we win, we expect to be rewarded. When we lose, we have the character not to wallow in a depression but to keep on fighting.

"I'll admit it. I'll complain too, sometimes. For my taste, this country has too much government and not enough Christ. But I swear to you, for every minute I spend criticizing America, I spend *hours* relishing how lucky I am to live here. Think about the alternatives to our democratic, capitalist formula. They're all failures.

"Take Marxism. Please! 'From each according to his abilities, to each according to his needs.' It sounded good. Then we saw it play out in practice, didn't we? One barbarous dictator after another slaughtering or exiling his countrymen whenever they didn't fit in with his plans.

"The Middle East? Give me a break. You can't even build a Christian church in Saudi Arabia. It's against the law, just like free elections.

"Then there's Africa—the land of poverty and AIDS. You'd think that place would make the progressives appreciate America, but you'd be wrong. They blame us for Africa's problems. Supposedly, we're obliged to turn Africa into Eden. Until we get that done, they'll tell us every way they can that America is run by a bunch of greedy swine. Marches, rallies, concerts, movies—you name it. There are as many vehicles for progressive venom as there are stars in the sky.

"Some of capitalism's enemies sound crazy, there's no question about it. But I want to be fair. Not every person who opposes capitalism is full of rage. Go back to the 19th century and you'll find peaceful utopians. They just wanted to live in small communities where everyone shares and shares alike. No gulags. Only love.

"Those utopians had their problems, though. How could they provide for economic growth, improve scientific knowledge, or make it possible for people to acquire consumer goods that would reduce the time spent on drudgery? The utopians didn't seem to care about the value of unfettered competition. They thought all we needed was wealth equality. Then we could enjoy equally and forever the benefits of state-of-the-art *19th* century medicine.

"I say this with all due respect, because I'm sure many of those utopians were kind people. But as a survivor of open-heart surgery, I say: Thanks, but no thanks!

"I don't get how anyone could live in the U.S.A. and not see the wisdom behind Adam Smith's ideas. And I'm thinking especially about the invisible hand of providence. Isn't it clear that God takes better care of us when we as economic producers serve our private interests than when we worry about the common good? Or that when we all compete to make as much money as possible for ourselves, we'll produce more, better and cheaper products, and in the long run this will benefit us all, almost *magically*?"

"Hey Art?" Allison said. "How many capitalists does it take to screw in a light bulb?"

Art thought for a second. "I don't know, how many?"

"None. The invisible hand will do it for them."

"Cute," he said, cracking a bit of a smile. Then he continued. "To me, the idea of the invisible hand is sacred. Maybe that's because I have faith in God and His providence. And everything I've seen in life only confirms my faith.

"I still remember when Ma Bell controlled the telecommunications industry. The progressives loved her. They said she made sure that everyone had the phone services they needed. Without her, the greedy entrepreneurs would take over, rich people would have lots of fancy telephones, and poor people would be left out in the cold.

"Well here we are, folks. It's been about 25 years since Ma Bell was hit with a nuclear bomb. And look what happened. We have cell phones, pagers, answering machines ... When I say *we* have them, I mean *all* of us. This stuff is cheap. The poor have them too.

"So no one seems to miss ol' Ma Bell. The progressives have

moved on to yell about other aspects of the free market—like the cars that are supposedly destroying our environment. They have no faith that car makers will come up with more environmentally sound technology. They have no faith *period*, and that's because faith isn't a progressive idea. Complaining is."

"Art?" said Allison. "I want to know more about this strawman group you're creating—the *progressives*. What percent of the U.S. would you include in it? All the Democrats?"

"I haven't thought about it," he replied.

"Think about it then," she demanded.

"I'd say most of the Democrats, yeah. At least a third of the country. Maybe two fifths."

"It's fun to build strawmen, isn't it?" Allison said.

"I wouldn't know," Art replied. Then he continued with his talk.

"The doomsayers predicted we'd all starve due to over-population. It never dawned on them that agricultural technology might improve. The doomsayers predicted that when nuclear weapons were developed, we'd all kill each other in some Strangelovian disaster. It never dawned on them that cool heads tend to prevail. Even now, the doomsayers say that sooner or later our chickens will come home to roost. I say we've been living the lives that God willed us to live—growing our economy, loving our country, and recognizing the hand of providence. Some of us have even tried to experiment with a bizarre concept: the guilt-free enjoyment of life."

"That sounds like you, Allison," I said, partially out of resentment. She gave me a scowl; she clearly didn't want to be associated with Art in any way.

"Can you imagine any idea stranger than living without guilt?" Art resumed. "I'm talking about celebrating God's creation without questioning whether we're righting every wrong.

No self-doubt, no fear. Try it for a year. Then decide whether to return to your angst. I know what choice you'd make."

Art closed his eyes and stopped talking for several seconds. Before he could continue, he had to wipe away tears. "My late father last visited this area five years ago, a month before his heart shut down. Now I want you all to picture the scene. Dolores and I live in Potomac, not far from River Road. It's a very expensive area to live in, and we own a couple of acres and a six bedroom house. The backyard is wooded, and a creek runs near the end of the property. That day, Dad and I were on the deck having a beer. Our black Lab was in the yard, catching balls and fetching them back to us.

"My dad was particularly happy that afternoon. I could see the pride in his eyes. When he grew up, his family had practically no money. They lived in Tidewater, Virginia, where the Navy was king. He joined up as soon as he was eligible, and he worked his butt off until the day he retired—as a captain. Meanwhile, he supported his three sons so that after a few years in the service ourselves, we could all go to college and earn a nice living.

"Each of us made a whole lot more money than he ever did. Believe me, that pleased him to no end. We'd offer to help him out, but he wouldn't take a thing. He wanted us to enjoy every bit of what we earned. He said his own material needs were limited.

"All us boys went into business. If someone had ever asked Dad if he were disappointed that his sons didn't work for Uncle Sam, Dad would have looked at him like a lunatic. 'Are you kiddin'?' he'd say. 'They're fueling the economy!' He would have never questioned the patriotic value of a career in business.

"When I think about that scene with my dad, I get choked up. But if a progressive were to witness that same scene, he'd probably find it offensive. Progressives have two nasty words for what I described—conspicuous consumption. Well, I say they're full of it. I earned every penny I've got, and no one can question my right to spend it as I please.

"When progressives aren't ridiculing places like Potomac, they're griping about the poor part of town. If you listen to them, you'd think the poor would be happier in Hell. All we hear about is how hopeless their lives are, and how they're denied a chance in life because of their poverty and the color of their skin.

"Let me clear up that junk right now. I've seen lots of blacks and Hispanics work their way up the corporate ladder. In America, if there's a will, there's a way. I can assure you of this— the people in Anacostia are no poorer than my dad was when he grew up in Tidewater. Most of them probably have five times the gadgets he had. I've heard my dad describe how he grew up; he had nothing! Nothing but drive and faith.

"I'd be willing to bet that our poor people today live a heck of a lot better than the middle class did in 1776. We all know why: our economy encourages competition to produce lots of high quality goods at affordable prices. That means we've always been looking for plenty of workers, especially people who've bought into the values that make America great—like an appreciation for hard work, the guts to take risks, and the faith in the inevitability of progress.

"America has always stood for those values. God willing, we always will.

"Let me end with this, and I say this mostly to the progressives in our midst: Complain if you'd like that our system isn't perfect. Just remember—no one's been able to improve on it. Personally, I'd suggest forgetting about perfection. It's a trap door. The truth is, the only places more perfect than the

USA are in our future. We'll keep making new discoveries—in medicine, environmental science, you name it. In other words, we'll *progress*. In the meantime, we can either take pride in our country or cry in our soup. The choice, ladies and gentlemen, is yours."

With that, Art Sherman sat down, collected a kiss and a pat on the back from Dolores, and awaited a response from his beloved Scott Shaw. Shaw's first response was visual, not oral. He took off his rugby shirt and revealed a T-Shirt underneath. It bore the inscription:

"The Poor Will Always Be With Us."—Jesus Christ, The Republican Party.

Shaw stood still near the window so that his audience could wallow in his irreverence. Then he smiled at Art, who couldn't stop shaking his head at the T-Shirt.

"Every era's had its Rome, its most glorious *empire*, and in every one of those *empires*, you'll find a ruling class." That's how Shaw began. When he said the word "empire" he stared straight at the camera. He had obviously prepared a rebuttal not just to Art but also to the Benefactor. "We've just heard a song of celebration on behalf of the latest ruling class in the latest great empire. You could hear the pride bounce off every wall. Hallelujah! All hail America! All hail its bourgeoisie!

"I know all too well the spoils of war. Don't kid yourselves, that's what this is about—bloodless class war. One of those spoils is the rulers' right to toast their own virtue. Another is their right to talk about their political ideology like it's a religion. We've just heard about the religion of capitalism. You'll forgive me if I've always somehow missed the holiness. I've seen the productivity and the cruelty, but never the holiness.

"Arthur has offered up the same smack talk that we've all heard a thousand times before, from economics professors, right wing politicians—really, from any businessman who takes the time to justify his existence. It's the same old stinkin' legal brief in support of their own heroism, the same tired old idea of the Chosen People. Only now, it's not the ancient Hebrews who are chosen. It's the modern-day country clubber.

"Arthur talked about competition. And why not? His social class has kicked some serious butt in their power struggle, so they want what's coming to them. They'll tell you to forget about all the poverty, elitism, selfishness, bigotry, infatuation with guns and shallow materialism. If you want to call them on what a load of bull they're peddling, you'll just get ridiculed as a 'doomsayer.' That's Arthur's terminology; Spiro Agnew preferred 'nattering nabob of negativism.' It means someone who's willing to speak the truth to the people in power. If that's the kind of person you are, they'll fight like hell to marginalize you.

"The fat cats know how to scare people. Once they get you to keep your mouth shut, they don't hassle you. But that's not enough to make them *like* you. They only like you if you buy off on all the B.S. they spew out of Madison Avenue. That's where they create human desires, like the desire to hang with a buxom blonde on the beach in Cancun, lounge in your chair with your cool shades, pick up a martini, and contemplate just how Goddamned glib you were last week in the boardroom. That's the life isn't it? That's what it's all about. Then you go home—to Potomac, Beverly Hills or whatever gated community you live in—and you have an orgasm at how well it's all turned out.

"Arthur talked to us about values. I've tried to note the ones he mentioned. There's courage, hard work, faith in divine providence, and the belief in the inevitability of progress. What do you say we take a closer look?

"The right wingers love to talk about their courage, especially the courage of an entrepreneur. Well, call me a skeptic, but I've seen how these entrepreneurs get started. They take their Wharton degrees, hook up with some money guy, and give it a go, realizing that if they fail they'll still be plenty employable—for surely they've kissed enough ass over the years to keep their connections. Or how about those Daddy's Boys? They call up and ask for a few hundred K to start a business. If it fails, they just call daddy again and get another half a mil. Look at George W. Bush. Really courageous what he went through as a businessman, isn't it? Make a couple of calls to daddy's friends, and the next thing you know, the world's his oyster.

"What about hard work? I'm all for it. But shouldn't it be a *means* to an end, not an end in itself? You'd think that as we become richer, we wouldn't have to work as hard—we'd have more time for leisure. Not true. The Man, the dude in the expensive suit, he doesn't want his workers having a lot of leisure. Then he might lose that all-important competition. So everyone's expected to keep working as many hours as possible, and the result is that we've seen an *increase* over recent decades in how much people work. It's hardly something to boast about."

"Are you denying we have more leisure time today than in the past?" Dolores asked.

"What do you mean by the past? The stone age? The time of Jesus? I'm not a historian. I only know we don't need to be killing ourselves for some CEO. We should be developing our creativity—artistically, intellectually. But there's no money in that, is there?"

"There can be," Dolores replied.

"Not for me. At least not yet," lamented Shaw. "So what's next? Faith in divine providence? In the inevitability of progress?

These two aren't even worth dissing. Just look at the 20th century. Are you telling me the providential God sent us Hitler or Pol Pot? Or that He *willed* the deaths of tens of thousands in Nagasaki and Hiroshima, while sparing, say, Kyoto? Give me a break. We've been through that debate before. I've got nothing more to say about it."

"Good!" Art said.

"What I *do* have more to say about is values," Shaw continued. "Arthur would agree that a society should be judged by the values it upholds. Let me throw out a few good ones.

"I'd like to talk about justice, compassion, dignity and respect. Some think those words are crutches for poor people to grab onto when they're not willing to work hard or compete. I don't buy that for a second. To me, those words are a whole lot more holy than anyone's God.

"You can't talk about justice in the U.S. without starting with the subject of *race*. Conservatives want to white-wash that word. They say bigotry's gone. A new day has dawned. I say they're not color blind, they're just plain *blind*!

"You know what the problem is? White folks just don't understand the sport of track. At least I assume they don't, because I never see a white boy compete in the 100 or 200 meters.

"Since most of you are white, let me help you out with this one. We're watching as they set up for the 200. If you've never seen that race before, it might look kind of funny, because the guy in lane one is standing several feet behind the guy in lane two, who's standing several feet behind the guy in lane three. You get the picture. They're all running a short race to get to the same place halfway around the track. What gives? Why the staggered start?

"They stagger it because the guys in the outside lanes have

to run around a wider circle. So if we're going to make the race fair, we've gotta do something to make it harder for the folks on the inside. We've got to move them further back from the finish line when we start the race.

"But that's track. It's a black man's sport. Arthur was talking before about a white man's game—the glorious competition for money, power and status. In Arthur's game, nobody but a white man has ever been elected President or Vice President. That's because the white folks rigged the game. On the White Man's Track, folks line up in a staggered position, only the guys on the inside are starting several feet *closer* to the finish line, not further back. It kind of makes it easy to win when you're starting on the inside, doesn't it? When you're on the outside, you've got to run a ways just to get to where the inside guy was starting, and then you've got to run a wider circle once you get there.

"On the White Man's Track, the positions have names. The inside lanes are called Beverly Hills, Scarsdale, La Jolla. Or Art's Potomac, upstream from George Washington's beautiful plantation. And the outside lanes, they're called Watts, Anacostia and Harlem. Oh, and the South Bronx. That'd be Lane 8.

"We've talked a bit about Lane 1, remember? We said if you start in that lane and want to become an entrepreneur, maybe, just maybe, you don't need the guts of a burglar. What about Lane 8? In that lane, you get to attend integrated schools, or so they say. But I'll let you guess how many White Anglo Saxon Protestants attend public schools in the South Bronx.

"What else do we know about Lane 8? You live in a shit hole. To get there from school, you've gotta walk past gang bangers and drug addicts. You see hookers too. Everywhere you look, the hos are out, just letting you know there's still a few ways left to make money. When you get home, Daddy's long gone. Mommy's there, barely literate. Maybe even on drugs.

She's trying to get you a square meal and hardly worried if you don't have all the books you need to master your social studies project. Computer? What's a computer?

"If you're lucky, you survive childhood. But even if you do, they'll say you're stupid, though it turns out you might actually have become smart, if you hadn't grown up in Lane 8.

"Now people, if you don't mind, I'd like to direct some comments to Sam and Allison.

"I hope you two know I'm not one of those Jew-hating blacks. But I gotta say something about Jewish neo-cons, the ones who hate affirmative action. They love to talk about how their ancestors came from Europe with nothing, so if they can make it here, anyone else can too.

"Those Jews are as full of crap as the Christian right. Their ancestors didn't come here with nothing. They came from a culture based on books—serious ones, like the books of the Talmud. Even if you leave the books aside, their culture was centered around verbiage, like the sales techniques they mastered in the markets of old Europe.

"When you think about it, it's not hard to believe that they could run in the Anglos' rat race, now is it? Because the race in this society is all about words. Did I mention business? Talmudic law? We're talking word games, aren't we?

"Compare that to the South Bronx. This is a culture of people who came from slaves. They didn't bargain for a living over diamonds. They picked cotton. Their names weren't Isaac or Jacob. Their names were *"Boy!"* If they were thoughtful, I mean lazy, they got a whipping. Strange that when they were freed from slavery and migrated to the South Bronx, their kids weren't interested in pursuing a career that would showcase their forensics skills."

"Why are you telling this to me?" Allison said. "I'm with you on affirmative action."

"So am I," I added. "I just wouldn't say that everyone who isn't is 'full of crap.'"

"I'm only telling it straight, brother. I'm not a diplomat. Anyway, let's move on. I want to talk about our society's compassion. *That's* what's really missing. The injustice is just a symptom.

"Back in the Reagan decade, lots of Americans made more money than they knew what to do with. Reagan said some of that wealth would trickle down to the bottom—Lanes 7 and 8. When that didn't happen, you'd hope our compassion would take care of the poor somehow. But I guess we decided we don't *need* compassion, not like we need VCRs, SUVs, 401Ks or summer homes. And not like we need our unforgiving puritanical morality. Now, when people die from AIDS, freeze to death from homelessness or overdose in a crack house, we can blame them, not us. Even if they're just kids, we don't have to feel responsible.

"My attitude is simple. If the white males who've bought out our politicians had enough compassion and commitment to human dignity, they could solve most of our poverty problems themselves. They could decide their luxury goods are wants, not needs, but the uplifting of Lane 8 is a need. So they could take their astronomical paychecks and spend it on refurbishing our cities—because they feel compelled to do it in their hearts, like a mom feels the need to protect her kids.

"I guess most of them just aren't hardwired that way. And why should they be? That's not exactly the attitude anyone's looking for in the Wharton Admissions Department.

"When you put all this together, what do you get? A need for a pretty big government, that's what—a very, very *visible* hand of providence. The invisible one seems to work only for some of us."

Shaw started walking back to his chair. Then he stopped himself. "Before I finish, I've got to address a pet peeve. Conservatives love to talk about how much progress we've made in this country. And I'll grant there's been a fair amount. But while the right wingers are taking credit, I have to ask them this: Were *they* responsible for the civil rights movement? Or were they too preoccupied with feathering their own nests to lift a hand? Were *they* responsible for improving environmental regulations? Or were they battling those regs, always in the name of the invisible hand? Have *they* been champions for successes in homosexual rights? Or women's rights? Or in the labor movement?

"A lot of those successes have come *in spite of* the barons of capital. And without their support, there's only so much the rest of us can do. The big money people are still the ones who arrange the track. They still decide how important the game is. And I'm afraid they're going to stay in charge unless we violently revolt. Arthur will be happy to know I'm not advocating that.

"There are no easy solutions. That's why we come here week after week—to listen, to learn. I'm willing to listen like everyone else. I'm just not willing to take a bow on behalf of my society. Not as long as there's a South Bronx. I'd challenge you religious people to find a single passage in the Bible to support your case.

"Remember what Jesus said about the rich man getting into the Kingdom of Heaven. God's boy said it would be easier for a camel to pass through the eye of a needle than for a rich man to enter that kingdom. I often wonder how our Jesus-lovin' fat cats stomach that one." I noticed Keister shake his head in agreement, while Art coughed in disdain, apparently willing to selectively interpret his beloved Bible on this point.

That was all Shaw had to say. As he hurled himself back into his chair, which was right between mine and Allison's, he was breathing deeply and visibly sweating. Then he turned his chair toward his nemesis and poised himself to continue the fight.

Linda had another goal in mind. First, she called for a short break; "no more than five minutes." Then she approached Shaw. "Listen Scott. I don't want to cramp your style. Just do me this favor. Cover that shirt!"

"What?" asked Shaw. "You can't take a little joke?"

"It's worn off by now, don't you think? Cover it."

Linda's edicts were the closest thing we had to the law of the land. Shaw mumbled something I couldn't make out and slipped on his rugby shirt.

Linda then turned to me and said "Let's take a walk, Sam." So I followed her down the stairs and into the living room.

"Did you bring your vocal chords tonight?" she asked.

"Are you referring to last week?"

"Of course. Don't you get it? We need you here. Last week, you wouldn't even discuss the schools. And you're a teacher!"

"Linda, you know what's going on with me."

"I know you dated a woman who doesn't want to date you anymore. Am I wrong?"

"No, but—"

"So you have so little self-respect that you don't think you can find someone who wants to be with you?"

"Come on, give me a break. I'm—"

"You're bringing your personal life into this house, that's what your doing. Look, we don't have much time left before we have to write our report. We can't afford to have you walking around semi-conscious."

"I was preparing to talk. Last week was an aberration."

"I'm glad to hear that," Linda said, looking at her watch. "We've got to get back up. Here's the deal. I'll let everyone else speak first; that will give you more time to prepare. Then I want you to talk, and I mean for a while. Point out stuff you agreed with in what both Art and Scott said. Point out what you *disagreed* with. Think Henry Clay. Bring this gang together."

Linda reached out and clasped my right shoulder while she looked me in the eyes. "Forget Allison. She's a friend. Just ... a friend. You'll do better. Trust me."

Returning home from the Creed Room on Leap Day, I thought about the fact that since Linda's "Move it, soldier!" lecture in the Benefactor's living room, I had probably spoken more than twice as much as anyone else. The night of the Shaw/Sherman debate, I critiqued both of their ideas. The next week, I gave the evening's presentation on the American Political System. On Leap Day, Dolores began a three-week discussion on "The World," which Keister would continue at the next session and Eileen would conclude the following week. Once again, after Dolores finished her talk, I had a lot to say. Linda's orders.

A few days after her pep talk in the Victorian, Linda and I got together for dinner. That's when she graced me with the following proposal:

I'd need to remain vocal whenever our group was in session. But my job wouldn't just be to say what I thought. I'd also have to identify and support positions that the group could rally around. Those positions would help form the foundation of our final report in May.

To succeed as a consensus-builder, I especially needed to co-opt the group's most outspoken members, Shaw, Art and

Allison. In other words, I had to work their ideas into my own statements.

On Leap Day, Linda would nominate me to serve as the lead scrivener for the group's final report and to direct a four member panel that would organize that report. The panel's three other members would be identified the following week.

Back in the fall, I would have jumped at Linda's proposal. But when Linda made it, my confidence wasn't exactly at an all-time high. Linda knew that, of course. She simply didn't care. She said that she had complete trust in me and that unless I was so strapped by other obligations that I didn't have the time to direct the panel, I'd better do it.

After thinking for a few moments about the proposal, I couldn't justify saying no, at least not according to Linda's criterion. My school duties were fairly demanding, but I was otherwise free. I had no wife, no children, not even a dog. So I accepted.

When Linda made the announcement, Keister gave me a thumbs up sign and said I was going to "kick some fanny." Allison told me I was definitely the best choice for the job. Art, for his part, whispered that he was relieved I'd be taking the laboring oar and not certain other people. Then he added, "I won't be much help to you. This crazy telemarketing bill is sending the whole industry into war mode. I'm already wearin' combat fatigues."

I wished him "good luck" but hardly meant it. After my discussion with Shaw, and given what I now suspected of Art, if it were left up to me, no piece of legislation could possibly have been harsh enough on the telemarketers. Maybe Dante could think of one, but I couldn't.

When I got home that evening, I finally felt good enough about my life to call Jamison. I knew I'd have to be the one to break the ice. He hated to deal with awkward situations and only called when there was something fun to talk about, like when our beloved Stanford Cardinal was on a winning streak.

If Steve were surprised to hear from me, he didn't show it. In fact, he acted as if nothing had happened in Brooklyn. When I asked what he was doing these days, he replied, "The usual—working, clubbing, skiing, watching roundball. You looking forward to March Madness?"

"You know it," I said, always able to kick into sports fan mode. Sports was my fantasy land, my favorite escape into an altogether different world. I can enter it at will whenever there is a game on the tube or another fan sharing the water cooler. If only for a moment, my stress or boredom vanishes. "I love our big men this year."

"Me too," said Jamison. "They actually give us a chance to win it all. I might even fly out to watch a game or two if we get past the first couple of rounds."

"Don't bet the ranch on it," I said, with my customary caution. "Our game is mental. We win so much early in the season because the other teams are still figuring out how to play. By March, it's all about athleticism. That's why we always suck in the Tournament."

"You're a downer, dude," he replied.

We talked a bit more about sports until Jamison asked me about Allison. "So how's it going with the poetry slammer?"

"That's history."

"As of when?"

"In my mind or hers?"

"How about in reality?"

"I think she decided to dump me back on New Year's Eve."

"I figured the over/under was about January 7th," Jamison said.

"You mean we didn't come across as the ideal couple?"

"I'll put it this way. Your frisky friend has a big mouth and the patience of a light beam. You weren't gone ten minutes when she asked if I wanted to head back to the City with her. I told her to give you another ten, but when you didn't show by then, we bolted. Then she started popping off about how she'd never seen anyone treat their mother like you did."

"So her little friends all come from perfect families," I said. "Isn't that sweet?"

"She talked nonstop about how disillusioned she was with you. She said that anyone who'd treat his mom like crap would be sure to treat his wife like crap too. And that you can tell how a man respects women from the way he treats his mother. I'm telling you, she was spewing out one piece of dime-store psychology after another—a regular Freud, that woman."

"Must be nice to feel so superior," I said, "especially when you come from tons of money and your parents chirp about like lovebirds. Screw her!"

"I thought about doing just that," Jamison said, laughing. "We went back to her friend's party and kept on drinking. At one point, I wondered if she were going to come on to me, but then she started flirting with some investment banker she knew from high school. So I took off and left the little preppies to themselves. Seriously, there was no way your relationship was going to last. You guys are from different worlds, and I think you *want* to be in different worlds."

How could I disagree?

Not ten minutes had elapsed after I finished speaking to Jamison when I was on the phone again. This time the call was incoming. It was Jamison's fan from Brooklyn.

She called with two purposes in mind: (1) to complain about her arthritis, and (2) to complain about her loneliness.

"It's so hard," Mother said, seemingly only half awake. "I lie in bed every night trying to sleep. It takes me forever. Then when I do get to sleep it's almost time to get up to go to work. I can't live like this any more, Sammy."

"What does the doctor say?"

"Oh, the doctor. She just gives me pills. They do more harm than good, believe me."

"Aren't you taking them?"

"I took one or two. They made me feel funny, so I stopped."

"Did you go back to the doctor?"

"I'm telling you Sammy, there's nothing a doctor can do for me."

"Damn it, mother! Do what the doctor says! If you don't like her, find another one."

"Sammy, don't scream, I'm too weak. I'm telling you, they don't know. None of them. The pills they give you all have side effects. I won't take them. I refuse."

"You'll just suffer then."

"Oh, I'd suffer anyway. I've got nothing left here to live for. I'd love to move down to Washington to be with you and Lenny, but I can't afford to leave my job. Not yet." Mother let out a long, depressing sigh. While I wanted to keep on her about the need to take her medicine, I simply couldn't bully her that night. She seemed too depressed to take the pounding.

"I've got some good news for you, Mother."

"You're back together with Allison?" she asked, without any hint of pain or fatigue.

"Forget about Allison. That relationship is as dead as a doornail. I was talking about school. There's news you'll like about school."

"Get back to Allison," she said, her voice weakening. "What happened?"

"You could see that for yourself on New Year's Eve. I don't want to talk about it. I want to talk about school."

"School? Why would you bring that up? I'm really not feeling well."

"That's the point, Mother. I'm trying to cheer you up. I'm starting to find things at school pretty intolerable. Now, doesn't that make you feel better?"

My mother's voice sounded stronger. "Well, maybe so. Sammy, I'm not sitting around hoping you're unhappy at work. It's just that I like to look at the future. I figure you'll have a better life if you burn out from teaching now than at 45 when your earning potential is shot."

"I'm not burning out, Mother. I'm burning *up*."

I came to the Creed Room with anticipation—not for the presentation or discussion, but for the selection of the other three members of the panel who would draft the final report with me. Linda said that she'd leave that task until the end of the session.

Keister's presentation that evening focused on a wide range of foreign policy issues. He tackled them from the perspective of "Nascar Ned." Keister had spent a couple of weekends preparing for his talk by attending conferences at local colleges. He decided that while the professors "know their stuff," they weren't talking about it in a way that could speak to Nascar Ned. "That's not Ned's fault, it's theirs," Keister said. "A professor's job should be to write books that grab people, like a Tom Clancy novel. Otherwise, what good's he doin'?"

Linda pointed out that a professor's job is to teach college students, not wake up Nascar Ned—that's Ned's responsibility. But Keister would have none of that.

"They're the foreign policy experts. If they don't talk sense into Ned, ain't no one else gonna. It's the Neds who pick our Presidents, so someone better teach 'em, don't cha think?"

I sure did. "Social studies and humanities profs really miss the boat," I said, lending my voice to Keister's. "The stuff they write about is incredibly esoteric. That's why I call them bibliographers. It's like their job is to come up with a new book or article that we can add to some imaginary library that houses all the ideas of the human species.

"Screw that. They ought to write for the masses like Fred said. They ought to fire people up!"

Nobody argued with me, but why would they? None of us was consumed with getting tenure or figuring out how best to impress our professional colleagues.

A few minutes before the session was scheduled to end, Linda announced it was time to round out the panel. She didn't ask for suggestions. She gave directives, and the gang obeyed.

First, Linda said, she was removing Art from the list of possible panelists. He had told her that he wouldn't have the time to do the panel justice, given the murderous demands placed on him at work. Second, Linda informed us, she was removing herself from consideration. As coordinator, she said, she's had more than enough influence already.

That left five candidates and three spots. Linda gave one to Dolores. If Art couldn't participate, Linda said, she at least wanted his wife to do it, figuring that Dolores would solicit Art's feedback and we'd get two Shermans for the price of one.

Next, Linda announced that one of the Georgetown students should be on the panel. So she selected the final two members by choosing at random between Allison and Eileen for one slot, and Shaw and Keister for the other. Linda's method was right out of grade school: the old Rock—Paper—Scissors game. Shaw and Keister squared off first and came up with scissors and paper, respectively. When he saw the paper, Shaw pumped his fist. We all knew he wanted to be on the panel, so his reaction was hardly a surprise. Keister simply shook his head and laughed.

That left the poet and the singer. Both were visibly nervous. Eileen seemed embarrassed about her tension, but not Allison. Her body language suggested aggression, as in "Gentlemen, start your engines!" When the time came for them to show their hands, the rest of us knew the result before they did. Then they opened their eyes. It was rock and rock. A do-over.

I realized at that moment how strongly I cared about the outcome of this stupid game. Allison had blown off our affair, and I had no passion to re-kindle the friendship. More importantly, I recognized upon seeing the two fists how much I wanted to get closer to Eileen. We all waited for the laughter to die down after the do-over. It was the laughter of stress— the same laughter you hear during a school exam after a long and loud stomach growl and before the other students think to themselves "there but for the grace of God go I."

While the laughter helped Eileen to relax, Allison's facial expression never changed. She stared at Eileen as if they were about to arm wrestle. I later asked Linda why she had decided not to round out the panel by flipping coins. "I don't know, I just felt like it," she said. But I knew the truth. She was curious to see the looks in her friends' eyes when it came time to compete.

After I heard Linda once again call out the count of "three," I noticed Allison's right hand first. It was a fist. Nietzsche would have been proud. But, as usual, pride goeth before a fall. The next image I saw was Eileen's outstretched hand, followed by that hand wrapping up Allison's, and Eileen sporting a big, ear-to-ear smile.

{>

After the final bell rang, I sat in my classroom for about 15 minutes putting the finishing touches on an upcoming U.S. History exam. The date was Wednesday, March 8th.

When I approached the corridor commonly known as jock hall, I heard a commotion coming from the boys' locker room. I had to use the bathroom anyway, so I walked in, curious about the source of the noise. It didn't take me long to see several students standing in a circle near the showers, hollering at someone in the center. It appeared to be another student kneeling down, though I couldn't make out the face.

About twenty feet away from the circle, I heard the words that I'll never forget: "Lick it! Lick it, damn it!" This was followed by taunts and jeers from the figures forming the circle, until once again I heard the first speaker's voice. "Lick it, you fucking twerp!" The words were shouted from the other side of the circle and delivered with pure venom.

I rushed over, too stunned to make a sound but alert enough to recognize my duty to stop the insanity. They never noticed me coming, absorbed as they were in the entertainment. Once I made contact with one of the creatures and threw him to the side, the panorama instantly became clear. The circle had been formed by several of the school's football players. Leaning over opposite me in the circle was my old buddy, George London. On the ground, between him and me, was little Jerome Haupt, the honor student. London's right hand clutched a wad of Haupt's hair. Haupt's face was inches away from London's reproductive organ.

For a moment, I completely froze. Even London, I thought,

Takoma Park's most blatant bully, couldn't possibly be capable of such depravity. Then, my instincts took over. I leapt to Haupt's side and sharply shoved London backwards as far away from Haupt as possible.

Candidly, it was a blissful feeling to give London's shoulders a good strong thrust. But the bliss was short-lived. I watched London stumble back a few feet, then slip on the slick floor and smack his head against a shower valve. He crumpled in a heap and lay motionless.

Immediately, a couple of the boys ran out of the locker room screaming for help. They returned shortly with none other than Ms. Cratchett, never my biggest fan.

Cratchett quickly called 911 on her cell phone. Then, as I stood speechless and in shock over the incident, Cratchett watched over London to make sure he didn't move his head. The ambulance came within minutes and took London away. It wasn't until I called the hospital in the evening that I learned his condition: the back of George London's skull had been fractured and there was bleeding inside his brain.

CHAPTER 11

DREAD

I was awakened the next morning in the middle of a nightmare. In my dream, Charlotte London, George's mother, was addressing her fellow school board members about the evil of one Samuel Kramer, who had murdered her son. She had said the word *murder* for a second time when I woke with a jolt to the sound of knocking at the front door of my apartment. This was no dream. It was Ericsson. When I saw him, I couldn't help but fear the worst.

"Relax," he said. "George is still hanging in there. The doctors say he can go either way. We're just going to have to say our prayers and let them do their work."

"I understand," I said. "I swear to you, I wasn't trying to hurt the kid, I only wanted to stop him. You know what he was doing, don't you?"

"Yeah, I heard all about it. I was working half the night on this. I spoke to some of the students who saw it happen, met with George's mother, talked to the doctors .... it's been crazy."

"Thanks for coming over and giving me an update," I said.

"It's not a problem. I can't even imagine how awful this must be for you."

"It hasn't fully hit me yet, I'm sure. I keep saying to myself, if we could only turn back the clock ...." I couldn't finish my own sentence.

"Uh, Sam," Ericsson began, his voice halting, "there is another reason I came."

"What's up?"

He started pacing. Then he turned to me and said: "I hate to tell you this. But I'm suspending you from your teaching duties, indefinitely."

"You're *what*?"

"You heard me."

"How can you suspend me? I was defending an innocent student. I didn't mean—"

Ericsson didn't let me finish. The stress and the lack of sleep had impaired his coping skills. "Just stop! Stop!" he yelled. "There'll be plenty of time for you to tell your side of the story. But I've got to make a decision before the school doors open. If I let you teach, Charlotte London will have both of our heads, and she won't be alone."

"Richard. Get a grip, will you? I didn't do anything wrong. I was protecting a defenseless child from sexual abuse by a bully. That's all. *He* caused what happened, not me."

"Like I said. You'll have your chance to make your case. Keep this in mind, though. There were a lot of witnesses. And they *all* say you used too much force."

"Wait a minute. Jerome Haupt said that?"

Ericsson stopped to think. "Actually, I don't think he opined about that. He did say he was glad you got London off of him, if that's what you wanted to hear. But all the other boys blasted you hard. They said you shoved George's shoulder like a blocking sled, and on a wet slippery surface. Trust me, you'll need the time off to deal with this. For now, you're still on the payroll."

"Thanks, that's gracious of you." I mumbled.

"Here's my advice," Ericsson said. "Get a lawyer. And I mean right away."

Gradually, it dawned on me that Ericsson's decision to suspend me wasn't only about covering his back side. He was concerned about me, too, and his advice that I hire a lawyer was clearly sound. Lord knows, Charlotte London was hiring one of her own.

I told Ericsson I accepted his decision and asked what could be done for my students. He said that he had my philosophy lesson plans and would teach that class himself. As for the others, they'd get a substitute teacher. "Relax about the kids, Sam, except for one." Ericsson added. "Say your prayers for George London. I can't tell you how much easier it would be for all of us if he gets better."

"No kidding," was the only response I could muster before Ericsson left.

As soon as he was gone, I went to bed and cried. I hadn't felt such torment since I walked into my father's blood-spattered study. Excruciating questions came into my mind and wouldn't leave. Did I really use too much force? Why didn't I just shout? How could I ever prove my innocence if the witnesses said I was guilty? If I were blamed for the incident, who would hire a law school dropout turned child abuser? Might I actually have killed London?

For the better part of an hour, I lay in bed, paralyzed by fear. Finally, I gathered myself and took my first real action: calling Mother.

For some stupid reason, I expected her to take the news calmly, with her natural maternal concerns being tempered by the fact that the incident could spell the end of my teaching career. I couldn't have been more wrong. She became unnerved from the moment I mentioned "internal bleeding." When she heard about the witness testimony, she went into a full blown panic attack.

I'd seen her have those attacks during the period right after my father died, but they went away as soon as she began taking meds. Eventually, she got off the drugs and the symptoms didn't recur... until I mentioned the witnesses. Then she said she was having trouble breathing. She also expressed concern that she was going to pass out. It was deja vu all over again.

Mother's panic attack unleashed my adrenalin. I called the police in Brooklyn and arranged for an ambulance to take her to the hospital. As much as I wanted to stay home and deal with my own issues, I knew I had to tend to my mother first.

The drive was long and dreary, complicated by not one but two accidents on the God-forsaken New Jersey Turnpike. When I arrived in Brooklyn, mother was back home, medication in tow. The attack was over, if not the stress that brought it on.

The trip turned out to be exactly what I needed. First, I was able to reassure myself that no one could successfully prosecute me *regardless* of London's fate. My heart was obviously in the right place in protecting Jerome. What jury would want to punish someone for coming to his rescue? Even if I did use excessive force, London provoked me. What he did was inhuman. All I did was shove him, and he happened to fall in the wrong place. Where's the criminal intent?

Second, I found myself a lawyer. On Mother's advice, I called my local teacher's union, which promised to pay for someone to represent me. Minutes later, attorney Karen Block phoned. She worked at a small litigation boutique in D.C. and was experienced in defending teachers on behalf of their unions.

The day after I went to Brooklyn, I came home to meet Karen. I also saw Joe Wong, who said he'd heard London had stabilized a bit, but his prospects for survival remained uncertain.

Joe did some heavy lifting for me that I could never repay. He gathered the witnesses' names and addresses and dropped off the information at my home. Thanks to him, by the end of the weekend, Karen was able to approach all seven witnesses.

Every time I saw Karen, I was struck by her sympathy and amazing attention to detail. She was determined not to leave my case to the whim of the fates. The more I reflected about her dedication, the more I laughed at myself. For years, I had filled my head with cynicism about the practice of law and romantic thoughts about school teaching. Now here I was, frustrated with the school bureaucracy and suspended from the classroom, only to be the beneficiary of legal services from a tireless advocate employed by a law firm. I could hear my mother asking why it was that I dropped out of law school. For a moment, fleeting though it was, I had no explanation.

That Saturday, a couple of my colleagues came over to help preserve my sanity. Then, on Sunday, it was my turn to pay a visit—to uncle Lenny's house. Unbeknownst to me, Mother had called him shortly after she got back from the hospital and cried about the mess I had made of my life—a life, she said, that once had so much promise, but had reached the point where I'd be lucky to stay out of the Big House. Knowing Lenny, he would have taken Mother's comments with a grain of salt, given her constant wolf-crying. Perhaps that's why he didn't seem especially disturbed when he called and asked to get together.

I intended to spend the whole afternoon at Lenny's. But when I put the keys in the ignition, my car could barely move. On the driver's side everything looked fine. On the passenger's side, however, both the tires and the body of the car were visibly slashed. In the back, my "I'd Rather Be Teaching" bumper sticker was ripped apart.

After surveying the vandalism, I returned to my apartment

to call Lenny. It was then that I noticed the *real* damage. Unfortunately for my landlord, I lived on the ground floor. That enabled my fan club to spray paint, in huge letters on the back wall: "I'D RATHER BE DICK SMOKING." They also left a baseball bat on the grass next to the wall. It looked like any other Louisville Slugger, except that it bore the inscription in small writing: "Kirby—watch your back."

Lenny came over right away. I expected him to chuckle at the reference to "Dick Smoking"—after all, he was the first person I had ever heard use that term. But he didn't laugh. Not in the slightest.

That night, I went outside one more time to survey the damage to my apartment. I didn't get angry. I simply felt weak and needy, and all I could think to do was pray. I'm talking about good old fashioned petitional prayers. The kind I supposedly didn't believe in.

Walking into the old Victorian for the next session, I was still groggy from spending the day in bed. No one called that day. No friends came over to show compassion. No landlord got around to covering up any spray paint. Then again, nobody threw any Molotov cocktails either.

I was the first guest to arrive in the Creed Room, which was nice, since I needed a few moments to transport myself back into reality. When I saw Eileen's face, I could tell how much she had been looking forward to making her presentation—her first since November.

Eileen led our third and final session on "The World." Because we'd spent two weeks on geopolitics, she avoided that topic like the plague. Instead, she spoke about a range of subjects concerning the environment and technology, including overpopulation, global warming, cloning experiments, and last, but far from least in her mind, ethical issues involving animals.

As with every other session, Linda began by introducing the topic and the presenter. But when Eileen walked over to take the presenter's customary place by the front window, Art interrupted with a question. "Eileen, if you don't mind, I'd like to raise an issue that has nothing to do with your talk. Should I do it now or at the end of the session?"

"I don't care," she replied. "You can do it now. That's fine."

Art looked down for a moment. When he lifted his head, a deadly serious look was on his face. "We need to talk about what happened last Wednesday at Takoma Park High."

"Son of a bitch!" I said, softly, but audibly. I knew right then I should have anticipated that London's mother might be in touch with Sherman. He had probably told her in the autumn that a teacher from her son's school was in our group, and she must have called him after The Incident to vent. How, I asked myself, could I be so clueless as to not put the Triumvirate on notice before the Creed Room met?

"You said it!" Art exclaimed, replying to my visceral utterance, while avoiding any eye contact with me. "Sam is in some deep, deep doo doo, in case you people don't know. I'm very concerned that, as the chair of the committee that's supposed to draft and present our report, he's going to be in *way* over his head."

I was too much in shock to fire back right away. But Allison wasn't so tongue-tied. "What are you talking about?" she asked Art. She sounded as accusatorial as she did concerned.

"Last Wednesday, in front of several witnesses and on school property," Art began, "Sam shoved a student so hard that the boy fell over, cracked his skull, and starting bleeding inside his brain. I know his mother. She serves with me on the County School Board. We spoke as recently as last night. Her son's life is in danger. They're hoping for a complete recovery but fearing the absolute worst."

"Sam, I'm so sorry," Allison said.

"Me too," added Dolores. "I was very upset when Art first told me what happened."

"I'm sure there's another side to this." Allison said.

"Of course there is," I added.

But no sooner did I finish my sentence than Art began his next one. "I've spoken to a mutual friend of the boy's mother. She's explained Sam's perspective to me. Apparently, the boy was bullying another student, and to his credit, Sam came to break things up. But from what the witnesses are saying, Sam went ballistic and attacked the young man with excessive force. The boy went flying across the room and hit his head. If another teacher hadn't come by right away, the boy might have died on the spot."

"What do you say, Sam? Did he get all the facts right?" Allison asked.

"That was the most one-sided summary I've ever heard," I said.

But again, Art was quick to continue making his point. "I didn't come here tonight to sit in judgment. Let he who is without sin ... right? Who am I to act as prosecutor?"

"What *is* your point then?" asked Linda.

"Simple. Sam shouldn't be writing our report. He'll be *way* too preoccupied."

"I ... I'll be fine," I stammered. "Trust me, I'll have plenty of time to write that report."

"*With all due respect,*" Art growled, facing me for the first time that evening, "if you're feeling cocky about the situation, you've got no clue what kind of trouble you're in."

"Look," I said, raising my voice and speaking quickly, "these bullies had formed a circle around a student. The student was being sexually abused by your friend's son. So I pushed him out of the way, and he stumbled and hurt himself. I'm sorry about that, but that doesn't mean I'm the culprit."

"Whether you're innocent or not, there are a whole lot of students pointing their fingers in your direction," Art said, and joined their ranks with a gesture of his own.

"Consider the source," I said. "Those are the same kids who formed a circle and watched as their buddy was about to get a blowjob. They're your witnesses."

"Not my witnesses, pal. I'm not your prosecutor. I'm only concerned about this group and its work product. Our host is shelling out more than $300,000 for us to write him one heck of a report. I can't imagine he'd want us to assign that responsibility to *you*!"

Art paused, as if he, too, noticed how condescending and hateful he sounded. That gave me a chance to respond.

"I suppose our host would want his report written by someone who would sit back and watch some bullies abuse and humiliate an innocent student. Is that what you think?"

As soon as I said that I realized that my logic was flimsy. Sure enough, Art pounced on it. "You want to know what I think? OK, I think you could have stopped the assault in its tracks just by yelling at the kids. You didn't have to shove the boy with all your might. You used too much force, big fella. All the students there will tell you the same thing. You've got some serious temper issues."

Art was certainly correct about that. Right then, I wanted to take one of his clients' telephones and smash his brains in.

"I appreciate that it might be good therapy for Sam to write the report," Art continued, in a more tempered tone, "but we've got obligations to the man who's paying the freight, not just to Sam and his psyche. We need to appoint another person to head the committee. This is an easy call."

Just then, I noticed Eileen's face, and my mind drifted back to when she had been singing in Allison's apartment. As our eyes met on the night of her performance, the world and its stresses slowed down to a waltz. The same thing happened after Art made his smug, "easy-call" comment and I looked at Eileen. All of a sudden, I felt myself relax.

For a moment, the Creed Room was completely quiet. Eileen broke the silence. "I only have one question. Sam, do you want to lead the committee and write the report?"

"Definitely," I said.

"That's it for me, then," Eileen shrugged. "I don't want to seem callous, and I certainly hope the boy recovers, but this story sounds like little more than a bully experiencing the laws of karma. Art, the next time you talk to your School Board friend, maybe you should suggest that she can't expect a teacher to come upon that scene and know exactly what buttons to push with her son.

"I'm convinced Sam can get out a quality report for us. But let me ask the other members of the committee. What do you think? Do you vote to replace him?"

The eyes in the room turned toward Dolores. Seeing that, Shaw deferred.

"I don't know how anyone can question a lot of what Art said," Dolores began. "Even Sam would have to agree he's in a pickle. Worrying too much about our report might not be what he needs to do right now."

"Maybe not," Eileen said, "but Sam's decided that he can take care of his personal issues *and* write the report. Isn't that his decision to make?"

Dolores paused for a moment. She had the look of a deer blinded by headlights.

That's when Shaw entered the fray. "Ain't nothin' like a schoolhouse bully. If I were in Sam's position, I'd have done the same thing to that punk. *You know* I'd love to write the report myself, but I wouldn't take that away from Sam just for standing up to a bully. Eileen's right."

"Thanks," I said to Shaw.

Again, all eyes converged on Dolores, and again, she was having trouble finding words. "If only *he* could let us know how he wants us to handle this," Dolores sighed, pointing at the camera. As our heads tilted upward toward the ceiling, the light began flashing on and off. It was Feaver's way of saying "How many times do I have to tell you to leave me out of this and make your own decisions?"

Finally, a look of clarity appeared on Dolores's face. "Art, tell Charlotte she'd better worry about helping her son get better, not ruining Sam's life. Yeah, I'm OK with going ahead as planned."

That was the cue Linda needed. "So it's decided. The committee wants Sam to be in charge. Art, *with all due respect*, as you like to say, my judgment as coordinator is that these are the people who ought to decide who gets to run their committee. They volunteered to be on it when you said you were too busy. Let's not forget that. Eileen, why don't you begin your talk?"

The remainder of the session went smoothly. I especially loved watching Eileen mix it up for the first time. Perhaps it was the subject—animals' rights—that got her juices flowing. Perhaps it was Art's attempt at a coup. Whatever the cause, I had a blast watching her slice and dice Keister's justifications for animal slaughter, or, as he would say, for preserving animal species either by thinning the herd or giving people a reason to raise animals in the first place.

I'd heard the debate before but never heard the animal rights side argued half as well. The effectiveness of Eileen's rhetoric shouldn't have surprised me. Allison once told me that Eileen had the best law school grades of the Triumvirate, in spite of her complaints about how much she loathed law school. "She doesn't talk a lot," Allison said, "but she's sharp as a tack."

That Creed Room session was a turning point for me, a heck of a cure for my depression and insecurity. I was exposed to two competing perspectives on my predicament at school—Art's and Eileen's. With each shot from Eileen's lens, Art's grew cloudier and cloudier.

He denied that he was putting me on trial. He claimed to be saying only that I'd be too preoccupied to write an excellent report. But that sham didn't fool me. The truth was that Art was indicting my character. As someone who failed to use proper restraint in a potentially deadly situation, I deserved, he felt, to be his latest object of condescension.

Thinking of Art stirred my resolve not to allow him or anyone else to deflate my self confidence. That resolve was made so much more potent because of Eileen. What prompted her to trust me so? To treat me with such respect? When people honor you like that, the last thing you want to do is let them down.

Early the next day, Ericsson's secretary called. She told me that George London seemed to be healing—no doubt, a testament to the recuperative powers of kids. It was the best news I could possibly have heard. I immediately passed it on to my mother, who sobbed tears of relief.

I was also told that Ericsson wanted to see my attorney and me on the following Monday. That gave me the rest of the week to enjoy as I pleased. During the next three days, I hit four book stores, two movie theatres and three museums. I also ran into none other than Paul Choulos. We spoke about the mess I was in at school, and I told him that I suspected Art Sherman of being an Empire Club plant.

"I'm not surprised," he said. "Sherman's—how do you say it? He's the redneck in the group, not Keister. He thinks he can hide that with his money. He can't hide anything."

Choulos asked me whether, given what I knew about Feaver and suspected about Sherman, I was only going to the Victorian for the money.

"Are you kidding?" I said. "It's the best thing I've got going right now. Look at my situation in school?"

"But you can only imagine what those pigs are going to do with the video tapes of your discussions," he said. "They'll make you sorry you ever opened your mouth in that room."

"You're just paranoid," I replied.

"You're just *young*, my friend. I'm a bit older, yes? I've seen more horrors. I know what happens when money and power get together. It's an ugly marriage."

Choulos' point rang true, but I was in no mood those days to face reality. After finally getting some good news from school, I craved even more of an uplift, not a cold shower. So on Friday morning, I found out Eileen's class schedule from Allison and took the subway to the Georgetown Law Center. Eileen didn't notice me waiting for her as she walked out of her classroom. "Counselor?" I said, from a few feet behind her, "why such a hurry?" She turned around and did a double take when she saw my face. Then, she smiled.

"My God. Wwwhat are—"

"I came to see you. Allison told me your schedule."

"Wow," she said. "It's such a nice surprise."

"You seem to be in a rush."

"Just to get away from that room, that's all."

"Great prof, huh?"

"They don't come any humbler. The joy we get when Brockman shows off her brilliance at a student's expense ... its infectious. Know what I mean?"

"Absolutely," I replied, recalling that Allison had told her friends I had dropped out of Harvard Law School. "Harvard's Ego Department is the largest in the university."

"Actually, most of the profs here are OK, but this lady's a shrew."

"Eileen," I said, changing both the subject and my tone, "I wanted to thank you for what you said on Tuesday night, and to see if you'd be willing to go out for lunch, my treat."

"Oh, you don't have to—"

"Of course I don't have to. I *want* to. I'd love to hang out with you today."

Eileen smiled again. "I'm free all afternoon. Let's go enjoy the city."

And we did. In fact, we spent the rest of the day together. I didn't get back home until a few minutes before midnight. Unlike Allison, Eileen was happy to let me set the agenda, except for meal times. Then, she was very firm: "No food cooked by white people."

"Come again?" I asked.

"I'm serious. I can eat Chinese. Japanese. Vietnamese. Indonesian. Thai. Indian. Middle Eastern. If it's not European, I can probably find at least a couple of dishes with a good amount of vegetable protein. The European restaurants usually have nothing."

"So you boycott them as a matter of principle?"

"I try," she replied. "If people want to eat meat that's their business. But I get ticked off when they open up restaurants and don't have options for vegans. We need our protein like everyone else. It's not hard to have a token bean or tofu dish on the menu."

Allison had told me that Eileen was completely vegan—she wouldn't eat dairy products or eggs, let alone animal flesh. "I didn't know there were any vegans in the Midwest," I said.

"Minneapolis is a bit of an oasis. Have you ever been?"

"The closest I've come is Chicago. Saw a slaughterhouse there as a matter of fact."

"Ooh baby," she said. "Love that big, broad-shouldered, manly kind of town. Love *any* town known for its butcheries."

"That meat made me good and hungry," I said, smiling.

"I'll bet. You know, I'd almost rather see a bull fight than go to one of those places. At least at the bull fight I could root for the bull. Who could I root for at a slaughterhouse?"

"Maybe for one of the workers to drop a meat cleaver on his foot."

"Hey," Eileen said, "you might be onto something there." No sooner had Eileen finished her sentence than we both started laughing, in my case at the whole idea of a vindictive vegan.

"I've got a question for you," I said.

"Shoot."

"Do you think the Benefactor sells fake art?" I asked.

Eileen thought for a moment. "Do you think Hillary Clinton's gay?"

"I don't know."

"Me neither," she said. And yes, I got her point.

I had a wonderful time that day. We checked out the Zoo,

the National Cathedral, and the Statecraft and Literature book store, which is one of the few sizeable bookstores left in Washington that doesn't have a sister franchisee in every soulless American suburb. I told Eileen that I hadn't been to Statecraft and Literature for a while, and the recent Creed Room discussions were whetting my appetite for political theory.

"I get kind of sick of that stuff, to be honest with you," she said. "I see law students all day, and D.C. law students at that. Anything political is *so* important to them."

"Shadows on the cave wall?" I said, harkening back to an image from Plato.

"Yup," she replied, smiling. "That would fit."

"I figured you weren't a political junkie."

"Don't get me wrong, I care about politics. I just don't like to think of it as our ultimate concern," Eileen said.

"When a big election is coming up, I definitely get carried away. It obsesses me, like when the 'Skins are in the Super Bowl. But that doesn't mean I think politicians are half as important as *they* think they are."

"It's not only politicians who think they're so important," Eileen said. "It's their staffers, and the media too. You'd think the fate of the cosmos turns on what they do for a living."

Listening to Eileen's critique of white-collar Washington, I could only muster the following response: "At least they're not apathetic."

"There you go again with apathy," she said. "Don't you understand we're all apathetic about a whole lot of things? Why does it bother you so much when you're interested in something and other people aren't?"

"Politics is different," I said, while thinking about the Jeffersonian ideal that in a republic, everyone needs to be educated and involved in the political process. "Let me put it this way. It's like we're all climbing a mountain together. If you don't give a damn about what we're doing, you'll make it that much scarier for the rest of us."

Eileen shook her head. "*You* might want to climb a mountain. That doesn't mean everyone else should want to."

That day, I didn't quite earn a Ph.D. in Eileen Mitchell but was well on the way to nabbing a Masters. For starters, I learned a lot about her upbringing. I had already known about her father's service with the FBI. Her mother, I was told, was a homemaker for years before becoming a preschool teacher. When Eileen was five, the Mitchells settled down in Edina, a Minneapolis suburb. Eileen had two older sisters, both of whom remained in the area.

Nominally Methodist, Eileen's parents rarely attended church and didn't expect their children to attend either. Politically, their only credo was that they voted for "the person, not the party," and they spoke little to their kids about current events. Dinner time at the Mitchell's consisted largely of the kids summarizing their days at school, Mrs. Mitchell talking about her volunteer activities, and lengthy spaces of time where the only audible sounds were the chewing of food ... or polite compliments to the chef. I'm sure Mr. Mitchell could have told some interesting stories about his job, but he didn't feel comfortable sharing them.

That was the sheltered life Eileen knew when she met a boy named Brad Flynn in high school. She was nearing the end of her sophomore year, and he was a junior. Quickly, the two became inseparable. He played guitar and sang, inspiring her to find those talents in herself. Then, midway through his senior year, Brad was "born again." He joined a church in a small town about a half hour south of Minneapolis where the members frequently spoke in tongues, engaged in faith healing and "witnessed" to strangers.

Before Brad's conversion, Eileen looked at him as the essence of cool. But that stopped when Brad joined the Church of the Nazarene. She absolutely hated his proselytizing. Still, she had trouble breaking up with him, as he treated her with as much affection as ever.

By the time Eileen finally ended the relationship before the start of her senior year, Brad had left an indelible mark. He proved to her that people's religious beliefs can totally transform their lives. His example also convinced her that someday, if she kept her eyes and ears open, she could have an epiphany of her own.

After her year with Brad Flynn, Eileen became a sponge. As a high school senior, she soaked up guitar chords, literary masterpieces and her teachers' lectures. Then, as a freshman at the University of Minnesota, she began a course of study in both Western and Eastern philosophy. By the time she graduated, Eileen had become well versed not only in those disciplines but in the humanities generally. In the "life of the mind and spirit," to use her words, she found her epiphany.

To help me understand her new attitude as a college graduate, Eileen quoted an unpublished statement that Nietzsche was said to have written to his sister: "If you want to find peace of mind and happiness, then believe; if you want to be a disciple of truth, then search." Eileen's point was clear to me: the search for truth is better than its possession. Lady Philosophy had claimed another victim.

We were sitting at a restaurant when Eileen quoted from Nietzsche's letter to his sister. As she finished her sentence and waited for my response, I experienced a powerful feeling—a distinct rush of pleasure that seemed, briefly, to penetrate every pore of my body and soul. I recognized the feeling instantly. It was the feeling of love—not infatuation, but love. When I had experienced it before, it had nothing to do with any flesh and blood human being, and certainly not with any of my old girl-friends. For all of the passion of my past relationships with women, I had never been confident that they'd last. My goals in life and those of my girlfriends had always been so different.

That evening, as the rush of pleasure came and went, its significance overwhelmed me. I knew enough not to count on Eileen sharing my emotions of love, but I couldn't help but recognize the importance of my discovery: if she were willing to have me, then I had found my soul mate.

So I reached out and, for the first time, touched her hand. And when I did, all felt well with the world.

CHAPTER 12

PRUDENCE

"*I*t's so nice to finally get this off my chest," Dolores said, walking into my apartment.

"Come in. Relax. Welcome to my humble abode."

"Nonsense," she said. "There's nothing humble about it. It's cozy. It's all anyone needs."

"I'd guess from seeing your house, you've got a bit more, huh?"

"Just a little," she said, smiling.

"So what's up?" I asked.

"Here's the deal. I'll tell you what I know. You were so nice to drive me home from Allison's party, and I remember you asking for this one favor in return."

"I figured you were too smashed to remember."

She smiled. "I can function better on liquor than you'd think. Listen, what I'm about to say, you've got to keep just between us. Do you promise?"

"Yes. Unless you give me permission later," I said.

"Deal. This is what happened. Art sometimes gets up in the middle of the night. When he's on his cell phone at that hour, I'm figuring he's talking to a member of his society."

"You mean a cell mate."

"Very funny," she said. "The other night, when he got up,

I eavesdropped. I stood in another room and listened. He didn't do much talking. But he said enough that I could tell he's been taking orders from someone about what to do in the Creed Room."

"Damn! That's what I was afraid of."

"I know. Me too. And I'm not just afraid for our group. I'm afraid for my husband. These people *own* him."

"How do you know?" I asked.

"Because I know Art, and I've picked up bits and pieces of conversations over the years."

"So everything he has been saying has somehow been choreographed?"

"I doubt it," she said. "I can tell you this: what you've heard from Art is the same stuff he's been telling me for years. But they're definitely putting him on a leash. The other night, just before he got off the phone, they made him swear that in the future, he wouldn't be too outspoken. 'I'll tone it down. I swear to you.' Those were his exact words."

"Who are these people?" I asked. "Why do they care about the Creed Room?"

"Sam, I really don't know."

"So where does that leave us?"

She paused for a while and then threw up her hands. "I guess we should just be ourselves. It's about us, not them, like you said before."

"I did, didn't I?" I said. "Now I'm beginning to wonder."

The bell rang to announce the end of sixth period. Karen Block and I were supposed to have met with Ericsson 15 minutes earlier, and I was getting impatient.

Just then, Charlotte London walked out of the principal's

office. As she proceeded past the waiting room where Karen and I were seated, she turned her head long enough to grace us with the look of a sworn enemy. At her side was a tall, lean man in a dark suit. I didn't recognize him by face but knew him by type. He was in his mid 40s, with dark hair that greyed around the temples. He passed us with his nose tilted upward and without even acknowledging our presence. The image was so repulsive that I chose instead to imagine him 20 years younger, attending classes at Harvard Law School, or perhaps Yale. Back then, he would have been dutifully attending to his professors' every word, much like his father did before him. Only after graduating and devoting the required seven or eight years before he could reach his manifest destiny (partnership) could he achieve his equilibrium state of absolute smugness. That's the face Karen and I saw gliding by.

Shortly after they left, another unfamiliar man emerged from Ericsson's office. "Hi, I'm Ralph Leeden," he said, shaking my hand. "I'm an attorney with the County. Hi Karen."

"Hello Ralph," she replied.

"We're not quite ready yet," said Leeden. "If you could bear with us for a few more minutes, we'd really appreciate it."

"Take whatever time you need," Karen said. Then, after Leeden went back in Ericsson's office and closed the door, she leaned over to me and whispered, "He's a son of a bitch."

"Great, just great," I replied.

"I've seen him operate too many times. I'll never trust him again."

"Pretty zealous advocate, huh?"

"As zealous as they come. Lots of lawyers specialize in misleading people, but most of them stop short of the outright lie. Leeden can lie as easily as he can breathe."

As we continued to wait, my thoughts turned away from

Leeden and toward Ericsson. Lenny had taught me never to trust a bureaucrat, even if he acts like my friend. "The smart ones," Lenny said, "the ones you'd like to trust, don't forget that they're survivors. They'll do what they need to cover their asses. *Anyone* under them is expendable. That's the iron law of bureaucracy."

Finally, after we were waiting outside his office for at least a half an hour, Ericsson invited us in and asked us to take our seats. "I've got some wonderful news," he said. "George London was just released from the hospital, and his doctors feel that he will recover none the worse."

I let out a long, audible sigh, before saying the obvious: "Music to my ears."

"We expect him back in school in two or three weeks," Ericsson continued. "He still has some recuperating to do and follow-ups with his doctors."

We spoke a bit more about the details of London's ordeal. Then Leeden began presenting the county's proposal. "First, you would be officially reprimanded for your conduct. I'm referring to the grossly excessive use of force, which could easily have caused a child permanent brain damage, *or even death!*"

"Second, you must attend 40 hours of anger management counseling. That's eight hours per week for the next five weeks. They hold them on Saturdays; we'll give you a schedule."

That's absurdly demeaning, I thought to myself, but quickly did the math and realized that I could finish those classes well before the time came to finalize the Creed Room report.

"Lastly, until further notice, you'd be required to submit your lesson plans for *all* your classes to Principal Ericsson at least one week in advance of each lesson. The lesson—"

"What?" I exclaimed, interrupting Leeden.

"Please, Sam, let him finish," Karen said. "Go ahead, Ralph."

"The lesson plans would be subject to editing by Principal Ericsson or curriculum specialists in the Superintendent's office. We'll brook absolutely no argument from you if you disagree with any edits made. We simply haven't the time for that."

I couldn't stop myself from reacting, even after Karen tried to stifle me. "What does the amount of force I used on George's shoulder have to do with the lessons I'm planning for class? This is insane!"

"We've talked before about the judgment you've used in the classroom," Ericsson said. "You've already been required to submit your philosophy lesson plans to me. Now this happens. Sam, it's not only about anger management; it's about your *judgment*. We're willing to give you another chance, but only if we keep you on a leash."

The conversation went on for a few more minutes. Karen had words with Leeden, who threatened that if I fought the county and lost, I could kiss my teaching career goodbye forever, "at least in the USA." This was my chance—and "a pretty darned generous one at that," I was told.

I left the room in need of an immediate anger management session. The bureaucracy was driving me crazier than ever. "They're telling me in no uncertain terms that they want me the hell out of this school," I told Karen. "They can't kick me out, so they're going to try to drive me out with their Kafkaesque rules. Am I wrong?"

"Who knows what they're really thinking? I need to know what *you're* thinking. Like how much it would hurt you to accept their terms. Or what kind of risks you're willing to take. I think we'd win if we fought them, but I can't guarantee anything."

I decided to sleep on the county's proposal for a couple of days before getting back to Karen. I hated both options and had no idea which one to take. I knew only whom I wanted to help make the decision.

Tuesday, March 21st was the first of two Creed Room sessions devoted to "Lessons from History." It was Linda's idea. She asked each of us to prepare to discuss those lessons from history that we found most notable.

In one mini-presentation, Keister spoke about the pacifist movements in the U.S. and Europe before World War II. Allison and I had discussed the same topic at Antietam—how the pacifists, had they been more persuasive, would have paved the way for Nazi rule. But Keister used that fact to justify America serving as the world's policeman. I took him to be suggesting that our destiny would be to bat down one third-world despot after another in a perpetual game of Whack a Mole. Keister didn't seem to think the Empire needed to worry about picking its spots. He said we'd always have the superior military force as long as we remained capitalistic and committed to peace through strength.

I expected at least Art to agree with Fred, but he was as cautious about military action as the rest of us. "It's about time other countries took care of their own problems," Art argued. "Why should our G.I.s bail them out every time they don't like their government? Someone should tell them that we don't have a War Department any more. It's called the Defense Department, and it's supposed to defend *us*, not *them!* The last thing we need is to blow a country to bits and then have to get involved in nation building."

"You don't get it, do you?" Keister said. "Them dictators got to be dealt with now or else they're only gonna get worse. Nukes, chemicals, you name it, they'll have 'em, and they'll use 'em against us sooner or later unless we act first."

Art rolled his eyes. "They wouldn't dare, Fred. It's no secret who's boss. As long as we keep our military strong, we'll be fine. We just can't let the liberals cut defense spending."

(A couple of weeks later, I asked Dolores how Art could be a member of an "Empire Club" if he's so isolationist. I'd always thought empires gobble other countries up. "States rights," she replied. "He's a big believer in state sovereignty. It's almost like he thinks of the U.S. as an empire composed of 50 semi-independent nations.")

After Art finished, a few of us continued to argue with Keister. We questioned why the U.S. should be trusted to decide which foreign regimes to topple and how many foreigners should die. We haven't exactly shown sensitivity in dealing with people who aren't white. If we're going to mistreat African Americans, Japanese Americans or Native Americans, how can we think we're qualified to act as the world's police force?

Then, something occurred that hadn't happened in the Creed Room before or since: a presenter said that the group's discussion changed his mind. That's right. Fred admitted he was wrong. We didn't give medals, but if we had, he might have deserved one that night.

My favorite "lesson from history" came from Allison. She spoke about the Jewish community after they were exiled from their homeland in the 2nd Century C.E. That's when the rabbis decided to write down the "oral law" that had been passed down from generation to generation as a complement to the Torah. Over the course of centuries, Allison explained, the written rabbinic code grew to form what is known today as the Talmud. Orthodox Jews credit it with divine inspiration and believe that it is every bit as binding as the Torah.

"As far as I'm concerned," Allison said, "the creation of the

Talmud was a tragedy. I know there's incredible wisdom in those books, but they never should have been written down as law and certainly not as the *completion* of the law."

"When a religion's holiest truths are all put in writing and accepted as the word of God, it becomes like a tree severed from its roots," Allison said. "A religion's lifeblood is precisely what *isn't* written down. It's the ability of each person to think for herself about what's sacred and what's profane, and to depend upon other people's *spoken* words to enlighten us. If it's oral, it's rough, it's unpolished. It's also flexible. That's what religion should be. You can't carve it all in stone, or else it stops being a guide and starts becoming a master, and we become its slaves."

As I listened to Allison, I felt myself agreeing with nearly every word. If only we could turn back the clock to the 2nd century and keep the "oral law" from being written down, I wondered, how different would Judaism—especially "Orthodox" Judaism—be today?

After the session ended, Eileen was halfway out the front door when I touched her on the arm. "I really need to talk to you about school," I said. "Do you have any time tonight?" From her initial reaction, I could tell that she didn't, but after some prodding, she finally agreed to come to my apartment on the condition that I'd drive her home afterward.

Eileen was all business from the minute she walked through my door. She had me recount my meeting with Ericsson. Then she wanted to know how I felt about my options.

I told her that winning a legal battle wouldn't give me some whopping thrill. I didn't feel the need for vindication. I knew I'd messed up, but I also knew it wasn't the crime of the century.

As for the problems with accepting Ericsson's terms, I confessed that it was the lesson plan monitoring that especially ticked me off. "It's sickening to have Ericsson edit my philosophy lessons. Do you think I want to be treated like a child for *all* my classes? I might as well come to school in diapers."

"Please Sam, don't you realize who you're talking to?" Eileen was preparing to work at the Minnesota Attorney General's Office, where her "superiors" would have to review all her proposals before they would ever see the light of day.

I told Eileen a story about Spinoza. Excommunicated at 23 by the Jewish community, he eked out an existence as a lens grinder and wrote philosophy during the wee hours of the night. A university offered to hire him as a philosophy professor, but he didn't accept. He was too afraid that the university would restrict his right to teach the "heresies" he believed to be true. So instead of growing old in a cushy academic job, he died at 44 when the lens particles he inhaled infected his lungs.

"I'm no Spinoza, but I'm entitled to a little academic freedom," I told Eileen.

"But you've already been submitting your philosophy lesson plans in advance. How will this be so much worse?"

"A matter of degree, I suppose. I see Ericsson, and I'm eaten up by resentment. There's no feeling more degrading than that."

I kept Eileen talking for almost two hours. When I saw her stifle a yawn, I looked at the time. It was almost midnight, and she was clearly exhausted. "Listen," I said. "I'll take you home if you'd like, but it's late. Why don't you stay till morning? You can have the bed. I'll be happy to take the couch."

"That's OK, I can go," she said, before yawning again.

"Look at you. You're practically asleep. Come on, stay the night. I promise to get you where you need to be tomorrow morning."

Eileen closed her eyes for a few seconds. "Alright," she

finally said. "Do you have something I can wear? And do you mind if I make a phone call? It'll just take me a minute."

While Eileen made her call, I rustled up one of my softest Redskins T-Shirts and a pair of flannel pajama bottoms and threw some clean sheets on the bed. Within seconds, she was out. I desperately wanted to crawl in beside her and not just to go to sleep.

My thoughts turned to Jacob, the Biblical patriarch. Even though he had to work for many years before he could marry Rachel, the time passed quickly because she was always nearby. For me, though, watching Eileen that night was pure agony. While she slept, I spent several minutes puttering around the bedroom—getting out my night clothes, closing drawers, setting the alarm clock, adjusting blankets. The idea of loving a woman in the spirit of Jacob struck me as masochism.

I didn't decide to accept the deal until the next evening. First, I spoke to Lenny and asked what he thought. He essentially told me I needed to choose my battles in life, and this shouldn't be one of them. "What principle is at stake here? The right for a teacher to really screw up, as long as his heart is in the right place?"

"What about a teacher's right to stand up for himself?" I said. "I'm not just talking about standing up to the bureaucracy. I'm also thinking about those thugs who vandalized my house."

"Forget about them," Lenny said. "I bet you those kids just wanted to get even. Now they've done it. You've got to let it go."

After I spoke to Lenny, Mother called. I told her that I was inclined to compromise. She responded by lecturing me mercilessly about being a "lemech," which is Yiddish for someone who lets other people push him around.

I was fine at first with her expressing her opinion. Believe me, I understood the urge to fight the school like a demon. But especially after talking to Eileen and Lenny, I realized that there really were two sides to this issue, and continuing the fight simply wasn't worth it. Anyway, once my mother weighed in and relentlessly ridiculed the idea of a compromise, I blew up at her, and at that point, the die was cast. "Anger management class," I said to myself, "here I come! Five sessions? Maybe that won't be enough."

A couple of days later, Karen and I announced my decision in Ericsson's office. He thanked us and said only that he looked forward to seeing me bright and early Monday morning.

"It's finally over," I told Karen, after walking her to her car. "I don't know what I would have done without you."

"You'd have been fine," she replied. "You're a prudent man."

"Only when I think before I act," I said. "Maybe one of these days, I'll keep that in mind."

Ever since my Thanksgiving visit to a Charlottesville synagogue, I had spent most Friday evenings at a Reform temple and most Saturdays relaxing and abstaining from work. That was about to change. For the next several weeks, my Saturdays would be devoted to anger management. Were they relaxing? Hardly. But neither were my Sundays, nor my Mondays ...

Art hit the nail on the head. I had become a very busy boy.

School demanded a lot of time. I needed to catch up on what the students had been doing when I was gone. Plus, I needed to draft a slew of lesson plans that could somehow meet my approval *and* survive the scrutiny of petty functionaries.

Believe me, that was no simple task.

My Creed Room duties were also mounting. From the end of March through early May, the Benefactor's Committee—as Eileen, Dolores, Shaw and I called ourselves—met each week on Thursday evenings and Sundays.

I was so busy during that time that I had to miss a ton of March Madness. That felt like a much greater indignity than spending hours during the Sabbath listening to psycho babble.

The transition back to the job of teaching went smoothly enough. Some students scowled at me, particularly the football players, but most of the kids were great. They told me how much they had been looking forward to my return and how badly they felt that I was ever suspended.

As for George London, he came back to school a couple of weeks after I did. When we first saw each other, he was holding court in jock hall. "Look out everybody," he said, sneering at me. "Here comes the Angry Man. I hope all you dudes are insured."

"Hello, George," I said, putting my new patience skills to the test. "Glad to see you're feeling better."

"I bet you are. If I wasn't, they wouldn't let you back in this building."

"Let's get over all that, shall we?" I said, gritting my teeth.

"You'd like that, wouldn't you? Tell me, how's your wrist?"

"What?"

"My mom said Ericsson slapped it a bit. Sure hope it's feelin' better. I'd love to slap it as hard as you slapped me. But I don't think the school would like that very much."

"I see your tongue is feeling back to normal," I said. Truth be told, a student's backtalk had never sounded better to me. His current behavior, directly in line with the unpleasant George London I had always known, suggested that he really didn't suffer any permanent effects from his head trauma. That possibility had seriously plagued my conscience over the previous few weeks.

"Oh, I'm back to normal alright. Fit enough to deal with the likes of you. Don't think I've forgotten how chicken shit you were to shove me when I wasn't even bracin' for a scrap. If you try that again, I'll be ready for ya'. I can see you comin' now."

"You can see me *leaving* now," I said, before heading down the hall and away from his line of sight. I had no choice but to ignore London completely from that point on. Any other path would be too combustible.

CHAPTER 13

HERESIES

The first Creed Room session in April was a bridge of sorts—the last week before Linda turned control over the group to the Benefactor's Committee. To honor the occasion, Linda the Coordinator gave way to Linda the Preacher. This was her swan song, and she made the most of it. During the first 45 minutes, she spoke without a break. She also didn't worry about pulling punches. In the past, I always felt that she held herself back so as not to compromise her ability to mediate disputes. That night, though, we witnessed pure, opinionated Linda. I didn't agree with many of her positions, but she delivered her views with such dignity and passion that I was disappointed when she stopped lecturing and opened the floor for discussion.

"Tonight," she began, "I want to explore the meaning of the word 'humanist.' It's a word my parents never used when I was growing up. Their lives were centered around heaven and God. My mama told me that life in this world is only a test. Pass, and you spend eternity without guilt. Fail, and you suffer even worse than you do on earth.

"My mama knew all about suffering. She worked like a dog every day. Daddy too. For as long as I've known him, he's held two jobs. He was too proud to let the family go on welfare.

"I first heard about Humanism with a capital H as a freshman at Boston University. A friend of mine grew up in Wellesley, and she took me to her family's church, which called itself Humanistic. The minister said that Humanism was all about taking responsibility for ourselves and our neighbors before we blow ourselves up or pollute ourselves sick. He mocked traditional religions, and he especially ridiculed fundamentalists like my parents.

"Going to that church became a guilty pleasure. The more I thought about how my parents would have reacted, the more I enjoyed it. 'Sinners one and all'—that's what they would have said. But I was intrigued. The church gave me a vision of the future where *we* control our own beliefs, not some holy man or book. The future that mattered to this church was in this life. And I liked that, for I couldn't care less about the hereafter. I wanted to think that people working together could solve the world's problems by appealing to logic and common sense—not *dogma*."

Linda winked at Allison, and then continued.

"I still love that vision. But social visions are easy to come by. They're much harder to implement. And that's where I parted company with the good people of Wellesley Humanist.

"To understand that place, start with one fact: everyone there is rich. You'd think they'd realize how little they know about poor people, but modesty isn't their greatest virtue. In fact, they're quite conceited. That starts with all the pride they take in their willingness to give money, either through private charity or high taxes. Call it noblesse oblige.

"The religion of Wellesley Humanism has both nobles and saints. The nobles are the ones who vote against their own wallets out of a sense of obligation to the underprivileged. The saints are the social workers or the teachers who work in the inner cities. Many are committed enough to pay the ultimate sacrifice and give up their affluent lifestyle, at least if they haven't married into money or inherited a bundle. They wouldn't have to move to Southie, but maybe to Somerville.

"Unfortunately, there's more to the religion than nobles and saints. We can't forget the poor people. You hear about them all the time in Wellesley—just not as individuals. They serve as objects, fragments of a homogenized mass. That's why the Wellesley church is guilty of false advertising. Their religion shouldn't be called Humanism, but Homogenism.

"At the heart of the Homogenist world are billions of people who are down on their luck. They don't have names, nor personalities. They're viewed generically—as beneficiaries of the world's nobles and saints. The do-gooders are the ones with personalties. They're the ones who are unique—*he's* a powerful fund-raiser, *she's* a devoted teacher, the other one's a loving social worker, the one over there is a brilliant medical researcher.

"If Homogenists were truly concerned about helping the poor, they'd study people, like my family, who've actually risen from poverty. We can tell you how to defeat it. We can tell you the key difference between Humanism and Homogenism: Homogenism focuses on the pride you get from helping others; Humanism creates conditions where poor people can help themselves.

"Do you know what Welleslyites can do to help? I mean *really* help? They can make friends with poor people. Hang out with them, empathize with them, have them over for dinner. But the *worst* thing the Wellesleyites can do is walk into a poor neighborhood ready to dole out presents. That just discourages people from working, and hard work is the only way poor people can set a positive example for their kids. The second worst thing is to spew anti-corporate rhetoric that makes people feel victimized. Poor people can't afford a negative attitude. They've got to respect their societies as much as themselves. They need the faith of Horatio Alger that with a little luck and a heaping of pluck, *any* American can reach her dreams. Talk to someone who's escaped from poverty. She'll tell you the same thing. There's no other way out!

"I won't deny that the government can do some things to reduce poverty. Create enterprise zones. Provide tax breaks. Offer scholarships to pursue an education outside of the ghettos. If the government is creative and smart, it can come up with any number of good ideas. Just hear this: none of that means anything if the nation's poor don't develop some faith in themselves *and* in America. Without that faith, they can't stay motivated, and without motivation, they'll never accomplish much of anything. But if they keep their faith, I have enough confidence in the rest of the human race that we won't let them down. I am, after all, a Humanist."

Linda went on to flesh out a conservative world view that fit well within the mainstream of the GOP—at least in its economic principles. When she finished, neither Shaw nor Allison jumped on her. They jousted a bit, but with the utmost diplomacy. I later asked Shaw to explain why the kid gloves. He replied that Linda was entitled to respect because "she came by her views honestly, not from the usual combination of self-interest and rationalization."

Who could disagree? Many people let their careers or social standing dictate their beliefs. Others are slaves to the views of their parents. Yet another group conforms to their circle of friends. It was as clear as day that none of the above applied to Linda. She selected her views in isolation, based simply on observation, inference and integrity.

At the end of the session, Linda fought back tears. She thanked everyone for treating her so respectfully, both as a coordinator and a pundit. Then she rummaged into her backpack and pulled out a baton. "Sam," she said, before handing it to me, "If your committee tries to give equal time to eight people, there's no way you can produce a coherent report. *Please*—don't worry about our egos. We're all adults.

"And now, your baton."

As Linda handed it to me, the group began to applaud. I put the baton down and joined them. Then everyone rose to their feet. There we stood, applause ringing throughout the Creed Room and, surely, throughout the house, for the better part of a minute.

It's about *us*, not *them*, I kept saying to myself. And I wouldn't let myself forget it. Just then, I felt so thankful for having Linda as our coordinator and so lucky for getting to know these wonderful people.

If there's no lower feeling than resentment, there's none higher than the sense of being blessed.

April in Washington is beautiful. It's definitely the best month of the year, at least when it's not raining. This is especially true when the cherry blossoms are out. Tourists flock to the Tidal Basin to see an impressive ring of white and pale-pink petals lining a small body of water. But Washingtonians know that the cherry blossoms are loveliest on the narrow side streets where the trees' branches engulf the road with their canopy of color. The area seems so peaceful then, so removed from the partisan bickering and ambitious posturing that often dominates the town.

Washingtonians wouldn't trade their cherry blossoms for

any plant in the world, but the pathos of these trees is hardly a secret and reflects much of what is unique about living in the D.C. area. The cherry blossom petals depart after only about ten days of blooming each spring. Then Washingtonians shake their heads at the idea that just as they have begun to appreciate their city, an important part of its beauty has vanished. Similarly, it so often happens that just as you make a new friend in the D.C. area, it's time for him or her to move out. Foreign diplomats come and go, as do many who staff the executive and legislative branches of our government. After a few years, they move back "home," which is presumably a friendlier, less career-obsessed existence. Even when they go to a bigger city, like Los Angeles or Chicago, they talk as if they were returning to a more bucolic environment. Such is the stress of life inside the Beltway.

Fortunately, as the blossoms recede, the moderate temperatures remain, and for the first time in months Washington is best enjoyed outside. During most Aprils, I would spend several days hiking in the mountains or visiting historical sites outside the city. In the April of 2000, however, my free time was so limited that I was only able to take a single road trip— a day excursion with Eileen to George Washington's plantation, Mt. Vernon. It's no Monticello, but if you only have a few hours available, it won't let you down.

"I remember very well your essay about growing up as an atheist," Eileen told me, while stretched out on the banks of the Potomac with her back to the mansion. "You never really explained how you grew out of that."

"I'm not sure how far I've grown."

"Oh please," she said, rolling her eyes. "Allison told me you even attend synagogue now. Why not the Ethical Culture society? What happened?"

I escaped answering by rolling down the grass hill where we were lying, wondering as I rolled whether to give the long answer or the Cliff Notes. How can a man whose career is about to implode justify spending the day talking about his past? Then I looked back and saw Eileen's plaintive look. It asked a question: Who are you? A student of philosophy wants to know.

Obviously, I had to answer.

I began by reminding Eileen that in college, I considered myself an agnostic. I studied religion then, but much like an anthropologist—curious about how religions have affected other people, but not especially concerned about finding a faith of my own.

When I went shopping for myself, I left the mall of religions and entered the philosophy store. As Allison has pointed out, they're not exactly the same place. With each philosophy course I took, my mind became exposed to more and more concepts. One of them especially influenced me: Kant's dichotomy between the noumenal and phenomenal realms.

"Love that philosophy jargon," Eileen said, laughing.

"Hey, you asked for it," I said, and then continued with my story. To Kant, I explained, the realm that we deal with on a daily basis isn't one that exists independently—it exists only in our consciousness. That's the "phenomenal" realm. It gets its name from the fact that it's based on the phenomena our senses experience. The "noumenal" realm, by contrast, is the realm of things as they truly exist in themselves. This realm underlies all of reality, even though we human beings can't come to know it through our day-in day-out experiences.

Once I started thinking hard about the concept of a transcendent, noumenal realm, I began to conclude that its existence was not only plausible, but likely. What attracted me to this view was the same thing that used to bother me about theology. Theologians say that people are created in the image of a God who honors us by directly intervening in our world. That sounded to me like B.S. From Kant, I came to infer that compared to the deepest, innermost aspects of life, people are small and limited, mere specks in the cosmos. I also came to believe that the realm we perceive—the "phenomenal" realm— is no more real than many other worlds we can't perceive.

In other words, we all experience reality through four dimensions: length, width, breadth and time, but who are we to say that no other dimensions exist? To posit a "spiritual" realm is merely to assert that there likely exist deeper dimensions that people can't perceive. Maybe those dimensions are appreciated consciously by beings who are more evolved than we are. The mere fact that we can't detect those beings with our senses or scientific devices says very little, once we accept that we're truly quite small and impotent relative to the cosmos as a whole.

So when I left college, I told Eileen, I had a vague sense of respect, even reverence, for the idea of the transcendent. But I didn't know what to do with this idea until I met some clerics. They knew all too well. They'd seen my kind before. They knew I was ripe for the plucking.

I noticed that Eileen's eyes were closed and wondered if she were sleeping, which I'm sure is what Jamison would have been doing. "Are you still with me?" I asked.

Eileen laughed. "You mean I don't look enthralled? Actually, I learned this technique when I studied Buddhism in Nepal. I'm concentrating entirely on your words, blocking everything else out of my mind. Go ahead. Please."

I went on to talk about my vacation in Israel during my year off between college and law school. My trip lasted only about 40 days (and 40 nights, as they say in that part of the world), but it changed my attitude about religion forever.

As soon as I got to Jerusalem, I checked in to a yeshiva. That's a place of Orthodox Jewish learning. Students at my yeshiva didn't pay for room and board and were accepted into the institution with few restrictions. I was told I could stay for a while, as long as I attended some lectures every day and kept my mind open to what the rabbis were teaching.

The first thing I learned was how "Jewish" I had become in college when I accepted the existence of the transcendent. Arguably, that concept is the basis of the entire religion. Yet it's one thing to believe in a transcendent, noumenal realm, and something else to accept the God of the Bible as your monarch. In trying to "convert" me into the Orthodox fold, the rabbis' success would depend on their ability to take the first belief and mold it into the second. Their tool was a logical fallacy, which I didn't perceive at the time: the fallacy of the excluded middle. They assumed that the question of God had only two possible answers and no "middle ground." I should have recognized the fallacy but was too emotionally needy to think critically. I deeply wanted to believe that I had found *the* truth. In other words, I was a typical post-adolescent.

So here's what the rabbis did, I told Eileen. They exposed us all to a fateful choice. We could believe that the world was created according to the will of an omnibenevolent, omnipotent, omniscient God. Or, we could believe that the world was produced by the random, meaningless interactions of sub-atomic particles, which have evolved into more and more advanced life forms, with humans at the very top of the evolutionary chain. Like the labor union activist who says "if you aren't for us, you must be against us," the rabbis implied that if a Jewish man doesn't accept the teachings of Orthodox Judaism, he must be a nihilist and an atheist. Self-proclaimed "agnostics," I was taught (and believe to this day), are people who live their lives as atheists, and simply refuse to accept that they have adopted that philosophy through their conduct.

Here's the irony of it all, I told Eileen. I nearly bought into this unnecessary choice because I happened to be reading Nietzsche when I came to the yeshiva. That's right, the great anti-religion crusader almost turned me into an Orthodox Jew. He was hellbent on sapping all the Judeo-Christian blood out of his readers' bodies, both by ranting against the "old God" and by praising atheism/nihilism as the only sensible alternative. So he and the rabbis obsessed about the same two alternatives—he simply chose the other one. As I sat in the yeshiva, the only question in my mind was whether the world of Orthodox Judaism was more or less compelling than Nietzsche's nihilistic world, where all is permitted and nothing commanded.

Eileen had opened her eyes as soon as I mentioned Nietzsche's name. She could have spoken for me when she said that no philosopher is more liberating to read than he. "Forget the Buddhists," she added. "If you're going to talk about Nietzsche, I'm not shutting my eyes."

"Well go ahead and shut them," I replied, "because I've got to get back to the rabbis." To break down our resistance, I explained, they combined their talk about cosmology with an appeal to our Jewish roots. The yeshiva was intended to be a microcosm of the community known as the Jewish people, which extends both through space and time. The rabbis created a relaxed environment where students cooperated instead of competed. The word we used was "learned"—we never "studied," we only "learned." We also visited the homes of Orthodox Jews outside of the yeshiva to drum in the notion that we all live as one large family—we love each other, pray together, and dedicate our lives to common principles.

"I guess what I'm saying," I told Eileen, "is that the rabbis hit us with a one-two punch. They appealed to our hearts through the sense of community and the idea that this community was in our blood. And they appealed to our minds through the concept of transcendence and by mocking the notion that we humans are the pinnacle of existence."

"It's not that different from the way *any* religious group hooks in new members," she said. "But you haven't explained something. You're sitting here lying on the banks of the Potomac with a blonde shiksa. What happened? Why did you leave?"

I laughed. "I like shiksas, what can I say?"

"Seriously. Why?"

"It's all about roots. The rabbis told me to return to my roots. But they were looking to take me away from my mother, and pull me apart from the philosophy of my father too. Heck, they wanted to rip me apart from my *self*. Everything that was unique about me—the things I loved, the things I hated—it was all shaped by a secular upbringing."

"So you left Israel because of the Redskins. Is that what you're saying?"

"Kind of. I can tell you this—when I did leave, I wasn't wearing a yarmulke, and I didn't feel guilty about it. But I was a changed person. I could appreciate more the value of organized religion. And for the first time in my life, I believed in God."

"And you've believed ever since?"

"Yes, in one way or another," I explained. When I came back to the States, I went to work as a legal secretary for a New York temp agency and had the time to take stock of my life, post-yeshiva. Religion had brought a new sense of meaning,

and it allowed me to accept God as a source of command-
ments. That's not to say I felt obliged to do everything the rabbis said, but I did feel "commanded" to honor God through the
way I live my life."

"What does that mean?" she asked.

"For example, I made a vow to pursue a career in public
service after I finished school. And I've honored that ever since."

My belief in God also enabled me to accept the existence of
an afterlife, I told Eileen. And once I came to believe in the
afterlife, I embraced the concept of soul-building, which is a
term I first heard at the yeshiva. It suggests that the better the
acts in this world, the bigger the soul in the next, meaning that
any moral act is an act of soul-building. So religion, to me,
became not just a source of obligations to God but also a vehi-
cle for rewarding my eternal soul.

I spent about five months working for the temp agency
before starting law school. Back then, God became more and
more concrete to me until I reached the point where I felt his
presence *all the time*. Let me be clear about this, I explained—
the God that I was worshiping was no different than the God
most Jewish *children* worship. He stood apart from creation
and molded it according to His will. He punished wrongdoing
and rewarded virtue. He loved us, in spite of our shortcom-
ings. But He loved us mostly when we acted within the dictates of morality.

"So let me get this straight," Eileen said. "You'd been thinking about God all your life, studied philosophy in college and
spent time in a yeshiva, and what you came up with were the
ideas of a typical ten year old."

"Pretty much. I wanted to believe in something that gave me
peace, so I went back to the basics."

Suddenly, a distinct and vivid recollection entered my mind

and overwhelmed my train of thought. I was recalling the rush of pleasure that I felt sitting across from Eileen at a restaurant when we spent our first day together back in March.

"What is it?" Eileen asked. She could tell something was up from my facial expression. "Ah, nothing. Nothing. Let me go on. One summer night at a Jewish service, I felt a sharp sensation in my heart—an intense, sudden feeling of pleasure. It can only be described as a rush of love. Just before I had this feeling, I had been contemplating only one object."

"God?" she asked.

"Yeah, God. After that feeling swept over me, I had no more doubts."

I was talking about God, but thinking about my feelings for Eileen. I continued with my story, but spoke very deliberately. "I took that sensation to be a clear sign that God was talking to me, telling me never again to doubt His existence. Today, if you asked where that feeling came from, I'd tell you my subconscious. But I'm not sure that matters. Ever since I've felt that feeling, I've been convinced that I should always love God.

"Have you ever ..." my voice trailed off before I could complete the question. I was struck by the thought that my affections for her weren't entirely reciprocated. Eileen made me feel valued, even adored, but not in a romantic sense. I wanted to know more about how she felt about me, but I dared not push my luck. Besides, I wondered, what was so bad about our relationship as it stood? It was the best one I had going, perhaps the best I had ever had. Then, for the first time, I felt a bit like Jacob.

Eileen could tell our conversation was starting to drain me, and she wanted me to save my energy for the Benefactor's Committee meeting that evening. "We can finish this later," she said.

"No, no, I'm fine."

She reached out and began massaging my temple with her fingers. "You take everything so seriously, don't you?" she said. "It's OK. We can finish or not. Your choice."

"I'd like to continue," I replied, finally gathering my composure. I certainly didn't want to leave Eileen thinking that my views of God were that of a ten year old.

"Do you remember those cartoons, where people get hit on the head and lose their memory, and then they get hit in the same place and their memory returns?" I asked Eileen. That kind of happened to me, I explained, about a week before I entered law school. I was walking down the street in Cambridge trying to make a bus. I was a couple of minutes late, and the next one wasn't scheduled to arrive for another 28 minutes. Just as I turned the corner, the bus left. If I had gotten there ten, maybe fifteen seconds earlier, I would have made it.

For the next few hours, I obsessed over why I had missed that bus and attributed it to God. He must have willed it, but why? Was He punishing me for something? I can't recall exactly when reality hit me later in the day, but it hit like a ton of bricks. A college-educated son of secular parents attributed the fact that he had missed a city bus to God's will. "Sam," I said to myself, "do you know what that makes you? A fucking imbecile!"

"After the bus incident," I explained, "I still believed in God but was confused about who or what to pray to. And I couldn't find a community that I felt comfortable in."

"Have you found one yet?" Eileen asked.

"Just this year."

"Do you mean at synagogue?"

"I meant the Creed Room."

"I kind of feel that way too," she said, smiling.

The whole enterprise of religion made me feel uneasy, I explained, until I read my first book by Spinoza. He couldn't give me a community, but at least he gave me a sense of being intellectually grounded. I needed to replace Jewish cultism with a measure of heresy.

"It's much more fun, isn't it?" Eileen said.

"Definitely." Merely mentioning the word heresy helped me relax a bit, and I realized that I wanted a break from the storytelling. "Let's take a walk," I said.

We left the mansion grounds and headed for the stable. Eileen had overheard that a colt had been born there yesterday, and visitors were allowed to come and see it.

Don't get me wrong, I thought the colt was cute and a whole lot bigger than I expected a horse to be in its first day of life, but after a minute, I was ready to move on. Not Eileen. She needed more time to coo over the animal. Finally, she jumped up, began walking back toward the mansion, and said "I want to hear about Spinoza. When did you first read him?"

"In law school," I answered. "Not long before I dropped out." I explained that he was the one who had finally set me free from the fallacy of the excluded middle. He showed me that we can reject the traditional conception of God without having to become atheists.

"I didn't hear much about him in college," Eileen said. "Just that he was a pantheist."

"Maybe I heard that much," I replied. "Maybe not even. But a law school friend told me he was pretty cool, so I bought a copy of his *Ethics*."

"That's his masterpiece, right?"

"I'd say he wrote more than one, but yeah, it's generally considered his greatest work. It's called the *Ethics* but it's about all sorts of things—psychology, epistemology, God. Mostly God."

"I can see I'm going to have to buy a copy," she said, much to my delight.

"The best way I can explain how Spinoza influenced me is to remind you of the night sky. Not the polluted D.C. sky. I'm talking the Wyoming sky. The one with lots and lots of stars.

"It's awe-inspiring to the eyes. And to the mind, it seems limitless. But astronomers can't afford to simply wonder and gaze. If they want to get paid, they'd better analyze. So they focus on bits and pieces of the sky. Constellations, say. Like Orion.

"To the Spinozist, all the traditional western conceptions of God are like planets and stars in the *same* constellation. God the Father, call Him Alpha Ori. Adonai, Beta Ori. Allah, Gamma Ori. They're all great, and unique too. But relative to this big beautiful sky we could be contemplating, they're just specks of light in a very limited part of space. When Spinozists think about God, we want to reflect on the entire sky, not just fall in love with one tiny constellation."

"I think I'm following you," Eileen said. "But I'm not sure."

"Try this. Theologians love to paint a conceptual picture of God. God is a *He*. He is all-loving, all-wise and all-powerful. He acts in accordance with a human-like will. He is separate from the world, which He alone created. He is incorporeal.

"This picture is known throughout the western world, right? Lots of people buy into it and say their prayers to more or less this same deity. Others think it's crap and say they don't believe in God at all. To a Spinozist, that whole debate is ridiculously narrow. It relates only to one little constellation in the sky, and we have a right to see God in any part of the sky we want to.

"In other words, we don't let other people define God for

us, we define God for ourselves. And we start with the principle of the sky—its awesomeness, its limitlessness, its grandeur. That's where we'll find *our* God."

"Are those Spinoza's words or yours?" Eileen asked.

"He never said those things explicitly. I bet, though, that a lot of other Spinozists gained the same inspiration from him that I did."

"OK, I'm with you." Eileen said. "But I want to hear about Spinoza, not just his disciples. Tell me about *his* God."

"You mean his favorite constellation?"

"Right. "

"OK," I said. "First, don't think about God. Think about the world. What have you got? Animals, plants and rocks. Beings and things. Each one unique, but not alone. We're all the product of some other being or thing—like our mothers, for example—and we're all affected, sometimes even destroyed, by the beings or things around us.

"That perspective is perfectly valid, Spinoza would say, but there are deeper ones. And the deeper we go, the more we'll find unity—complete unity of substance. That unified substance is Spinoza's God. He's not a being among beings, or a thing among things. God is *Being* itself. He encounters nobody outside Himself. That's because there *is* nothing else.

"Every one of us and every part of us is in God. We all *comprise* God—we, and everything that existed before us and that will exist after we're dead. And aside from us and other stuff that shares the same substance we do, God doesn't exist at all. Nothing does."

"You told me some of this before, in the Creed Room," Eileen said. "God isn't simply in us. We're in God."

"Precisely. When we want to think about Spinoza's God, we don't turn God into some force of good battling the forces of evil. And we don't think of God like the Deists do—as someone who acts at certain times but not others. In fact, when we want to focus on God most clearly, we stop thinking about breaking the world into chunks of space or units of time. To use Spinoza's words, we perceive God *'under the form of eternity.'* Whenever we think about what's eternal and limitless—whenever we think about 'Being' with a capital B—that's when we get our strongest glimpse of Spinoza's God."

"And you see this God as somehow more awesome or grand than the traditional God?"

"In a sense. The traditional God is limited by His conscious desires. He only creates what he *wills* based on his benevolent personality. And when he does create, he makes things outside of Himself—like human beings, for example—and we become junior partners in God's universe. Spinoza's God is greater, for my money, because Spinoza didn't limit God's powers in any way. Life to Spinoza is an infinite array of *expressions* within God that occur quite naturally. I can quote you Spinoza's exact words: God's nature is 'so comprehensive as to suffice for the production of everything that can be conceived by an infinite intellect.'"

"That quotation makes Spinoza sound so mechanistic, like his God is churning out stuff in a factory," Eileen said. "Is that the way you read him?"

"Others do. I don't. Spinoza is telling us *not* to restrict God's power or greatness, that's all. So we don't project our ideals onto God. And we don't think of God as some sort of mindless power source either. Believe me, there's more to the universe than humans and machines."

"Like colts with horns on their foreheads ... and wings," Eileen said.

"Now you're catching on. By the way, do you want to know

what Spinoza said that drives his interpreters crazy?"

"What's that?"

"In the final part of the *Ethics*, he said 'God loves himself with an infinite intellectual love.' And 'God, insofar as he loves himself, loves mankind.'"

"Anthropomorphisms, anyone?" Eileen said, laughing.

"You got it. Some people think those statements contradict everything else Spinoza taught. But I like them. They show he wanted to have a fulfilling relationship with God. What's wrong with that?"

"So even though he was excommunicated, he was a good Jew after all," Eileen said.

"Let me put it this way. Maybe he didn't go over the line of treating God as one of us, but every now and then he walked right up to it."

I went on to recite for Eileen another passage, only this time it wasn't written by Spinoza but about him. In Bertrand Russell's *A History of Western Philosophy*, Russell referred to Spinoza as "the noblest and most lovable of the great philosophers. Intellectually, some others have surpassed him, but ethically he is supreme. As a natural consequence, he was considered, during his lifetime and for a century after his death, a man of appalling wickedness." Russell went on to point out that the people who knew Spinoza loved him. And, in fact, so have some very prominent thinkers who lived long after Spinoza died. For years, Goethe carried a copy of the *Ethics* with him wherever he went. Then there was Einstein. He made a pilgrimage to Spinoza's house in Rijnsburg, Holland, a suburb of Leiden.

"My favorite description of Spinoza is from the German philosopher, Novalis," I added. "It was common to call Spinoza an atheist; Novalis called him a 'God-intoxicated man.'"

"You could talk about him for hours, couldn't you?" Eileen said. "He sounds like he plays the same role for you that Jesus plays for a Christian."

"To a degree. But I don't view him as divine. He made some stupid remarks. You'll like this one: he wrote that women weren't fit for positions in government. Oh yeah. He also staged fights between spiders."

"Nice. Then again, if we knew the historical Jesus, we might find he had his share of human frailties too."

"You'd think so, wouldn't you?" I said. "To follow Spinoza is to reject the idea that *any* being who has taken human form is worthy of deification."

I could have spoken longer about Spinoza, but Eileen let me know she'd had enough to think about for the day. "We'll continue this later," she said, before giving me a peck on the cheek and as warm a smile as I'd seen in ages.

Leaving Mt. Vernon that afternoon was painful. It had been so difficult scheduling time to be with Eileen, and I knew it could be a while before we'd be alone again. But I had no right to complain, not after reading the *Ethics*. As we returned to the parking lot, I reminded myself of its final words: "All things excellent are as difficult as they are rare."

"Where the hell is she?" Shaw asked, finally losing patience. The committee was meeting for the fourth time since we'd last seen Eileen, before she flew to Minnesota during her spring break. She told us she'd be at the meeting but was already a half hour late. Then, out of my peripheral vision, I saw her approach us. She looked drawn and terribly sleep deprived.

"I'm *so* sorry I'm late," she said.

"That's OK," Shaw said, obviously relieved to see her.

"I'm just happy you're back," said Dolores.

I wanted to chime in with an amen. Lord knows it would have been heartfelt. Yet I couldn't, not then. The face that had previously represented for me the height of serenity was driving me to distraction. I had no idea what I could do for her, but I had to do something.

At the end of the evening, while the others were getting ready to leave the Friendship Heights Deli where the committee always met, I asked how she had enjoyed her week off.

"Oh, you know, it was alright, I guess."

"You seem worried about something," I said.

"I have a lot of stuff going on these days, that's all."

"Care to talk about it?" I asked.

"I ... I probably better not. But thanks for asking."

Eileen smiled and then started walking toward the door of the Deli. It was a beautiful evening, and I asked if she wanted to take a stroll down one of the side streets.

"I think I'd better go home and get some sleep," she said. "Sorry."

During the following weeks, Eileen and I spoke nearly every day, sometimes for over an hour at a time. Invariably, though, the conversations were by telephone—her choice, not mine. I'd often try to make plans to see her alone, but she'd always come up with some half-baked excuse as to why that wouldn't be possible. It reached the point where I'd ask her out not because I expected to see her but because I was curious to hear what kind of excuse she'd think of.

When our committee work got started, I viewed Eileen almost like my assistant. During our evening conversations, we spoke a fair amount about school or our families, but mostly we discussed the goings on in the Creed Room or with the committee. She'd allow me to explain my thoughts at length and would occasionally punctuate them with her own suggestions.

Then, one night, I thought I'd vary the routine. I came to a committee meeting determined to listen to my colleagues and speak very little. What I found, what we *all* found, was an Eileen Mitchell in full bloom. Her comments were succinct but insightful, often summarizing in a few sentences what the rest of us would have taken minutes to say. When the session ended, Shaw came up to her and said "Damn it, lady, you're brilliant." It was exactly what I was thinking. Brilliant, and beautiful.

Less than an hour later, Eileen called me at home. She wanted to talk shop. This time, I was too much in awe to flap my gums incessantly, so I listened, just like Eileen usually did. Then it hit me. She's not afraid of life, she's *awed* by it. That's what keeps her so quiet most of the time. It wasn't shyness at all.

From that point on, Eileen's days as "my assistant" were over. I realized that I had more to learn from her about philosophy than she from me. We became partners, and sometimes I simply acted as her scribe. Instead of pontificating (my natural state), I'd try to draw her out with open-ended questions. She shared her own observations and discussed the teachings of her favorite thinkers from the East and the West. I especially enjoyed listening to her talk about the one modern Jewish thinker whom she had studied in depth: Martin Buber.

I had read Buber before—not as much as she had, but enough to get his drift. Many consider him to be the 20th century's greatest Jewish philosopher. Yet in some respects he was an anti-philosopher. He contrasted his own teachings to those of thinkers like Spinoza who analyzed relentlessly. In fact, Buber tried to do the same number on Spinoza that Allison did to me when I gave my first presentation. To Buber, life must be encountered with the entire spirit, lovingly and openly, not just dissected into concepts.

Listening to Eileen talk about Buber's work and reflecting on the time I'd spent with her, I realized how much she followed his teachings. Like Buber, she was more than capable of striking back when her principles were offended. Art had seen that side of her. So had Fred. For the most part, though, she inspired with her mouth closed—simply observing, respectfully and attentively.

Coming from a family where the three of us often spoke at the same time, my ears and eyes weren't as trained as my mouth, and that wasn't about to change overnight. But thanks to my new role model, I had some motivation to change. I wanted to listen better to my students. I wanted to treat Art with dignity—at least to hear him out before I peppered him with counter-arguments. I wanted to reflect whenever I heard something interesting, rather than immediately reacting with a comment. In short, I wanted to be more like Eileen. And gradually, I felt myself putting that desire into action.

For all that Eileen did for me, however, I seemed to be able to do nothing for her. That was my biggest frustration of the spring. The more time I spent with her, the more I noticed that something was disturbing her equilibrium. She avoided talking about it with me, just like she avoided seeing me alone, but there was no mistaking the facts: Eileen was a troubled soul.

The last Saturday in April was my final anger-management session. Determined to celebrate my "graduation" with Eileen, I told her a few days earlier that I had to see her that Saturday evening and couldn't accept 'no' for an answer.

"What's so special about Saturday evening?" she asked.

"We can celebrate my release from the prison of psycho-babble."

"That's your last session?"

"That's it. They're pronouncing me cured. Or at least they'd better, if they don't want me to rip their balls off. Calmly, of course."

"Well it just so happens that I'm performing that night, not far from where you live."

"In Rockville?"

"In Bethesda. The Shamrock Pub. They're doing a tribute to five new D.C. area music acts, and I'll be one of the performers. Supposedly, I'm on stage from about 9:30 to 10:00.

"I'm there," I said. "How about dinner before the show?"

"I better not. This is my first public gig. *Ever*. I should probably relax alone at home before the show. You don't want to see me get sick up there."

Every day, a new excuse. But this one made sense to me. Before we hung up, I made sure Eileen knew that I wouldn't miss her show for the world. In fact, I spent much of the remainder of the week, and nearly the entire anger-management session, anticipating it.

When I arrived at the Shamrock, it was already packed to its capacity of about 250 people. I didn't feel very social so I headed straight for the bar and ordered my usual: ginger ale. I had barely taken a sip when Allison walked over and basically dragged me back to her table.

Nine Georgetown students were seated there, and Allison felt the need to introduce me to each one, throwing out names at warp speed. Near the end of the introductions, she came to a familiar face. "Oh, and Sam," she said. "This is Linda Smith. She used to be the Creed Room's Big Dog. Now she's just a spectator waiting to see if your committee's worth all the money."

"Allison's jealous," Linda replied.

"Of whom?" I asked, smiling. "Me or Eileen? I may be the head writer, but Eileen's the one who kicked butt at rock-paper-scissors. It still hurts, doesn't it?"

It must have, judging from the look on Allison's face. Before she could respond, Linda was all over my comment. "Yes indeed," she said. "The great Creed Room chess match. Paper wraps up rock. Checkmate. You never could outsmart Eileen, could you?"

Allison didn't acknowledge Linda's comment. She simply turned her attention to another person at the table. "Sam, there's one last person I'd like you to meet. This is my boyfriend, Amos. Amos Steiner."

"How ya' doing, Sam?" he said in a rich baritone, giving me a handshake worthy of Hercules. Amos stood about 6' 4" and obviously kept himself in superb physical shape. He was also, just as obviously, Jewish. That was apparent not only from his name but also his facial features. His self confidence was palpable—presumably the product of a care-free upbringing in an affluent suburb where he had surely excelled, athletically and academically, before matriculating at an Ivy League school and joining a fraternity.

He was quite the Irving doll.

"So Amos, you're at Georgetown Law?" I asked.

"Sure am. I graduate this spring, just like Allison. We're headed up to New York. I'll be at Hamilton Mead. Corporate Department."

"That should bring in some Benjamins," I replied, in the lingo I instinctively associated with Steiner.

"Damned straight," Steiner said, laughing. "I'll have to work my ass off to get 'em, but that's OK. Between my paycheck and

Allison's, we'll be able to afford a pretty sweet apartment close in. Maybe Brooklyn Heights. Maybe even in the City."

"Great," I said, feigning pleasure. "So you'll be able to go to Rabbi Schwartz's temple."

"That's the plan," Steiner replied. "The rabbi can't wait to get Allison back in the fold."

"Truth is, Amos has been one of those two-days-a-year tribesmen," Allison said. "That's going to change, though, isn't it, dear?"

"If that's what you want, baby." He said that, but I wasn't convinced. I still figured he'd be more at home drinking brews with his frat bro's at a local strip club than listening to Reb Schwartz lecture on Deuteronomy. Fortunately, that was Allison's problem, not mine.

At 9:45, Eileen came on stage—just her, a microphone and her acoustic-electric guitar. She began by announcing that, in honor of the Shamrock Pub, all of her songs would be related to the Emerald Isle. First, she covered Van Morrison's "Sweet Thing." Next, U2's "One." Third, she played the Cranberry's "Ode to My Family," and she followed that with Clannad's "Journey's End." She performed each song without any talking in between. In fact, after every number, while the audience was applauding, she closed her eyes, just like she did in Mount Vernon.

With each passing tune, I couldn't get over her vocal range. I also wondered more and more why this woman was toiling away in law school. If she were anyone else, I'd have assumed it was the money. But Eileen wasn't materialistic. So how could I explain her decision to write briefs, when she could be making music instead?

After she finished the Clannad piece, the entire Shamrock was buzzing. Then, for the first time since she introduced herself at the beginning of her set, Eileen addressed the audience. "The next song is my favorite traditional Irish tune. It might be my favorite song, period." She played "Molly Malone." I had never heard it sung better.

After her ovation died down, she addressed the audience again. "I'd like to close with a number by an Irish-American law student. None of you have heard it before—because I only wrote it a week ago. I hope you enjoy it."

She sang about a battle with illness, one that devoured the body of a man and the joy of the woman who loved him. Strangely, though, by the time she finished, I felt uplifted, even empowered. Overriding the grim facts of the illness was a message of hope. Eileen, the songwriter, refused to accept defeat, even if the sickness were to end in death. She wouldn't admit that the love we build in our relationships is any less eternal than our own souls.

When Eileen strummed her last chord, the applause grew quickly to a deafening crescendo. I wasn't alone in appreciating its message. It was reminiscent in style of one of Dylan's efforts at prophecy, something like "A Hard Rain's A-Gonna Fall," though Eileen's ode had a very different message. Dylan painted a picture of our world's impending apocalypse if we don't usher in an era of justice. In Eileen's portrait, all of our obsessions with death, destruction and conflict would be washed away once we've accepted the role of the eternal in our lives.

For a moment, I wondered if the song was inspired by our conversation about Spinoza. Then I realized how absurd and self-centered I was being. Could it be possible, I asked myself, that this woman actually had a life of her own outside of our conversations?

After her performance, Eileen sat at the table of honor next to the stage. She was joined by many of the evening's other performers. The other acts that night were reasonably good, but *nothing* compared to Eileen's.

Once I finally had the chance to talk to her later in the evening, I asked what prompted her to write her new song.

"What prompts anyone to write a song like that? I wrote from my heart."

"I'm sure you did. But I'm asking if something happened that inspired you."

"Did you like it?"

"Well yes, but—"

"I was afraid it would be too depressing. I didn't mean to depress anyone, but I think songs should express how you're feeling. That song expresses my emotions these days."

It must be nice, I thought, to be able to express your emotions and watch people applaud like crazy. It must *really* be nice when you can keep that applause from going to your head.

We talked a bit longer before Eileen told me that she had to go. When she got up, she gave me a gentle kiss on the cheek. Then her hand touched the spot that she kissed. As long as I live, I won't forget that kiss, her song or, for that matter, any part of her performance.

That night, I was too upset with myself to fall asleep. It's one thing to panic and shove a bully when a mere shout could have sufficed. It's something else to live for 30 years without having once stood up to a woman—other than my mother, of course.

I wasn't second guessing the way I treated my old girlfriends, not even Allison. None of those women was right for me. Eileen was. And yet I was letting her get away without a fight. I was letting *everyone* get away without a fight—other than my mother.

"It's about us, not them." That had been my mantra when it came to the Creed Room and the Empire Club. But that night it hit me. It may have been about "us," but it was certainly never about "me." I was always the one to react to other people—to let them set the agenda. Even when I left law school, I did so at the urging of a friend, whose logic I found compelling. It's time, I thought, to start listening to myself.

The members of the Empire Club had their secrets. So, too, did Eileen. I wasn't overly concerned about uncovering their secrets. Let them do their thing, I felt; I'd do mine. But, as I lay in bed that night, I realized how desperately I wanted to know about Eileen. I had to find out why, if I thought we were so obviously perfect for each other, she was walking away from happiness.

The next evening, I camped out in front of her apartment until she showed up. Then I didn't ask, I *directed* her to tell me why she'd been keeping me at a distance. Eventually, she relented. She invited me into her living room and poured us both some coffee. "OK Sam," she said, after a long silence. "If you must know about my life back in Minnesota, so be it."

Eileen explained that she'd only had one boyfriend aside from Brad Flynn. Her second relationship started in college and involved a professor, Jim Gustafson. He later told her that it was her fascination with philosophy that he noticed most about her when she took his Intro to Epistemology course during the spring of her freshman year.

At the time, Eileen was 18. Gustafson was 43. "He was handsome and young looking for his age," Eileen said, "*but he was 43! How could I fall for a man that old?*"

She didn't right away. They were nothing more than teacher and student. But she was an incredibly enthusiastic student. After nearly every class, when the other students were long gone she'd still be asking him questions. When he had office hours, she was usually there too. "Trust me. I wasn't being a suck up. I just wanted to learn philosophy."

One afternoon, Gustafson suggested that they speak about Eileen's questions over dinner.

"I take it you went."

"Absolutely. It was a nice innocent meal. Totally Platonic. But for the first time, he started talking to me about his personal life. I learned that he had been married for a couple of years until he caught his wife cheating on him with one of the other philosophers at the U."

"It's nice to know all that ethics training didn't go to waste," I said.

Eileen explained that she took another Gustafson course in the fall of her sophomore year, and they got together then for a couple more "innocent" dinners. But she decided against taking a third course from him in the spring. "That would have looked too weird," she figured. Then, during her semester break, she examined her feelings and realized that she had fallen in love. So there she was, obsessed with a professor, only without any plans to see him.

As it turned out, Gustafson was equally obsessed with her. On the day she came back to her dorm for the spring semester, he called to ask her out to dinner. She accepted, and within a week they had become intimate.

Eileen and Gustafson began their closeted romance in January 1993. They continued secretly to see each other until she graduated from college in June 1995. Then, they felt no more need to keep the relationship under wraps, so she moved in with him.

"Everyone could tell how much passion we had for each other and how much we had in common. At one point, I seriously considered becoming a professional philosopher."

"Why didn't you?"

"Oh, I don't know. I guess I wanted to see the world outside of books. That's why after I lived with Jim for a few months, I went to Nepal."

"What did he think of that?"

"He totally supported me. If it means helping me grow, he's always supported me."

"I'm impressed," I said, wondering how I could compete with this guy, except maybe in terms of life expectancy.

Little did I know how easily I might win that competition. "They discovered the tumor when I was overseas," Eileen said. "It was in his prostate. He didn't talk to me about it at first. He didn't want to screw up my experience in Nepal. Finally, after about seven months, he broke down and told me, and I came home right away. I lived with him until I began law school."

"I have to ask. Why did you go to law school in D.C. if you two were so close?"

No sooner had I finished my question than Eileen's eyes welled up. "I wanted to go to law school at the U, to be with Jim. He wouldn't let me. 'If you pick a law school with me in mind, I'll never speak to you again. You're not going to spend your 20s nursing a sick middle-aged man.' Those were his exact words."

"But why law school at all?" I said.

"Why did *you* go to law school? Why does anyone?"

"Because they don't know what they want to do, and it's supposed to open a lot of doors."

"Don't forget the other reason," she said. "Because our families think it's a swell idea."

Each summer during law school, and every spring and winter break, Eileen lived with Gustafson and once again became a caregiver. She vowed not to get romantically involved with another man as long as he was alive. "I didn't make that promise to Jim," Eileen said. "I vowed that to myself."

Eileen said that recently Gustafson's condition had improved, thanks to a new drug. So she had hope for a recovery. But she also knew the cancer could prove fatal.

"This past winter," Eileen said, "he told me he felt like an old married man who had lived a long, happy life and is finally ready to go. I cried my eyes out. You've got to understand that I could never even look at another man right now. Jim's been *so* good to me. Like an angel."

I did understand. And while I began the conversation intending to fight for her, I realized that this wasn't the fight to pick. Not then. As Jacob would say, maybe in seven years.

The April and early-May sessions at the Creed Room were information-gathering exercises for the committee. We reviewed the ideas that the Gang had played with throughout the year and introduced some new ones too. Scott and Dolores led discussions on ethics, psychology, economics and politics. Eileen and I handled metaphysics, spirituality and organized religion.

The person who was most marginalized during the last few sessions was, not surprisingly, Art. I knew from what Dolores told me that he wasn't going to pitch a fit no matter what we did, but I tried hard to include his views in our final product. It just so happened that on most issues, we were able to reach as close to a consensus as possible if we took exception to his beliefs.

On one occasion, Art gave us a hint of what he was truly thinking, though without the passion that he often brought to our earlier meetings. "You people are just kicking around a bunch of crazy liberal ideas, that's all. Do you think your stuff has any appeal to a Christian conservative? Do you realize how many of us there are in this country?"

"No more than I know how many cockroaches are in my apartment," Shaw said.

Art ignored him. "I thought we were trying to come up with something that could unify America."

"There is no way we can think of a coherent philosophy that everyone in this room can believe in," I said. "It's just not possible. We're all too different."

"Answer my question," Art demanded. "If we're not trying to find some kind of consensus, or some unifying philosophy, what are we doing here?"

"We're bringing together as many of our ideas and values as we can. Yours too," I said.

"I don't buy that for a second. You might be trying to figure out how to bring together the *Democratic Party*. But your coalition will never include conservatives."

"Art," Linda replied. "I'm sorry you feel left out, but I think the rest of us are satisfied."

"Go ahead, people, have it your way," he shrugged. "Just remember—you're not nearly as open-minded as you think you are. You have no idea how to deal with traditional values. Or with Christianity. But you'll have to, soon enough. We're going to take over this city again. Then you'll have all the time in the world to study the New Testament."

CHAPTER 14

THE SYNTHESIS

We were told to arrive on May 23rd no later than 6:45 in the evening, and not a soul was late. McDonald greeted each of us at the door and asked us to take a seat in the living room. The video camera that had previously been in the Creed Room had been moved downstairs. As we sat in our seats, making polite conversation, the camera light was on. Finally, a grandfather clock announced the arrival of the new hour. Within seconds, I could hear a door open above us and the sound of footsteps walking down the hardwood floor toward the stairs.

Slowly, the footsteps descended the stairs until, at last, we were all staring the Benefactor in the face. He was accompanied by McDonald. "Hello everyone," said the Benefactor, smiling. "My name is Charles Feaver, but please, call me Chuck." He was short, perhaps no taller than 5' 6", and slightly overweight, both in the face and the body. His pale skin was wrinkled, suggesting an age of at least 80. The Benefactor—and to this day, that's what I call him—was dressed in a dark blazer. He was the only man in the room without a tie, including McDonald.

After the Benefactor finished shaking everyone's hands, McDonald led him to his seat and pulled up a chair next to him. It was the first time McDonald had sat down with the

Creed Gang all year. "I can't tell you how much I've looked forward to this," the Benefactor said, addressing the group. "I'd like you to do whatever it is you want to do. I'm just going to shut up and listen."

With that, all eyes turned toward me, and mine turned toward Eileen, who walked to the front of the room. "Mr. Feaver—Chuck," she began. "Tonight, we're presenting a single creed—a philosophy that we as a group can rally around and that each of us can use to grow over time. We'll state our creed in the first person plural, as if *we*, the group, subscribe to it, hook, line and sinker. But don't be fooled. None of us agrees with every single thing that's going to be said tonight. There may even be a person or two in the group who'll disagree with *most* of what you're about to hear. That couldn't be helped.

"We want to thank you for everything you've done for us. Hopefully, we'll be able to show you that we've taken your project very seriously. That means that you'd better relax, because we've got a *lot* to present.*

"With that introduction, I give you tonight's featured speaker, Mr. Samuel Kramer."

What follows is the transcript that I passed out at the end of the evening. The group heard the Presentation for the first time on May 23rd. I had kept a good deal of it a secret from all of them, even Eileen.

---

* Just as Choulos once warned the Creed Gang, I must now warn you, my readers. Much of the Presentation, and all of Part I, is quite abstract. If you're in the mood to read a story, it is definitely *not* for you. Before beginning the Presentation, I might suggest first taking a walk with your head in the clouds, like Socrates. Or, you can feel free to skim it now (enough to get the gist) and digest it later.

Presentation of a New Creed
May 23, 2000
Garrett Park, Maryland

I. The Underlying Components of the Creed

We're here to celebrate, above all else, two aspects of the human spirit: our rationality and our empathy. The first without the second connotes frigidity, intransigence, perhaps even conceit. The second without the first connotes Pollyannaism, manipulatability and weakness. We need both, or it might be just as well if we possessed neither.

A. Rationalism

The first thing we're going to do is tweak a word. It's a word philosophers love to use, and they use it in different ways. Sometimes, it's a veil behind which they bash theology. Other times, it has been contrasted to a different kind of religion—the worship of the scientific method. It has also referred to a type of optimism that proclaims the power of science and education to improve the human condition. That last sense is the closest to our usage, but it doesn't quite cut it either.

By calling ourselves *rationalists*, we wish to affirm—yes, to celebrate. We celebrate our capacity to live in thrall. Other types of rationalists proclaim themselves free thinkers. We do too—but only to a point. We wish to be free to live consistently with reason, not to evade her truths.

We love reason largely because of how much she respects our power and autonomy. Even her judgments of "right" and "wrong" are delivered modestly. She speaks to us privately, as a quiet, serene voice inside our heads, inviting us to decide for ourselves whether to obey her voice or ignore it. Reason, then, speaks to us as if we were her master, but we, the disciples of rationalism, know better. Hers is the voice of experience, objectivity, wisdom. We would be well advised to listen whenever she is audible.

Reason talks to us on two very different levels. On the more basic one, she appeals to us as selfish animals. Nature has armed us with the drive to meet our biological needs and gratify our emotional desires. But when you think about it, much of that drive has evolved into an impulse to consult reason. She explains to us how to subdue other animals, build buildings, predict the weather, treat illnesses. She's been kind enough to give us lordship over the earth.

On this level, reason judges not. She merely provides us with utensils.

Whenever we try to help our family members or friends we remain on this first level. We're simply treating those others as extensions of ourselves. On Level One, we're often willing to disregard someone else's interests so long as they get in the way of our parochial goals.

Please don't think that we're disparaging the importance of this first level. Only a fool wouldn't recognize any person's rights to feather his own nests or those of his children. Thank God reason helps us in these ways. But she offers gifts that are so much more beautiful, even though comparatively few people appreciate them.

We've come here today to praise reason's *second* level. When we encounter her there, we're not content to act selfishly or parochially. We seek instead to be vessels—vessels for truth, and particularly moral truth, in the broad sense of that term. We seek to view the world from an Olympian standpoint and to act in a way that does that perspective justice.

On the second level, people stop talking about "*my*" interests being pursued only at the expense of *"yours."* We now seek to become members of a universal community committed to the highest goals imaginable—like the aim of treating all people with respect, dignity and fairness. It is to this level that Immanuel Kant was referring when he framed his first so-called Categorical Imperative: "So act that the maxim of your will could always hold at the same time as a principle establishing universal law."

Those words by Kant remind us of the voice of reason. They call us to rise above our present limitations and aim toward *universal* truths. When John Stuart Mill suggested that we always act so as to produce the greatest good for the greatest number, he too was speaking as a Level Two disciple. Perhaps he heard her right. Perhaps not. But at least he was listening.

On Level Two, rationalists grapple with the timeless questions at the heart of philosophy. Who is God? How did life originate? How should our societies be governed? Do human beings possess natural rights that ought never be violated? We also ask specific, context-laden questions, such as: is it just and proper for one country to invade another given a particular set of historical and geopolitical facts? These latter questions give us a reality check. No rationalist philosophy is worth anything unless it can be applied successfully to the real world.

The questions are easy enough to ask. But when we try to answer, our limitations are striking. Limited by space, time and a whole lot of emotions, the questions are much bigger than we are.

On the second level, reason forces us to recognize and transcend our limitations, not to repress them. When we address any of the great questions, we must take steps to note our biases and ensure that they don't swallow up our philosophies. That means double checking our conclusions whenever they coincide with our personal interests.

For example, when considering the theory that life sprang from the conscious choice of a single intelligent being, we rationalists must think twice about whether that theory resulted from our own wishful thinking. It is, after all, a more comforting idea than, say, the alternative that attributes every life event to utter randomness. So when we contemplate this theory, we must ask the question: are we simply satisfying our emotional needs? Or are we following the path of reason wherever it leads?

While the goal of rationalism is clear—to be bound, *commanded*, by reason's dictates—we mustn't fool ourselves into thinking that this is a simple task. Reason is a curious commander. No Patton, she's not even a Vince Lombardi. Like anyone who communicates through whispers, she's easy to ignore. Reason is never shrill, but on her second level, her voice is more muted than on her first. Typically, once ignored, the advice is gone, and our powers of rationalization rush upon the scene, blotting out with abandon any semblance of reason's dissent.

To be a rationalist is to grab onto reason's whispers and not let go. And when we do err and stray from reason's proposed path, rationalism requires that we recognize our mistake ASAP. There are few better signs of a rationalist than one who is willing to admit to his mistakes—and unwilling to "rationalize" them.

Rationalism is about balance. It has to be, or else it would be better termed lunacism. On the one hand, we find ourselves with emotional desires and biological needs. On the other, we find ourselves with a brain—and the capacity to seek universal truths.

The rationalist lifestyle is about seizing the best of both worlds. We need to eat, drink, make love, hear beautiful music, commune with friends ... the list of our personal needs could go on and on. But we don't have to tend to these needs 24 hours a day. We also have time to consider the great questions of philosophy and construct our own beliefs largely on the basis of logic. Just as importantly, we have time to use our brains to make an impact on the world at large—in our occupations, our selections at the ballot box and through our avocations. In those domains of life, we are faced with a fateful choice: do we attempt to meet the world parochially or as universalists? Reason awaits her answer.

Candidly, entering the second level is hardly a sacrifice. As we make a habit of seeking reason out, she responds with greater and greater regularity, and we come to recognize how instead of trying to subdue the planet, we have the capacity to live in harmony with it—to nurture it and allow it to nurture us. Further, rationalism isn't simply the path of inner peace; it's also the path of liberation. Only by transcending our creature constraints and meeting reason on her highest level can we fully unleash our mental powers.

So rationalism can do wonders for the individual. Yet perhaps its greatest gifts are for the society. When it comes to the ultimate questions, we live in a world of strong opinions that divide people in all sorts of ways. The consequences of these divisions are stark—they run the gamut from uncivil conversations, to job discrimination, to rape, to murder, even to genocide.

Rationalism tends not to excite people generally, but it excites us, particularly the role it could play in bringing the world together. Warring camps could unite in pursuit of a common goal—to locate objective truth, or as much of it as we human beings are capable of grasping. We might differ on how to reach that goal, but we can at least agree on the objective. And we should also agree that those who are serious about that objective must demonstrate their ability to see all sides of an issue and their willingness to concede to their opponents whenever logic requires. In realizing the need to think and speak logically, we can also agree on a common language.

In short, our rationalism impels us to come together respectfully with our fellow human beings, regardless of our differences. How else can we rationalists develop our *common* sense? And if we can't develop our common sense, how can we seriously call ourselves rationalists?

Even on her second level, reason is a temptress. My God, what a temptress. She never gives us one choice in response to any philosophical question. The more we seek her, the more choices we hear. And somehow, we must figure out a way to discard some of them.

Perhaps after we die we are reincarnated as an animal or person here on planet Earth. Perhaps. But *she* tells us that other "plausible" conceptions are more reasonable, so we rationalists don't buy into that one.

Perhaps the Bible is literally true, and the world was created from a state of nothingness several thousand years ago by a being who lives in a place called heaven. Perhaps. But *she* tells us that other "plausible" conceptions are more reasonable, so we give that one a pass too.

Some rationalists call themselves servants of truth. We'd rather see ourselves as reason's servants. She doesn't always counsel telling the truth, you know. If, for instance, we have the opportunity to hide a fugitive from the murderous hands of a fascist government, reason tells us to go ahead and protect the fugitive, and lie if we're ever confronted about him. Still, a rationalist should never lie to *oneself*. Any decision to adopt a particular viewpoint when another is more reasonable would require either giving up rationalism or lying to oneself. To a rationalist, neither is acceptable. *Ever.*

We rationalists don't know if we can handle the truth. But at least we're willing to try. And try again, and again ...

While we're on the subject of truth, how's this for irony? Many anti-rationalists claim to be truth's disciples. Ask the most dogmatic, closed-minded theologians about rationalism, and they'll say it's bunk. But they'll call themselves servants of the truth. Their truth, you see, is only known in the heart. It can't be known in the mind—at least it can't be communicated in the language of logic.

The world is now replete with these self proclaimed truth-disciples, none of whom seem to be able effectively to reach out beyond their own parochial groups. They may like the sound of the word "truth," but they don't look for it very diligently or in many places. They know it only from studying their own Scriptures and certain interpretations of those Scriptures.

Apparently, they've never learned the lesson about the Tower of Babel: we mustn't take any one building, language, culture or religion so seriously as to think it monopolizes the truth.

The lifeblood of rationalism is the devotion to *principles*. Rationalists seek out all manner of principles—mathematical theorems, natural laws, moral doctrines, sociological patterns. The wider their application, the more we cherish them.

Rationalist principles are born of reflection, tested by the crucible of experience and applied based on common sense. They need to be nourished in an environment that recognizes every situation as unique and judges it accordingly. "Ideologues," in other words, aren't rationalists. Their minds are closed.

Still, despite the risk that principles will blind us to the facts on the ground, we must consult them whenever an important decision or philosophical choice is made. Otherwise we'll miss much of what reason is whispering in our ears.

Grounded in reality, but at once uplifted *and* bound by principles—that is the way of the committed rationalist.

For many people, it's also the path not taken. Just consider the realm of ethics. Level Two moral principles are violated as often as people change underwear. They're easy to ignore because a person faced with a moral decision can always find ways that his life is distinguishable from others, so conventional rules need not apply. Thus, for instance, a politician could justify committing marital infidelity by rationalizing that traditional mores shouldn't apply to those who have to live with unusually great stresses and demands. But that's nonsense. From the rationalist's perspective, it is difficult to envision any acceptable justification for marital infidelity—however important, or self-important, the would-be adulterer might be.

We chose the example of marital infidelity because that prohibition comes from the Bible, a source of many invaluable principles. Make no mistake—we take that book to be more than mere "literature." For centuries on end, it has formed the bedrock of civility in Western culture. To ignore its ethical precepts is, to say the least, extremely dangerous. Nevertheless, to be a rationalist in our sense of the term is to avoid letting any book, even the Bible, become our *ultimate* source of moral authority. That is reserved for the voice of reason itself—that still, small voice that distinguishes right from wrong and truth from fiction.

So, you see, we love reason, and we're happy to follow her wherever she leads. But we only love her because she'll level with us, even about her own limitations. She's told us that she alone can't bring us wisdom. How could she, given that some of her greatest disciples have held such radically different beliefs and exemplified such radically different values?

Wasn't the great Plato one of reason's greatest followers? But Plato also taught that in an ideal society the government would practice censorship and establish what amounts to a caste system. Do we really want to adopt his values as our own?

And what about Marx? He was a devoted rationalist who viewed his theories as "scientific." His critique of capitalist societies was brilliant; his theory of history, fascinating. Yet many of his teachings are an affront to the conscience—like the idea that the ends justify the means, so violence against peaceful people is acceptable as long as it would help the working class. For all of his genius, aren't we thankful that we don't live in a Marxist world?

We also have the example of Martin Heidegger. Arguably the 20th century's most profound philosopher, his ruminations on the nature of *being* are majestic. But he was a German who flirted with Nazism at its outset and never could condemn it squarely, even decades after its demise. Somehow, his doesn't sound like a profile in courage or humanitarianism.

We toast Plato, Marx and Heidegger for all that they've fed our cerebra. But we're looking for role models who feed our entire souls. Clearly, then, our philosophy must go beyond the mere celebration of rationalism or the intellect. In fact, we would be hard pressed to praise the intellect at all—unless it is coupled with another characteristic that is far more sacred in our eyes. That characteristic is empathy.

B. *Empathy*

We've spoken of a life devoted to reason. Now, we turn to a life devoted to empathy. The first suggests the preeminence of the mind; the second, the heart. Historically, this has been viewed as an either/or, a choice between forks in a road. Mister Spock or Mother Teresa. Whoever attempts to have it both ways will drive himself crazy, or so the story goes, just as Spock did whenever he gave his emotions a try.

Perhaps we're already crazy, but we believe these two faculties aren't just compatible, they are crucial complements of one another. While we're committed to honoring all of reason's dictates, she usually isn't giving dictation, so we're generally free to act as we please. We can think of no better way to use that freedom than to emulate the world's greatest empaths.

Rationalism teaches how to transcend our limitations as human beings. Empathy teaches us the beauty of humanity.

If reason is about thinking, empathy is about opening our hearts with love. We said before that disciples of reason are devoted to thinking about *universal* truths and applying those truths to their lifestyles and philosophies. Similarly, empaths strive to open their hearts universally and not just to a narrow range of beloveds.

Every human heart is open to somebody or something. Most of us open our hearts to family members or friends. We might also sympathize with people who are poor or sick, or who share our interests or backgrounds. Even Hitler opened his heart to attractive Teutons, or, for that matter, to dogs.

To a degree, then, we're all capable of love. But some people stand out in the depth and breadth of their willingness to empathize. They're the ones worthy of the term "empath."

Empaths try to open their hearts not to some others but to *the other*—in other words, to whatever or whomever is outside their own egos. They don't always succeed. Often, distance remains, perhaps even dislike. But never is an empath's heart fully closed. Not even to Hitler.

You can judge an empath more by his incapacity for coldness than by his capacity for love. That's why history doesn't judge Ramses II by the extent to which he opened his heart to Egyptians but rather by the extent to which he closed it to the Hebrews.

The cornerstone of empathy is the encounter. We can recognize empaths by the unusual way in which they encounter or meet the *other* in its many forms.

Perhaps Seinfeld's Bubble Boy is an exception. But for the rest of us, life is best viewed as a series of enounters. Whether we come across a person, a book, or an oak tree, we find ourselves with an opportunity for one of these meetings. Obviously, they don't fill up all of our time. But when we're not encountering the *other*—as when we sleep—we're probably digesting the relationships our encounters have forged.

Empaths bring to these meetings a certain type of love—love laden with respect. An empath approaches the *other* realistically, refusing to let his prior expectations distort the way he sees the *other's* face; after all, no other attitude would be respectful. Combining love and respect, the empath shows deep, compassionate concern for the *other's* needs and wants. These respectful, loving, caring connections—these powerful relationships fully experienced in the light of day—are the ultimate marks of the empath.

Love, respect, concern. They comprise much of the blood of

the empath's veins, yet none of these words captures empathy at its heights. The greatest empaths bring to the meeting another element—that of enchantment.

We all know what it means to be enchanted. It's an emotion we've felt on special occasions, like when we visit the Sistine Chapel or the Grand Canyon. Many take pride in their ability to appreciate exceptional beauty. But we say, "Big whoop!" Who can't appreciate the *other* in its most wondrous forms? Empaths don't stop at that. They're enchanted by the *mundane*.

That's why whenever an empath encounters a human face, even one that lacks unusual intelligence or classical beauty, empaths are moved—perhaps by its unique features, perhaps by its similarities to other faces, perhaps by any number of things, but in any event, they are moved.

Empaths aren't in love with an honored few. Empaths are in awe of life itself.

Yeah, we know. It all sounds good in theory. But who has the time to be empathic 24/7? The fact is that everyone has choices to make. Even the greatest empaths can't encounter everything, or every one, empathically. In fact, no matter how empathic the soul, at times he will encounter a person whom he finds distasteful. We're talking eating-a-bad-tomato distasteful. Perhaps the person is a malicious gossip or a pathological liar. Perhaps he's just plain violent.

To be empathic in these situations doesn't require turning the other cheek. Sometimes people have to be confronted and stopped in their tracks. Yet, even in the darkest of encounters, an empath must act respectfully toward the *other*. He must recognize that this distasteful or violent person is a human being, cut from the same basic cloth as the empath himself.

When encountering a walking, talking bad tomato, the situation is no different from when the empath recognizes something about himself he doesn't like. He doesn't wallow in self-loathing. Where's the respect in that? For the same reason, he shouldn't wallow in hatred for others.

That said, if it turns out that an empath finds himself in the same situation that a certain writer did in *A Clockwork Orange* and is forced to witness the *other* raping his wife before his very eyes, we suppose a heaping handful of hatred is in order. But even then, the pilot light must at least be flickering.

To illustrate what it means to be an empath, we wish to turn to the golden age of rabbinic Judaism and the struggle between two schools of thought—the House of Hillel and the House of Shammai. Shammai was a parush—someone who keeps a distance from that which is deemed sinful or unclean. Hillel, by contrast, was a hasid. We use this term not as it is typically used today to refer to a member of certain Ultra-Orthodox communities, but in its more traditional sense as a pious person whose piety comes from love, not fear. Hasids are distinguished by a visceral affection for God and people, *all* of whom they strive to encounter with gentleness, patience, compassion and respect.

Buddhist spirituality discusses the goal of eliminating the "I." The hasidism of Hillel does not. Hasids rejoice in the encounter between the self and the *other,* and they recognize the importance to each of us of having strong, secure egos, lest we treat the *other* not with respect, but fear or resentment. Hasids aren't afraid to embrace the *I.* They only want to jettison some of its typical features—like selfishness, self-centeredness, and their triplet, conceit.

Consider a meeting between Hillel and some undistinguished member of his community. Each would be profoundly concerned about the other. Each would be experienced by the other as unique and worthy of honor. You might expect this attitude from the nondescript man who meets the great Rabbi Hillel. What we wish to stress is that this man would be equally honored in the mind of the rabbi. To Hillel, being in the presence of an average Joe is a joy and a privilege. We can imagine no greater joy or privilege than to be in the presence of an empath like Hillel.

People resembling Hillel are around today. Sometimes they're children; sometimes, adults. Whenever you meet one, you ask yourself "what have *I* done to deserve so much of his esteem?" You've been born the child of a human mother—it's as simple as that. Those who live in the spirit of Hillel respect all life forms but reserve a special place in their heart for people. Merely by finding yourself in that category, you receive the same kind of concern from hasids that they would show a great sage or a political prince.

Unfortunately, the Hillels of the world are a rare breed. As a result, people's standards for empathy are low. All it takes is a smile and a kind word to be called "polite" or "civil." If you go out of your way to shoot the breeze with your neighbor, you might even be called "friendly" or "nice." Those are considered fine compliments.

Far be it from us to criticize acts of politeness or friendliness. But neither of these concepts begins to touch the level of the empath. Neither does justice to a Hillel. If one word were to be used to describe an empathic encounter it would be *warmth*. Empaths exude it with every facet of their spirit. Only with warmth are they able to establish the connections that give their lives meaning.

It takes a lot of courage to routinely act warmly outside of your family or your circle of friends. Some people are put off by it—they'd prefer the privacy that is born from distance. Presumably, the empath would respect that preference, but not without some frustration. The natural state of the empath is to be affectionately drawn towards other people with the force of a magnet.

ᔓ

Was Hillel not just an empath but a rationalist too? He was certainly an intellectual. It is said that one night, a young Hillel was too poor to pay his way to enter the House of Study. So rather than missing two great rabbis debate, he climbed up on the roof and listened. He was so absorbed in what they were saying that he didn't notice the snow falling around him. The next day, he was found unconscious on the rooftop skylight.

Hillel, then, was a lover *and* a thinker. But was he a rationalist? Candidly, we don't know enough about him to say. We don't know, for example, whether he was willing to follow the path of reason wherever it took him, or whether he instead felt bound by his Judaism to a set of doctrines that he dared not question.

In other words, we don't know whether Hillel was the kind of theologian who believes that if you open your mind too much, your brains will fall out.

That's not our attitude. We've come here to toast a philosophy where questioning is always encouraged, always mandated, and where no cows are sacred. For lack of a better expression, we'll coin this philosophy *Empathic Rationalism*. Rationalism is the noun, because ultimately we must always follow reason's dictates wherever we hear them. But remember, she is usually silent. And when she is, we hope that the direction of our life will be empathic. This is the route in which we are impelled to move from day to day, minute to minute.

To explain Empathic Rationalism, we have focused on Hillel in large part because he is such an uncontroversial figure today. As a result, Hillel may be studied without prior biases interfering with our thinking. The fact is, however, that only decades after Hillel modeled his empathic philosophy to the Hebrews, another man came who, together with his followers, spread a compatible philosophy throughout the planet. This is a man who is known to us all—indeed, he may be the most pivotal figure in human history.

Exemplifying numerous virtues, and none more than empathy, Jesus of Nazareth has come to be seen by a billion or more as their Lord and Savior. But to a growing number of others, the religion associated with his name has become an object of distaste, even hatred. Christianity is now widely associated with bigotry and divisiveness. The irony is palpable, given that the historical Jesus came to preach such a universalistic, benign message. When we contemplate his brief life on Earth, we see the quintessential example of the loving humanitarianism at the center of Empathic Rationalism.

Undeniably, faith in Jesus as the Christ has permanently uplifted legions of wayward souls. In that sense, he has truly served as a savior, perhaps the greatest savior of all. Yet with no disrespect intended to those who worship him, we as a group have not come to honor Jesus as a Lord or as the one and only savior of humankind. In other words, we are not all disciples of *Christ*. But we hope that some day every person will be a disciple of *Jesus*.

C. Passion

Our creed has a label—Empathic Rationalism. But the commitment to empathy and reason doesn't fully express what we have in mind. One final concept is needed: *passion*.

We fully recognize its dangers. How could we not? Observe human rage, and you'll see the face of passion. Hide a camera in an adulterer's hotel suite, and you'll see it again—more vividly than in the bedrooms of most married couples. The fact is that passion fuels many an act of horror or vice. If nirvana's your thing, passion's your enemy.

In discussing reason, we spoke of inner peace and harmony. With passion, we think instead of *sturm und drang*—great victories and agonizing defeats, miraculous births and devastating deaths, blissful unions and unrequited loves.

Perhaps we should look passion in the eye and say "thanks, but no thanks." That's what a blood pressure specialist might suggest. And yet ... as you might have gathered by now, we're here to salute passion just the same. It has an honored place in Empathic Rationalism.

That's how we see passion—as combined with the other facets of our creed. Apart from them, passion's a threat. As part of a life devoted to reason and empathy, it's a godsend. Empathic Rationalism is designed to limit passion's potential for devastation. This is a creed of moderation; it extols sanity. Empathic Rationalists never want to know the abyss up close and personally.

Thankfully, life isn't a mere minefield. There is much to celebrate: our spouse, children, friends, social causes, religion— you name it. Whatever manifestation of the *other* we find to be uplifting and meaningful is a potential object of passionate joy. The memory of this joy helps us persevere through even the worst sorrows. As we experience and recall our ecstasies, we fashion our uniqueness as individuals and make our egos strong and secure.

Armed with these assets, Empathic Rationalists are prepared not only to face the world but also to transform it. To nurture the soul of this planet, hard work must be done. Hard, inspired work. We know of no better motivational tool for making this happen than passion. It gets the blood flowing, the eyes focused, and the hand poised for action.

Passionate Empathic Rationalists are vigilant. They are so entranced by the prospect of redeeming the world that they are compelled to watch closely and identify any way possible to work toward redemption. But again—they don't simply watch. They make things happen. They don't feel that they have the luxury of failure.

There you have it. Contemplation. Compassion. Action. Why settle for less?

Sadly, we recognize passion in the face of violent fanaticism. Taken to an extreme, it is no better for the Earth than for the individual. But we'll take the chance that we can keep our passion at a sane level. As would-be Empathic Rationalists, we need to have that much self-respect.

Ultimately, the issue for us isn't whether to embrace passion, but what causes to become passionate about. This brings us back to the centrality of the *encounter*. Whenever we find an opportunity for a meaningful, wholesome encounter, the prospect exists to forge a passionate relationship. We hope to be passionate about confronting the great intellectual questions. We hope to be passionate about the individuals whose lives intersect with our own. And perhaps above all else, we hope to be passionate about lending a hand, a heart, and a mind toward the further evolution of our planet.

Frequently, the passionate encounters we seek will lead to

suffering. Such is the nature of the beast. But if we're to be Empathic Rationalists, we mustn't worry about reducing our suffering to a bare minimum. We'll strive for fulfillment—not perpetual euphoria. That, we'll leave to the utopian dreamers. We've got work to do.

⁊🐦

Please allow us to summarize our philosophy in a simple sentence:

Let passion be your sail,
Reason your keel,
And empathy your rudder.

⁊🐦

II. Applying the Creed

We've been trying to paint a picture—a vision that can guide both our beliefs and our actions. Now, we'd like to give examples of how we'd apply this vision in practice.

Our goal will be to demonstrate how an Empathic Rationalist might approach some of the basic issues in public policy and religion. The key word here is *might*. Empathic Rationalism stands for one thing above all else—the need to rid ourselves of dogma. So however we apply our philosophy today, we could apply it very differently tomorrow. We must never become so in love with our current beliefs that they keep us from opening our minds to something deeper.

A. Fundamental Freedoms

Let us begin by announcing our support for civil liberties. By that, we mean freedom of *action*—the liberty to express our tastes, interests and beliefs however we want to.

A huge part of our society lives so conventionally that it doesn't worry about the majority deciding what conduct is acceptable and what isn't. Many are also offended by acts of "sin"—since, of course, they never engage in it—to the point where they would gladly enlist the government in wiping it out.

We can't condone the government's prohibiting "sin." But there remain other sensible reasons to restrict conduct. Certain actions directly threaten other people or are cruel to animals. Obviously, they should be prohibited. In some situations, we're even willing to prohibit conduct that harms nobody but the actor, such as attempted suicides.

Our Empathic Rationalism doesn't take an extreme libertarian position. It's not a philosophy of extremes. But it does have a center of gravity, and that's foursquare in support of liberty of conduct. We consider it breathing room for the soul. Any government that wishes to restrict it better have a pretty compelling reason.

The more rationalistic we are, the freer the thinkers we become, and the more apt we are to march to the beat of our own drummers. That's one reason we're civil libertarians. We don't trust conventional mores to form the basis for government prohibitions.

Similarly, Empathic Rationalism compels us to adopt a fair amount of humility. No person can possibly appreciate all the needs and desires of his fellow citizens. To treat others with empathic respect is to assume, absent clear evidence to the contrary, that they're in the best position to decide how to live their own lives. Moreover, we can't justify telling adults what they can and can't do simply because our holy books might prohibit their actions. Remember—we recognize reason, not the literal words of Scripture, as the ultimate arbiter of truth.

In addition, for one part of a society to restrict the civil liberties of another would breed the latter's resentment, and possibly even destroy its self esteem. Empathic Rationalism would never flourish in such an environment.

Finally, our form of rationalism thrives only when we're deeply sensitive to the perspectives of people who are very different than we are. The question to ask is: what kind of world would we wish to live in if we knew nothing about our own preferences? If we didn't know whether or not we had homicidal tendencies, for example, we'd still be forced to prohibit murder. But other forms of social "deviance" aren't patently destructive. If we knew nothing about our sexual preferences, and we weren't letting the literal words of Scripture control our conduct, isn't it obvious that we wouldn't tolerate laws that discriminate against homosexuals?

That brings us to the first issue we'd like to address—whether gay marriages should be permitted. To us, few issues are more cut and dried. Yet, somehow, we have staked out what most people would consider a "fringe" position—not only because we support the right of gay people to get married but because we think this right is such an important one.

We know of no institution more conducive to human welfare than marriage. It makes our lives stable and secure, and it provides a wellspring of love that carries over well beyond our families. We can't imagine denying that institution to *any* pair of consenting adults. And that hardly distinguishes us as humanitarians: even slave holders commonly permitted their slaves to partake of this holy tradition.

If Empathic Rationalism stands for anything, it stands for the need to honor *and empower* people whenever they find love in their lives, whether it is via the conventional route or some alternative lifestyle. Homosexuality is not inherently violent. It isn't hateful. And it shouldn't be threatening—except for gays who are trying to deny the truth about themselves. Rather than prohibiting gay marriage, we might wish to *encourage* it instead.

The majority view is that marriage is an institution with a definite historical meaning, one that entails the permanent union between a man and a woman. Once we allow gay people to marry, the argument goes, we've torn the institution apart by its roots. What would stop us from allowing groups of three or more people to get married, all in the name of encouraging permanent unions among loving adults?

Our response is that the *essence* of marriage has nothing to do with gender. While it is true that marriages traditionally have been between a man and a woman, it's also "traditional" that married couples come from the same race or social class. So what? What makes marriage holy is that it supports two consenting adults who wish to pledge their love and companionship to each other for the rest of their lives. Whether they're black or white, rich or poor, men or women is irrelevant to their entitlement to the spiritual benefits associated with matrimony. It's also irrelevant that two men or two women can't have a baby together; if that were a requirement, infertile heterosexual couples wouldn't be eligible for marriage either.

Some would say we're arguing about semantics—the meaning of the "essence" of marriage. But this isn't just about semantics. Our interpretation of Empathic Rationalism requires us to respect freedom of action as a fundamental principle. That means we must place a high burden of persuasion on those who would deprive people of the right to partake in *any* institution that is half as enriching as marriage. When in doubt, society must be inclusive, tolerant and willing to embrace the *other*. Why would we ever tell homosexuals, who've already suffered so much discrimination, that we wish to stop them from partaking in our most beloved social institution simply because of a semantic construction that is arguable at best?

We're often amazed by how little the majority feels that it owes to groups who have been victims of discrimination in the past.

❦

The gay marriage issue is so easy for us to resolve largely because no one is victimized by those marriages other than the sensibilities of the intolerant. In that sense, the issue differs from many other civil liberty debates, where acts of free expression lead to innocent casualties. Those situations give us pause; we can't sit idly by and allow people to harm the innocent. Nevertheless, if the issue is strictly one of *law*, we generally tend to support the path of freedom.

For example, we'd permit all law-abiding adults to retain certain firearms despite the potential of these weapons to kill or maim. This is a society that, since its inception, has recognized the rights of citizens to own guns in order to protect themselves or hunt animals. Those rights are embedded in American culture, not merely in our law. Under the circumstances, taking those rights away would almost seem like bringing back Prohibition.

As the garden variety handgun is typically used only for self-defense purposes, people should be allowed to possess them in their homes. Similarly, as traditional rifles are primarily used to hunt wild animals, not people, citizens should be permitted to own these weapons as well.

As another example of civil libertarianism, we're generally pro choice on abortion. Late-term abortions are truly savage and should be prohibited, but those procedures are relatively rare. The main issue is what to do about abortions during the first trimester. It's a difficult issue, since abortion always involves a killing of another human life. Yet this living being isn't necessarily a *person* in the conventional sense of that word, other than in late-term abortions. More importantly, it is growing inside a woman who presumably has a say over what happens within her own body. This creates just the kind of balancing act between fundamental rights that we view the law as ill-equipped to resolve. Moreover, when we consider extreme forms of the "pro life" position, the issue becomes particularly clear. Rationalism can hardly countenance forcing a rape victim who is psychologically unable to carry the fruits of that rape for nine months to risk her own life in some sort of back-alley procedure. After all, that rape victim could be our own sister or daughter.

So what does that make us? Pro-gun and pro-abortion? Actually, we are neither. To reiterate—we've been speaking solely of what behavior should be *legal*, not what behavior we view as appropriate or wise. Americans today have an annoying habit of reducing all issues of public policy to questions of legal rights. Should handguns be legal, yes or no? Are you pro-abortion rights, or against them? Find out which politicians agree with you, send them to Washington, and be done with the whole matter.

If the issue is one of legality, we vote with the permissive brood. But if the issue is whether our leaders need to *raise consciousness* in our society against destructive conduct, you'll find us on the anti-gun and anti-abortion sides.

People need to be educated about whether guns in the hands of ordinary citizens tend to save more innocent lives or *take* them. We suspect the latter. People must also be asked how they can believe on Sundays that "life is sacred," while spending Saturdays killing innocent animals purely for the "sport." We understand that sometimes the herd has to be thinned for the greater good, but how can hunters actually enjoy the shooting of an animal? Like the executioner's, the hunter's task should be a solemn one, not a pleasure.

As for abortion, we must realize that unprotected sex can result in a *needless*, tragic choice between nine months with an unwanted pregnancy or the killing of a human life form. Those who trivialize the human fetus and use abortion as a form of birth control hold their species in utter disrespect.

As much as the pro-choice movement protects the choice to terminate a pregnancy, it also protects the choice to wantonly risk a human life—by engaging in irresponsible sex. We who call ourselves "pro choice" had better do something to ensure that this happens as rarely as possible.

In short, America must remain the land of the free. But it doesn't have to remain the land of gun violence or abortion epidemics. How do we minimize these horrors? By taking the fight out of the courtroom and into the culture. That entails that we all recognize one basic fact—the horrors we've been discussing will continue on a massive scale unless we reduce the amount of poverty in our society.

Poverty is at the heart of our problems. Not freedom.

B. The Marketplace and Its Lessons

Now, we'd like to turn to a second set of issues. They all revolve around one common concept—the marketplace. As would-be Empathic Rationalists, we're big fans. No matter what manifestation of the marketplace is under discussion—be it the economic marketplace or the marketplace of ideas—Empathic Rationalism supports it wholeheartedly.

In economics, the marketplace refers to a space where people attempt to peddle items of value to the public. Depending upon the public's reaction, the items will either skyrocket in value and usage, or die on the vine. We enter the marketplace of ideas whenever actions are taken or proposals made and the public is given an opportunity to evaluate them. The marketplace of ideas is alive in forums such as newspapers and magazines. It is perhaps most alive in times of free elections involving a genuinely engaged electorate.

In any marketplace, ultimate power is given to the public. Whoever contributes to the marketplace must disclose enough information about their own products or ideas to enable the public to make a fully educated choice. The marketplace encourages experimentation. First, the public shops, then it buys, then it utilizes what it purchased, and, finally, it evaluates the purchase. This process applies whether a society is considering a widget or a new approach to world peace. Thanks to the marketplace, choices need not be made based on the speculation of elites, but, rather, on the actual experiences of the public.

There are many reasons why the marketplace is one of the darlings of Empathic Rationalism. To begin, the empathy and humility at the heart of this philosophy are built on respecting *all* people. No mechanism for evaluating ideas and products respects the power of the masses more than the marketplace. Further, any serious rationalist recognizes the value of experimentation and experience as guides for future choices. This is ironic, because rationalism would appear to support the value of pure reason, or the capacity of the human mind to determine truth based on logic alone. Then again, appearances can be deceiving. Rationalists wouldn't be behaving sensibly if they placed no value on the benefits of human experience. Reason demands that her disciples take advantage of every tool at their disposal.

It follows from what's been said that Empathic Rationalism would support the institution of a market-based economy, rather than one built on the judgments of a small number of central planners, as in a Marxist regime. Because market-based economies require lots of competitors who are willing to risk complete failure for the chance to remain in business, these economies must create handsome incentives for those who succeed. That means that substantial wealth disparities are inevitable. Like them or not, and we don't, they're the price we must pay for the prosperity that only the marketplace can bring.

To say that we love the marketplace, however, is not to say that we worship it. Marketplaces often require regulation and, inevitably, powerful forces are in place to prevent the regulators from doing their jobs. Before leaving the subject of the marketplace, we would like to offer an example of a market breakdown. We were tempted to discuss the awful global threat to our environment. But we've chosen to focus instead on another problem, one that we consider to be at least as horrific. We're back to talking about poverty.

Poverty is a sign that every competition has its losers. It's fine to praise the great economic competition that fuels a market-based economy, but unless someone steps in to help those who come up short, poverty will be here to stay. Finding it in any society is sad. Finding it to be *rampant* in a society as wealthy as ours is unconscionable.

That's our lament. Who could disagree with it? Even the anti-tax crowd wouldn't try. "Poverty?" we could hear them saying. "Sure it's a terrible thing. Can you pass the veal, please?"

Nobody's proud of rampant poverty, but a whole lot of people are prepared to tolerate it. So are our political parties. The political marketplace of ideas isn't set up to reward statesmen who care about poverty, since so many of the poor are too alienated to vote and few, if any, can raise significant campaign funds. Without voting constituents or fundraising support, how could anti-poverty politicians expect to get elected, let alone re-elected?

If you want to hear people talk about poverty in our country, you're most likely to hear it addressed by the business community. Businesses love to toot their own horns about their charitable walk-a-thons and celebrity golf events. It's good for company morale and doesn't hurt their reputation with the public either. Unfortunately, these charitable events are mere ripples in the ocean when we compare the money they raise to the funds needed to fight poverty on any sizable scale. Only the government can oversee a massive, sustained, frontal attack on poverty's infrastructure. To defeat poverty, it needs tax dollars, the very dollars that much of the business community is lobbying *not* to have to pay.

That means our nation's poor are left in the hands of apathetic politicians and businessmen who give *dimes* with their left hands while refusing to pay *dollars* with their right. Yet the politicians call themselves compassionate, and the businessmen call themselves charitable. Chutzpah, indeed!

Empathic Rationalists ask the questions: *Dare* we put up with rampant poverty? And if not, are we as a society prepared to invest our blood, sweat and tears to eradicate it? No matter how pessimistic we get, we must keep asking these questions. Otherwise, we'd have to hold ourselves personally responsible for the problem.

The fact is that few things viscerally affect an empath as much as the need to obliterate poverty. Whenever empaths encounter affluence, they're reminded of the joy people derive from material wealth. Decent homes, vacations in beautiful places, you name it—modern life can't be fully enjoyed without them, and they, in turn, can't be obtained without money. Truly empathic souls have difficulty enjoying their own wealth as long as so many of their brothers and sisters are poor.

The rationalistic component of our creed is equally intolerant of poverty. On this topic, reason poses a clear challenge: "Assume you don't know where you'll be born or how rich you'll be," she says. "Would you be prepared to give up the chance to live like a king for the security of knowing you won't live like a dog?" Merely to ask this question is to answer it.

Our creed gives us one choice: to urge that we all band together and mobilize our national strength in a fight against poverty—one waged as furiously as if we were fighting a foreign army. Is that such an absurd thought? Belligerent foreign dictators mobilize us by triggering our fear and hatred. Why couldn't our hope and love fuel a very different war—one fought in the spirit of America's Declaration of Independence, which claims that everyone by virtue of their humanity is endowed with the right to pursue their happiness? Clearly, that right is being denied to virtually every child born today in the South Bronx.

Is it realistic to say that poverty can ever *completely* be eliminated? Of course not, but that isn't the point. Our poverty problem is rampant, and rampant poverty is needless. America has enough resources to provide decent educational and job-training opportunities to most of our nation's poor, and to incentivize the business community to employ them at liveable wages.

In fighting poverty, the government needs to place most of its resources in initiatives designed to help the poor work themselves out of poverty, rather than to depend on handouts. That way, our efforts should bear permanent fruit. And besides, as long as poor people are willing to work hard, taxpayers won't balk so much at subsidizing them. Of course, we mustn't forget the need to create a safety net that supports the dignity of all people—even those who won't help themselves. Many of these "deadbeats" happen to be the parents of innocent children.

With whom should the government work to alleviate poverty? We say, *all* organizations that are sincerely devoted to serving the poor, including faith-based organizations. That's right. Even if the organizations proselytize, we'd support them. In this context, the idea of a Chinese Wall between religion and government is something our society can't afford. Those who feel to the contrary may or may not be religious, but we're reasonably sure they've never lived in poverty.

For the government to avoid partnering with religious charities isn't sound public policy, it's liberal paranoia. If we're really going to fight poverty in earnest, we'd better use all the weapons at our disposal. Remember, we're talking about *war*!

In the short run, the idea of a war on poverty is a bit fanciful. But we have faith that, in the long run, this war is inevitable. People on both the left and right would be hard pressed *not* to enlist in it if somehow they could be forced to put their money where their mouths are. Liberals claim to be humanitarians and advocates for the underprivileged. How, then, could they justify ignoring the cries of the poor if these cries enter into our nation's consciousness? Conservatives frequently claim that their greatest concern is eliminating cultural decadence—meaning violent crime, drug use, dead-beat fatherhood and abortions. How could these conservatives, or anyone else, possibly doubt that reducing poverty would be the best way to keep such decadence to a minimum?

In order to unify America in support of this common war, all we need are a few good men and women—charismatic and thoughtful leaders, much like the leaders who met in Philadelphia during the summer of 1776. These new leaders must be prepared to inspire a movement. The movement would issue challenges to politicians: how *dare* you allow rampant poverty to continue and think you possess moral authority on the other issues you like to talk about? The movement would also challenge the media: how do you justify reporting ad nauseam on the O.J. Simpson trial or the Monica Lewinsky scandal and treat our poverty problem as old news? The future leaders will figure out a way to make this problem seem urgent and, therefore, newsworthy.

We have enough faith in our country to believe that a war on poverty will be waged in the not too distant future. And yet the war we have in mind would necessarily be a limited one. It would be confined to the borders of the USA. That's a shame, as our species' worst poverty problems are overseas. But Americans can't fight that problem yet as a *war*—at least not the kind of total war we've been talking about, one worthy of William Tecumseh Sherman. This country must learn to crawl before it can walk.

First, the South Bronx. Later, the world.

C. God

We come now to a word that we've rarely mentioned during this talk: God. We associate that word, above all else, with the unity of life. And yet somehow, this same word has become an incredibly divisive force in our society.

Even among those who "believe," speaking about God can breed disrespect. Protestants ridicule Catholics for the way they venerate Mary and the Pope, but are ridiculed by Jews for the way they venerate Jesus. Then again, the same Jews who mock Christians are mocked by their fellow Hebrews. The Orthodox say the Reform dishonor God's word, whereas the Reform say the Orthodox are antiquated, superstitious cultists. And so it goes. All those people may believe in "God," but they mean largely different things by that word. And more often than not, they're all too certain that their own conception of God is objectively superior.

Must we state the obvious? How can anyone speak with authority about who God is or *whether* God is? We're only human. What do we know about the ultimate truths of reality? And if we don't know much about that, how confident can we be in what we think about God?

Maybe we can agree that *all* God-speak is presumptuous. That wouldn't alter the fact that it can also be incredibly meaningful and fulfilling. It sure is for us. Our empathic side clamors for us to *believe*, to encounter the *other* not only as it appears in finite, discrete forms, like "dogs" or "rocks," but as it shines in its grandest glory, as the reflection of cosmic unity—the limitless, timeless, wondrous *Being* that has always existed and will exist forever.

Ah, but rationalism is the noun, and empathic the adjective. We can't allow ourselves to cleave to whatever portrait of God tickles our emotional fancies. Any perspective we adopt on this issue must be the one that's the most sensible. So even if we'd love to believe that God is a talking horse, should one emerge next year in Churchill Downs, as long as we think that belief conflicts with the dictates of reason, we can't go there.

Does that mean our thirst for emotional fulfillment has no role to play in our choice of beliefs? Not necessarily. If a particular perspective on God is *the* most sensible, we're stuck with it. But what if we find no single optimal perspective? What if we find two or three that excel to an equal degree when submitted to the crucible of reason? That's when we can choose the perspective that works best in our lives—in other words, the one that lets us live with the most fulfillment and meaning.

Reason gives us that freedom. She calls it her principle of *pragmatism*.

It's time now to check some philosophies of God off our list. Where better to start than with the traditional God that we've all heard about since we were in diapers?

Each of us has read what Christians call the Old and New Testaments. And we're familiar with the God-character that emerges from these books—why He created the world, what His personality is like, which races of people He decided to reward, which ones He punished, and why He sent His own Son to walk the earth in the form of flesh and blood.

Sorry, but it's too darned anthropomorphic for us. What can we say? We're rationalists. The Biblical portrait of God smacks of wishful thinking on the part of human, all-too-human authors. Who are we to posit a God who's so much like us? A god maybe, but *the* God?

The Bible depicts a deity on a mission: to inspire a world where "good" reigns over "evil" without depriving human beings of the freedom to determine their fates. We refuse to believe in the concept of a divine mission of any kind—especially not one that is so simple a ten year old could understand it. It's insulting to think of God as that transparent. Besides, how can *this* world, as full of strife as it is, emerge from a single omnibenevolent will? Oh sure, it's plausible. But is it sensible?

Occasionally, we suspend our disbelief and imagine that an omnipotent, loving mind is truly responsible for all that happens on earth. We say to ourselves, "Since God grants us free will, we're at liberty to trash the world as we see fit. If *we* take that liberty, why blame it on God?" So we let God off the hook and think of His world as one of cosmic justice and human injustice. Then we're reminded of two words—pediatric oncology.

So much for cosmic justice.

The Biblical portrait of God isn't the only one we must dismiss. We shall opt out of *any* conception of divinity grounded in myth—at least as the basis of a philosophy of God. Take, for example, the classic Kabbalistic story attributed to Isaac Luria. In the beginning, Luria taught, there was God and God alone. Then He withdrew within Himself, creating an empty space. A personal manifestation of God came to fill the void, embodying the basic ideas and structures of our world. But these structures couldn't withstand the divine light that flowed through them, so they broke. Now, we human beings are left with a holy mission: to restructure and heal the world and, in that way, bring back the original divine energy throughout all of existence.

It's an intriguing story. And a beautiful one. But how could it possibly satisfy us as rationalists? Again, the problem is its presumptuousness. We're being bold enough whenever we speculate about the existence of a God, *any* God. To weave an intricate web about the deity in human-like terms strikes us more like writing fantasy literature than doing philosophy.

Implicit in our reasoning is the rationalist principle known as *parsimony*—or Ockham's Razor, if you wish to attribute this principle to its source. William of Ockham wrote in the 14th century that "what can be done with fewer [assumptions] is done in vain with more." We think that approach makes sense, especially when talking about issues as speculative as whether God exists. We want to keep our assumptions minimal.

The more we think about parsimony, the more we open our minds to another perspective. We call it the "what you see is what you get" approach. It also goes by the name of atheism.

Atheists try to see the world just the way it presents itself to our eyes. We don't see the Red Sea parting or hear voices coming from burning bushes. Our senses experience a plethora of animals, veggies and minerals, not a single divine power that underlies them all. We might want to believe such a power exists, but our senses don't tell us that. They give us nature, not the supernatural. They give us multiplicity, not unity.

Tell an atheist that all advanced life forms share the same chemical constituents, and he'll say, "Agreed." Tell him that we're all subject to the law of gravity, and he'll say, "Absolutely." Point out that we're all subject to the principle of evolution, and he'll say, "Precisely my point. We all evolve, but we're still just *beings*—unique, separate, occupying a distinct portion of space and existing for only a limited time. So what if we share the same basic chemical makeup or are subject to the same natural laws? What does that have to do with God? Or even cosmic unity? When I see proof of unity, I'll believe in it. For now, I just see a food chain."

The atheist's outlook on life is easy enough to understand.

And parsimonious too. That attracts us. But this perspective doesn't *satisfy* us. Not emotionally. Not intellectually either.

The fact is that we don't merely have sense organs. We also have minds, and they allow us to *infer*, to look beyond where our eyes and ears can take us. That's when we begin to sense unity and to recognize the connections that link *every* being—living and dead, large and small.

Don't just take our word for it. Scientists who've explored the universe have found more and more connections that transcend what we can pick up with our naked eyes. That's what led Einstein to say, "I believe in Spinoza's God who reveals himself in the orderly harmony of what exists," and to write that "the eternal mystery of the world is its comprehensibility."

The idea of hidden unity makes logical sense. To a microbe crawling inside our bodies, our neck and thigh bones seem like two thoroughly separate entities. It's only because our perspective is broader that we can tell there's a unity that underlies those bones.

To open our minds to the idea of transcendent connections is to come to a fork in the road, a *fateful* fork. On the one hand, we can choose to believe solely in the world of multiplicity that appears before our eyes. On the other, we can ground that world in a hidden unity that reveals itself with each discovery of a "law" of nature. Think about the microbe; it tells us that the broader our perspective, the more of life our minds can grasp, the more apparent it will be that the "natural laws" we know about only scratch the surface of the ways in which we're all connected. From that realization, we require few leaps and bounds to conclude that, from the standpoint of Olympus, all of reality may be viewed as but a single entity. You can even call it a unified *organism*, because it's very much alive.

Behold, then, another alternative to the perspectives of the myth-based theologian and the atheist. Call it the belief in *cosmic unity*, or if you prefer, the *Absolute Being*. Is "It" worthy of the term "God"? That's not yet our concern. For now, we only want to identify world views that are at least as reasonable as any other. And this one appears to fit the bill.

From this perspective, all the *beings* we know—people, plants, you name it—are related in much the same way as our hands are related to our feet. We're all part of the same *Being*. Of course, in some respects, we humans are quite different from the Absolute Being. We're finite—limited both in space and time. With some things we live in harmony, with others we clash, but in any event, we're the product of our encounters with whatever's outside of us. Not so the Absolute Being. It's eternal. Infinite. Omnipresent. Ultimate. Nothing has ever, or *could* ever, exist outside of It. For It consists of the sum total of everything that is, *plus* whatever connections link beings together. It includes the all.

We don't feel qualified to speculate about the Absolute Being's inner mind, at least not seriously. We certainly don't want to call it conscious. That sounds too much like a person. We'll refer to It instead as *supra-conscious*. That suggests mystery and transcendence.

And that's pretty much the bottom line. We won't limit the Absolute Being in any way—neither Its mind nor Its body. It exists on such a scale that we couldn't possibly exaggerate Its greatness even if we wanted to. We know Being as the *ultimate* in every possible domain. Our job is to open our eyes, minds and hearts to the true meaning of that word.

Here's the honest-to-Absolute-Being truth: of all the perspectives we've discussed, the last one seems to us to be the most reasonable, more so at least than the alternatives grounded in theological myths or the one preferred by atheists. As rationalists, though, we've got to be aware of our biases. That means we have to recognize that we may be discounting atheism because of our hearts, not just our minds.

At a minimum, we must credit the atheists for their parsimony. Even so, their perspective makes no more sense than that of the Absolute Being. And that's the key point from which our entire philosophy of God follows. Remember—in order to adopt a perspective, we don't have to believe it's more sensible than every other. As long as it's no *less* sensible, we can throw ourselves into it, with faith and passion, if it's the one we find most fulfilling and meaningful. In this case, once we start talking about fulfillment and meaning, we'd say the choice between the perspective of the Absolute Being and that of atheism is as clear as crystal.

There you have it then: our argument for believing in unity, in ultimacy, in Being. It's certainly something we can study intellectually. That's what we do when we learn like scientists and logicians and serve as reason's disciples. Absolute Being is also something we can appreciate empathically. In that latter sense, we've stopped *analyzing* an It and begun instead to *encounter* that which is worthy of the term God. In the terminology of Martin Buber, God shouldn't be primarily viewed as an It, an object of study. God is best *met*. And met as a *Thou*.

We would-be Empathic Rationalists are struck by the emotions that overcome us when we think about *beings* in terms of their origin in *Being*. When we see a sunset or a waterfall, we no longer think about them as mindless. Now we're struck by both as expressions of the same supraconscious Being—sheer limitless greatness on the grandest possible scale. When we see a breathtaking face, we no longer think about the fact that it will someday wither with age. Now, we see through the face to its origin in Being, whose majesty will never dissipate and is truly ubiquitous.

But what do we see when the sun sets and the night sky emerges, just like it did the evening before and the evening before that? And what do we see when the face in front of us doesn't take our breath away, for it has already been ravished by age? If we're thinking about their relationship to the *Being* that links night to day, or age to youth, we remain just as awed and amazed as if we were looking at the most exceptional beauty.

Looking at *any* being in terms of its origin in *Being*, how can we not feel love and gratitude for our greatest benefactor, the donor of life?

Once these feelings overcome us, what choice do we have? We simply must give this Being a name. People all over the world have come up with so many words for the Thou of Thous. Coming as we do from America, you'll forgive us if we use the name God.

It is, of course, the same name venerated by millions of our countrymen who've deified the *Ultimate* in their own ways. Does it really matter if our view of God isn't identical to those of most other God-loving Americans? The similarities in the way we all worship God are much more profound than the differences. We all want to express our awe, respect, and reverence for the unlimited. We all want to express the humility that stems from recognizing our own limits. Above all else, we all want to express gratitude to the One who deserves it most of all.

The idea of God brings us peace, security and warmth. It

also helps us appreciate our incredible fortune at receiving the gift of life. We can speak until we're blue in the face about the imperfections and injustices in this world, yet a simple fact remains: we choose to live another day. Every day that we opt for a tomorrow is a day that we show our appreciation for God.

Once named, our God may be approached as studiously and empathically as any other. The beauty of *studying* our God— contemplating the divine as might a scientist or philosopher— is that everything we learn in life, everything at all, is about God. Sure, our knowledge consists primarily of only a small number of God's finite, temporal forms. But the better we understand them, the clearer a glimpse we get of the eternal *Thou* in whom they reside.

God is the subject of the book of life that we read every day. The more excited we are about reading, the more of God we'll come to appreciate.

So, from the standpoint of knowing God, there's much value in reasoning. But reason will be the first one to tell you that if you want to understand divinity, you'd best be willing to *encounter* God as well.

Few things are as blissful or as enlightening as when we meet the divine with an open heart. We're talking about addressing God directly, either in the form of words or simply by allowing ourselves the joy of recognizing the eternal, the limitless or the unity in life. But the direct encounter is hardly the only way to deepen our emotional relationship with God. Every time we enter into an I-Thou rather than an I-It rela- tionship with the *other*, be it in the form of a dog or a tree, we're forging that same bond with the divine.

In short, whether or not we focus directly on God, our willingness to treat the *other* as a Thou allows us to become true students of divinity—honor students, you might say. We honor God and God's expressions, and are repaid with enlightenment—such as the awareness that in any I-Thou encounter, the magnet pulling the two together is nothing less than the Holy Spirit at work.

For most of us, I-Thou encounters are rare. But if we want to know and love God, that had better change. In these encounters, the *other* is met openly, lovingly, warmly. She's fully present for us, as we are for her. In meeting her, we don't attempt to characterize the *other* to suit our biases or our desires. We wish instead to encounter the *other* in her uniqueness—as she *is*, not as we would have her to be. That's called treating the *other* with respect. That's called honoring her nature, rather than using her for our own purposes.

We've heard people tell us that we had better believe in the traditional God—because if we don't, we won't feel commanded to live virtuously. That argument bores us. Our commandment is to behold God precisely as we find God—not to utilize the deity for our own selfish purposes.

To know God, to love God, to honor God—just as we find God, not as we would like to find "Him." This is our goal. It's easy to announce, but hard to accomplish.

Think about the way most of us treat our pets: as if they're human beings. Surely, we all have a tendency to want to treat *any* beloved, human or not, as one of us. But as rationalists, we also believe in our ability to transcend our limitations once we understand them. And when it comes to God, we simply can't allow ourselves to treat our beloved as just another person.

To be sure, we could continue to call God our "father" or

claim that we are "created in His image." We could even mold "Him" into the image of the human ideal. Then, we could go on to discuss earthly events in terms of whether they violate or harmonize with "His" will.

But what would have become of our God?

If we respect God, why should we feel the need to re-create divinity based on human values? Shouldn't we prefer to let the facts speak for themselves? We came to God based on a recognition of cosmic unity, not human supremacy, and we see in God a beautiful name for recognizing that source of unity. God, to us, is the ultimate, the unlimited, the omnipresent. The more such words are used, the more we realize how far they are from the human realm. To believe the opposite is to lose any semblance of humility. And that, of course, is the ultimate irony of the conventional approach to religion—it champions humility as one of the most important virtues, yet posits a God created in our own image.

Coming to love the God that *is*, not the anthropomorphized version, "with all our heart, with all our soul and with all our might," is perhaps the fundamental challenge of Empathic Rationalism.

All that said, what if we are wrong about what kind of "Being" underlies reality? What if, in fact, this world has been shaped from the outside by a loving, merciful, incorporeal will who made human beings in His image and will someday decide to redeem our societies? Let's say that's true. It still wouldn't affect the fundamental point we're making about God.

Our analysis begins with two indisputable facts—(a) nobody knows for sure "the truth" about God, and (b) many people would like to erase the word entirely from our collective vocabularies. The first fact can't be changed. But we'd love the opportunity to change the second.

We maintain that only if society allows the term God to be defined broadly and flexibly so as to include conceptions like ours will it be able to sharply reduce the number of atheists and agnostics in our midst. Non-believers have rights too, and they've exercised their rights to reject the traditional deity. But have they rejected the concept of divinity itself? Have they been exposed to all robust formulations of that concept? We doubt it. And we are confident that many who are turned off by the Bible's God will be open to the Absolute Being.

To traditional theologians and their followers, we must ask this: Do you want more people to open their eyes to divinity? Or do you want to send a message to all who search: 'It's our way or the highway?' Even if you are right about "God," why not encourage people to come to God as they please and let the power of your Lord work His magic? What do you have to lose? Are you worried that if people don't adopt your *precise* portrait of God, their souls will be condemned? If you truly think that ... let's just say we're at an impasse.

D. The Great Political Divide

We've said most of what we have to say about the sacred. Our next, and final, topic involves the profane.

You don't have to be a de Tocqueville to notice great divides that threaten modern American society. Everyone perceives schisms in the context of class, race or religion. But this being Washington, D.C., our group is especially concerned about the divide in the arena of politics—in the chasm between the unabashed "liberals" and the self-proclaimed "conservatives." Empathic Rationalism can hardly survive in such a polarized environment.

Turn on the tube and see it for yourself. Politicians and pundits are defining their ideas less by what they embrace than by whom they battle. The fight just keeps getting meaner and the disdain more palpable. As a result, the love and respect critical to empathy have become nearly impossible to maintain. And open-mindedness is a casualty as well; when you're a soldier in an ideological war, that's a luxury you can ill afford.

So far in this talk, we've taken positions on a number of public policy issues and have opined on matters of theology. On each subject, we haven't so much been searching to find a middle ground as a *synthesis*. Any student of King Solomon can tell you that the one is often quite different from the other.

On most public policy issues our synthesis forces us to side with the liberals. Even on matters of theology, our views are hardly conservative. And yet, with respect to the phenomenon of the Great Political Divide, we couldn't be more alienated by the liberal community.

All too frequently, when liberals contemplate their opponents' teachings, all compassion goes out the window. Instead, they become a simple-minded fighting force that clings to one strawman after another in describing conservatives and their motivations. Greedy. Hypocritical. Bigoted. Those three words are supposed to summarize the leaders of the American Right to a T.

That attitude isn't empathic, nor is it rational. Cathartic, maybe, but also tragic, for as long as it engulfs our society, we will be incapable of accomplishing great feats, such as taking on poverty, root and branch. That job requires unity.

Rather than maligning the Right, serious American liberals must embrace them *and* much of what they stand for.

"Conservatives" who are true to their moniker are merely trying to nurture the values that have enriched western civilization for millennia and brought incredible prosperity to these shores. These same values are at the heart of Empathic Rationalism, and we would argue that they are harmonious with many of the ultimate goals of liberalism.

American conservatives claim to be turned on by the acceptance of responsibility for one's own actions, by the value of free enterprise and free expression, by the security that results from a commitment to law and order, by fidelity to institutions that have stood the test of time (like marriage, not mere "civil unions"), and by an overarching reverence for that which transcends human life. Those are terrific values. Wouldn't the liberals agree? So why aren't they opening a dialogue?

To all liberals, we say: Meet your conservative counterparts face to face. Recognize their basic teachings as compatible with liberalism. Recognize their mentors as yours. Don't treat them with disdain; try to complete their mission. *Their* mission. They're trying to conserve the great mosaic that is embedded in Isaiah, Plato, Jesus, Jefferson and so many of the other great minds of history. Your job should be to help learn with them about what the great minds truly stood for.

When conservative statesmen bring their religious inspiration into their political speeches, liberals have got to stop wincing. Think about what Martin Luther King would have done had he survived Memphis and run for office. We bet he'd talk about his Christianity. Why shouldn't he? The separation of church and state is meant to protect intellectual freedom, but it can be taken too far. When we deny politicians their right to express their inspiration from religion, we've thrown out the baby with the bathwater.

֍

Liberals, then, must respect conservatives, learn from them, and take particular care to tolerate their talk about religion. In fact, if liberals hope to relate to their conservative colleagues as partners, they must do more than simply "tolerate" religious references in the public domain. Liberals must embrace the mixing of religion and public life. That's right: *embrace* it!

To many, such an embrace is sacrilegious. We've already alluded to the issue of whether the government should support faith-based charities that proselytize. "Can't have that," most liberals would say. "The government shouldn't be in the indoctrination business." We agree 100 percent. Public schools, for example, must go out of their way to avoid indoctrination. They should strive to be neutral in the way they treat different religions. But that doesn't mean they should avoid talking *about* religion or spirituality. We think it's a tragedy that kids today almost never hear about those topics in 13 years of public school. It helps explain why so many adults have no use whatsoever for the realm of the spirit, and why so much of the "art" that Hollywood peddles flies in the face of *any* venerable religious tradition—including Secular Humanism.

We hope that someday, even atheistic liberals will speak in favor of spirituality and religion. Just as we defined God broadly to encompass a deity that is more pantheistic than the traditional Lord, atheistic liberals can define religion and spirituality broadly enough to include, say, faiths like Secular Humanism. To define "religion" so as to respect human diversity is to clarify that we're *all* religious and spiritual people, or at least those of us whose concerns extend beyond our own hedonistic goals. Being fully human, in other words, means being religious and spiritual, in the expansive sense of these words. The alternative appears to be moral relativism, secularism run rampant, and a spiritual void as large as Jupiter. That attitude repulses cultural conservatives. Perhaps it shouldn't repulse liberals. But if they hope to play a role in shaping this country during the next century, it had better, at least, depress them.

In short, liberals will accomplish precious little until they're willing to meet conservatives as equals and recognize that the conservative foundation is a darned good place for the dialogue to start. In fact, it's the necessary place to start—for Americans are generally conservative people. Yes, liberals might forget bridge building and still manage occasionally to find a fellow traveler with the charisma to be elected President. But he won't be elected with any mandate for change; he'll only be elected because of the cult of his personality.

Such a President could make the liberals proud that he or she has kept the society from "getting any worse." But think about what the word "liberal" means: a change agent. How can a liberal be satisfied just by making sure things don't get worse? If a person is afraid of change, how can that person call himself a liberal?

We Empathic Rationalists demand more. We are people of hope. We proclaim metaphysical unity, and we wish to see it reflected in social unity. Homogeneity we don't want, but fellowship, we need.

Tolstoy may have been right when he said that all happy families are the same. So, in a sense, are all would-be Empathic Rationalists. Every one of us wishes to govern ourselves not by fear, but by hope. And love. All the rest, as Hillel would say, is commentary.

CHAPTER 15

THE BENEFACTOR

*A*s soon as the applause died down, Feaver stood up. "Bravo!" he said. "Excellent. It's definitely a philosophy I can sink my teeth into." He walked up to me and vigorously shook my hand. Then he turned to the rest of the Gang. "I had no idea what to expect when I sponsored this group. But you've all worked so hard. You've given me everything I could have asked for. And now this. Thank you so much."

"Well thank *you*," Linda said. "You're the one who made this happen."

"Please excuse me," said the Benefactor. "At my age, the master bathroom becomes your favorite room in the house. David, would you mind helping me? Oh, and you can cut the camera." With that, the stoic McDonald left his seat and accompanied the Benefactor up the stairs.

As soon as the two were out of sight, several of my colleagues rushed up to me. Allison was the first. "I'm proud of you, Sam," she said. "I wish my dad could have heard your talk."

Then Shaw appeared with a high five and a clenched fist. He was followed by a glowing Eileen Mitchell and then Fred Keister. "I heard a smidgen of myself in your talk," Fred claimed. "At least you're gettin' the message on gun laws."

"Actually, you had a lot more influence than you might know," I replied. "When I started drafting this up, I wanted to sound like a professional philosopher. Then I remembered your talk about academicians—how they'd rather speak to each other than the public. So I took out a lot of obscure references and jargon." It's true. Keeping Keister's comment in mind, I had decided to target my presentation to high school students— not the George Londons of the world, but the bright, intellectual teenagers I loved to teach.

After speaking to Keister, I noticed that the camera light had gone out. Then I looked in Art's direction. He was pacing alone near the other end of the room, clearly annoyed. I thought I'd give him the chance to vent, so I walked over to him. "Sorry if I pissed you off," I said. "I hope you know that wasn't my goal."

"I don't want to make a big stink about this tonight," he grumbled. "You said what you said, and I'll have to live with it. At least *I* didn't have to pay for that one-sided pile of ...." Sherman's voice trailed off.

"Look, I did my best to—"

"I don't want to hear it! I 've had to sit here all evening and listen to your B.S." Then he walked away.

At that point, Linda reached out to me and pulled my arm in the direction of the front door. "Let's get a breath of air," she said.

When we were alone outside, Linda turned to me and said, softly, "Sam. I'm gay."

"You're ... I didn't know," I stammered.

"I hope not. When I tell people, I swear them to secrecy. That applies to you too."

"Of course. That's nobody else's business."

"I'm letting you know because of what you said tonight

about gay marriage. I remember you talking about it in the Creed Room a while ago. I could tell then how strongly you felt about it."

"I'm Jewish. Discrimination is very real to me."

"Believe it or not, some of the most anti-gay people in America are black," Linda said. "They don't look at it as a matter of discrimination. To them it's all about religion."

"Sad, isn't it?"

"I want you to know I appreciate what you said, that's all. When straight people care about us, it's good karma for them. That's what Eileen tells me."

Before we left the Victorian, McDonald handed us our end-of-the-year checks. Mine totaled $31,500. It would take me the better part of a year to earn that much as a school teacher.

The next time I saw Chuck Feaver would be the last, though I didn't know it at the time. He arranged to have separate meetings with each member of the Creed Gang to discuss our experiences. Our meeting took place on June 24th, only a week after two emotional farewells.

Friday, June 16th was the final day of school at Takoma Park High. I'll never forget how hard it was for me to say goodbye to the kids. Their enthusiasm and affection after I came back from my suspension did wonders for my psyche. During my teaching career, I don't think I've ever felt closer to my students than I felt that June afternoon.

The next day was just as intense. It was Georgetown Law Center's graduation and my last chance to see the Triumvirate before they went back to their home towns. Linda said she hoped to return to Washington after a few years. She made no bones about it: she wanted to be in Congress. A black Republican, a

Congresswoman from Boston? I didn't see it, but she wasn't like too many GOP politicians—she cared more about helping the poor than gorging the wealthy. She simply didn't believe in the anti-poverty programs the Democrats had promoted back when their leaders gave a damn about the problem.

Who knows? I thought. I'd never voted Republican before but always have wanted to do it at least once in my life. For Linda, I wouldn't just vote for her; I'd donate to her campaign.

Linda spent most of her graduation afternoon with her family, so I didn't see too much of her, nor much of Allison. I greeted Allison's parents, but just long enough to be polite. Playing the role of the discarded boyfriend didn't appeal to me, especially given that my replacement was strutting around like the cock of the walk. I made sure to re-introduce myself to Steiner, mostly to see how "damned glad" to meet me he'd pretend to be. Sure enough, he shook my hand with enthusiasm and wished me the best at Takoma Park High.

"Good luck at the law firm," I replied, with as much warmth as I could muster.

None of Eileen's relatives came to the graduation, so she and I had a chance to talk for a while. When I first saw her that afternoon, she mentioned briefly that Gustafson wasn't doing well, and she felt like an idiot for having stayed in D.C. rather than flying back home. A bit later, though, she turned to me and said that she was glad she stayed. "I needed to see you one last time," she told me. "You've been such a big part of my life these past few months."

Eileen said that she'd be studying for the bar exam that summer in Minnesota, but she still ought to have plenty of time to write.

"Nice long letters, I hope," was my only response, spoken from the heart.

The Benefactor smiled warmly as he welcomed me into the Victorian. We were alone—except, of course, for McDonald. Always McDonald.

Sitting in a large reclining chair in the living room, the Benefactor proceeded to go through the motions of filling and lighting a pipe. "You're the last one," he said, after taking a long draw. Even when he wasn't smoking, he spoke more slowly than most people I know; listening to him talk between puffs was definitely a leisurely pursuit. "I wanted to meet with the others first. I was curious to hear what they thought of the Presentation, especially the ones who weren't on that committee of yours."

"I don't suppose Art Sherman claimed credit," I said.

The Benefactor laughed. "No. He told me you were full of it."

"What can I say?"

"You don't have to say anything. I already knew what people like Art thought. I wanted to hear from people like you."

"So you liked the Presentation?"

"I told you that already. It made me think. I'm fond of anything that makes me think."

"Do you have any suggestions?" I asked. "Something we could have added? Something that got on your nerves?"

"I want to know about you, first. Did you have any epiphanies from our little project?"

"Probably a few."

"Give me one," he said.

"Well let's see. I learned this about myself: a year ago, I would have said that my favorite thing in life was to think about the great philosophical questions. Now I realize I only want to think about them in a way that somehow grips my emotions. That's when I feel like a whole person. Maybe it's the only time I do."

"Have you had a lot of those experiences around here?"

"Definitely," I replied. "Honestly, this group was probably the best thing that's ever happened to me—the people, the discussions, everything. It's been incredible."

"I'm glad," he said, and seemed sincere in saying it. "I didn't want you to remember this just for the money. That would have been a shame."

The room was silent for several seconds. I kept wondering if he were going to let me in on why he sponsored the group. No such luck.

"You asked for my comments about your talk," he resumed. "I've got to tell you, I've been watching you all year on tape and then for a couple of hours in person. I'm just a heck of a lot more conservative than you are."

"OK," I said, not knowing how to respond.

"That time a while back when you talked about white people begging the Demon of Greed for charity so they could rip off minorities, I couldn't believe what a leftist you sounded like," he said. "I expected that from Scott, but I had thought you were more balanced."

"So you're not big on redistributing wealth," I replied, egging him on.

"We just need some tax cuts, that's all," he said, laughing. "But let me try to look at your talk from *your* perspective. I'd have to say I found it interesting that you spoke so little about dreams, especially when you addressed passion."

"I don't get what you mean," I said.

"When I think about passion, I think about dreams. That's where it all starts. And if passion is the sail, and dreams are the starting point of passion, dreams should be put at the front of everything you're talking about."

"Wait a minute," I said. "I feel passionate about rock music, but I wouldn't say it has anything to do with my dreams."

"Wouldn't you? Maybe rock n' roll sets you free. That's what these paintings and sculptures do for me."

"Alright. I see what you're saying now," I replied, nodding.

"The only time you mentioned dreaming was when you mocked it."

"When was that?"

"You made some point about utopian dreaming. Then you contrasted it with doing work that actually matters."

"Oh yeah. I remember."

"Where do you think the *real* work starts? Where do you think great discoveries begin? Always with dreams. Just because people don't understand them doesn't make them utopian."

That comment struck a chord in me. I've been a dreamer all my life but often thought that dreaming was foolhardy and impractical. Just then, I imagined hearing my mother's voice telling me to get a life, until it was drowned out by the Benefactor's, telling me to *live* my life, and let my mother live her own.

"Are you a dreamer?" I asked him.

"Sure. Any successful person is."

"This project, this Creed Room idea, was it a long-time dream of yours?"

"Actually, it came to me not long before I placed the ad."

"So tell me," I said, tired of waiting for him to bring it up, "why did you decide to sponsor us?"

The Benefactor paused while he drew on his pipe. "I own a house in Tampa and another in Milwaukee—just as big and expensive as this one. I've got other investments too. What I don't have is anyone to give my money to. My wife's no longer with us. I have no siblings, no children, no family at all—except David. I help him out, believe me. I'm just not keen on giving him all my money. We're, uh, not exactly kindred spirits. Do you know what I'm saying?"

"Sure. But there are a lot of ways to donate money. Why sponsor a group like ours?"

"Curiosity. Basic curiosity."

"About what?" I asked.

"I wanted to see what a group of random people would come up with when they wrestled with their ideals and then had to reach some sort of agreement. I figured it would be like buying a crystal ball."

"I'm not following you," I said. "Our ideals and our future are so different."

"We become what we want to become. At least that's what I think. If I'm right, you may have given me a look into the future. You can probably tell mine isn't going to last much longer. Just look at me and watch me smoke." When he finished his sentence, he began to laugh.

"You seem healthy enough," I said, before his laughter turned into coughs.

"Please," he replied, after clearing his throat. "I'm old. I don't take great care of myself. My kidneys are about to fail. My rheumatism is acting up. I've got the longevity of a goldfish."

"Why didn't you take part in the group yourself?" I asked.

"You've got to be kidding."

"I'm serious."

"Do you honestly think I could pay people to sit in a room with me every week? I'd feel like the clown of the century. Every time I'd go to the bathroom, someone would snicker about having to wait one more time for old money bags to relieve his prostate. Maybe it would be different if I could do this with friends. But most of mine are in the ground."

"I'm sorry."

"It's the price of living long enough, I guess."

"Have you thought about going back to college? Getting another degree?"

"*Another*?" he asked. "I never got the first one. I've never even been to college."

"Oh. I just assumed—"

"My college was the streets of Milwaukee. I grew up there in an orphanage and came of age during the Depression. I worked every odd job I could and then went off to war. That was my grad school—Omaha Beach. I got a degree in how not to count on *anything*, not even waking up the next morning."

"Do you mind if I ask you a personal question?" I said.

The Benefactor grinned. "Do you want to know about my sex life?"

"What?" I said, laughing.

"Go ahead, ask your question."

"If you grew up in an orphanage and then went off to war—"

"How did I get my money?" The Benefactor finished my sentence for me.

"Yup. That's what I was going to ask."

"Luck. And I had a couple of talents. After the war, I began working for the father of a buddy from the service. He got us into the computer business back when it was just getting started. About a decade later, his son and I invented a new computer language called RADIC. They used it in the defense industry and, later, the space program. We made a killing."

"Impressive," I said.

"I heard from your friends that you know about my exploits in the art business. That's how I made most of my money. I have an eye for Dutch and Flemish art, especially portraits."

"You'd have no way of knowing this, but that's my favorite kind of art," I said, recalling how much I enjoyed walking into the Victorian for the first time. "I can't tell you how often I've stared at the paintings here."

"You've been staring at reproductions."

His statement took me aback.

"Cat got your tongue?" he asked.

"No. I'm ... I'm just surprised ..."

The Benefactor laughed. "I know you've heard I sold some fakes. It's true. But I sold them *as* fakes! I can't help it if some-one tried to palm them off as originals. As soon as I heard that was going on, I made sure I never got rid of another one again."

"That's good," I said, still looking for the right words.

"I know an artist who can copy the old style so well only an expert can tell the difference."

"So if these are reproductions, where are the originals?" I asked.

"I either sold them or gave them to museums. My days as a speculator are over."

Just then, McDonald announced that dinner was served. While the Benefactor and I had been talking, his personal chef arrived and began preparing food. We were fed an incredible four-course meal.

During dinner, the Benefactor commented that he was sur-prised that the Shermans were the only members of the group who were married. "Correct me if I'm wrong," he said, "none of the rest of you is even engaged?"

"That's right. Fred's a widower. Everyone else has always been single."

Suddenly, the Benefactor became very serious. "It's been 11 years since the death of my wife, may her soul rest in peace—11 years and five months, to be exact. She was with me since my early days in the computer business." He pointed out two different photographs of her.

"Nancy was born and raised in the D.C. area," he continued. "That's how I came to buy this house—she wanted to spend the springtime and fall here.

"We traveled everywhere together. More than 60 countries. You name it, we've been there. She'd always asked where I wanted to go, I'd tell her, and then she'd plan the itinerary."

"Did you go back to France after the war?"

"Sure I did. Paris. The Riviera too."

"What about the beaches up north?"

"Never," he said, suddenly intense. "I love my country. And I can't tell you how proud I am to have fought for her. But to me, that place is all about death and always will be."

"'A free man thinks of death least of all things. And his wisdom is a meditation not of death but of life,'" I said. "That's a direct quotation from Spinoza's *Ethics*."

"It's a good one," he replied.

"You know, we heard other rumors about you aside from your selling fake art."

"Of course I know that."

"Who told you?"

"Do you think I burn my sources?" he said, smiling.

"We heard you're a member of a secret society called the Empire Club. We were told it was composed of a few hundred ... how should I put it ... would-be plutocrats."

"What's a plutocrat?" he asked. "Remember, I didn't go to college."

"Is it true?" I said, ignoring his question. "Are you a member of the Empire Club?"

"If I were, I couldn't tell you, now could I?"

"Should I take that as a 'yes'?"

"Take it any way you want to," he said, once again drawing on his pipe.

"What would the Empire Club want with people like us?" I asked.

Rather than answering, he responded with a question of his own. "Let me ask you this. Assume that this thing you people did upstairs was some sort of Empire Club activity. And that for some hidden motive, I paid you a few hundred thousand dollars to give me and my fellow—what's that word, *plutocrats*—some information. Would it still have been worth it to you? Or would that depend on how we'd use the information?"

"That's what I've been wondering," I said.

"Stop wondering. Seize the opportunity. Why don't you take this whole project as one big challenge? See if you all could benefit so much from the experience that you'd say it was worth it, no matter what."

"How can I think that if I don't know what you're doing with our work? This is totally unfair."

"Is it?" he said. "Think back to when this all got started. I promised I didn't know any of you. And that was true. I promised I'd keep your videos out of the public eye, and you can count on that too. Those were the only promises I made. I *never* said what I'd do with the information you've given me. If you made assumptions, that's your problem, not mine."

"A plutocrat is one of the men in charge of a society totally controlled by rich people," I said. "You're beginning to sound like one."

"I'm telling you, my conscience is clear. And so is my challenge. You go out in the world and do your thing. I'll do mine. May the best creed win."

All I could think about was how much the Benefactor's world sounded like the White Man's Track that Shaw discussed earlier in the spring. "It's not a competition," I said.

"If that's your attitude, so much the better," he replied. "You can't say I didn't give you your chance."

After visiting the Benefactor at his home, I went nearly a month without hearing from anyone associated with the Creed Room. Then, on July 20th, a phone call woke me up.

"I've got to see you," she said, with an assertiveness that was out of character.

"Where are you?"

"Minneapolis, at home."

"Did something happen?"

"Well, yeah. There's a lot we have to talk about. Can I please see you?"

"Of course. I've been thinking about you, hoping you'd write."

"I didn't feel like writing. I still don't feel like writing. I just want to see you."

"I want to see you too," I said. "You know I do."

"Sam, when can we get together? I've got to take the bar exam this week. After that, my schedule couldn't be more open. They're not expecting me at work until the end of August. I can come to D.C. if you'd like."

That wasn't necessary. I wanted to get away from D.C. We agreed to meet in the city of Fort Wayne, Indiana, a place that neither of us had been to and saw no particular reason to visit, except that it was halfway between D.C. and Minneapolis and we'd both be traveling by car. Eileen told me not to worry that Fort Wayne was no tourist Mecca. She said we'd have more than enough to talk about to occupy our time. I didn't argue; I simply began counting the days.

Seven, to be precise. It took me nine hours of driving before I reached the Marriott on Fort Wayne's north side, where we had arranged to meet at the hotel bar. I was seated when she walked in, wearing cut-off jeans and a University of Minnesota T-Shirt. No makeup, no hair spray, no jewelry, just a fit body and a face that captivated me more and more each time I saw it.

Eileen didn't hang out for very long that evening. She said she was exhausted from the drive and wanted to get some sleep. But I could tell how happy she was to see me. "I've found a great place for us to visit tomorrow morning," she said, before turning in for the night. "It's a state park, about a half hour away. There are a bunch of lakes, hiking trails, canoeing, swimming ... it sounds just like Minnesota."

Leave it to a Midwesterner to find a nice spot in Northeast Indiana. It's a bit like picking a needle out of a haystack—or, in this case, a pile of corn stalks. Chain O' Lakes State Park, near Albion, Indiana, is a beautiful set of seven watering holes. Had I been more accustomed to the finer things of life, I might have noticed all sorts of reasons why this state park didn't measure up to its counterparts in New England and the Upper Midwest. Fortunately, my taste wasn't nearly so refined, so I thought it was just a perfect place to spend a day with my favorite person.

When we got to the park, we headed for the biggest lake and swam for nearly an hour. Once we were back on the beach, Eileen told me the news I had been expecting to hear.

"You probably figured it out," she said, tears beginning to roll down her face. "Jim died on July 1st."

I tried to comfort her as she continued to cry. "I've never let you see me like this," she said, finally, struggling to fight off the tears. "I haven't really let you in."

"That's OK. I understand."

"All the things you talked about when you were describing the hasid—that was Jim. He was a tall, blonde Swedish hasid."

Eileen could barely utter those words before she broke down once again. I held her in my arms, but still she cried. "I could tell that from the way you described him in the spring," I said.

We spoke about Gustafson for a few more minutes until Eileen decided she'd had enough. My heart went out to her for the incredible suffering she must have endured. But another part of me was relieved. That's right, relieved. The same guy who wrote in praise of empathy had taken note of the opportunity he was given by another man's death. Only my disgust at the way I felt after learning of this tragedy allowed me to show Eileen the compassion she deserved.

When we got back to the Marriott late in the afternoon, our attention turned to dinner. Fort Wayne didn't have many options for Eileen. Many places served veggies, but few served vegetable *protein*. Luckily, we found an Indian restaurant not far away. Eileen assured me that every Indian restaurant in this galaxy can accommodate a vegan, despite all the dairy products on the menu.

Over dinner, we discussed our meetings with the Benefactor. Hers mostly involved answering his questions about our presentation. He especially wanted to know which parts of the creed moved her the most. She asked him several times why he sponsored our group, but he kept ducking the question.

As Eileen listened to me describe my meeting, she became

more and more vocal in criticizing Feaver. "Talk about using people as means to an end," she said. "It's so immoral, what he did. Why do you still call him the Benefactor? Choulos was right. He's a malefactor."

"He could be both—at least if we take our work seriously. I'm telling you, he issued me a challenge to make our creed count. As long as that has meaning to me, I'm going to think he did us all a favor."

Gradually, I eased the conversation away from the Benefactor and toward the topic of Eileen's future without the man she called her "hero." I asked her a couple of open-ended questions, just something to get her feeling comfortable talking again. She had trouble finding the words at first. Then, she looked me in the eyes, and said, "I can't tell you what a hole I have in my life. Thinking about the future totally depresses me. I only want to live in the present and be with people I'm close to. Like you."

I may never have felt more confused about what to say or do than at that moment. I wanted to kiss Eileen. I wanted to hold her and not let go. But I didn't know if that's what she needed. I hadn't a clue what she needed. So I sat in silence, in paralysis.

"Be patient with me, OK?" she asked.

"Of course," I said, regaining my voice. "Just let me say one thing. Take all the time you need to figure things out. About *us*, I mean. But whatever you decide, *always* be my friend."

For the rest of the evening, neither of us brought up anything heavy. Instead, we planned for the next day and got just the comic relief we needed. As it turned out, while the Fort Wayne area might not offer much in terms of scenic beauty, art or history, it truly had a hidden jewel.

I'm speaking of the Dan Quayle Center & Museum, which

is located southwest of the city in the town of Huntington. It styles itself the nation's only Vice Presidential museum. After we stopped laughing at the brochure, we realized that this place might be a hoot to visit. Besides, Quayle seemed like an especially timely character. Given that George W. Bush was the GOP's choice for President, Quayle had definitely set a trend: the rise of the C student in American politics. The end of egghead rule. Eileen asked if I thought they had a wing devoted to statesmen who had blown off their studies or if that was the theme of the entire museum.

"Obviously we've got to find out for ourselves," I said.

We spent the next morning at the Quayle Museum. When we walked inside, I expected to laugh at Dan Quayle, but the real joke was on me. I learned that the museum gets about as many visitors in one month as the Spinoza House in Holland gets in a year.

My mind wandered to Jefferson and his idea that a few years of schooling is all we need to educate a wise electorate. Two centuries later, we had a nation of high school and college graduates, and they're electing Quayle. I'd love to hear Jefferson's reaction to that. Or Darwin's.

With each passing day that Eileen and I spent together, it became clearer that she was committed to living in the Twin Cities for a long time. Her parents had been supportive of her relationship with Gustafson, and that support meant the world to her. She knew they wanted her to live near to them and felt she owed it to them to stay.

Our original plan was to stay at the Marriott for four nights. After the fourth night, having exhausted the area's bucolic and comedic attractions, it was high time for both of us to leave, but to where? And alone or together?

I hadn't a clue how Eileen would answer those questions, but I didn't feel the need to wait for her answers, for I knew my own. Takoma Park High expected me back on August 22nd. That would give me two weeks to play before I had to be in the D.C. area preparing for class. The fact is, though, that I wasn't thinking about playing; I was thinking about my future. The choice between another year with Ericsson and company and the chance to live near Eileen was cut and dried. I was convinced that I wouldn't meet another Eileen as long as I lived. It's true that she never suggested that she wanted to be my girlfriend, let alone my wife. But she didn't have to. I knew how compatible we were. And I had faith that if I moved to Minnesota and gave her enough time to mourn Gustafson's death, we'd never again be apart.

"So this is our last night here, isn't it?" Eileen asked during dinner—this time, at one of Fort Wayne's only Thai restaurants.

"That was the plan."

"I should probably get back to Minneapolis. I can't tell you how much I've loved seeing you, but I'm starting to get homesick. I hope it's not that long before we can get together."

"Oh, it'll be soon. I'll come up to Minnesota."

"Seriously?"

"Yeah. I want to see you in your native habitat."

The next morning, she headed northwest, and I headed southeast. I allowed her to assume that I was preparing for another year at Takoma Park High and would be making only a brief trip to Minnesota in the fall. In fact, however, I was already trying to figure out how best to free myself from the east coast.

Leaving the school in the lurch wasn't an issue. Prospective social studies teachers were knocking themselves out to teach in a Chase County high school. It was my mother who concerned me—specifically, the prospect of moving halfway across the country from her. But it couldn't be helped. I wanted ... I needed to be with Eileen and was willing to work hard to move my mother to Minnesota or at least make sure that I'd see her often enough in New York. What I wasn't willing to do was give up my best chance at happiness.

In the words of Rabbi Hillel, repeated more than once by Rabbi Schwartz's daughter, "If I am not for me, who will be?"

EPILOGUE

Years have passed since I last set foot in the old Victorian. It is now December 2004, and much has changed—both in the lives of the Creed Gang and in the world around us.

Eileen and I got married nine months ago. In *so* many ways, I couldn't have asked for a more perfect wife. And yes, I do give credit to the Benefactor for bringing us together.

After I left Eileen in Fort Wayne, it took me six weeks to get to Minnesota. I intentionally gave her no inkling that I was preparing to move to the Twin Cities. Even after I arrived, she thought of me as a visitor until I escorted her to a high rise in Minneapolis and showed her my new apartment. The look on her face was priceless. I live for moments like that.

Unfortunately, they don't come cheaply. I couldn't get to the Land of Lakes without first paying my dues in Brooklyn.

"It's not enough that you threw away your Harvard education. It's not enough that you threw away your job, such as it was. Now you've got to go to the North Pole chasing some shiksa. And for what, the unemployment insurance? Is that what you're getting out of this, Sammy? What about your mother? What happens to me? Do I just sit here all alone? No friends, no family, just me, picturing my husband with a bullet in his mouth, or my son in Minnehaha watching T.V. all day?"

Mother went on like that for nearly a half hour, yet I didn't cuss her out once. The fact is that I was ready for her insanity. Sometimes, a Jewish mother's gotta vent.

During the three weeks that I stayed in Brooklyn, Mother probably averaged about two mini-tirades a day. For the most part, I just stood there and took them. It was the price I was willing to pay for my freedom, and it wasn't really as excruciating as it sounds. In the past, Mother would drive me crazy after I had made an important decision because she'd always take exception to it, and I'd wonder if she were right. Not this time.

Occasionally during those three weeks, my mind would turn to Dolores's comments about romantic love and her idea that, when we fall in love, we see something in our beloved that captures our sense of the human ideal. I didn't have to think hard to figure out what it was about Eileen that I loved so much. It was her values and how true to them she behaved. I trusted in those values even more than my own.

Dolores was also correct about the importance of honor to a successful romance. When I reflect today on my relationship with Eileen, I feel, more than anything else, a sense of being honored and the need to honor her in return. Maybe I don't deserve it. Maybe she could have done a whole lot better. Then again, as Motl the tailor might say, even a poor nebesch like me is entitled to a little happiness.

Eileen and I moved in together one year and a day after the death of Jim Gustafson. She puts up with my messiness. I put up with her animals—four of them, at current count. I promised her before we got married that I wouldn't eat any more animal flesh. She promised that the kids—who don't yet exist—would be raised as Reform Jews, and that no matter how poor we got, she'd never ask me to give up my subscription to Direct TV and the National Football League Sunday Ticket. No Redskins, no relationship.

Eileen is still at the Attorney General's office, where she's a consumer protection lawyer. More importantly, though, she's formed a folk-rock band with three old friends from high school. As the band's lead singer and guitar player, Eileen got to choose the name: *The Empaths.* They've already released one CD, and a second is coming out in the spring. Who knows? Maybe, someday, they'll be known outside of the Twin Cities.

As for me, I've been working at the Mall of the Americas, the world's largest shopping mall, for nearly four years. My store is called The Bibliophile's Bungalow, which is an ironic name, as we're one of the largest independent book stores in the nation.

My title is Assistant Manager, but I don't care much about the "managing." What I enjoy is the chance to moderate the Bungalow's biweekly discussion group that meets year round. When I'm not needed to supervise anyone, I research the upcoming discussion topic. If I know a topic well enough, I even feel like I'm back in the classroom teaching.

Candidly, the main reason I took the job at the Bungalow instead of looking for work at a school is because I didn't want to take my job home with me. Don't listen to the scoffers—good teachers put in their hours, even at home. By contrast, as a bookstore employee, unless I'm doing prep work for my discussion group, my job has literally no claim on my energies when I'm away from the store. That allows me to pursue the one vocation I've discovered that I enjoy more than teaching: *writing.* This book, for one thing, was made possible by my reduced work load. When I'm done with it, I plan on pumping out another. Maybe, someday, I'll earn enough money as a writer to pay for my mother's psychoanalysis; God knows she needs it after my two career moves.

Speaking of my mother, since I moved to Minnesota, I've seen her perhaps four or five times a year. With a couple of exceptions, Eileen and I have spent all of our vacations in New York. She loves to visit the city as much as I do.

Mother is re-married now, can you believe it? Perhaps my career "tragedy," as she calls it, shook the foundations of her world, and she felt the need to do something drastic. Her husband is a Jewish neo-con. When we get together, we agree about nothing. I mean *nothing*. Eileen suggests that someone ought to film our family gatherings and make a sit-com out of it—"All in the Jewish Family" or something like that. I told her that would be impossible. Once she had turned me into a vegetarian, I couldn't properly play the role of Meathead.

When we go to New York, we don't just see Mother and her new hubby, but Lenny too. That's right—he, a septuagenarian, moved north to Brooklyn. Not Boca, Brooklyn. It goes to show that people aren't nearly as predictable as birds.

One person who *is* predictable is Jamison. He's still living by the Pacific Ocean, still accumulating treasures and still single. Some day in the distant future, his heart will stop, but until then, it will be smooth sailing. The Fates will care for him in grand fashion. Don't ask me why they work that way; they just do.

While I have less confidence in the fate of Choulos, nor do I have bad news to report about him. I've heard nothing at all about him since I paid his jewelry store a visit shortly before leaving for Minnesota in the summer of 2000. We spoke about the Presentation, and I told him all I knew about Feaver. Lately, I've thought a lot about calling Choulos and updating our conversation. I can't say I'm looking forward to talking to him, but I resolved to make the call before the end of the year. It's the least I can do, given the efforts he took to warn us about Feaver, and how sensible he turned out to be.

As for the other six Creed Roomers, they're all alive and kicking, though some are definitely doing better than others.

Keister recently tied the knot again. After the wedding, he and his wife moved to a small town near Pittsburgh, where he's got a job at a construction site. They both go to church regularly, and he credits the Creed Room, and especially Dolores, for his renewed commitment to Christianity. I'm sure Dolores was honored to hear that. I won't try to speculate on Art's reaction.

Allison has worked for the same New York law firm since she left Georgetown, only now when she leaves the office, she doesn't have to come home to Amos. The guy actually traded up, can you believe it? The word is she's just as Semitic as Allison but even more affluent. Don't worry about Miss Schwartz, though; she rebounded quite well. The way Eileen tells it, Allison shortened her skirts another notch, hit a couple of Midtown Hebe-Hops, and found herself a neurosurgeon fresh off his fellowship at Hopkins. Jamison was impressed when I told him about Allison's catch. "That's a *great* specialty," he said. "They *really* do well. Good for her."

OK, OK. I shouldn't be so catty. The truth is that Allison's fiancé is both nice and engaging. Besides, if Rabbi Schwartz can marry a rich doctor, why shouldn't Allison?

Her wedding is set for next March at her father's synagogue. I'm looking forward to hearing the rabbi speak. Anyone who has studied closely under the great Heschel surely has a lot to teach me about Judaism—or Empathic Rationalism, for that matter.

The biggest news about Linda is that she's outed herself. It can't be a coincidence that she's now as happy as I've ever seen her. Linda claims to have faith that by the time she's ready to put her hat in the political ring, her lesbianism won't kill her chances. "Not where I'm from," she said. "Look at Barney Frank. They love him in Boston."

Linda has been working at a law firm, though we've recently learned that she's heading south. She'll be working on the majority staff of the Senate Judiciary Committee and has already started looking for a home to rent on Capitol Hill.

As for Shaw, he changed jobs—he's now working for an anti-poverty lobbying group—but he's still unattached and continues to write screenplays that Hollywood has yet to pick up.

I've got to give the guy credit for persistence.

When Shaw came up for our wedding, he raved about Minnesota: the mega-mall where I work; the tunnels that connect all the downtown buildings so that winter-wimps needn't go outside; and, finally, the people—fresh-faced, down-to-earth and progressive. "Maybe I'll move here," he said. "Everyone's white, yet they've always voted Democratic after '72. It's the longest streak in the country. I'm impressed." I'd love for Shaw to move to Minnesota, but I don't see it happening. He needs to be in D.C., fighting the good fight on a national level. It's in his blood.

That leaves the Shermans—or should I say, that leaves Art Sherman and the future Dolores Bell. They're already separated. It happened November 3rd, when the networks officially announced the winner of the Presidential election.

For a while after our Creed Room presentation, Dolores stayed devoted to Art. But the Benefactor wasn't the only Curious George in the Victorian. The more Dolores wanted to know about her husband's late night conversations, the more adept she became at eavesdropping. She confirmed that Art and Feaver were indeed members of the Empire Club, though in different cells. The two didn't know each other before they met on the night of the Presentation but were linked by a "brother" in the organization. He made sure that the Benefactor got what he asked for before agreeing to shell out the money on a creed room—an articulate Christian conservative who would provide balance to what would likely be a highly secular and liberal group of people. After all, Garrett Park, Maryland isn't exactly middle America, is it?

Dolores also learned that our creed room was but one of several. The Club sponsored others in Boston, San Francisco, Chicago and Seattle. That's right—five creed rooms in five very liberal cities. Each had a plant just like Art—ignorant about the project and the sponsor, but directed to show up and "be himself," as long as he didn't take control of the festivities.

The creed rooms all had different personalities. Ours became known—and ridiculed—as "Philosophy Corner." The Club found our concept of God quite amusing, for example. But they didn't spend nearly $2 million just for the laughs. They did it for the information—in other words, the intelligence. They wanted to know what was important to Blue America.

Obviously, they could have spent less money infiltrating union meetings or even Unitarian study groups. But they fixated on the idea of creed rooms—small, diverse collections of people seeking unity—as places where Democrats would get together in an attempt to reach relatively moderate positions on issues of religion and politics. They saw these positions as a basis of a possible secular, liberal/moderate coalition that could threaten to shift American culture and win national elections. They needed to understand what such a coalition might look like so that they could defeat it and preserve their vision of

America.

Not all five creed rooms bore fruit, but ours sure did. We highlighted the gay marriage issue during our presentation because, even though Fred and Art dissented, the rest of us, including Dolores, felt *extremely* strongly about the issue. I later learned that one person after another drummed that point in during their exit interviews with the Benefactor. That, apparently, was all he had to hear. He didn't even bother to talk to me about the topic. He simply reported the results of his experiment to the Club's central body, and through its network of contacts in conservative churches, the Club spread the news that marriage as an institution was at risk.

By the time the Massachusetts Supreme Court came out in favor of gay marriage, the conservatives were loaded for bear. And when the Club hit on the idea to place a gay marriage initiative on the ballot in Ohio for the 2004 election, they guaranteed for themselves a huge conservative turnout—one that the party of the donkey couldn't possibly compete with.

So, we have four more years of Republican rule. And poor Art will soon have to look for another wife.

With the passage of time, Art's continued participation in the Empire Club was becoming too much for Dolores to take. She figured he stayed with the Club out of fear, more than kinship, but that was cold comfort for her—not after what the Club put us through. Before the recent election, she confronted him about how appalled she was that she and the rest of us were manipulated like pawns. "If your candidate wins on November 2nd," she threatened, "I'm gone. I won't sit back and let your people make a monkey out of me."

After the election, Art begged her to stay, but her need for self-respect was too strong. "They *own* you," she told him. "If I stick around, I'll feel like a mob wife."

Dolores told me just the other day that she hasn't had any second thoughts about leaving Art. Yet I can tell that a big part of her still loves him and always will. She surprised me when she gave me permission to write "the truth, the whole truth and nothing but the truth" about the Creed Room.

That brings me to the Benefactor and his cousin. Since the summer of 2000, I've been getting reports on the Benefactor from Dolores, who received her information from Art. Dolores told me that the Benefactor's kidneys made a miraculous recovery. Though his rheumatism didn't completely go away, it too eased considerably. And that happened before the election. I can imagine that watching John Kerry go down in flames made him feel even stronger.

But when you're talking about Charles Feaver, an eternity has elapsed since election day. I'm writing these words on Monday, December 13, 2004. This past Saturday night, Dolores received a phone call from her estranged husband. She was told that the Benefactor and his cousin were driving not far from their house in Florida when they were struck head on by a drunk teenager in an SUV. The teenager survived. The Benefactor and his cousin did not.

Charles Feaver was 87. David McDonald, 51.

Dolores got her call the day after the accident. She immediately phoned the rest of the Gang to say that the funeral would be held on Wednesday in Tampa. Eileen said there was no way she was going. But I intend to show up, mixed feelings and all.

To many, the worst thing anyone can be called is a hypocrite. As a lover of Jefferson, one of the world's most blatant hypocrites, I must disagree. It is easy enough to avoid hypocrisy by saying little and accomplishing less. But whenever we aspire both to philosophize about life and leave our marks on society, some hypocrisy is inevitable. Certainly, it would take quite an Ubermensch to proclaim a creed as high-minded as Empathic Rationalism and then always live consistently with it. A bookstore employee could pretend to pull it off easily enough, but the real trick would be to practice that philosophy as a statesman or a baron of industry. Good luck!

The Benefactor's hypocrisy isn't hard to see. He claimed to be a patriot, a defender of the soul of America against all enemies, internal as well as external. Yet isn't that soul best illustrated by Jefferson's principle that America must be governed by a devotion to the free, open marketplace of ideas? "Give the people ideas to debate in the light of day," Jefferson might have said, "and we can trust in the majority's judgment. Keep ideas from the people, and we'll assure ourselves of tyranny." Unfortunately, the Benefactor's society refused to do anything in daylight. They were so hell bent on winning their battles that they refused to risk a fair fight. They demanded to know their opponents' ideas, all the while keeping their own a secret. It goes to show that while Nixon's body may have died, his spirit is alive and well.

So the Benefactor and his band of would-be plutocrats were clear hypocrites. But I refuse to demonize him entirely. The fact remains that I have him to thank for so much that's good in my life. And while Eileen would disagree, I think he honestly wanted to help each of us personally. I saw how happy it made him when I mentioned what the Creed Room experience had done for me. I'll also never forget that he went out of his way to put me on notice of the battle that his group was about to